REDEMPTION UNDER THE MOON

The Lycanthrope Protection Agency

Book 5

CJ Ravenna

Editing by Carta's Editorial Services

Copy and line edit by Jennifer Smith

Proofreading by Lori Parks

Beta reading by Rare Bird Beta Reading

Cover designed by www.doelledesigns.com

The story, all names, characters, and incidents portrayed in this production are fictitious. No identification with actual persons (living or deceased), places, buildings, and products is intended or should be inferred.

This book contains sexually explicit materials only suitable for mature readers.

First edition 2023

CONTENT WARNINGS

- On-page death of children, which is discussed throughout the story

- Themes of grief

- Graphic violence, including descriptions of murder and gore

- Suicidal ideation

- Substance abuse

- Violence against shifters in animal form

Please read at your own discretion.

A Note

Ben and Isaac's book mostly takes place in the past. I have been deliberately vague about what years the LPA series takes place in. A modern world, for sure, just one that I imagined to be a little further into our future. If I were to set Ben and Isaac's book in the year 2023, then a chunk of their history would have spanned 2001-2002. I choose to keep the era of their past vague but still futuristic. So there are no mentions of any events or technological developments specific to the 2000s era. This was deliberate and not an oversight.

Chapter 1

A Savage Wolf

Isaac Bennet took a gulp of cold, bitter gas station coffee and reminded himself that this late-night drive would be worth it when he saw his son. The vibrations of the car tempted him toward sleep and his headlights chased the darkness in a never-ending hunt. He dragged on his cigarette and breathed smoke out the window, then threw the burned-out cig into the night.

The headlights illuminated the woods around him, empty as the road ahead of him. An approaching car occasionally blinded his eyes as it whizzed past. Tomorrow they'd be unveiling his newest drinks at the bar where he worked. His boss had been hesitant to give Isaac's cocktails a chance, but Isaac had persisted. Finally, he was beginning his career as a mixologist.

If his babysitter didn't kill him, that was. He was over an hour late getting home to relieve her of her duties. Jessie was honestly a saint. He'd be sure to pay her twice her usual rate.

Poor Beau. He felt terrible for being late to his birthday dinner. How was his son already eight years old? He still remembered the day he was born as if it had happened yesterday.

Throughout high school and into college, his life had blurred together, each year the same as the last. He'd been directionless, partying hard and drinking harder. Breezing through life without a care as to what he'd do after graduation.

Then his girlfriend Melissa had come to him and told him the news that had changed his life; they hadn't been quite as careful as they'd thought, and she was pregnant. She'd told him she wanted to keep the baby, and he could be as involved as he wanted to.

Isaac had never given parenthood much thought. He'd been raised by a single mom, a good, hardworking woman who'd loved him. But he'd seen how hard she'd had to work to support them, and it had made him second-guess parenthood for himself.

But this would be different. He'd loved Melissa—or so he'd thought at the time—so they'd decided to get married. They would do this together as partners. Their child wouldn't want for anything. Suddenly, Isaac's world hadn't been about him anymore. He'd had a reason to start planning for the future; he was going to be a dad. So he'd stopped drinking and partying and had ruminated over what jobs he'd wanted after college, and he'd realized he was wasting his time and money trying to get a degree.

He'd always loved the hospitality industry and meeting new people at the bar he'd worked at, so he'd dropped out of college and committed himself to the bar. He'd done a bit of everything, from serving, to cooking, to mixing drinks, and had even worked his way up to management, though nowadays his passion was behind the bar.

Beau had changed his life for the better. It was his goal to be the best dad he could be for his son. Tonight, though, he was doubting himself harder than usual. He worked long hours, and his marriage with Melissa had fallen apart. He had custody of Beau, and Mel saw him on weekends. Isaac had his regrets, one of which was being late to his son's, and his *own,* birthday dinner. He and Beau shared the same birthday. Like father, like son.

When he parked outside his home in upstate New York, the lights were on inside the house. Grabbing the present for Beau from the seat beside him, Isaac left the car and jogged to the front door. He was wrestling with the key in the lock when the sitter answered the door.

Jessie smiled at him, though it was laced with annoyance. "Hey, Mr. Bennet!"

"I am so sorry, Jessie. Thank you so much for staying late." Isaac counted out some money and handed her extra for the trouble.

She laughed. "It's okay. He's not bad company."

"He behaved?"

"Like an angel, as always."

An angel who'd gotten in a fight at school today. Beau had been too worked up to tell him why. They still needed to talk about it.

"Do you need me to walk you back?"

She snorted. "I live across the street. It's no big deal."

Somewhere in the distance, a creature howled.

Jessie's eyes widened. "Creepy! I've been hearing that all night."

"Must be some werewolf out for a run." Isaac knew there were a few werewolf families on this street. He couldn't say he was comfortable with the idea of a wolf running around in the dark, even if it wasn't a full wolf.

"Goodnight, Beau!" Jessie called over her shoulder.

"Night," came Beau's distracted reply from the living room.

Despite the short distance from his house to hers, Isaac still watched until Jessie made it safely across the road and in through her front door. He locked the door behind himself, shivering when he remembered the wolf's howl.

Over in the living room, Beau sat in front of the TV watching *Jurassic Park*, his favorite movie. Isaac came up behind him and grabbed his shoulders. "Surprise."

Beau groaned. "I totally knew you were there!" The boy laughed when Isaac tousled his hair. "What the heck took you so long?"

"I'm sorry, bud. Work stuff. Have you eaten?"

"Yup. It was really good. There's leftovers on the counter."

Isaac winced. "I'm—"

"It's fine, Dad. Geez. I'm not codependent, you know."

"Technically, you are."

Beau crossed his arms and grinned. "You wouldn't even remember to eat without me."

Isaac raised his hands and conceded. "That's true."

Smiling, Isaac went to the kitchen to reheat the homemade mac and cheese he'd prepped the night before. Armed with a steaming bowl of cheesy noodles and some Brussels sprouts, he rejoined Beau on the couch. "Scoot your boot."

Beau giggled and moved over, and together they watched a T. rex chase people around a park. Isaac always got nervous during the scene where the dinos stalked the kids in the kitchen, and he reached over and touched Beau's head, his parental instincts triggered just watching two kids in distress.

"Scared?" Beau teased.

"Nuh-uh. I could take those dinos, no problem."

"You'd throw out your back, old man."

"Hey!"

Beau erupted into laughter. While his son was distracted, Isaac took the present out of his pocket. "Here you go, bud."

Beau's face lit up. He snatched up the gift. "Thanks, Dad." He smiled bashfully.

"No problem. Don't forget the card."

When Beau opened the card, he laughed at the lame dinosaur pun. "Thanks. I love you too," he said, giving Isaac a quick hug.

Isaac kissed his hair. "You too, kiddo."

"Now can I open my present?"

He snorted. "Yeah."

Beau tore apart the wrapping paper and grinned. "No way!" Isaac knew he'd made the right choice. Beaming, Beau held up the two tickets to Disney World like they were Simba from *The Lion King*. "When are we going?"

"As soon as school's out for the summer."

"Yes!" Beau flung his arms around Isaac's middle and squashed the breath out of him. "This is so awesome. Thank you!"

Pride warmed him, and Isaac gave his son a one-armed hug. "It'll be fun."

Squirming out of the hug, Beau said, "I got something for you too. Wait here!" He tore up the stairs like a little tornado. Seconds later, Beau thundered down the stairs and returned with his hands behind his back, his sandy blond hair as messy as if he'd run through a hurricane.

"Taa-daa!" Beau held out the clumsily wrapped box.

"What is it?"

Beau rolled his eyes. "What are you even—just open it!"

Chuckling, Isaac unwrapped the box. Inside was a pocket-sized notebook.

"You're always writing down ideas for your drinks on napkins or other stuff, and you get annoyed when you forget. So, I got you this."

How had he raised such a thoughtful son?

"Don't forget the card," Beau parroted, and Isaac laughed.

His son had folded some printing paper and drawn a picture of two dinos on the front. "The T. rex is me, obviously, and you're the raptor."

"I do love raptors."

Inside, Beau had written *Happy Birthday to the best dad ever. Thanks for always working so hard for our family. Love, Beau.*

Tears pricked Isaac's eyes.

"You're not gonna cry, are you?" Beau sighed like he was about to be subjected to torture.

Chuckling, Isaac wiped his eyes. "Thank you, bucko. Look, I know I work a lot and for a long time, and I'm sorry."

Beau shrugged. "It's okay. I mean, I don't want us to be homeless or anything."

"This summer, it'll be all about us and Mickey and Minnie. I promise."

Beau held out his hand, and Isaac gave him a high five. They both laughed, and then Beau curled up on the couch. "Can we get back to the movie?" he asked, cuddling into the crook of Isaac's arm. He was sure going to miss his snuggly son. Beau was already so sassy, he figured he was in for some rough teenage years.

"In a moment, once you tell me why you and Steven got into a fight."

Beau groaned. "Mom told you?"

"Yup. Kiddo, what gives? You never start fights."

Beau folded his arms over his chest. He shrugged.

"Hey. Come on and tell me. I know you're a good kid. You wouldn't fight unless you had a good reason to. So can you tell me what happened?"

Heaving a sigh, Beau glowered into his lap. "Steven made fun of Katie for having two dads. He made her cry. I told him to leave her alone, but he kept teasing her. So I hit him. And I don't feel bad about it." He gave Isaac a challenging look, his blue eyes blazing. "He was being a bully."

"He was," Isaac agreed, trying not to show how proud he was that Beau had stuck up for his friend. "But you know that hitting someone is wrong."

"Yeah, so is making someone cry."

"It is, but there are other ways to handle situations like that. You could have gotten an adult to help you."

Beau nodded glumly. "Yeah, but it was happening right in front of me. I needed to help. So I hit him and told him there was nothing wrong with having two dads—or two moms. You and Brian liked each other, and he was really nice. It was like he was calling *you* a freak, and it made me mad."

God, he was proud of this kid. He was good, better than Isaac would ever be. The world needed someone like him. Isaac pulled him close to kiss his hair. "You're right. There's nothing wrong with Katie's parents. It's a good thing that you stuck up for your friend. If it happens again, can you promise me you'll get an adult?"

Beau nodded. "Okay, Dad. Can we watch the movie now?"

"You bet."

With Beau cuddled up against him, Isaac resumed the movie.

His son was going to do amazing things. Isaac couldn't wait to see it.

WHEN ISAAC OPENED HIS eyes, the DVD had returned to the main menu. Beau wasn't sleeping next to him. Stretching, he sat up and turned around. The sliding glass doors into the backyard were open. His heart dropped into his stomach. "Beau?" Isaac crossed the room in seconds, not bothering to put on his shoes. Cool grass tickled his bare feet. "Beau?" The dark woods spread out in all directions, and nightmares of Beau wandering lost haunted him. "Beau!"

"I'm here, Dad!" His son stood farther down the yard to Isaac's left. He had a familiar sheepish look that said he knew he was in trouble.

Willing his heart to calm the fuck down, Isaac sucked in a gulp of air. "Beau, what are you doing out here? You know you're not supposed to come out here at night."

"I saw a shooting star."

"Beau, you should have woken me up. What if—"

"Look, there!" The little boy ran to the edge of where their backyard ended and the dark woods began. Grinning, he pointed into the night sky.

Sure enough, streaks of light flew across a blanket of star-strewn indigo. It was pretty enough that Isaac relaxed a little. "Beautiful, huh?"

"So cool!" Beau crowed, spreading his arms wide.

"Don't forget to make a wish."

Beau wrinkled his nose. "That's baby stuff."

"Nuh-uh. If you wish upon a star, your dreams will come true."

"Wishes aren't real."

Isaac put his hands on his hips. "Says who? I wished upon a star once, and I got just what I wished for."

"What did you wish for?"

"I wished for a beautiful house, an amazing job that I love, and a cool kiddo just like you." He'd gotten everything he could possibly want. Maybe some things had gone off the rails like his marriage, but he wouldn't trade any of it for the world. "So make that wish, son. If you want it badly enough, it'll come true."

Giving him a skeptical but teasing look, Beau closed his eyes and turned his face to the night sky. A big smile bloomed over his cheeks. "I wish for…"

Twin green lights shone in the darkness of the woods. Fireflies, Isaac thought. Until twigs snapped, and a growl like thunder rumbled in the trees.

A dark shape tore free of the shadows and lunged for his son. Beau screamed as the beast locked its jaws around his ankle and ripped him off his feet.

His son's name tore from his throat, and his feet slammed the grass as he ran.

Beau screamed for him as the beast dragged him on his belly. He grabbed leaves in his little hands, kicked and flailed, but the shadows devoured them both as the beast hauled him into the woods.

"I'm coming, Beau!" Isaac roared, already running back toward the house. He crashed through the doors and lunged for the kitchen drawers. Beau's screams echoed in the night. He grabbed a flashlight. Fumbled and dropped it. Cursed and yanked it off the ground. Beat it against his palm until the damn thing turned on. His gun was in the safe upstairs, but there was no time. He grabbed his butcher's knife. This thing, the dog or wolf or whatever the fuck it was, was going to regret harming his son.

Charging into the backyard, Isaac threw himself into the darkness. "Beau! I'm coming. Hang on!"

Beau screamed within the tangled woods, his voice seeming to come from everywhere all at once. Isaac only knew where to go because of where the ground had been disturbed when that fucking monster had dragged his son through the dirt. Rocks stabbed his bare feet, and splinters punctured his skin. He followed the trail, first of flattened grass and scattered leaves but then the trail turned to blood glistening wetly on the leaves.

Oh God.

Beau's screams went from terrified to agonized. Ferocious snarls echoed in the night.

"You fucker! Get away from my son!" Isaac roared into the darkness.

Beau's screams got closer.

A root snagged his ankle and Isaac crashed to the ground. His head struck a rock, and white spots burst in his vision. The knife flew from his hand and tumbled into the leaves. The flashlight rolled to a stop some feet away, and the wide cone of light illuminated Isaac's worst nightmare.

His son, lying on his back, feet skittering in the leaves, pale hands tearing at the ground.

Blood on the leaves, spattered over rocks and tree trunks.

There was so much of it.

A beast stood over Beau's small, vulnerable body. A wolf—jet-black fur matted and wet with blood, green eyes flaring in the dark. Beads of blood dripped from the long, pointed snout and dangled off white fangs.

The beast looked up at him and smiled in a way no animal should be capable of.

Isaac lunged to his feet. "Get away from my son!" He bent over and grabbed the knife.

When he looked up, the creature's tail was disappearing into the trees.

Beau made a sound of pain that Isaac never wanted to hear again. On his knees, he gathered his son's body into his arms. There was so much blood. Beau whimpered. He shook. He sobbed.

"I've got you, baby boy. I know, I know, *I know*. It hurts. I'm so sorry. It's okay. It's going to be okay. I'm here. I'm going to fix it. It's going to be okay."

Beau stopped shaking. His cries fell silent. His blood left Isaac's hand crimson when he cupped his little blond head.

"Baby boy? No. No, no, no. Don't do this. Oh God. Please don't do this. Please, please, please. Oh *God*."

A shooting star flew across the night sky, and no others followed.

THE NEXT TIME ISAAC saw his son, he was cold in the morgue.

Someone had cleaned his hair and stitched his wounds. Without a trace of blood, he lay so still, like he was sleeping. Isaac kissed his cheek. His skin was cold and taut. It felt wrong in a way that made him shake down to his bones. He and his ex-wife Melissa stayed for hours, crying over him, talking to him. Saying nothing at all. The mortician came in a few times, telling them they were closing soon. No one made them leave.

The mortician asked if they wanted to come back again tomorrow, but Isaac couldn't do another day of this. He kissed his son and told him he loved him for the last time.

His neighbors sent him flowers and cards. Plates of food. Isaac found himself fixing a plate of food for Beau without really knowing why. His son had liked cheese and ham and crackers, and Isaac couldn't bring himself to throw it out. It sat there on the counter until the cheese dried out and the ham began to stink.

Isaac had never believed in God, but some nights he prayed to someone, anyone, who would listen. *Give me my son back, and I will be the best father in the world. Give me a second chance. I'll do better. I'll be what he deserves. I promise. Just please, please give me my son back. Don't punish him because I wasn't good enough. I'll be good. I'll be so fucking good this time.*

Sometimes Melissa called him after she'd had one too many. She screamed through the phone, "I told the courts you were unreliable! He should have been with me! You're the reason he's dead! This is your fault!"

Isaac didn't fight back, at least not all of the time. Sometimes he gave as good as he got. Other times, he let her words crash over him and believed all of them.

It rained the day of the funeral, a Friday. Isaac burned through a whole pack of smokes and a bottle of bourbon before the ceremony, but nothing could sufficiently numb him. They held the service at a tiny church near where Isaac lived upstate, so he could visit Beau whenever he needed to. His coworkers came to the service. Melissa's extended family came to hold her and console her while she sobbed. Isaac shook hands and thanked people for coming to his son's funeral.

This didn't feel like his life. He felt like an observer outside his body, witnessing someone else's tragedy. It wasn't his life. Couldn't be his.

"So sorry for your loss."

"Such a beautiful boy."

"I'm so sorry."

"What a tragedy."

Sorry. Sorry. Sorry.

The condolences were never-ending, each one more meaningless than the last. He never knew what to say, how to respond.

"I'm so sorry—" a woman said, a cousin, or aunt, or something. Her son stood behind her. He was close to Beau's age.

"You're sorry, huh?"

The woman blinked at him.

"What the fuck for?" It was the first thing he'd said since the ceremony. His voice was slurred. "Your children are alive. You'll get to see them grow up and go to college and get married and have kids of their own. You'll get to meet all the friends they make, the special boy or girl they bring home for dinner. You'll get to learn what their favorite subjects are and hear all about who they want to be. I'm sorry too. I'm sorry that I'm still breathing the air he should have breathed! I'm sorry that it isn't *me* who's dead in the *fucking* ground!"

He walked out, and the crowd let him go in deathly silence.

He stayed by the grave long after the congregation had gone inside, oblivious to the rain on his suit. The cold gnawed at him but he couldn't be bothered to move. He wished the ground would swallow him up. A hand fell upon his shoulder, warm and gentle.

"Your son is with the angels, Mr. Bennet. God will care for your sweet child like his own until you are reunited again." Father Donovan had overseen the burial. His sermon had been moving and empathetic.

Isaac made a strangled sound he didn't recognize, incapable of speaking.

Fuck the angels. Fuck God. I'm his father. He should be with me. He wanted to scream those words, but he'd lost the ability to speak.

"The loss of a child is unspeakable." The father's voice trembled with raw emotion. "The pain you're feeling now, that gaping wound in your heart, is God's way of telling us that we loved deeply and were loved in return."

Isaac swallowed around the ache in his throat.

The father handed him a card with his name and number. "Call me anytime you need to. I will always answer." His warm brown eyes sparkled, his hands soft and gentle, and it was difficult for Isaac not to burden the father with his grief. "Come inside out of the rain."

Wordlessly, Isaac followed him inside the church.

"Isaac... A biblical name." Don led him to a pew by the altar, his robes sweeping over the tiled floor with a whisper. Isaac sat beside him.

Father Don turned his face toward the ceiling and smiled, bringing color to the apples of his cheeks. He couldn't be much older than Isaac's twenty-nine years, but there was a wisdom in his eyes Isaac felt he lacked. The colors of the stained glass glimmered in his hair, neatly combed and slicked back. With not a hair out of place or a wrinkle to his robes, his hands folded with ease in his lap, he was the image of patience and order. Isaac envied him that.

"Isaac means 'laughter' or 'he will laugh,' reflecting the laughter of Abraham and Sarah when God revealed they would be blessed with a child. Of the three patriarchs, he was the longest-lived." Don's wide mouth smiled with surety and hummed with quiet laughter. He touched Isaac's shoulder. "You will laugh again, Isaac. In the face of great adversity and pain, you will find joy again."

Isaac hung his head, not wishing to be rude.

"You don't believe me. You can speak your mind. God does not pass judgment."

Isaac didn't know what made him open up to the father, but they were alone, with no one to overhear them. "I don't want to laugh. Or be happy."

Father Don hummed, his face etched with patient understanding.

It was Beau who deserved to laugh and be happy, not him.

"You were a good father. Willing to sacrifice as God did when he gave his only son to us."

"If I was a good father, he'd still be here." Isaac slumped, his elbows on his knees and his head hanging toward the ground. "A... a wolf killed him."

Don's eyes widened. "I think you and I were meant to meet."

"Yeah? Why is that?" Isaac didn't really care.

Don touched Isaac's back and took in a deep breath. "I'll tell you something, a secret I only tell my closest friends. My wife and son, God rest their souls, were killed by werewolves." Isaac's shock must have shown for Don's lips trembled. "Yes. It's true. The beasts came into my home while I was away. Killed my wife. My son, he... he'd been violated. The monster forced herself on him, marked his neck like he was her property. So I hunted her and her pack down and made sure they never hurt another innocent family again."

His confession shocked Isaac into silence for a moment. Don was so kind and soft-spoken, he couldn't imagine he had a capacity for violence. But Isaac was in no position to judge him. "I can't even imagine... I don't blame you at all." Isaac's heart ached for him. "I just... keep thinking about everything I could have done differently." Isaac's voice cracked, and he wiped his eyes.

"I know, my friend. I know."

"It's all my fault. He'd still be here if I'd just..." Isaac couldn't look at Don, ashamed as tears burned his eyes.

Don shook his head. "No. You can't blame yourself for the savagery of wolves. Think about it, Isaac. We live in a world where men who can shift into monsters at will are allowed free rein. This system failed you. It failed your son. It is *not* your fault."

And wasn't he right? Wasn't it strange the way werewolves were allowed to live among them? They could turn into wild animals, for fuck's sake! They were dangerous. "You're right," Isaac whispered. "Fuck, Don. You're right. It's fucked up." How had he never stopped to consider how stupid this society truly was?

Don nodded grimly. "Every day, I hear stories like yours. The government sweeps it all under the rug and insists we live in a civilized, equal society. You did not fail your son. Our world did."

"You're right... Fuck! I didn't do anything wrong." Isaac's voice shattered in his fury, but it wasn't Don he was angry at. "It was that *thing*! That wolf! He took my son from me and—" Grief overran his fury and he couldn't get another word out.

"Of course none of this was your fault." A tender hand fell upon his shoulder. "And... where did the tragedy happen? If it isn't too much." Isaac's skin prickled. Don's gaze was attentive, intensely so.

"In White Plains. In my own backyard."

"Ahhh..." Don sounded as if this were somehow very interesting. "There have been wolves howling there. Animal carcasses stripped of flesh. Children dragged from their homes and into the woods. Nobody has been able to catch the killer just yet."

Don sneered. "That's the way of this wicked new world we live in. Unfortunately, all werewolves, no matter how kindly they seem, are at constant risk of losing themselves to their inner beasts. Many call this 'going feral.' Feral wolves never recover their humanity. They become mindless, bloodthirsty monsters. God above, some even *rejoice* in the loss of their humanity! When they do inevitably lose themselves, they become a danger to this society, and must be put down." Anger tightened Don's voice.

A shudder ran through Isaac. "Oh my god. I never knew that." Sure, he'd occasionally heard stories on the news about werewolves attacking humans or running fully shifted through the city, but he'd had no idea of the deeper meaning behind such instances. If werewolves were ticking time bombs waiting to go off, then why were they allowed to roam freely among humans? "Is there a cure?"

"No. Only death can cure their madness."

Isaac would have almost felt sorry for werewolves, but there was no room in his heart for anything but grief.

The father crossed himself and looked to the statue of Christ. He frowned thoughtfully, wetting his lips. "If you could get vengeance for your son, would you?"

Isaac sucked in his lips, his fingernails digging into the denim of his jeans. He stood, his shoes squeaking over the tile. "I want to kill the beast who took my son from me." He couldn't look Father Don in the face when he said it, and his voice broke from rage. His body quivered, and he gnashed his teeth to hold himself together. "Kill the monster with my bare fucking hands before he hurts any other children."

"You can," Don said, his tone deathly serious. "Just as I got vengeance for my family."

"What?" Isaac's voice was a whisper. "How?"

"Do you want to avenge your son?"

Isaac's breath caught. "I—"

Don whirled toward him and took him hard by the shoulders. His breath was sour against Isaac's face, his eyes wide as they locked with Isaac's. "Ask yourself, son. Would you die for your son, Isaac? Would you take a life for him?"

"Yes," Isaac croaked. "Tell me how."

Don's sweaty hands framed Isaac's face. "You can avenge your boy, Isaac. There are ways. Meet me at the Cathedral of St. John the Divine tomorrow at midnight. I will show you the way."

And he left with a swish of his robes, sweeping his disheveled hair back into place. Isaac let him go, speechless and stunned. He trembled, scared by this new side of the kindly father he'd just met.

Would he die for his son? Would he take a life for his son? Yes, and yes.

And so he found himself sitting on the steps to the cathedral the following night. The sun set and the moon rose full and bright in a cloudless sky. The streetlights came on, the crowds thinned, and he found himself alone as midnight drew near.

"You can avenge your boy, Isaac."

The air froze in Isaac's lungs, and a shiver ran down his spine. *"There are ways,"* he'd said. Don could be crazy for all he knew but he had to meet with him tonight. He had to understand just what the father had meant, unravel the promise in those whispered words.

"You've come, son," said a voice to his right.

Isaac's heart slammed against his ribs. "Holy shit!"

Don's wide mouth stretched into an apologetic smile. "Once you've recovered, follow me. It isn't far."

Don led Isaac through the graveyard, passing sculpted angels with their faces hooded in shadow. Isaac shivered, desperate to leave. He stumbled into Don, who'd suddenly stopped. "Ah. Here it is." The dim light of Don's phone illuminated a crypt with a heavy stone door padlocked tight. Isaac froze, confused and unsettled.

"Don?"

The father turned an iron key in the lock and the padlock clicked open. He gave it a push, and the door opened with a hair-raising grinding noise. Isaac held his breath, expecting to see a coffin, and instead there was a gaping passageway and a stone staircase descending into darkness.

"Watch your step," Don advised. "It's very dark."

Morbid curiosity compelled Isaac on. What kind of graveyard needed a hidden passageway leading to who only knew where? For all he knew, Don would kill him the moment he set foot in the dark.

And what does that matter, Isaac thought. *I have nothing to lose.*

His son was dead, and he was divorced with little to no prospects. His boss would replace him in a week. His mother was dead and gone from cancer and his father was out of the picture, having run off with the woman he'd ruined his marriage with. His ex-wife surely wouldn't miss him, and he didn't have anyone at home wondering where he was. His death would be inconsequential.

Still, he suppressed a shiver as his phone's light revealed a seemingly endless stairwell sprawling into shadow.

"Close the door behind you," Don ordered.

Isaac did and the darkness closed in on him. Their footsteps echoed with every step and it was an effort not to slip on the smooth stone. He shuddered at the thought of rolling all the way to the bottom. The darkness closed in, impenetrable beyond the small cone of light his phone produced.

The stairwell looked longer than it was, but he made each step slow and deliberate to avoid losing his footing. Sooner than he'd hoped, he breathed a sigh as his feet touched the ground. Fiery light chased away the dark as torches blazed in sconces nailed to cold stone walls. It was such an unexpected, archaic sight that Isaac momentarily forgot his fear, swept up in sudden wonder. "This way, Isaac." Don eased open a door at the end of the tunnel.

Torchlight scorched his eyes, burning so bright it turned the cavern walls yellow. The cramped tunnel opened up into a vast underground chamber with marble pillars and elaborately tiled walls and floors as impressive as Grand Central Station. It looked like an extension of the cathedral itself with rows of pews to sit in and even an altar over which Christ was suspended in judgment.

Every step echoed as he passed display cases with Bibles, and the items within only became more elaborate. Silver swords and daggers gleamed, the edges far too sharp to convince Isaac they were anything other than genuine. He just couldn't understand what a father and his clergy needed them for.

Silver crosses shimmered in display cases, nestled reverently upon small satin pillows. Each cross was fitted with a tiny ruby, probably to symbolize the blood of Christ, Isaac assumed. Not exactly something he would wear.

An enormous creak made Isaac jump. A door at the rear of the chamber opened and a group of men in black militant garb marched into the torchlight. They wore body armor and a utility belt full of weapons from silver grenades to daggers like the ones in the display cases. Some even had crossbows. Silver crosses glittering from their necks. The sight sent a shudder down Isaac's spine.

His mouth fell open as a wolf limped into the torchlight, a rope tied around its neck. An armed woman yanked on the rope, causing the wolf to yelp and stumble faster. Blood matted the wolf's fur and the creature shook pitiably.

His stomach turned over. It looked like the wolf he'd seen crouched over his son's crippled body, its blood-soaked snout hovering over his son's pale throat. The wolf who'd torn out his boy's throat while he lay too weak to even scream.

Don grabbed Isaac's shoulder. Don had shed his coat, revealing the same militant outfit he wore beneath. "I told you there was a way. We are the Silver Cross, and it is our holy mission to hunt the beasts that prey upon mankind."

Father Don was a werewolf hunter. Isaac felt as if he'd stepped into some bizarre dream... or nightmare.

"I have brought the beast who murdered your son to you, Isaac, to confess his sins."

Isaac's knees buckled, and he nearly collapsed. He forced himself to suck in a gulp of air as he swayed, lightheaded. Don reached out and laid a hand over the wolf's snout, removing a muzzle. "The beast of White Plains has haunted the community long enough. For too long the people have lived in fear of their own neighbors and tonight that reign of terror ends. This beast has claimed the lives of women, children, and Isaac's son, Beau. Speak, beast!"

The wolf's wide green eyes found Isaac's. Before his eyes, the body shifted and changed. The paws became clawed hands, the face somewhat more human, though twisted and savage. "Screw you humans!" The boy panted, coarse snarls interrupting the flow of his words. "I'll tear your throats out!"

The fury in his voice made Isaac's blood boil. The werewolf was young. He couldn't be older than fifteen. How could someone so young be so barbaric?

Don sneered. "What monster would harm an innocent child of God? Only a savage animal is capable of such mindless violence!"

The hunters cheered their agreement. Isaac remained rooted in place, sweat cold all over his body. "Let me speak to him. *It*," he amended. Don stepped aside and Isaac's legs shook as he approached the altar, peering into the face of the monster. "You." His voice came out a croak. "You tore out my son's throat. You dragged him from my backyard and murdered him!"

The boy sneered. "You people kill us all the damn time! He deserved it!"

Fury made Isaac shake.

"Silence, beast!" Donovan injected the werewolf with a needle full of purple liquid. His eyes closed and he collapsed onto the altar. "This beast is on the path to becoming feral. Soon, he will be unable to shift back, and he'll be lost forever." Donovan extended a blade to Isaac. "Take it. Avenge your son and all the other children he's killed."

Isaac's hands trembled. The blade glinted, sharp enough to split his skin with the slightest touch. Did he truly have it in him to take a life?

"Do it, Isaac." Donovan's warm hand touched his shoulder, his dark brown eyes boring into Isaac's. "He will go feral. It is only a matter of time. Once he loses himself, he will kill and kill again. You heard how callously he dismissed the murder of poor Beau. There will be more fathers like you, waking up each day with a hole in their hearts. You can end more heartbreak before it can begin."

Isaac's hand trembled so badly he nearly dropped the blade. More children like his Beau could be spared this creature's violence. Tears burned his eyes.

"If only there'd been someone like you, Isaac," Don whispered, his eyes full of sympathy. "Your boy might still be here if someone like you had stopped this beast before he claimed innocent lives."

If he had the power to change things for the better, then what kind of man would he be to step back and allow more pain and suffering?

When he looked up, the boy was gone and a wolf had taken his place. There was nothing human left in the creature. It was just an animal to be put down.

He pressed the dagger in, piercing through dense fur to the soft flesh beneath. The beast died with a groan. The dagger clattered from his numb fingers, and he dropped to his knees in the warm blood pooling at the base of the altar.

The hunters uttered a prayer, crossing themselves. Isaac exhaled and slumped over, forehead to the cold altar. Tears spilled hot down his face, and a broken noise escaped him. It was over. He had avenged his son, and yet… nothing had changed. Beau was still gone. What was the point?

"Well done." Don's voice was gentle, empathetic. "It's always hard the first time. I know. But we do what others will not. We are protecting our fellow man from the beasts that stalk among us, disguised as sheep." Steady hands helped Isaac to his feet. Long fingers cupped his cheek. "Will you do something for me now, Isaac?"

He wiped his wet eyes. "Yes. Anything, Don."

"Join us. You will make an astonishing hunter, Isaac. I knew it the moment I heard your story; you have exactly what it takes to be one of us. You were sent by God himself. Isaac"—he urged Isaac to meet his gaze—"join us, and we will make the world a better place. Together."

Don drew the blade across his own palm, then waited for Isaac to offer him his hand. "The Cross is for life, Isaac. Do you understand?"

For a moment, Isaac thought about saying no and walking away. He'd accomplished what he'd wanted to do. What was the point in becoming a hunter, Isaac wondered hopelessly. It was too late for Beau, too late for all the other children this monster had killed. He bowed his head, submerged in a wave of grief.

"I know, my son." Don guided Isaac's head to his shoulder. "It's too late for those we have lost to these animals. But you can save others like Beau, and I will be there every step of the way."

He waited, dagger outstretched. The breath left Isaac's body in a shuddery exhale. He wouldn't refuse. He had the power to help. If he didn't act, then he was responsible for every man, woman, and child that fell at the fangs of werewolves. "Okay, Father. I'll join you. I want to fight. I want to make a difference. For... for Beau."

Isaac reached out and clasped the hilt, the metal warm from Don's skin, and sliced open his palm. "I'm in, Don. For life."

"Then welcome, Hunter Isaac of the Silver Cross." A cross glittered, swaying from a silver chain. Isaac bowed his head and Don slipped the chain over his neck.

CHAPTER 2
DON'T TRUST THEM

"I'm going to miss you, Ben." Heather Brown's eyes sparkled with tears.

"You too." Benjamin Stroud tried to smile. "Thanks for waiting with me."

She laughed softly. "Figured you needed the company. Your pop's been gone a while, huh?"

Ben nodded. "You've gotta work soon, right? You don't need to wait around until he's back."

"I can wait a minute more."

Jackson, one of their own pack members, had gone missing in the woods. His dad had left hours ago, and Ben worried about what his father would find. He hoped Jackson was okay. Ben would have gladly joined his pops in the search, but he'd had to pack for his flight to NYC. Now all he could do was sit around and wait for his dad to return with news, good or bad.

"Won't it be scary moving to the big city? There are so many humans there."

"Sure," Ben admitted. "But it's the right thing to do."

"I hope it's worth it."

Ben winced, not missing the hurt or the jab in her words. "Heather..." Damn. He didn't know how to apologize any more than he already had.

She tried to smile. "It's fine, Ben. You were right. We care about each other, but we aren't meant to be. It's for the best." She checked her watch. "I've got to run to work. Let me know about Jackson, okay?"

"Will do."

She patted his knee. "Stay in touch, city boy." With one last smile, she stepped off the porch and walked away.

The forest around the pack territory spread out in all directions. Skies that were normally a deep blue were choked by angry gray clouds. A storm was coming. Ben took in a deep lungful of the green trees, the air dense with moisture, and breathed it all out in a sigh. No matter where he went, the world smelled the best after a shower of rain. He hoped New York City would smell just as wonderful after a storm.

The porch creaked beneath him as he stared down the worn dirt road at the long stretch of town that was the Appalachian Pack territory. It was a tiny community, couldn't be more than a hundred werewolves packed into this little town, but he knew every face that smiled his way. He could raise a hand and wave, and the gesture would be returned without hesitation.

These were his people. He knew the butcher who greeted him by name and always had his family's Saturday roast waiting for him. He remembered how angry Anthony had been when his son Kenny had told him he wanted to live in New York instead of working in the family's general store. He knew Willie, who owned the bar where he'd had his first whiskey cocktail. The lake where he and Heather had had their first kiss beneath a shower of rain.

He'd spent all thirty years of his life in this tiny town. It held a lifetime of memories, from his first day at Pre-K to his graduation from college, the memories a mix of good and bad. In New York, he'd be a nobody, just one face in a sea of thousands. And there would be humans, lots and lots of humans. He knew little about humans. There wasn't a single human in town, not even a hybrid, and there'd been an uproar when the daughter of the Jamison pack's alpha ran off with her human mate to live in Dayton.

Humans brought complications and danger and Ben had seen for himself the damage they could do to shifters.

He checked the time and his stomach did a flip. His flight was three hours from now, but he would leave in an hour so he could get through security early like his mother had suggested. His time in this small town was drawing to a close.

His dad had texted him and Ben's heart lurched.

Dad: Found Jackson. It's not good. Do me a favor and grab me a cheeseburger at the diner. Haven't eaten all day. After I take you to the airport, I'm gonna stay at the hospital for the rest of the day with him.

Shit. Pushing himself up, Ben walked down the street and bought himself lunch at the boxcar diner called Moonbeam. He ordered the same thing as always: meat loaf with a side of mashed potatoes with gravy and a whiskey cocktail. The drinks weren't as good as Jack's Bar, but they did the trick. He ordered his dad's cheeseburger to go.

"Our boy's growing up," said Debbie with a sigh, handing him his last cocktail. "I still remember when all you were drinking was soda and milkshakes. Now look at you…"

"An alcoholic, right?" Ben cracked a grin.

She rolled her eyes and smacked him with her dishrag. "You got someone to stay with in the city?"

"Nope but I'll be fine." He'd bought his own place in Brooklyn with the money he'd saved up working in the Ohio branch of the Lycanthrope Protection Agency, an organization his family established years before he was born. His parents had been ready to pay for all his expenses, and with their money they certainly could, but Ben had wanted to have some independence.

"All alone in the big city. I'd be terrified, especially with all those humans running around."

Ben's whiskey went down the wrong way and he coughed into his sleeve. He *was* terrified. He'd never lived among humans before or been so far away from his family. And then there was the business to consider, his parents' lifework they were entrusting to his care. Could he exceed their expectations? Or would all the years of preparation and training be wasted on him?

He downed the last of his whiskey, wishing the doubts would go with it. "The shifters in NYC really need the agency's help. Crime against shifters is up more than it's ever been. This new branch will be a good thing for all werewolves."

"Don't think I'm not proud of you, Benji. We'll just miss you is all." She patted his cheek and then jumped. "Oh, before I forget!" She bustled to the kitchen and returned with a paper bag. "Take a little bit of the Moonbeam with you to NYC." Inside was a container with an extra serving of meat loaf and potatoes for dinner. Ben smiled, his heart squeezing like a fist in his chest.

"Thanks, Deb."

Heart and stomach full, Ben strode from the diner for the last time. Sirens howled and his father's familiar pickup truck hurtled past, the lights on the roof flashing. Ben's lunch became a queasy lump in his stomach. The townsfolk recognized his dad's truck and came running after it.

"Shit..." He jogged after the truck and followed the familiar road to the agency, the biggest building in town that served not only as a hospital but also as the HQ of the LPA in Ohio. Ben hurried through the gates to his father's truck in the courtyard. His dad climbed out and slammed the door. Throwing off the tarp covering the truck bed, his father revealed an enormous cage. "Ben! Give me a hand."

The smell of blood and dirty fur made Ben's stomach twist, and the sight of the wolf in the cage almost paralyzed him. The brown wolf was unmistakably Jackson, his enormous paws twitching, his sides heaving as he panted. A ring of blood formed around his neck, the fur parted to reveal a deep cut that encircled it.

"Hurry!" his father barked. "Help me get this cage outta the truck!"

His dad grabbed the front of the cage and pulled. Ben's arms shook as he grasped the bars and carried it toward the building with his father in the lead. Nurses were waiting, armed with a rolling stretcher. Ben and his father unloaded Jack's body onto the stretcher and the doctors sped the wolf away. Ben and his father jogged to keep up.

"He's lost a lot of blood and he's got a silver bullet in him, so he ain't healing!" Ben's father shouted, voice hoarse as he kept pace with the medics. "He'll need a transfusion, stitches if his body refuses to heal itself."

"Got it, Mr. Stroud!" The nurses rushed the patient into the operating room. Ben caught his breath, feeling sick. His father dropped onto a bench and leaned his head against the wall.

"Fucking hell." As the founder of the LPA, Jonathan Stroud possessed a commanding air. Today, though, he looked a hundred years older and exhausted. Ben went to get him some water from the cooler. "'Less that's beer, boy, I don't want it." He sighed. "It's exhausting, Ben." His father's shoulders slumped heavily. "Thing about this job is, you think you know how low humans can stoop. Then they trap and almost kill a kid." Jonathan glowered into his lap, his mustache bristling. "I'll stay with him until his parents arrive. You can go home. Nothing more we can do for him now."

Ben didn't move. Jackson was part of his community, and Ben was an agent of the LPA. He couldn't leave, even if the sight of the injured wolf tore a hole in his heart. The wound never healed. Every murder, every attack reopened the wound and it bled afresh. He should stay, for Jackson. He could handle it—he should.

"Ben. Go home."

His throat ached when he tried to breathe. The blood-soaked fur wouldn't leave his mind. He didn't get why this was affecting him. He barely knew Jackson from anyone else, but just knowing someone had driven a knife into their peaceful community—the pain was like a hot poker under his ribs.

His father was right; it was exhausting.

His dad's warm, calloused hand grasped the back of his neck. "Keep it together, soldier. Go home, get your luggage. I'll drive you to the airport."

Ben stood. His father suddenly grabbed his arm.

"That pain you're feeling, that anger—it never goes away. You just get better at handling it."

Wordlessly, Ben left, sucking in a gulp of air once he was outside. The coppery smell of blood still clung to his nose. He swallowed, his stomach spinning like a washing machine. His mother, Meredith, rushed toward the HQ in her surgeon's scrubs. The sunlight hit her, making her silver hair glow. She sniffed and bounded to him, reaching out to touch his face. She stopped long enough to give Ben a hug and a kiss. "Goodbye, sweetheart. I wish I could see you off, but—"

"Jack needs you," Ben said. "I get it. Can you believe it? Humans trapped him."

"I know. Your father texted me." She shook her head in disbelief but that was all the indication he got that this was upsetting to her; his mother was in doctor mode, her emotions compartmentalized. "Call me after you land, okay?"

"I will." Ben squeezed her tight. "Love you, Ma."

She returned his smile. "Love you too. I'm proud of you!" she called over her shoulder, already running through the doors.

Ben wished there were something he could do, but he wasn't a doctor. He knew how to restore a feral werewolf's humanity, how to give orders and keep his head in times of crisis. But what little he could do was useless tonight. Besides, how useful would he be if he let an injured wolf break his heart? Maybe he wasn't the man his parents thought he was.

With his flight in three hours, Ben walked home to his little house at the end of the dirt road where he'd lived for the past five years and did a last-minute sweep, making sure he had everything packed away. He'd thought about having one last run through the woods as a wolf before he departed for the city, but after what happened to Jackson, he was too weary to shift in peace.

Downstairs, he heard the loud beep of his father's truck. He exhaled, his stomach writhing. It was time. He grabbed his bags and took one last look at his room. With all his belongings gone, the room was devoid of character, a blank slate for the new owner who'd make it their own. With a lump in his throat, he closed the door and turned away.

Outside, his father waved out the window at him. "Are you all packed up?"

"Yeah."

His father patted the truck door invitingly. "Hop on in."

Ben threw his suitcase in the truck bed and buckled in. Some trashy country love song filled the interior of the truck. Ben rolled down the window and breathed in the smell of the forest for the last time. He watched as the buildings sped past, knowing each one at a glance.

They drove past Heather's house. The lights were on and they were probably all sitting down to dinner. When they'd first started dating, he'd thought for certain she was the one; that they'd settle down and start a family. But she wasn't his fated mate. Whoever they were, they were out there somewhere.

The buildings disappeared, transitioning to sprawling woodlands, then to vast plains. Ben looked over his shoulder one more time and watched as the town disappeared behind him.

His dad sighed. "It never gets easy, Ben."

"Will Jackson be okay?" He didn't know Jackson personally, as they had a big age-gap between them, but he was a part of the pack, same as anyone in town.

"I hope so. I still remember when he was a little kid. He had that stutter. Couldn't get out a sentence. His parents will be devastated..." With sudden anger, he ripped the pewter badge from his shirt and slammed it onto the dashboard.

"Pops, you did everything you could."

"You can tell that to Jackson's parents. Their son could die, and I couldn't save him."

"What even happened out there?" Ben didn't understand. "I thought he was going hunting."

"He was." Jonathan's jaw stood out sharply as he gritted his teeth. He did that often, and his clenching had changed the shape of his face, giving him a wide, hard jaw. "Till he became prey. Humans did it. I smelled them. They were stalking around our territory. They set traps. Shot him, but he got out of range. Then he got caught in a snare. He was half-dead when I found him. He nearly suffocated to death."

Ben couldn't speak, fury leaving him too angry for words. The wolves of his town never hurt anyone. They kept to themselves and avoided humans, yet humans sought them out, trespassed in their territory, and trapped and killed any who left town. The cruel hatred of it all tore Ben up inside.

Before he was ready, they were at the airport in Columbus. His father jumped out and popped open the trunk. Ben and his father carried the bags into the terminal and stopped near the first security checkpoint. His father said, "It's not easy for your mother, you know. Me neither. Sending you off into a city full of humans, especially after what happened."

Ben rolled his shoulders. "I'll be careful, Pops."

"That's the thing. You can be as careful as you like, keep calm and quiet, have a handle on your wolf, be respectful of the law, but there'll always be folk who look at us and see nothing but animals, Ben. That's just the truth of it."

Ben nodded heavily.

"And yet here I am, throwing my only son into a city full of humans..." His father scratched at what little hair he had, a sigh seething between his teeth.

Unsure what else he could say to ease his father's nerves, Ben dragged his feet toward the checkpoint. The line was long and a thousand different smells hit him all at once, perfumes and body odor being the most promi-nent. A big, hulking security guard marched up and down, sniffing the air. A werewolf, scenting for illegal or dangerous materials.

"Damn, I left my cocaine at home."

His father rolled his eyes. "That's not funny, Ben."

Ben faced him, suddenly at a loss. His father used to seem so tall. Now Ben towered over him. His father opened his arms and Ben held him tight as his father clapped him on the back. "Call us when you land or your mother will panic. I will too."

"I will." Ben felt suddenly as scared and unsure as a little boy and held on tight before his dad could pull away. When they did part, his father smiled, a tremor in his lip that made his mustache quiver.

"Love you, son. Have a good flight. Be careful, hear? Don't trust humans. Not a one."

Ben returned his smile. "You too. I'll be careful, I swear." He grabbed his bags and turned away before his father could see the tears he was fighting back. He took the first steps away from his father and before he knew it, he'd passed through the gate and was farther from his family than he'd ever been.

For a time, he was distracted as he passed through security, holding his breath as he focused on not getting arrested or searched. He sweat it out when security clipped his nails as was customary for werewolves—couldn't have them growing claws during their flight. He checked his ticket for the gate number and to his relief found it with ease. With time to kill, he snacked on Deb's meat loaf and read a cheesy thriller novel he'd packed for the flight.

The time came to board. Ben passed his seat and had to double back, squeezing past grumbling passengers who shot him nasty looks. Ears burning, he dropped into his seat by the window.

The rain finally came, pouring down from the skies and streaking the windows. The plane took off down the runway, and as they left the ground, Ben felt weightless when they took to the skies. Rain lashed the windows but he looked hard for where he knew the Appalachian Pack was, hidden among the trees.

He thought of his mother and father. He thought of Jackson and his heartbroken family. He thought of Heather, who he'd loved once. He leaned his head on the window with only the rain to witness his sadness and allowed the tears to fall down his face.

BEN TOOK A YELLOW taxi from the airport. On the horizon, the New York City skyscrapers dominated the sky. He rolled down the window and leaned closer, unable to stifle a smile as he glimpsed the famous Empire State Building. His apprehension and nerves were swept away in a rush of adventurous excitement. Who knew what kind of life awaited him in the city of dreams and opportunities?

Perhaps he'd find love, the real true love of a fated mate, and start a family. Perhaps the LPA would flourish and become the home and safety werewolves needed more than ever. Perhaps he'd make his family proud and honor their legacy. The car soared over the Brooklyn Bridge and a train roared like a dragon below his feet, screeching across the tracks that carried it over the bridge.

The driver dropped him off on a quiet street. The air stank of exhaust fumes, garbage on the corner, and stale urine. The pack town sure hadn't smelled like this. The air had been cleaner for sure, but all these new smells invigorated his senses. What was stinky and intolerable to humans was thrilling to werewolves, and he desired nothing more than to investigate every new smell. A homeless man slept in the doorway and Ben had to squeeze around him to reach the door.

His first apartment was... humble at best. He could already hear the rats in the walls when he walked in. He uttered a growl that filled every empty corner of the room and practically heard them shit themselves with fear. He doubted he'd see much of the critters. His furniture hadn't arrived yet, so the apartment was vast and empty and every step echoed. The living room and kitchen was one big room with a tiny bathroom and bedroom on opposite ends of the apartment.

It was a far cry from his little house and even his living quarters on the HQ grounds back home, but it would do. He would likely be spending most of his time at the new agency in Fire Island. True to his word, he called his mother and father while he waited on a pizza delivery.

"How was your flight?" his dad asked.

"Did you get anything to eat on the plane?" his mother said, fretting.

"It was pretty smooth, and yes, Ma." Ben sighed and supposed they'd always look at him and remember when he was a little tyke crapping in diapers.

They talked until the pizza arrived, and he reclined against the counter and ate, ravenously hungry after a day of traveling, while he listened to his parents. Outside the windows, the sun descended over apartment rooftops. Though he was glad to hear their voices, there was something to his father's prolonged silences that made Ben uneasy. Either his father was tired, or something had happened.

"Everything okay, Dad? You're awful quiet."

"Jackson didn't make it, Ben." His father's voice was heavy with remorse.

His mother sighed shakily. "I missed the signs of aconitum poisoning."

"Wolfsbane?" Ben's heart sank.

His dad said, "We found a dead deer in the woods that Jackson had snacked on. Hunters must have poisoned it with wolfsbane. He survived the silver, but the poison..."

Ben's heart ached for the boy's family and for his own parents as they warred with their grief and guilt. "You did everything you could. Both of you."

His father made a hoarse sound. "Don't trust them, Ben. Not a single one. They'll only see you as a monster. Stay safe."

Ben hung up with an ache in his chest.

Fuck sleeping. He needed a drink.

CHAPTER 3

RAIN CLOUD EYES

THE NEAREST BAR STILL open at this hour was a pizza joint on Flatbush and Sixth. It was only five minutes away but in the dark in a new neighborhood, it felt like longer. There were very few people out and about, save for a few people in need sleeping in the doorways of shops. The bar's neon lights streaked the pavement, glimmering in puddles.

Ben sniffed, scenting tomato sauce, cheese, yeast—and humans. He hesitated, his fingers closing into a fist inches from the knob. With an exhale, he told himself as long as he didn't wolf out he'd be okay.

The bell jingled as he entered. Heads turned his way before looking away in disinterest. A handful of people sat at the tables grabbing a late-night bite to eat or working on their laptop with a slice of greasy, cheesy pizza by their keyboard. An empty stage waited to be used, a microphone standing like a lone actor beneath dim periwinkle lights.

He thought about leaving until he smelled it.

Wet asphalt. Clouds heavy with moisture. Wet grass and leaves.

The scent had him spellbound. His wolf rumbled low in his chest, every instinct flaring to life. He couldn't leave. He had to find the source of that scent right now. He knew what this was. What this meant. Someone in this bar belonged to him. His fated mate.

"Welcome," the bartender said, but Ben swept past, sniffing the air frantically.

33

Where was this person? Were they a man, a woman? He had to find them, had to know.

Following the scent to the bar, he pulled up a chair and sat. He looked up and down the bar, trying to figure out where that scent was coming from. There were only four people seated at the bar tonight, two of whom were talking.

A guy sitting to Ben's right snagged his interest. He thought the guy was asleep since he was slumped over the bar with his head on his arm and wearing a gray hood that obscured his face and hair. Ben sniffed, wondering if the scent was coming from him or someone else at the bar.

"Another one?" The bartender took the man's empty glass away, the ice melted to water.

The guy jolted awake, running a hand down his face tiredly. His fingers rasped through wiry stubble a few days thick. "Yeah. Why the hell not?"

Something glittered around his neck. A silver cross, fitted with a blood-red ruby.

The bartender smirked, splashing bourbon in a glass. "Boss's not gonna like you drinking on your off days."

He just hummed, not looking like he gave two shits either way. With a grunt of thanks, he tossed back his drink like it was water, ice cubes clinking against the glass. He was human. Ben could tell at a whiff even over the scent of rain that clouded the bar.

Hooded eyes beneath a low brow glanced his way. Something like electricity shivered down Ben's spine. His eyes were a deep gray flecked with slivers of blue, like the sky just before the storm clouds broke.

"Anything for you, sir?" The bartender splayed his hands on the bar before Ben.

Jolted out of his stupor, he cleared his throat. "Bourbon on the rocks."

The bartender splashed whiskey over ice in two glasses. "Hey, think you and this guy should be friends. You guys like your whiskey the same way."

A smile tugged at the guy's lips but didn't quite reach his rain cloud eyes. "A man after my own heart. Cute too." He spared Ben an approving look. Ben swallowed his bourbon down the wrong pipe and choked, heat springing to his ears. "Sorry." The guy thumped Ben on the back. "Didn't mean to almost kill you there." Shaking his head, Ben mumbled that it was fine, fixing his eyes on his whiskey. "Think I'll make this my last one." The guy motioned for the bill. "Or I'll be hitting on the wallpaper next. I am sorry, man. I get stupid when I drink."

"Don't we all?" Ben laughed, though his face still felt hot with embarrassment. He wasn't accustomed to meeting new people.

"You sayin' I'm stupid?" Hooded blue-gray eyes scrutinized him.

Ben growled, squirming in his seat. *What the hell?* "No, I meant... It's just a—"

Laughter rumbled from the man next to him. A smile broke through the stormy exterior, lighting up his face like a ray of sunlight. Ben suddenly forgot what he was flustered about. He forgot everything that had driven him to this bar. In that moment, all he wanted was to make this beautiful man laugh again.

"I'm bein' an asshole. My bad. Let me buy you a drink to make up for it?" He tilted his head in invitation, wavy dark locks swaying against his cheek. For a human, he really wasn't that bad, and not hard on the eyes either. He'd looked so dour and unapproachable until he'd smiled.

Ben downed the last of his whiskey, enjoying the burn. "Got work tomorrow, but fuck it."

"That's the spirit." The guy waved over the bartender. "Gerard, one for my new friend here." He nudged Ben. "What's your name?"

"Ben Stroud." Ben leaned in to sniff him, then realized how odd that might look. He froze with his face inches from the man's. Isaac smelled like bourbon, ashy cigarette smoke, and the clean scent after a rainstorm... It was him. This man was the source of that amazing scent. It took everything he had not to sniff him again.

His fated mate was... a human? No. This had to be a mistake. He couldn't be fated to a human of all people. Sure, this guy smelled nice, but that was all. It had to be.

"What's your name?" Ben asked, voice rough as the scent of rain flooded his senses. He needed to know.

"Isaac Bennet." The guy extended his hand, and Ben shook. Touching him felt like being zapped by lightning. "You're totally not from the city, are you?"

Ben took a sip of whiskey chilled from the ice. "How'd you figure that?"

"You got that wide-eyed puppy dog look most of us had stamped outta us. Where you from?" Isaac leaned an elbow on the bar.

"Ohio," Ben answered with a pang of homesickness. By now, the coyotes would be howling with the wolves as they hunted for prey. The diner would be closing soon, the neon sign of the full moon glowing almost as bright as the real thing. The stars would blanket the sky, shining bright without city lights to wash them out. "Some little town. Probably can't find it on a map," he added before Isaac could ask. He wasn't about to tell a human where he could find the pack, not after what happened to Jackson. "I just moved in today."

"Welcome to New York. Cheers." Isaac raised his glass, though it was empty. Ben returned the gesture with a clink. New Yorkers were friendlier than he'd thought, at least when they were drunk. "You in the neighbor-hood?"

Ben glanced at the door toward where his apartment sat about five minutes away. "Yup."

"Me too. I work here. What brings you to the city? Fame, fortune?"

How to explain? He squeezed his glass. "My family has a big business. I'm running the new branch in the city."

"Impressive, Mr. Businessman." Stormy eyes appraised Ben from his head to his torso as if he were envisioning Ben in a suit instead of a tank top with grease stains and baggy denim jeans.

Heat tingled down south. "Have you lived in Brooklyn long?" Ben realized he hadn't asked Isaac much about himself. Realized with some surprise that he wanted to know.

"About a year." Isaac gently bit the rim of his glass, an unconscious gesture but one that made Ben wonder how those teeth would feel against his skin. "Used to live upstate. Wanted to be close to my ex-wife. For my son's sake."

His voice wavered subtly enough that some might have missed it but Ben's preternatural hearing didn't. The scent of Isaac's sorrow washed over him in waves, drowning him. Ben understood at once. He was missing his son deeply. It was why he was here drinking, why he seemed so open yet so closed off. Something clenched in Ben's gut.

"Sorry," Ben said, his own voice wavering.

"For?"

The scent of Isaac's sorrow made Ben want to do anything to fix it. What an odd thing to feel for a stranger. "I know what it's like, missing someone."

Isaac's eyes widened, and he looked so vulnerable he might break in two. He cleared his throat roughly. "Thank you, 'ppreciate it." Isaac motioned for another drink.

"Think you've had enough, Isaac." Gerard put a hand over Isaac's empty glass protectively.

Isaac shot him a frustrated look that mellowed into somber acceptance. "Ass. Fine, you're right. Hey, guess there's still hope for me; I didn't trash the bar and rage out." With a sardonic smile, he stumbled out of the bar seat and landed on his ass.

Ben winced. "You okay?"

He grabbed onto the bar for support. "Shit. Almost forgot. Here you go." He slapped some cash on the counter. "For his drink."

"Isaac, wait! I'll walk you back!" Gerard called.

"I live five minutes away, man." Isaac teeter-tottered to the door. "Can walk myself home, thanks."

Something about Gerard's offer made Ben's wolf growl. Who was this guy to Isaac? A boyfriend? And why did Ben care? "Where do you live?" he asked, choking down a growl.

"Over on Prospect Place."

Ben paid for their drinks. "I live on the same street. I'll walk you back."

"Yes, please," Gerard said. "Don't want him to run out in traffic after I plied him with drinks."

Isaac flipped Gerard off. "Can go myself."

Ben scoffed. "At this time of night, you'll get robbed before you're halfway home." His father hadn't raised an idiot. He knew when someone needed an escort.

Isaac squeezed Ben's biceps. "Big, burly guy like you'll scare off all my would-be robbers. Don't worry, Gerry, he'll keep me nice and safe."

Ben had been expecting to get flipped off too. Feeling strangely pleased, he accompanied Isaac outside. Isaac suddenly lurched away from him and puked his guts up behind a trash can. Coughing and spitting, he stumbled and Ben snagged him under the arm before he could topple over.

"Fuck. Sorry." Isaac wiped his mouth on his sleeve. "Good thing I didn't have another whiskey..."

Ben tried not to cough. Isaac smelled like the entire bar and vomit. "Let's get you home. Uh..." He suddenly realized he didn't know where home was. He growled, embarrassed and annoyed. How was he supposed to look like a gallant protector if he didn't even know the way home?

"Take a left," Isaac suggested, pointing the way.

Ben took a left and, checking both ways, crossed the street. The occasional car rumbled past and sirens howled—far away, thankfully. Light from the streetlamps pooled around them. Isaac's hood had slipped down, revealing a mop of black curls that framed his face.

When he wasn't smiling, Isaac's face was unreadable. His eyes were clouded, his lips set in a permanent frown—at least, until he caught Ben looking. A tiny smile curled Isaac's lip. He had nice lips, soft and full, but his beard presented a rugged contrast that was quite appealing. Ben quickly looked away. He was supposed to be a gentleman—gentle*wolf*. Not checking out a drunk guy he barely knew. "Thanks." Isaac nudged Ben's shoulder. "Gerry was right; I'm a mess."

His breath smelled foul, like whiskey and puke, but underneath that was still the pleasant scent of the streets after a rainfall. Ben gritted his teeth, strangling down the urge to lean close and sniff, wrap himself in that scent with all the joy of a wolf rolling around in wet leaves. "Yeah." Ben grunted, not thinking. "I mean, not that you're a mess. Just... happy I could walk you home, is all." Why did he make a fool of himself every time he opened his mouth?

Isaac chuckled humorlessly. "You're sweet." His voice trailed away, his eyes glazing over as they walked.

Ben swallowed, suddenly warm all over. "Sweet" sure as hell wasn't a word he'd ever apply to himself, though he'd been called it more than once. He had no idea what to make of this man. Humans were weird.

"Hold up. We're here." Isaac stopped and Ben stumbled, tugging Isaac with him. He turned, and his mouth fell open at the familiar doorway.

"You live here?"

"Yup."

"So do I."

"No shit? Small world." Isaac fumbled for his keys and dropped them. "Damn it."

"Let me—"

Their fingers touched as they both bent to grab the key. It was like a zap of electricity went up Ben's finger and into his spine. Isaac glanced at him, his hair falling into his eyes. Up close, his eyes really looked like streaks of blue breaking through a cloudy sky. Realizing one of them had to break the stare, Ben snatched up Isaac's keys and turned them one by one.

"It's the big one." Isaac leaned unhelpfully against the wall, head back and eyes closed in a liquor-induced daze. He glanced at Ben through hazy, slanted gray eyes, and something in Ben's stomach fluttered.

The door clicked, and the pair made their way up the stairs. Ben counted the flights.

One, two, three, four, five—

"Finally. Home sweet home. And I didn't break my neck on the stairs. Go me." Isaac wobbled over to a door—directly across the hall from Ben's. With a curious hum, he glanced at Ben. "What?"

He looked from his door to Isaac's and back again. "I live right there."

Isaac dropped his head against the door with a laugh. "No fucking way."

Shoving his key in the lock, Ben wrenched open his door for emphasis. Isaac smiled. "Welcome to the building, neighbor. And thanks. Nice to know chivalry ain't dead."

Ben smiled back and raised a hand. "Night."

Isaac waved. "G'ni—" He stumbled through the door and nearly fell on his face. Ben laughed—he couldn't help it. Isaac laughed with him, his face split in a grin, and Ben's breath hitched. His smile really was like the sun, the kind of smile that made it damn near impossible not to smile back. "Goodnight." Isaac emphasized each syllable and, still smiling, closed the door. Ben lingered until the lock clicked. Isaac's smile and rainfall scent were imprinted on his mind.

He scoffed. "Humans," he muttered.

Not all of them were so bad.

"HUMANS AREN'T ALL BAD," Ben said the next morning. "You've lived among humans a while, haven't you?"

Greg Harris panted exasperatedly as he lugged the last box of Ben's weights into the living room. Sweat stained his chest and underarms, drenching his T-shirt that was strained by his plump belly.

"Don't die on me, man." Ben slapped him on the back.

Greg flashed a teasing smile, wiping sweat from his forehead. "Why didn't you warn me you live in a five-floor walk-up? I'm getting old for this shit." With his big glasses and slicked-back hair, he had a scholarly look about him.

Ben scoffed. "You're my age. Lay off the donuts and you'll be fine."

"I'd rather die. You ever been to that donut shop by the park?" Greg plopped down and reclined against the last of the boxes. "You and me gotta hit up that donut place before I leave for the monastery."

Ben gawked. "I'm sorry, the what now?"

"Oh, my pops didn't tell you? Mandy and I broke up, so I'm taking off to live with some monks in Italy."

"Sounds terrible."

Greg looked at him like he were the crazy one. "They invited me! This is a big thing! They're so secretive it's hard for anyone to get invited into their circle. We're gonna meditate under the moon, read tons of tomes on werewolf history, study old relics, and meditate some more probably."

"And the Council's all right with you taking off?" Greg had worked as the Council of Lycanthrope Affairs' historian for years now. He, like many teachers in the paranormal studies field, learned shifter lore and history by working with the Council so they could better educate the masses on the misunderstood supernatural entities that were werewolves.

Greg grinned, round cheeks full of rosy color. "You kidding? They're paying me time off. They'll benefit tons from whatever I learn with the monks."

"Congrats. Just be sure to jerk off tons before you go and kiss your internet goodbye." Ben couldn't imagine anything worse than being stuck in a temple for months.

"Ye of little faith." Greg patted him on the knee with each word. "I can survive just fine without internet and cell phone service and... baser pleasures. It'll be a nice little break."

Ben scoffed. "Guess they'll have you walking around naked too? To strengthen your connection with the earth or whatever."

Greg rolled his eyes skyward. "Hardy-har-har. Get me some water, you grump."

Ben fetched them both water from the tap and rejoined Greg on the floor. His friend downed his glass in one go. "Why'd you ask about humans?"

Ben shrugged, watching the water lap at the rim of his glass. He had no idea how to tell Greg he suspected a human was his mate. He wasn't even sure he'd fully accepted it yet. Seriously, how could that be right?

"That's not helpful."

Ben sighed, reluctant to relive it. "Remember Jackson?"

Greg pursed his lips. He shook his head. "Nope. Oh, wait!" He raised a finger in a moment of *eureka*. "The banker's son! Yeah, I remember him. Why?"

Ben took a much-needed gulp of water. "He died. Humans killed him."

"Shit, man." Greg sighed. "That's rough. Bet that scared the hell outta your folks, huh?"

"My pa warned me to keep to myself, said folk here'll just see me as a monster. You think he's right about that?" His stomach twisted uncertainly and he drained the last of his water.

"Sure. I mean, not all humans. But yeah, you should keep that beast of yours under wraps. Unless, that is, you find someone you know will be cool with it. Crime's up in New York more than ever against wolves. Tons of humans think they can get away with hurting people like us." He gave Ben's shoulder a nudge. "But hey, maybe the LPA will show them how wrong they are."

Ben hoped so.

Greg suddenly chuckled. "I don't know. Humans are fun. I haven't had any trouble. But they're so delicate! They can't heal like us and they're a lot weaker. I'm telling you, I was with this girl once and we were horsing around and I think I broke her finger."

Ben's eyes widened. Humans were really that delicate compared to a werewolf's strength? What if he accidentally hurt a human?

"Shh, Benny," Greg cooed, rubbing his shoulders. "You're sweatin' it out, man. Breathe!"

Ben wriggled out of Greg's grip with a growl. "It's not funny." The last thing he wanted was to draw attention to himself, especially on his first day in the city. "Thanks for the help, Greg. I gotta start the commute to Fire Island."

"Oh, right, your first day!" Greg grinned and bounded to the door after him. "Good luck, Alpha Stroud!" He tousled Ben's hair and jogged to the stairs. Ben watched him go, feeling both lighter than before and worried. It occurred to him he had to plan exactly how he was getting there. He didn't have a car yet, so driving wasn't an option. He would have to take a train and then ride the ferry. Seriously, why couldn't the agency be closer to the city?

First, food. His fridge was empty, so he'd have to grab something to go once he arrived at East New York station. He walked out into the hall and locked the door behind him.

Another door closed at the same time as his. He turned and his stomach gave a pleasant jolt as Isaac stepped out carrying a bag of trash and wearing the same thing he'd worn the night before, his hair a bedraggled mess. Isaac froze at the sight of him, tired, bloodshot eyes widening. Ben gave him a smile. "Hey." Nodding curtly, Isaac grunted something. Ben turned away and locked the door. "Hungover?"

"Yeah." Isaac's voice was gravelly. He'd likely just dragged himself out of bed.

Ben turned back slowly and found Isaac looking away, shuffling his slippers. He was a different person in the light of day—and when he was sober. The friendly man from the night before was now completely closed off. They had been strangers before, yet they'd been drawn together in their eagerness to learn more about each other. What were they now?

"See ya." Unsure what he could say and disappointed by that fact, Ben turned away. He supposed it really had been the drink talking.

"Hey," Isaac blurted.

Ben whipped around, hopeful. He held his breath as Isaac ran a hand through his wavy hair, which was coming loose from its ponytail. "I don't know if I thanked you. For making sure I got home safe. Everything's kind of a blur."

Ben smiled, relieved. "You did," he assured him.

"Oh. Good. I'm not that much of an asshole at least, even drunk."

"Not at all." Okay, maybe a little. But Ben was okay with that.

A smile broke through the gloom on Isaac's face. "Where you off to?"

Ben jumped and checked his watch. "Work. I gotta get to East New York station."

Isaac whistled. "I don't envy your commute. You got a car? 'Cause taxis are hard to get this early."

Ben frowned. He hadn't thought about what he'd do if taxis weren't running. "They are?"

Isaac laughed. "Uh, yeah?"

Ben hummed, troubled. He'd be late if he didn't catch the seven thirty train, and it was half past six.

Isaac said, "I could drive you?"

"You'd really do that?"

"Of course. Just let me throw on some clothes first and throw this trash away." There was a smile in Isaac's voice, as if he were genuinely pleased to help Ben out.

"I'll wait outside," Ben assured him, already excited for their trip together.

Maybe humans really did hate his kind. But this one?

Ben liked him quite a lot.

Chapter 4

A Bright Light

Most of last night was a blur. Isaac remembered his ex-wife Melissa calling him up. Used to be, they couldn't talk without screaming at each other. Ever since Beau's murder however, Melissa would call him to talk about their son.

They'd talk for hours, reminiscing over Beau's toddler days. It was bizarre to be able to have a normal-ish conversation with her after years of animosity between them. Why couldn't they have made their marriage work? Why couldn't they have been better for Beau? The guilt festered inside him, until Isaac had to end the call so he didn't fall apart.

Alone in the apartment with nothing but guilt and despair eating him up from the inside out, he'd decided to go get shit-faced at the bar where he worked. To hell with what his boss thought. *Maybe I'll have one too many and let alcohol poisoning work its magic. Who would miss me?*

The world would be better off if he wasn't in it at all.

"Isaac?"

He jumped, car keys in hand. He'd been staring blankly into the window of his car.

Ben stood opposite the vehicle, waiting expectantly. "We going?"

"Yeah. Sorry. This hangover's fucking with me." Snorting, Isaac opened the car doors and let them both in. "Where'd you say you were going, Grand Central?"

"East New York station. Or is that the same thing?"

Isaac laughed. "Okay, I'm insulted. East New York ain't got nothing on the Grand."

Ben doubled over with a snort, a warm smile softening his face.

Isaac felt an unexpected fluttering in his stomach as he drove from the parking space.

"Sorry," he said, rolling down the window. "If I knew I'd have a guest, I'd have aired out this thing." The interior smelled of smoke and Ben's nostrils kept twitching. Heat warmed Isaac's cheeks. "You smoke?"

"No," Ben stated, wrinkling his nose.

Isaac bit back a sigh. He really wanted a cigarette, even if he'd already smoked two with his meager breakfast of coffee and two Advil.

Sudden silence enveloped the car. Ben looked out the window and Isaac focused on the road. Every so often, his eyes strayed to Ben, a prickling at his neck. Each time Ben would look away so fast he'd hear his neck crack.

It must be awkward for Ben to ask Isaac of all people for help. He'd made a fool of himself last night, he was sure. Knowing how loose his tongue was when he drank, he'd likely hit on Ben multiple times and made him uncomfortable. Well, his drunk self had good taste, at least. Because Ben was smokin' hot.

On top of that, Ben had wanted to make sure he didn't walk out in front of a speeding car. He'd cared enough about this idiot drunk he barely knew to walk him home. Isaac swallowed, a lump in his throat. His life was worthless and meaningless, but Ben clearly didn't think so—*hadn't* thought so. Who knew what he thought now in the light of day? Regardless of where they stood this morning, he wanted to cling onto that memory for a while and bundle himself up in it like a blanket.

They stopped for the light. There was heavy traffic but they had time. Isaac drummed his fingers on the wheel.

"Lotta traffic," Ben remarked. He glowered with his chin in his palm, low brows sweeping over piercing silver eyes that brought to mind the shimmer of moonlight over a bank of snow. He had beautiful eyes, even when they were narrowed in a scowl. Isaac had seen them soften and light up when he smiled.

"We've got time," Isaac assured him, hoping to soften that frown. "I'll get you there."

Ben hummed, his mouth twitching into a small smile. "Thanks."

Isaac stomped on the gas. He blinked, suddenly emotional for reasons he wasn't sure of. How long had it been since he'd felt useful? Needed? It was stupid, but knowing Ben was relying on him right now... it meant something to him. How pathetic.

Ben had a nice smile. Usually the guys or girls Isaac hit on in one of his drunken stupors turned out to be less attractive than they'd seemed after one too many drinks. Ben, though? Ben was as handsome when Isaac was sober as he'd been when Isaac was drunk.

He was tall, the top of his head just barely scuffing the roof of the car. On top of that, he was built like a wrestler with big, strong arms bronzed with a tan from days under the sun. His neat beard was the stuff of envy; Isaac was far too lazy to care for any facial hair he grew. Maybe it was his strong nose and high, flat cheekbones, those piercing eyes the color of moonlight, or the way he wore his chestnut hair long and loose, but he reminded Isaac of a Viking warrior.

His stomach lurched when he looked into those silver eyes. He looked away fast, focusing on the road. "Where do you work?"

"Over on Fire Island."

"Whoa." Isaac sure didn't envy his commute.

"Not all of us can live five minutes away from our job." Ben's tone was teasing. A smile broke through his broody façade, his bright teeth unnaturally sharp beneath the curl of his lip. Fuck. Why did Isaac want to ask Ben to bite him?

"What do you do for work?"

Ben looked down into his lap and shrugged. "Uh, I just push papers for human resources."

In the quiet that followed, Isaac felt as if the pair of them were wrapped in a bubble nothing could puncture. The cars started moving again and they made idle conversation when the need possessed them. Ben didn't initiate conversation, but he opened up and met Isaac halfway. He learned Ben was an only child and his parents wouldn't stop calling to make sure he hadn't been struck by a cab. They sounded like good people.

Ben had been born and raised in a tiny Ohio town, where he'd also gone to college and earned his master's degree in social work. He'd done his field placement in the town's medical clinic and schools. No wonder he was so overwhelmed by city life after spending all his years in a small town. Isaac admired his bravery. It took guts to leave behind the only life you knew in pursuit of something new.

So he was good-hearted, handsome, and wanted to help his fellow man? That was sexy as hell. And way out of Isaac's league, he reminded himself, trying to tamp down the pull toward Ben.

The station grew closer.

"Where are we?" Ben's low, gentle voice asked.

Isaac peered out of the window. "Here we are." He pulled into a parking spot just outside the station.

"And with time to spare too." Ben fished in his pockets and held out twenty dollars.

Isaac pushed it away. "It was no problem." Ben smiled sweetly and returned the money to his pocket. It was his pleasure, really. Driving Ben through the city was way more enjoyable than sitting around at home brooding.

His stomach growled. He hadn't eaten breakfast.

"Hungry?" Ben eyed him knowingly.

Isaac gaped, outraged. How had he heard that? His hearing was insane. "A bit, yeah."

"I'll buy you breakfast. Where's a good place to eat around here?"

Isaac checked the time. They'd need something fast. "There's a McDonald's across the street."

Ben squinted. "A McWhat?"

Isaac blinked at him. "You've never… Don't tell me you don't know what a McDonald's is. I don't care what backwards little village you grew up in."

Ben continued to look confused.

"Wow." Isaac was stunned. "Okay. We're fixing that. Now. Follow me." He grabbed onto Ben's thick arm and dragged him toward the fast-food chain. If Isaac hadn't believed Ben had never been inside a McDonald's, he certainly believed it now; the guy appeared shell-shocked as he gaped up at the menu. As a variety of smells wafted through the restaurant, Ben sniffed the air with zeal. He did that a lot, Isaac had noted. Maybe it was a tic or a medical condition?

"Hey, hurry it up! I got a train to catch!" a lady barked behind them.

Ben's eyes widened and ruddy color sprang to his cheeks. "Sorry." He took a wide step to the side. Isaac let a few people go before them while Ben decided.

"Tell me you've had a burger before."

"Yeah… Just not sure about all this other stuff. What's a Happy Meal?"

Isaac tried not to laugh. He really did. He coughed instead. "How about a breakfast sandwich?"

"There's so many…"

Isaac decided to help the guy out and ordered them two breakfast sandwiches, assuring Ben that he would love it. Ben shoved some money at him, red in the face and looking flustered. Isaac let him pay. He was sure the guy was embarrassed. Food in hand, they went to sit on the platform to wait for Ben's train.

"So what do they have in your town instead of McDonald's?" Isaac asked.

Ben shrugged. "A diner. Best meat loaf you've ever tasted. A barbeque place. All the meat's locally sourced, fresh as if you're eating right off the carcass itself."

"Sounds great." Isaac had suddenly lost interest in his food.

Ben smiled, a dreamy look in his eyes. "It is…"

"Huh. Maybe I should visit sometime if the food's that good."

Ben choked on his food. "You can't!" Isaac gaped at him, surprised by his outburst. Ben deflated. "It's... boring," he added much more calmly, flushing red to the tips of his ears.

Ben's train roared into the station, shattering what might have been an awkward silence. Isaac smiled and waved. "Have a good first day. Thanks for breakfast."

Ben raised a hand. "You're welcome. Thanks for getting me here."

Isaac walked to the stairs and looked back. The crowd had already swallowed Ben. The train pulled out of the station, and Isaac walked back to his car.

Isaac's new neighbor was... a lot of things. He was a grumpy giant with the heart of a kitten; he really liked to sniff just about anything like a big dog; he was kind and gentle, though a bit easily flustered; he was handsome, very handsome; he made Isaac laugh and smile when he thought he'd never do so again.

Isaac liked him a lot. Ben was a bright light in a very dark place, and Isaac hadn't realized just how badly he'd needed the sun until Ben came along.

BEN THOUGHT A LOT during the ferry ride to Fire Island, mostly about Isaac. He was on Ben's mind more than he thought he should be. They were still in the getting-to-know-you phase but Ben knew enough about him to know one thing was certain: he liked Isaac. He knew Isaac had his problems—that much was clear. He drank like a fish and was prone to making poor decisions, and he had the habit of downplaying himself.

It didn't take a genius to see he'd been through a lot. Sometimes, he'd get all quiet and a darkness would cover his face like a heavy cloud. Then when he smiled, it was like the sun coming out. Ben wanted to see more of his smiles; he wanted to learn more about what Isaac liked, what he was passionate about, discover all the things that made him happy.

More than anything, his wolf liked Isaac. The beast was so close to the surface around Isaac, content and excited. It was frightening because Ben wasn't sure how Isaac would feel if he knew what Ben was. He couldn't help it; his wolf liked the way Isaac smelled, and he growled deep in Ben's chest at the thought of anyone causing Isaac pain. His inner animal wanted to protect Isaac. It was a feeling Ben had never felt before, not even with Heather. He supposed it might be because Isaac was the only connection he had in this big city, and Ben felt safe with him.

Even if he could never know what Ben was.

His heart clenched in his chest. If Isaac was his mate, how would that work, especially if humans were as delicate as Greg said? Ben had been extra careful not to touch Isaac in case he hurt him. He would have to keep the wolf under control so he didn't lose Isaac's friendship.

It was a short walk to the agency's gates from the ferry. Ben's jaw dropped at the sight. Nestled within a vast forest of palm trees, the new Lycanthrope Protection Agency was by far their biggest location to date. It boasted hundreds of acres of space for the rehabilitating wolves to roam and hunt, and housing construction was underway for doctors and staff farther in the woods. There was an enormous courtyard in the back with a garden, swimming pool, and an open space.

However, Ben's delight faded as he strode farther down the driveway. A crowd of people, all human by the stink of them, surrounded the front gate. They carried signs and shouted into megaphones. "Go back to the fucking woods!" a bearded man screamed, red-faced.

"You will not replace us!" a woman bellowed, shaking her fist at the gate.

Ben's claws lengthened, and a growl rumbled in his throat. Humans dominated society, yet the moment the rights of his people were brought into the spotlight for a change, humans felt insecure about their place in the food chain of life.

Inside the gates, shifters in human form snarled, flashing their claws and baring their fangs, their faces and arms covered in fur. At their sides stood shifters in their wolf forms, their ears flattened and their fangs bared defensively.

Ben massaged his temples. No way. Not today. The new agency had just opened its doors, and it was too damn early for all this drama. Sucking in a breath and summoning a growl, he unleashed a roar so loud it strained his throat. The crowd fell suddenly silent, their heads whipping around as anger turned to fear.

Ben smiled, showing off his fangs, and raised a clawed hand to wave. "Problem?"

The humans seemed to shrink back, all but one brave soul. The bearded man shuffled forward. "Your... your kind doesn't belong here."

Ben folded his arms, almost respecting the fool. He opened his arms again, motioning to the woods around them. The humans flinched back. "Case you haven't noticed, folks, we are in the woods. You're the ones trespassing. I want you gone on the count of three. One. Two."

The humans took off running, throwing down the megaphones and signs. With that annoyance taken care of, Ben radioed in for someone to come clean up the trash.

On the first floor of the three-story manor was a clinic in cases of emergencies and a big kitchen and massive dining room where buffets were served to the agency's patients and staff. There was also a gym Ben had every intention of using, as well as a variety of recreational rooms.

Kennels for feral wolves to rest and recuperate in while they awaited the Humanity Restorative Treatment as well as bedrooms for shifters in their human form occupied the second level. On the top floor, there were several offices, a library for research, and labs. Ben dashed to his office, eager to go over his notes.

He would have to do a full sweep of the estate, check in with the doctors and staff, meet with patients, make sure the trainers were all here to manage the catchers responsible for rescuing ferals off the street. That was a tough job; they had to be fast and strong, skilled with nonlethal weapons to tranquilize feral werewolves before they could hurt themselves or others.

With a shaky exhale, he gripped the back of his chair tight and hoped he was up to the task.

Pushing his doubts aside, Ben puffed out his chest and over the intercom he called all staff who were available for a meeting. There were a lot of them, shifters of all skill sets, all passionate about helping make New York State a haven for their kind. He cleared his throat.

"I'm Ben Stroud, leader of the agency. Just Ben, okay? I hate that alpha wolf rubbish. I'm not gonna sugarcoat it. Politicians all over the country are emboldening others to lash out against werewolves by stereotyping us as monsters."

Many states had passed dozens of laws against werewolves. Some politicians were dead set on preventing shifter kids from participating in school sports because they falsely believed the competition would provoke a werewolf's prey drive, causing them to attack their fellow students. Other states banned books that showed werewolves in a positive light or punished teachers trying to educate their students about wolves. Politicians in New York boasted that the city was a safe haven for shifters, but hate crimes against werewolves were fifteen percent higher than in recent years.

"More than ever, we're being targeted by humans just for being what we are. Werewolves have more power and presence around the country than ever before, and they can't stand it. You're angry and hurt. I am too, damn it. But we are gonna do something about it." He paced, his eyes scanning over the faces. They whispered and shook their heads, faces grim and eyes burning. They wanted change. "We are a voice for any wolf who feels ostracized. And we're gonna prove to humans that America is our home too. They can try and break us, but we'll come back tougher than before."

The crowd cheered, their eyes shining with emotion.

Ben bit back a smile. "Now, get back to work. I'll stop by the kennels and clinic, visit the new catchers. You'll be seeing a lot of me."

The crowd dispersed slowly.

"Mr. Stroud?" There was a knock at the door.

"Come in."

Ben instantly recognized the man before him—tanned and Hispanic, with glossy black hair, a neat mustache, and warm, twinkling brown eyes. A sniff told Ben he was a wolf and more than that, he was half-human too. A hybrid. At his side stood a human woman with olive skin and a bright smile. Hiding behind her legs was a little girl with pigtails. Next to his father's side was a preteen boy who was tall and curly-haired, his nose buried in his phone.

"Councilman Manuel Reyes. My wife, Veronica." Ben knew who he was without any introduction needed. Manuel Reyes was the first hybrid to serve as the representative for New York on the Council of Lycanthrope Affairs.

Ben jumped up to shake their hands. "It's an honor to meet both of you."

"My kids." Manuel laughed, ruffling the little girl's hair. "This is Isabella. Izzie, say hello."

Little Isabella poked her head out from behind her mom's leg. "Hi. Um. Hola." She hugged her wolf plush close. Ben smiled. She was so cute.

"Very good, kiddo." Manuel chuckled and stroked his daughter's hair. "We've been teaching them Spanish. Never want them to forget their roots, even if they're growing up in New York."

"Gabriel. Hey. Put that away and say hello." Veronica motioned to her son.

Gabriel jumped and shoved his phone in his pocket.

"My son, Gabe," Manuel said.

Gabe raised a hand and smiled awkwardly. "Hey." He was cute too, in the gangly way preteens could be.

"Go sit down outside, kids." Veronica ushered them to the door. "We'll just be a minute." Izzie whined but Gabe took her hand, not looking like he cared either way and eager to get back on his phone.

Veronica's eyes sparkled. "We just wanted to congratulate you, Alpha Stroud. This organization... it means so much to our family."

"Just Ben, please. I'm glad to hear it." Ben didn't doubt her for a second. Werewolves were discriminated against, but hybrids were treated even worse—not just by humans but by werewolves as well, because of some werewolves' bigoted belief that any wolf with human blood wasn't a real shifter at all but a traitor for breeding with their oppressors. It was bullshit, all of it. It infuriated Ben that such hatred could come from their own community when they should be working together.

Veronica clutched her husband's arm and continued, voice wavering. "We worry about the kids, you know? They have to grow up in a world where they could be mistreated. It's such a hard thing to have to tell your child that someone won't like them for reasons that aren't their fault. And..." She wiped her eyes.

Manuel held her close. "We're very grateful for your agency's presence, Ben." His voice, thick with emotion, wavered. "It gives us hope that after we're gone, there'll be someone looking out for our kids when they need it." He clasped Ben's hand again and squeezed tight. "Thank you. For everything that you do. It means the world to families like ours."

Their heartfelt words made Ben misty-eyed. He held Manuel's hand tight. "That's why the agency's here, Mr. Reyes. It's a hard job but knowing our work's made even the smallest difference reminds me it's worth it."

People like Manuel and his family were the reason Ben would never give up the fight, not until there was true peace within their fractured community and with humans.

CHAPTER 5

DEATH TO ĤYBRIDS AND ĤUMANS

THAT EVENING, MANUEL AND Veronica invited Ben over for dinner.

The Reyes home was quaint and well-loved, with crayon scrawled on the wallpaper and the walls covered in photos of Gabe, Izzie, Veronica's family in Spain, and Manuel's pack in Mexico City.

Ben sat down at the table, which was loaded with chicken, potatoes, and vegetables. "Looks delicious, Veronica."

"Kids, turn off the TV," Veronica called over her shoulder. "Dinner is ready!"

"Where's Pops?" Gabe asked, coming to sit down. Izzie was fixated on the TV.

Veronica smiled, but there was something off about her scent. She smelled worried. "He's running late with his meeting."

Ben could smell Manuel somewhere in the apartment, probably a home office.

Just as the kids sat down at the table, Manuel emerged from the bedroom. He waved at Ben and smiled, but it didn't reach his eyes.

"Everything good?" Gabe asked around a bite of chicken.

"Chew your food, Gabriel," Veronica admonished lightly.

Gabe rolled his eyes, which made Veronica roll them right back, and they both laughed.

"Yeah, mijo." But Manuel didn't sound convincing to Ben's ears.

56

Dinner was delicious. Gabe told them all about soccer practice. Izzie was excited about Thanksgiving, which was a few weeks away. Manuel was oddly quiet. After dinner, Manuel cleared the table while Veronica told the kids to brush their teeth. A heavy rainstorm poured down outside.

"Ben, would you like to stay the night? The couch folds out into a bed," Veronica said.

"Oh, no, I couldn't."

"Please. It's no trouble."

Ben accepted her offer. Once the kids were in bed, Veronica served them all some wine and they sat together in the living room. Manuel set his glass down and cleared his throat. "Alpha Hanson gave me troubling news today. Jacob Morgan, a Moonborn cultist, murdered a human-werewolf couple and is currently on the run from law enforcement."

Veronica's face paled. "That couple was murdered in our neighborhood. You're telling me there was a cultist prowling our streets?"

Manuel shivered. "Yes."

A growl rumbled in Ben's throat. The Moonborn cult were full-blooded werewolves who despised human-werewolf couplings and the hybrid children born from them. Their twisted religious beliefs dictated that hybrids tainted the divine connection all werewolves had to the She-Wolf, the deity who'd created all wolves. It was disgusting and wrong.

Veronica looked ready to start breathing fire. With a sigh that was fortunately lacking flames, she glowered into her wine, her plucked brows pinched. "We should move, leave the city."

Manuel shook his head. "What kind of lesson is it going to teach our children if we let fear dictate our lives, V? Nowhere is truly safe for people like us. It's simply the way of the world."

Veronica's eyes filled with tears. "What if the children get hurt, Manuel?"

"They won't." Manuel squeezed her hand. "We will never let that happen."

Ben said, "I know how you feel. My family's been threatened more than once. I've been on the receiving end of violence. It's a dangerous business, challenging the way loud, angry folk think things should be. But if we don't do it, who will?"

The conversation died a miserable death. Veronica set up some blankets on the sofa and Ben settled in to sleep. He was grateful not to have to navigate his way home in the torrent of rain lashing the windows. A door creaked open, and tiny bare feet slapped the floor. He heard frustrated mumbling.

He turned on the lamp and little Izzie gave a start. Ben waved his fingers. "Need help?"

"I can't reach." She pointed to the cabinets. "Someone took my step stool."

Ben untangled himself from the blankets and went to the kitchen. He opened the cabinet and reached up.

"That one," Izzie said, pointing out a plastic cup patterned with wolves.

Armed with the cup, Ben asked, "What'll it be, miss? Water, juice, warm milk?"

"Milk, please."

Ben heated her some milk in the frother and made some for himself too. He needed the serotonin after this stressful day.

"You're too big to drink milk."

Ben grinned. "Says who?"

She shrugged and accepted the milk. She hoisted herself into her chair and Ben sat beside her. He took a warm, grateful sip, and Izzie giggled, her eyes slanting when she smiled in a way that resembled Veronica. "You've got milk in your mustache!"

Ben licked his upper lip and poked her nose. "So do you."

She burst into a fresh wave of giggles. Izzie's infectious laughter made it hard not to smile.

They drank in silence. Ben noticed that her eyes were red like she'd been crying. "Everything all right, kiddo?"

Izzie kicked her little legs back and forth. Her toes didn't quite touch the ground. Big brown eyes glanced at him. "Is the bad man who killed those hybrids going to try and hurt us?"

Ben winced. He supposed she'd been eavesdropping. He shook his head and smiled at her. "No, kiddo. Your parents will protect you."

"I'm scared." Her face scrunched up, big pearly tears in her eyes. "What if someone hurts my mom and dad, or my brother?"

Ben sighed, gazing down into his frothy milk for answers. "I know the feeling."

He told her about how, one night, his father had needed to leave. His parents had fought before he left; his father had wanted to drive to the neighboring pack where there'd been an attack against the wolves there. His mother hadn't wanted him to go. She couldn't go—she'd had to stay and watch Ben—and she'd told him this work was going to get him killed. Why couldn't he think of their family? His father had left and even after the sun set, he hadn't come back.

Ben's mother had told him not to worry, but he'd heard her pacing and restless, and she'd sat on the porch most of the night. Unable to sleep, Ben had gone and sat with her. He remembered it had been a hot night. His skin had been sticky with sweat and from nerves. He'd sat on the bench beside the rocker where his mother sat. Moths had swarmed to the porch light, making little buzzing noises when they'd tapped against the light.

"Is Papa coming home?" he'd asked.

She'd smiled but it was fragile. She'd opened her arms and bundled him up when he ran to her. "I don't know, pup."

Ben had wished he'd never gone. "Why didn't he stay?" He should have stayed. What if something had happened?

"Because his work is important to him."

"Does he love work more than us?"

She'd looked at him in disbelief. "No. Not at all. Ben, it's because he loves us that he works so hard and puts himself in danger." She'd held his face in her hands, blinking away the tears in her eyes. "He wants you to grow up in a world that's safe for our kind. That's why he—" Her voice had trailed off with a gasp of relief as a light had flooded the porch.

A familiar truck had parked in front of the house, and though it was dark, Ben had recognized his father's tall silhouette at once. He'd smelled like blood but when he'd turned to them, he'd smiled despite the blood on his forehead. Ben and his mother had run off the porch and into his arms. All the fear and worry had evaporated.

"If it was so dangerous, why'd he do it?" Izzie asked.

"Because he had to. As grown-ups, it's our job to make sure the world is a kind and safe place for kids like you."

Izzie smiled, easing the worry pinching her face. "My papa is a hero. He helps werewolves."

Ben grinned and touched her shoulder. "He sure is."

"And you are too!"

Ben snorted, his ears warming. "Nah."

"Mama told me you help werewolves who get hurt by humans. So, you are a hero." Who was he to argue with her? Done with her milk, Izzie jumped off her chair and waved. "Goodnight, Mr. Stroud," she whispered loud enough for him to hear. Ben waved.

The door closed and Ben sat and finished his warm milk, watching as lights from passing cars below streaked across the ceiling and faded into shadow. The house was still and quiet, full of the smells of the Reyes pack.

He was unsure what the future held but one thing was certain. The Reyes pack, from Manuel to Veronica down to little Izzie and her brother—they were pack. His pack. And anyone that had trouble with them, even Moonborn cultists, would have trouble with him.

IsAAC KNEW THE MINUTE he woke up that today was going to be a shit day. He took some Advil for breakfast, smoked, and seriously considered drenching his alcohol-deprived brain with more liquor, societal norms be damned. He was half-tempted to call out of work and sleep the day away. He didn't want to talk to anyone or do anything. As Thanksgiving grew closer, he got more and more withdrawn. He hated the holidays more than anything since Beau was killed.

There was a knock at his door. Who in the hell? Isaac squinted through the peephole. His heart galloped at the sight of Ben. Shit! He'd forgotten they'd made plans to hang out this weekend. He ran his hands hastily through his bedraggled hair and checked his breath. He smelled like cigarette smoke.

"Just a minute!" He bolted to the bathroom and scrubbed his teeth with copious amounts of toothpaste. He knew Ben hated cigarettes, so he didn't want to drive him off. Drenching his fingers under the faucet, he quickly detangled his hair into what he hoped was a presentable state.

Ben smiled brightly at the sight of him when Isaac answered the door. "Hey." His ears were red, his smile sweetly shy. "Figured I owed you breakfast." He held up a container of food, homemade from the looks of it and delicious by the smell.

"Didn't you pay?"

Ben faltered. "Yeah, but..." His brow furrowed low. "You want it or not?" Ben shoved the food at him.

Isaac chuckled. "Sorry, I—thanks, Ben. I appreciate it." Of all the guys who could live across the hall from him, he was so happy it was Ben Stroud. "Do you want to—" He stopped himself at once. His apartment was a disaster but he didn't want to just slam the door on Ben. "Wanna head to the park? We can eat there."

"Sure. I'll meet you downstairs."

Isaac smiled and shut the door. He slumped, burning up from embarrassment. He was such a mess. There was Ben, looking gorgeous and so put together at ten o'clock in the morning on a Saturday while Isaac had just dragged himself out of bed. He threw open his drawer, carefully sniffing each article of clothing he picked. He had to do the laundry; he was running out of shirts without stains.

Just the fact that he cared about his appearance gave him some sense of normalcy. For the past year, he hadn't cared about anything except hunting down feral wolves that had slipped under the police radar. Now it seemed like he cared about spending time with Ben too.

Is that okay? A stab of guilt suddenly hit, churning his stomach. His chest tightened painfully and breathing was hard. Was it all right that he'd found some small semblance of happiness? It was Beau who'd deserved happiness and yet he was gone and Isaac was breathing his air, experiencing moments of joy Beau would never have.

Should he go? He likely wasn't any fun to be around. Still, he wasn't such an asshole that he'd leave Ben hanging after he'd generously prepared him breakfast. He should count himself lucky Ben was even giving him a second thought. He tugged on a mostly clean sweatshirt and sought Ben out by the entrance to Prospect Park, smiling with an ease he hadn't expected at the sight of Ben, who was scowling as he chewed.

"A squirrel poop in it?" Isaac peered into Ben's serving of eggs and breakfast sausage.

"Eggs are rubbery." Ben sighed.

Isaac didn't want to laugh at him. Really. But he almost did. "So?" He reached for the plastic container and Ben clutched it to his chest.

"Maybe we oughta go to a restaurant or something..."

Isaac snorted. "Come on, it can't be that bad." His fingers brushed Ben's as he took the second container. His skin came alive with sensation, tingling like he'd been shocked. He was close enough to Ben to hear his breath hitch.

"Thank you. I'm sure it'll be good." He took a seat on the bench beside Ben and dug in, finding the eggs to be better than Ben had made them out to be. He could faintly taste Worcestershire sauce, a generous helping of pepper and salt, and some butter too.

Ben's massive frame was impossible not to notice from the corner of his eye. Long, sleek strands of brown hair falling across his face, he stared into his lap, opening and closing the hand Isaac had touched. Isaac smiled at the sight of him, as brooding as a warrior inspecting a wound. He hoped he hadn't made Ben uncomfortable. He was shyer than his gruff looks implied.

"You okay?"

"Hm?" Ben's moody face softened into a warm smile. "Yeah."

"You one of those guys who never cooked until after he moved out from home?" Isaac speared a sausage and took a bite.

"Why, is the food bad?"

Okay, no making jokes around you, Isaac thought. "No. It's good. Just wondering... 'cause I was one of those guys."

Ben grunted in understanding. "I moved out when I was twenty-five, though I spent most of my life in the same town as my family, and it wasn't a big town. Might as well not have moved out at all. When did you leave your pa—*home*?" Ben visibly cringed, shaking his head for some reason.

Casting his mind back, Isaac looked up to the sky. It was a clear day, bright and blue. "I was seventeen. Went to live with my aunt and uncle."

"That's young."

"My mother had died. Cancer. She left me enough money to put myself through school, but hell if I knew what I was passionate about or interested in. I started working in a bar to pay for school, decided I was into it, and dropped out of college after my girlfriend became pregnant."

Ben chuckled as if he were impressed. "My folks woulda killed me if I'd done that."

Isaac shared his humor. "I don't regret it. I've worked in bars all over the city. The pizza joint is okay."

"Favorite place you've ever worked?" Ben asked.

Isaac smiled. "This taqueria, without a doubt. I almost became a mixologist there. They were going to let me make my own drinks. It felt like... like all these years of hard work was about to pay off, and..." Isaac wet his lips, his appetite diminished.

"Fell through?" Ben guessed.

"Got fired. Um... there was a..." Isaac closed his eyes tight as pictures of Beau's little pale hand burst into his mind, flashing in and out of sight with every blink of the flashlight. He couldn't tell Ben about his son; it was too soon to bare his broken heart to a stranger. The reminder of Beau had him reaching for a cigarette. "You mind?"

Ben shrugged, though his brows knit. In disgust or worry, Isaac couldn't tell. He lit up and sucked in smoke.

"You should quit."

Isaac's mouth twitched at Ben's concern. "I'll quit when I'm dead."

Ben frowned. "Might happen sooner rather than later."

It didn't matter. Isaac exhaled smoke, his knee bouncing up and down.

"You okay?" Attentive silver eyes took his breath away. The man was so intense, but only in good ways. The leaves on the trees shivered in the air. It was cooler than it had been weeks ago.

"How're you liking New York so far?" Isaac asked, eager to change the subject.

Ben leaned back against the bench, gazing out at the skyscrapers like mountains on the horizon. "It's big, loud, smelly. I love it. Don't think I'll ever live anywhere else."

Isaac was pleased Ben wasn't quite as homesick anymore. "Here I thought a country boy like you would never settle in."

"It hasn't been that bad. My friend Greg's in the city for a while and I met a nice family. Good people. Hard not to feel at home." Ben opened and closed his hand as if he were still feeling Isaac's touch. Isaac flexed his own fingers and swore he could still feel Ben's. "Then there's you." Ben didn't look at him but a smile softened his hard mouth.

Isaac laughed breathlessly. "What about me?"

Ben fidgeted, scratching at the back of his head. Some hair came loose from his ponytail and swayed against his face. "Well, you coulda just let me get to the train station myself, but you didn't. You showed me places to get food."

"I wouldn't eat at fast-food joints all the time."

"I mean I'm—" Ben slumped with a sigh, not appreciating Isaac's joke. Or perhaps just flustered. "I'm glad we're neighbors." Ben's voice was quiet, nearly carried away by the gentle howl of the wind, but Isaac heard every word as if they were meant for him alone. From anyone else it might have been such a simple, casual thing to say, but Ben's face went so red it was clear he meant every word.

Isaac's fingers twitched, aching to reach out to him, to show him how much it meant to him that he had Ben's friendship. Knowing Ben was the best thing that had happened to him in a long time. It only occurred to him that Ben might not want to be touched after his fingers settled on Ben's knee. His knee jerked and Isaac held his breath.

Shit! What had he done? If Ben wasn't into guys or wasn't even remotely touchy-feely like Isaac was, this would be a huge mistake. "Sorry." He looked up into wide silver eyes but there was no revulsion or discomfort. His eyes were like gentle pools of moonlight. Ben's throat rippled as he swallowed, his wide eyes never leaving Isaac's.

Ben's fingers settled so lightly over the back of Isaac's hand it could have been the touch of the wind. Isaac thought he felt those big, warm fingers tremble as Ben's hand moved, covering the top of Isaac's as if to protect it.

Isaac's phone rang and Ben jerked his hand away. Unable to look at him, Isaac yanked his phone out and put it to his ear. "Sorry. I need to take this." He walked a short distance away and answered the call.

"Isaac, it's Don. We have a problem."

Isaac's heart sank. "What is it?"

"Werewolves are planning a 'peaceful' protest at Union Square."

Isaac scoffed. "Protesting what?"

"Oh, who knows? Their right to slaughter humans and encroach upon our species? If things take a violent turn, the scent of blood could make them go feral. We need to get down there and put down the dogs."

Isaac swallowed, his food a lump in his stomach. "Got it."

"I need you at the scene. Get to high ground where you can watch the goings-on and track down any stragglers that might escape the police's attention. Bring proof of your kill, as always, and you'll be rewarded."

Isaac glanced at Ben. "Don, I... I can't right now."

"What?" Don's surprised voice made him wince.

"Look, you know how passionate I am about our cause. But I'm kind of in the middle of—"

"Isaac, I'm disappointed in you," Don said, and his words were like a blow to Isaac's chest.

"I'm sorry, Don. You know that any other day, I would be there. But this is important." He glanced back at Ben, who offered him a sweet smile. He didn't want to walk away from Ben. Not when he felt happier than he had in a year. Finally, there was something more to his life than hunting and grief.

"What could be more important than the hunt?" Don asked, and Isaac wanted to crumble when he heard the disappointment in Don's voice. "Than protecting innocent people? People like your son?"

"Don, I..." Bile rose in Isaac's throat, and he wanted to slap himself. Of course, he was being so selfish. Don was right. He had to put the needs of others above himself. "Never mind. You're right. I'll be there, okay?"

Don sighed, the sound pleased and relieved. "Good. I knew I could count on you, my son."

Isaac hung up. He hated to leave, but this was important. Innocent people could get hurt. It was a dangerous day for anyone when werewolves decided to ignore the laws that kept their inner animal in check.

He walked back to Ben. "Sorry, Ben. Something's come up. I gotta run."

Ben frowned. "Everything okay?"

"I think so, just some disaster at work they need me for." Isaac smiled, though he felt terrible for ditching Ben. "So, uh..." He leaned down and kissed Ben's cheek. "Thanks for breakfast."

Ben blinked, color rising to his cheeks. "S-sure. No problem!"

Isaac squeezed his hand, his heart galloping in joy. "You have today off, right?"

"Yeah. I'll be around all day." Ben nodded, still looking pleasantly stunned.

"I'll knock on your door later."

"O-okay. Sure."

Isaac took a few steps backward, reluctant to turn his back on Ben. "See ya."

Ben waved and offered a bright smile that nearly made Isaac walk into a tree when he managed to pull his gaze away from him.

Isaac jogged to his car. He checked the trunk and found his gym bag where he kept his crossbow and silver pistols. He slammed his foot down on the gas and drove toward Union Square Park, soaring over the Brooklyn Bridge. His stomach churned like a washing machine, heart slamming fast against his chest.

He hadn't woken up today wanting to kill, but he would if any of the monsters endangered innocent human life. It was his duty to prevent as much suffering as he could at the hands of these animals.

Nevertheless, his stomach still hadn't settled by the time he arrived at Union Square. The square was closed off to the public by police cars and NYPD barricades. The furious howling of wolves sent a shudder down his spine as he stepped out of his car, gym bag across his shoulder. He needed a decent vantage point.

There were several apartments that dotted the area, so he backtracked to an apartment building. The fire escape ladder hung rather low. He took a running start and jumped, grabbing onto the ladder. It creaked and wobbled in protest but Isaac hoisted himself off the ground and climbed, footsteps slamming on the metal steps. Once on the roof, he maneuvered from rooftop to rooftop toward the park, where at last he found a suitable vantage point.

The park sprawled below him. A crowd of werewolves in the square proudly displayed their fangs and claws and some had fully shifted to wolves, but they weren't growling and sat calmly by their comrades' sides. The shifters who were in their human form carried signs that declared *Hybrids are wolves too!* and *Equality for weres and humans!* among other signs. So far, things seemed peaceful, though knowing werewolves' volatile tempers, shit could go down any minute now.

It seemed they were protesting the murders committed by the Moonborn cultist a few days ago. Moonborn—just the name of the cult made him shudder. As Don put it, the cult's name was a reference to the belief that pure-blooded werewolves were descendants of the She-Wolf, their lunar deity, and that any who dared pollute their bloodline—by reproducing with humans, in this case—was a traitor to the species.

The werewolf protestors booed and snarled in rage as a group full of humans marched up to the square carrying banners and signs. Isaac's heart raced when he realized they were armed with silver baseball bats. A wall of police shielded them from the werewolf protestors.

The cops wore riot gear of all things. Isaac thought that was a bit excessive but pushed down the thought. Werewolves were always dangerous, even unarmed ones. One of the counterdemonstrators shouted into a megaphone, "You fucking dogs need to get out of our city! Nobody wants you or your shifter disease. You and your Moonborn friends!"

A werewolf snarled, "They do not represent us! We're not Moonborn!"

Isaac retrieved his crossbow and laid it across his knee. He hesitated to arm it. So far, the werewolves weren't doing anything wrong. If anything, it was the humans who were bound to stir shit up with all their yelling. Until they'd arrived, the shifters had been protesting peacefully. Now, things were beginning to heat up.

What would Don want him to do? No doubt, Don's priority would be the humans. Still, there was a sour taste in his mouth as he armed his crossbow with a bolt tipped in silver. He dipped several of his darts in a bottle of aconitum. It would weaken the beasts and kill them before they had the chance to do much damage. But he'd only use it if they attacked.

One of the humans threw something over the heads of the cops. It exploded in a burst of flame near the paws of one of the shifted wolves. A Molotov cocktail! The wolves yelped and snarled in rage. One of the half-shifted protestors let loose a furious roar and stormed toward the counterdemonstrators.

The cops in front of the humans fired a rubber bullet into her ribs, causing her to double over. Furious snarls split the air as the werewolves rushed to protect her, only to be met by a wall of tear gas.

"Jesus Christ," Isaac muttered, alarmed as a fight broke out below.

As the werewolves lost themselves to their fury, they shifted entirely to wolves. Frightened onlookers ran. Humans raised their bats and shoved their way through the cops to get at the shifters while some demonstrators fled the scene. The cops hid behind riot shields and deployed tear gas on most of the protestors, though some were able to avoid the spray and clash with the humans.

Shit. The wolves would go feral, and this situation would become a bloodbath.

"Help me!" The scream echoed from an alley between two buildings nearby, close enough that it was isolated from the pandemonium below. Isaac leaned over the railing dividing the rooftops and peered below. One of the humans had his blood-soaked baseball bat ripped out of his hand by a half-shifted werewolf.

"Hey!" Isaac roared.

Two blazing eyes set their sights on him. Isaac fired and the bolt flew free and struck the wall with a shower of sparks as the werewolf dodged. The werewolf shouted at a fully shifted wolf nearby. "Get out of here, hurry!"

The shifted wolf limped away.

"Face me, hunter!" The beast-man charged, leaping up the fire escape to reach him. Clawed hands swiped madly, latching onto Isaac's leg, and Isaac lost his footing. He fell in a blur of sound and color, crashing into the bloated garbage bags overflowing from the dumpster. They ruptured like pustules, spewing garbage across the floor. Isaac rolled onto the pavement and lunged for his crossbow, only to have it kicked out of his reach as the werewolf landed on two clawed feet.

Leering down at him through a mouthful of fangs, the creature came closer, claws sharp and dripping blood. "Hunter," the werewolf snarled. "Leave our kind alone! We've done nothing to you!"

Isaac's hand closed around the silver dagger in the holster around his thigh. "You animals murdered my son!"

Isaac howled as the wolf lunged, and his jaws locked around his wrist, fangs ripping the flesh from his arm. Behind the wolf, the man Isaac had tried to rescue lurched to his feet, bat in hand.

With a shout, the counterdemonstrator swung his bloody bat at the wolf's backside. The silver began its work, turning the werewolf's fangs blunt and making his claws shrink. The werewolf hurled Isaac into a wall, then took off after dodging a swing from the man.

"You good, brother?" the man asked. "God damn animals. This city has lost its mind."

Gasping for air, Isaac pressed his back to the wall and cradled his shredded arm to his chest. "Just get out of here." The blood wept freely, soaking his shirt, and Isaac cut off a scrap of his sleeve and tied it around the wound.

The blood seeped through. He had to stop the bleeding, fast. Isaac stumbled to his gym bag which had fallen down with him and rifled through for bandages. The process was clumsy with only one arm to work with but he managed to drape bandages over the wound and draw them tight. The gauze soaked up the blood.

Shaking and faint, Isaac slumped against the wall. The howls of wolves and yells of humans, the roar of helicopters, and the scream of police sirens filled the air. It was like a fucking war zone out there.

He wished he'd never left Ben's side.

Chapter 6

BEN THE SECOND

The punching bag crashed into the wall and Ben's claws flew into it when it came flying back. He clutched onto it, clenching his jaw until it hurt. "Fuck."

After human terrorists attacked Union Square, because how anyone could call that march anything other than an act of terror against wolves Ben wasn't sure, there'd been a surge in patients. The police had sided with the humans and helped fuel the violence against the shifters.

What had started as a peaceful protest in solidarity with hybrids had ended with dozens of injuries and five shifters and one human tragically dead. Of course, the media fixated on the human injuries and the single human casualty. Go fucking figure. Nobody was even sure if she'd been killed by shifters or in the ensuing chaos.

Ben hated this world sometimes.

Checking the clock, he realized it was time to head home. He'd never been happier to leave. With the clinic finally under control and all the patients recovering, Ben hoped he'd be able to relax and get some sleep.

Ben did sleep, at least a little. He drifted off on the train ride to his apartment and the shapes of wolves ran across the backs of his eyelids. A rush of indistinguishable voices, the images of nurses pushing stretchers, the sensation of running—

His eyes flew open as the conductor announced East New York station over the intercom. He grabbed his coat and lumbered off the train, yawning into his fist. It was almost one in the morning. His eyelids were heavy and he thought about just curling up on a bench and sleeping. Why had he even left the estate? He'd just come back in six hours and do it all over again, and it wasn't as if he could compartmentalize the stress of the day. His very bones were heavy from the things he'd seen and heard today, the stress like a sickness manifesting in his body.

He rented a cab from the station and rode it to his apartment. He hoped he didn't get so exhausted that he shifted right in the back of the cab. Last thing he needed on this shitty day was to become a statistic of violence himself. That would just be the flies on top of the pile of horse crap that was today.

The cab dropped him off outside his apartment and Ben lugged himself up five flights of stairs one heavy step at a time. He slipped on something wet, and his stomach sank at the spots of crimson blood dotting the marble steps. "Shit." He'd seen his fair share of blood today. He jumped the steps two by two and caught his breath on the fifth floor.

The trail stopped right outside Isaac's apartment. Ben's hand shook as he raised it and knocked. It was a lot of blood. What had happened to him? How badly was he hurt? Who had done it, or was it simply an accident? A drunk at the bar who'd gotten too rowdy and smashed a glass near Isaac, or maybe some cyclist ran him over, or—

"Isaac?" Ben called. He knocked again. The silence grew heavy, the scent of blood more and more potent. His breath turned to pants and he barely stifled a whine. Fuck. His wolf was close to the surface, restless and panting, longing to come out. He took in a deep breath and rang the doorbell this time. "Isaac, you all right in there?"

Come on. Answer the door!

If Isaac didn't answer, he'd have to kick it in. There was no way he was walking away and leaving Isaac to his fate when he didn't know how badly he was injured. His claws left painful indentations in his palm and his breathing got sharp and short.

His fangs cut into his lip and drew blood, and a growl rumbled deep in his throat. Thick hair sprouted across his arms. Alarmed by the intensity of his wolf, Ben closed his eyes tight and took in a deep breath. He'd never lost control but somehow when it came to Isaac, he had none.

The lock clicked. Ben panicked as his clothes ripped and tore. He hurled himself toward the stairs and fell on his way down. The hallway spun around him and when he crashed to the bottom, his hands had turned to paws and his skin to dense fur.

"Ben?"

The wolf's ears flicked and his tail wagged. His mate's voice. His mate was safe. Shaking his pelt free of any uncomfortable scraps of fabric, the wolf bounded up the stairs, heart racing.

A familiar face peering up and down the hallway sent the wolf into a rush of excitement. Isaac gasped, freezing as their eyes met. Fear filled his scent. "Shit." He raised both hands slowly. "Stay back, okay? Easy."

The wolf sniffed the air, tail wagging so fast his bottom wiggled. He smelled like wet asphalt and rain. Like his mate—and blood. His mate was hurt. Why was he hurt? He wanted to make it all better. He padded closer and stopped when Isaac backed away. "Stay back!" The wolf lay down, trying to make himself small and nonthreatening. "Are you... friendly? Huh. A normal dog, then? Want a treat?"

The wolf's tail wagged, and he cocked his head. Treat? Food? Yes, food!

Isaac ducked into the apartment and returned with a piece of something. It smelled like meat. "Here, boy." He knelt, holding out the meat. The wolf's mouth salivated and he charged. Isaac yelped as the wolf flattened him onto his back, chowing down on the meat—*so juicy, so salty, so good!*—and nosed around his hand expectantly.

There was no more food, but it didn't matter. His mate smelled better than all the food in the world. The wolf plopped down on top of Isaac and licked his face. His beard was scratchy under his tongue. Isaac's chest heaved when he laughed, warm hands settling softly on the wolf's dense fur.

"Well, I'm still alive, so I guess you're friendly. Must be only part wolf, then. Phew! Scared me a second there. Where's your collar, buddy? Who do you belong to?" Big hands felt curiously around his neck.

You, the wolf thought. *I belong to you, and you belong to me.*

"Off, buddy. Off!"

The wolf didn't understand, not until Isaac wriggled and freed himself.

"Damn. I can't leave you here. Come on in." Running a hand through his hair, Isaac motioned for the wolf to follow him inside the apartment. The whole apartment smelled like Isaac, like rain-washed pavement and wet leaves, moisture and ozone.

Isaac winced, clutching his arm. Some bloody bandages had come loose. The wolf trotted to him, nosing worriedly at the injury. A growl rumbled in his throat. Another wolf had touched his mate. He would find them and kill them.

"Hey, no growling. I'm fine."

The wolf nosed worriedly at the wound and licked the skin. It smelled like pus, and the flesh was warm. But from the smell of Isaac, he hadn't been turned by the bite.

"Ew. Don't do that. You'll get it infected."

Dejected, the wolf leaped onto the couch and couldn't resist rolling around, wrapping himself in Isaac's rainfall scent.

"Hey, off the couch!" His mate pointed an accusatory finger at the wolf. With a huff, the wolf laid his head on his paws, far too comfortable to even think of moving. "Ugh. Fine. Guess I might as well make you some food. You're probably hungry. Think I have some sirloin somewhere."

Soon enough, the apartment was full of the smells of roasting meat. The wolf dozed while the meat cooked. Now that the excitement had faded, the more mundane thoughts of *food, comfy,* and *sleepy* were overpowered by *Happy now, you damn wolf?*

Ben took the reins, and the simple thoughts of the wolf were overrun by total embarrassment and fear. He couldn't believe he'd let the wolf take control so easily. What if Isaac had caught him shifting? He might have endangered their friendship. The last thing he wanted was to chase Isaac away. Speaking of Isaac, he raised his head and peered over the arm of the couch. His mate was humming in the kitchen, spatula in hand, as he flipped the sizzling steak.

Ben's tail wagged. *Damn it, stupid tail.* Isaac was a good guy. Many would have freaked out or guessed he was a werewolf and called the police, but Isaac's first instinct had been to take care of him. Just like Ben's first instinct was to take care of Isaac.

Never had his wolf instincts been so powerful before. Even now, he wanted to bolt from the couch and tend to Isaac's wounds. He should. The wound was clearly getting infected, but because of his stupid wolf, he was stuck in this form until Isaac went to bed.

He sniffed the air and singled out the smell of blood and pus—but no werewolf venom. Whoever had bitten him hadn't done so with the intention of turning him. He could only wonder then who had bitten him and why. Isaac didn't have a boyfriend, did he? A shifter boyfriend? A growl rumbled in his throat. If some asshole was abusing Isaac... The thought made him bristle with fury. That might explain why Isaac seemed so down and reclusive. He bared his fangs, longing suddenly for something to bite.

The stove clicked and Isaac's footsteps came his way. "Here you go, boy. Left the inside a little raw for you. Figured you'd appreciate that."

Tail wagging, Ben wished he could tell Isaac just how much he did appreciate the gesture, and the one making it. Isaac sat beside him and laid the plate between them. He'd cut the steak into thick strips, the outsides brown and crisp and the insides juicy and pinkish. Isaac grabbed a piece and handed it to the wolf. Ben took it carefully, minding Isaac's fingers.

"Wow," Isaac whispered. "Your eyes are such a pretty silver color. That's so cool. I had a dog that looked just like you when I was a kid. A Czechoslovakian wolfdog. You look so much like her." He smiled fondly and played with the fur on Ben's cheeks.

Ben was grateful Isaac was impressed and not suspicious. On any other night, Ben would have been in control of his shift, but Isaac's blood had brought out the beast in full force. It scared him to realize how easily he could lose control around Isaac. To ease his nerves, he licked Isaac's fingers and tasted the juices of the steak.

Isaac chuckled and ran a hand through Ben's fur. His touch was warm and soothing. "You're friendly. I hope you belong to someone in the building. I'd hate to send you to a shelter. I'll help you find your owner first thing in the morning. I hope you don't live with the assholes in 3E. They're too shitty to own a cool dog like you."

Isaac's smile fell away as he ran his fingers through the thick fur on Ben's cheek. "I'd take you in if I could, but truthfully I'm not much better than the 3E a-holes. I got no time, and let's be honest, I'd be a shit dog owner."

Ben whined and nudged Isaac's hand. Isaac was amazing. He was kind and funny and he had a wonderful smile. Isaac ran a finger along the length of Ben's snout, gray-blue eyes staring into his as if Ben weren't a wolf at all, as if he knew Ben understood his every word. But that couldn't be possible.

"I couldn't keep my son safe," Isaac murmured, his eyes dark with misery. "I'm not qualified to take care of anyone." A flash of understanding burned white hot in Ben's heart. "I wake up every day and expect it to hurt less. At first, maybe I feel okay. Then I remember he's not gonna run into the room and jump in bed with me, pestering me to get up, get up. I used to hate that." The little smile the memory of his son had inspired trembled and cracked. "Now I'd give anything for him to wake me up again."

Ben understood now why Isaac was so quiet and withdrawn, why his rare smiles looked like a ray of sun through dense gray clouds. He was grief-stricken and alone. Ben longed to change back and hold Isaac tight but understood that would do more harm than good. The last thing Isaac needed was a heart attack. So Ben laid his chin on Isaac's knee and listened as he talked.

"It makes no sense that the world just kept turning without him. It's not right. The world stopped for me but everyone around me's getting married, having kids, getting jobs, or quitting old jobs or... And here I am, trying to remember what I was even doing with my life before he..."

He swiped a fist across his cheek, smudging away a tear. He sniffed and sank his fingers into the fur on Ben's head, running his thumb up a pointed ear. It tickled but Ben only twitched his ear in protest and didn't shake him off.

"He was my life, you know? Of course you don't. You're a dog." Isaac snorted, blinking hard. "All the work I did was so I could help him succeed in life. In case one day he grew up and decided he wanted to be a... a lawyer or a doctor." Isaac rubbed his eyes but it was no use as tears streaked his face.

The scent of his heartache made Ben's own heart hurt. Was this what it was like every night for Isaac, coming home to an empty apartment, surrounded by photos on the walls of the family he'd had and lost? Ben hated that he lived right across the hall from Isaac and yet had been totally oblivious to his grief and loneliness.

"Fuck. I need a drink." Isaac attempted to stand, sniffing hard.

Ben growled. *Like hell I'm watching you get drunk by yourself.*

He sat up and shuffled close so he could lick away the tears on Isaac's face. Isaac made a sound between a laugh and a sob, putting a hand around Ben's snout to make him stop. Despite it all, he smiled, so encouraged, Ben licked his face some more. While Isaac was distracted, Ben tackled him, bringing one hundred eighty pounds of wolf down on Isaac's body. He groaned, crushed underneath Ben.

"Holy fuck, you weigh a ton!"

Ben huffed, satisfied.

Giving up, Isaac put his arms around him and held on tight, burying his face in the wolf's shaggy fur. "Good boy," he whispered, his voice tender and frail. Ben laid his head on Isaac's shoulder, shifting his weight enough so that he was lying completely on top of Isaac.

The couch was too small for both of them but Isaac draped a leg over Ben, using him as a makeshift body pillow. Isaac's body trembled and he broke down, burying his face in Ben's fur as he fell apart into gut-wrenching sobs. Ben soothed him the only way he could, by licking his face and letting Isaac hold him tight without squirming. Within minutes, Isaac's hand stilled in Ben's fur and his breathing slowed.

Ben licked the last of the tears from his face and closed his eyes.

On that tiny couch with Isaac's arms around him, Ben slept better than he had in weeks.

ISAAC WOKE TANGLED UP beneath the afghan. He sat up, surprised to find that the enormous wolf-dog was gone. How? He rolled off the sofa and checked the door. In all the excitement, he'd neglected to lock it. He scratched his head. Was he supposed to believe the dog had just turned the handle, opened the door, *closed* it, then walked right out? No, Isaac supposed he'd forgotten to close the door in his surprise.

Damn. He hoped the dog found its way back to its owner. He had to ask around, just to be sure. Perhaps he could even convince the owner to let him pet sit. He'd liked that dog. He hadn't realized how much it would mean to him to have someone else to spend the evening with. Especially someone that offered comfort without speaking and listened to a grown man sob without judging him.

At first, he'd feared the huge dog was a werewolf. It was only when the wolf-dog revealed his friendly nature that Isaac had realized there was no way he was a werewolf. Werewolves were all aggressive and dangerous once they shifted or went feral. If that wolf-dog had been a shifter, Isaac would have been killed in seconds, no doubt.

The hallway was cold as the heat hadn't been turned on yet. Shivering, Isaac supposed he ought to start with his neighbor. He knocked on Ben's door and waited. He recalled hearing Ben's voice the other night only to open the door and see no one. Before he could wonder, the door opened and Ben dominated the entryway.

"Isaac?" Ben wore a T-shirt and gray sweats.

Isaac hoped he hadn't woken him. "Hey. Sorry to bother you... Just wondering if you'd seen a dog? Big, like a wolf."

Ben smiled brightly. "Yeah, actually. He belongs to a friend of mine. I was pet sitting."

Isaac almost sighed his relief. "I found him wandering around the building last night." He couldn't believe he hadn't run into such a big dog by now, but then again, he and Ben were on different time frames throughout the day.

Ben slapped his forehead. "Ugh. I'm so sorry! The big bastard's too smart for his own good. He opens doors at night if I forget to lock him in his room."

"Oh, okay. Sorry, I wish I'd known. I'd have knocked on your door. I let him stay at my place for a while."

Ben rolled his eyes. "What a pain!"

"No, no. He was great company. Feel free to bring him by again. What's his name?"

"Ben."

Isaac squinted.

"My friend named him after me!" Ben blurted. "He's got the same eyes," Ben supplied as an explanation, eyes fixating on a spot above the wall. "I call him Ben the Second."

Isaac laughed. "That's cute."

"What happened to your arm?"

Isaac jumped to conceal it, but it was too late. "I got bit. A dog—not yours."

A big hand reached out, fingers settling gingerly over the bandages. They were coming undone, exposing the wound. Ben's eyes narrowed. "You gotta clean this! It's getting infected." His large hand covered Isaac's wrist but his touch was gentle as if afraid Isaac's wrist might snap under his fingers. He pulled away, not liking the thought of Ben going out of his way. He wasn't such a wreck he needed someone else to take care of him.

"It's okay, I can—"

"Shut up and come on in." Ben didn't force him but left the door open.

He exhaled, looking around. Ben wasn't much of a decorator and it was only furnished with the essentials: a sofa and an armchair, a TV, a tiny table for two by the window. No rugs or pictures—the air was musky with the unmistakable odor of wet dog, and plenty of fur covered the couch.

"Sorry 'bout all the hair." Ben glanced apprehensively over his shoulder. "I need to buy one of those lint rollers. You can sit at the table if you want." Ben shuffled into the bathroom and Isaac heard a cabinet door squeak and then quiet mumbling.

He came back with bandages and disinfectant. "Your apartment layout is similar to mine." Isaac sat at the table and Ben knelt on the floor before him. Isaac's face warmed. It felt unreal to have a big, burly guy like Ben on his knees, taking care of him, without Isaac even having to ask.

Ben held out a hand and Isaac placed his wrist on his palm. Grabbing a cotton ball, Ben said, "This'll sting." Isaac stayed quiet while Ben dabbed the wound and bubbles frothed around the bite marks. Ben's brow furrowed, his lips in a thin line as he cleaned the wound. Isaac's shoulders relaxed, touched by Ben's attentiveness.

"Thanks for looking out for me."

Ben's mouth twitched. "If you'd just be more careful, I wouldn't have to."

Isaac found it in him to grin and kick Ben's foot. "No one's making you look out for me. You coulda walked away."

"Maybe letting you die from tetanus would teach you to dress your own wound," Ben grumbled. "What were you thinking? Did you even clean this?"

Isaac snorted, finding Ben's grouchy concern endearing. "'Course I did. I'm not a moron, Ben."

Ben growled, binding the bandage tight. Isaac winced—a bit too tight. "There. Your arm shouldn't turn green and fall off, but if it does, well, you probably deserve it." He got to his feet and went to the kitchen.

Isaac grinned. "Someone's worried."

Ben whirled around, seething. Isaac might have been intimidated if he weren't red up to his ears. "I—you—it's not funny, Isaac! You think I don't know a werewolf bite when I see one?"

Isaac's breath hitched. "How—"

Ben folded his arms over his big chest. "What were you doing to piss off a werewolf that it bit you like that? You could have been turned if there'd been venom in his bite!"

"What was *I* doing?" Isaac floundered for a response that wouldn't betray the reason he'd been at Union Square yesterday. "You think I just walked up and shoved my hand in a fucking werewolf's mouth and told him to bite me? That it?"

"No! I—" Ben looked ready to combust. Breathing hard, he paced away, then back to Isaac. "Fuck..." He breathed in deep, shoulders losing their tightness. "I don't know, Isaac. Did you *want* to be bitten? You think your life will get better if you change who you are?"

"No," Isaac said through gritted teeth. "There's a lot I wish I could change, but I'd never—just no." He'd never want to be one of those monsters. He'd rather die than lose control of himself like that and hurt other people.

"What would you change?" Silver eyes peered at him from beneath strands of chestnut hair falling free from his ponytail. "'Cause from where I'm standing, you're the sweetest man I've ever met." The wind went out of Isaac's lungs. Ben really thought that way about him? Face coloring, Ben coughed. "Y-you don't have to tell me, not if you don't want to. Just..." Ben's lips thinned and he looked away. His hand tapped softly against a denim-clad leg and Isaac sure wished Ben hadn't drawn attention to his thighs. It was suddenly harder to notice anything else.

The floorboards creaked. Isaac hadn't realized he'd looked down until he looked up and Ben was standing over him. The silver of his eyes was like twin pools of gentle moonlight. A quiet exhale fell from his lips, and big, warm hands took hold of Isaac's fingers. Gently, always gently. Isaac breathed in and smelled the woodsy aroma of Ben's beard oil.

Producing a napkin from his pocket, Ben grabbed a pen on the table and scribbled something. Ben handed him the rumpled napkin with his number written on it.

"I may be gone a lot, Isaac, but if you call, I'll pick up. Day, night, whenever. If you get lonely, or bored, or just want someone to talk to, or—" Ben's throat clicked as he swallowed. Slowly, his fingers left Isaac's hand and hovered just inches from his cheek. "Or if you can't talk at all and you just need someone, for whatever reason. Doesn't matter. I'll always answer."

Isaac wished he could say something, anything, but words would be a waste. He'd never noticed the shape of Ben's lips before, how they could be hard and thin in anger one moment, then so soft and supple when he smiled. Now, Ben's lips were all he could notice and he didn't know how he'd been so blind. Isaac didn't know who moved first—perhaps he started it, leaning his head into Ben's hand and feeling those fingers soften to cup his cheek.

The floorboards creaked again, and the toes of their boots bumped together. The slow but heavy wafts of Ben's breath hit Isaac's mouth. Unmistakable desire left his eyes dark and heavy-lidded. The scent of him blanketed Isaac's senses and the warmth of his body shielded Isaac from the draft in the room.

A low chuckle rumbled in Ben's throat. Almost a growl. "Your heart's racing."

Isaac kicked the toe of Ben's boot lightly. "Is not." He hadn't kissed anyone in a year. Since his son died, he'd felt like a zombie, living without feeling alive. The thought of doing something so normal was almost unsettling. He'd never thought he'd actually want another person, that he would feel something like desire or joy again. Then Ben had come along. "Your hands are trembling," Isaac countered.

Ben made a strange sound and touched their foreheads together. "Don't wanna mess this up."

Isaac scoffed. His hands, stationary like much else in his life until now, came alive and fumbled up along Ben's shirt, holding on tight to the fabric. His chest was hairy—he could feel the soft fuzz underneath and the hard muscle tightening at his touch.

"Don't think you could mess up if you tried," Isaac said, nudging Ben's toe with his boot.

Isaac surrendered before he'd realized it, closing his eyes as he leaned in. The last thing he saw was Ben's own eyes falling closed. Ben's breath tickled his lips, and the shaking hands holding his clung on tight.

Isaac's phone shattered the silence between them. With all the annoyance of waking before the best part of an exciting dream, Isaac groaned and his eyes flew open, finding his frustration mirrored on Ben's scowling face. Ben shut his eyes with a soft laugh. "Fuckin' technology."

"I can throw it out the window if you like."

"Please do." Ben's big hands gripped Isaac's waist. His scent of clean clothes and that attractive musky male scent that not even freshly washed skin could erase was making Isaac's blood run hot.

Despite it all, Isaac had the feeling he should answer in case it was Don or another member of the Cross. He stepped out of Ben's arms and felt as if he were waking from a dream. His mind was clearing with every step he took, desire dissipating and leaving his neck hot with embarrassment. What had he been about to do? *Kiss Ben Stroud, that's what,* his cock reminded him with an approving twitch.

Kiss Ben. His neighbor. His only friend. And then what? He hadn't given any thought to what would happen after their lips met but he, a single divorced man of twenty-nine, didn't have a great track record with romance. Yet all it had taken was a smile that softened those stern features and gently rumbled reassurances to convince him to make what would undoubtedly be a mistake.

Before he could answer, the call had already gone to voicemail. Don had been trying to get in touch with him. Before he could wonder why, a message popped into his inbox.

Don: Come to the cathedral now.

Isaac's stomach turned over. What had happened this time? More protests or brazen attacks in the streets? *Someone's gotta leash these damn animals,* Isaac thought. He turned, trying to think of what he'd tell Ben. Ben looked like a different man, his expression dark and brooding in contrast to his gentle shyness from before. Isaac cleared his throat. "I need to run. Work stuff."

Ben nodded with a vague understanding noise.

Isaac scuffed his boot on the floor, his neck burning. "Thanks," he blurted. "For the..." He motioned to his arm when words failed him.

Ben met his gaze and offered a smile. It seemed forced but his attempt at sincerity made Isaac hopeful that he hadn't ruined things between them for good. Then they just stood and stared, expecting something neither was sure the other could give. Realizing it was hopeless, Isaac turned and made for the door.

"Wanna take you out." Ben's ears were bright red. "After your 'work stuff.' We can grab dinner, go for a walk."

Isaac wet his lips, at a loss. So he hadn't just ruined everything between them? Should he be happy about that? His mind was already made up, though, struggling to hide the smile trying to rupture his face in two. "Sure. That... that sounds fun."

Ben made a happy sound between a laugh and a sigh, his eyes twinkling. "Cool. I'm gonna grab dinner with some friends but I'll text when I'm done. Wanna meet back here, or—"

"Yeah. Yes. Definitely." Things would be ruined for good if Ben spotted him walking out of a crypt with a bunch of other guys.

Wearing what Isaac was sure was the stupidest grin of the century, he turned and walked right into the door. Face burning up, he quickly excused himself. The door closed and he wasn't sure if he should hit himself or jump up and down.

"Yes!" came a roar from the other side of the door.

Isaac slapped a hand over his mouth to stifle his laughter.

Fuck his worries and fears. He was going on a date with his hot, sweet neighbor, and it was going to be a blast.

"We have learned of the Moonborn's attack plans. They will strike tonight," Don said, his youthful face made haggard by eyes heavy from sleepless nights and the hard lines of a scowl at his mouth. He sat in the center of the throng of hunters.

The Cross's hideout was packed with them. Hunger for the hunt filled the room, thick as storm clouds.

"Will John Stone be participating in the attack?" Isaac asked.

John Stone was the leader of the Moonborn cult. He was highly evasive, managing to avoid police and Council of Lycanthrope Affairs detection ever since he'd gone rogue from the Council a year ago.

"Not to my knowledge. The cowardly wolf doesn't usually join his fellow beasts," Don sneered. "No, he always has his lackeys attack for him. However, Jacob Morgan will be there. The monster responsible for killing innocent humans must be stopped!"

"What's the plan, Father? The abominations have to die!" one of the hunters declared.

Don crossed himself. "In God's holy name, the monsters will be cleansed tonight."

Isaac was pleased Don was taking the Moonborn threat seriously. "How?"

Don shot him a look as if offended by Isaac's lack of faith. "God," he stated, one finger raised, "has sent me a sign." Rumblings of amens rippled among the hunters, the sleeves of their robes whispering as they crossed themselves one after another. Don stood, arms open to his congregation. "The attack at Union Square was a travesty but it was a sign, my brothers and sisters! A sign that God's work is not yet done! New York, the world itself, will not be safe until we have cleansed the abominations and restored order to this great country!"

As always, Isaac appreciated Father Don's passion for the hunt, but the man sure loved to hear himself talk. Bored, his mind tugged him toward Ben and those dancing silver eyes, the warmth of his hands on Isaac's body, the strength of his chest beneath Isaac's palms. Now, Ben he would worship without question...

"A travesty? That's what you call it?" A woman's voice cut through Don's speech. A hunter Isaac recognized as Gina shouldered her way to the front of the gathering. "The wolves at Union Square yesterday were *not* Stone's Moonborn cultists. And yet I watched as our brothers and sisters slaughtered and shot them."

Don laughed, unruffled by Gina's anger. "I fail to see what your issue is, Sister."

Gina crossed her arms. "My issue, *Father,* is that I thought the Cross's duty was to protect citizens from wolves like Stone's Moonborn cultists. But your hunters killed and hurt wolves who were protesting his cruelty! Shouldn't we have been on the same side?"

An uncomfortable pit yawned in Isaac's stomach. That was true, he had to admit. Those wolves hadn't been the ones to start the riot. The humans had. Perhaps Gina had a point. Guilt gnawed at him for even admitting such a thing to himself.

Isaac cleared his throat. "Look, Gina, a lot was happening. In the heat of the moment, if there's a wolf coming at you, you've got to act."

Gina waved a dismissive hand at him. "Oh, really? We were there to protect civilians, but you lot were chucking silver grenades left and right, not caring who you hit! How are we any better than wolves like Stone if we throw aside all disregard for human life?"

Throat dry, Isaac looked to Don, interested in seeing how he handled her accusation.

Don paced up and down. "Of course, I expect better from you, my hunters. We mustn't lose our heads in the heat of battle and forget the people we're sworn to protect. Sister, I don't know what it is you want to hear from me. I trust you all to have done what you thought was best."

Gina shook her head, eyes blazing. "Don, those wolves at the square were on our side. They wanted Stone and his cult gone as much as we do."

Don barked a laugh, looking around at his hunters. Many joined in. Isaac didn't know why he couldn't. "Perhaps, Sister, you should go and take a wolf's bite if you feel so empathetic toward them! By all means, Sister, go join a pack and see how long you last. They'll kill you in seconds. Or bite you and make you their slave. I guarantee it. They are animals. Never forget that."

Scowling, Gina glared at the floor.

Clearing his throat, Don said, "If we're quite done wasting time, I do in fact have a plan to stop these beasts. Unless you'd prefer to question me more." He narrowed his eyes at the gathered hunters. No one spoke up. "God did send a monster into our flock, my brothers and sisters. The creature trailed one of our own from the square the way a wolf stalks a lamb!" Gasps and frightened whispers spread among the flock. Don smiled, pleased by his ability to engage and rile up his audience. Gina scoffed and turned away. "Fortunately, Sister Jocelyn defended herself and brought the beast to heel. Sister, tell us what the servant of Satan told you."

Sister Jocelyn lurched to her feet with all the eagerness of a schoolchild about to answer the teacher's burning question. "A servant he was! Straight from the depths of hell itself. But the beast betrayed his own master's plans when he witnessed God's righteous might, wielded through me! God's holy silver drove the devil out of the beast until he was just a man at my feet. He told me everything. The Lord is all-knowing! Hallelujah!"

The crowd echoed her with some clapping and others bowing their heads in reverence.

"And, Sister?" Don arched his brow high. "What did the beast tell you?"

Thankfully, Jocelyn must have sensed his impatience. Her face went the color of a tomato. "Moonborn beasts will gather in Inwood Park at midnight."

Isaac's stomach clenched. Inwood Park was massive, with so much of it still preserved in its natural state of tangled woods. It was the perfect place for wolves to meet and plot. And they would have the advantage. They could move swiftly and quietly, passing easily over uneven ground where hunters might trip or stumble. They would be at home in the woods, and the hunters? They would struggle to keep pace in the dark and twisted forest, possibly to their own undoing.

"Father." But one look at Don silenced Isaac.

Don smiled and this time it was riveting as he bared his teeth in unbridled excitement. "The Silver Cross will be there to confront these wolves. They will bear witness to God's wrath, and any who dare stand with him!" The hunters of the Cross echoed him in praises of the Lord. Isaac stayed silent, feeling sick.

As the crowd dispersed, Isaac pursued Don through a sea of hunters. "Don, it's too risky."

Don turned, looking tired and unappreciative of Isaac's concerns. "I'm aware of the risks, Isaac. It's true that some of us may die tonight, but we will be reborn again by God's side. He will honor our sacrifice. Go, Isaac. Don't forget. Inwood Park. Midnight. God's speed, my son."

Isaac took a step back, surprised by Don's dismissal of his own hunters' sacrifices.

The father turned, robes swishing, and left Isaac alone with a lump in his stomach.

If the cultists weren't stopped, more parents might know Isaac's pain when their families became targeted by feral wolves. Pain fueled his resolve, and he pushed away his doubts. Isaac would do whatever it took to save innocent lives.

Chapter 7

Don't You Let Him Go

The Slaughtered Lamb, styled after the pub of the same name from the iconic *An American Werewolf in London,* bustled with activity. Waiters tangoed between the crowds at the bar, carrying plates of various sizzling meat dishes to tables of hungry fanged and furry patrons.

Ben felt right at home for the first time since coming to New York. He'd never imagined there'd be havens within the cities for his kind alone but here he was, not a human in sight, surrounded by shifters in their human form with fangs and excess hair, and others in their full shift, howling and walking around on all fours and sniffing about with zeal.

"Liking the place, my friend?" Manuel had just arrived, his shoulders dusted with snowflakes.

"It's snowing? Already?" It was only November. "Does it snow early in New York?"

"Oh, no. This is very rare weather, trust me. The pups were ecstatic." A server rushed over with a beer served with a shot of tequila on the side. Ben assumed Manuel was a regular since he was the one who'd recommended the place. "Know what you want to order?" Manuel asked.

"Torn between the burger and the pork sandwich. How's the Angry Werewolf's Balls?" It was a cocktail.

"Pretty good. Definitely order their burger. Best in the city by far."

Ben was sold.

"Hey, guys!" Greg dropped into a seat beside Ben and gave his head a shake, scattering snow everywhere. Ben shoved him, not appreciating the wet flecks of cold. "Manuel, my man!" Greg reached across the table and shook his hand. "What did you wanna talk to us about?"

Manuel smiled darkly. "I called you both here for a—" He sighed as a server cut him off, notepad and pen at the ready. Manuel ordered "the usual." Ben chose the venison burger. Greg ordered the pulled pork sandwich and extra fries for the table and they each ordered a drink.

Greg sighed. "Been forever since I've been to the Lamb. I really oughta come more often. This place is crazy on a Sunday."

As he spoke, a couple of werewolves got into a fight at the bar, bowling into each other and falling to the floor. Quick as could be, the enormous bouncer stormed over, seized them by the scruff of their necks, and hurled them out into the snow. Grinning, Ben clapped and Greg whistled.

Ben checked the time. Thanks to the weather, it was dark and seemed later than it really was. It looked like eight out there but was only a quarter past five. He still had plenty of time to plan a proper date for him and Isaac. The waiter brought Ben and Greg their drinks.

"Hey, Manuel, you know humans, don't you?"

"I married one of the best," Manuel answered with a dreamy smile that could have made Ben barf. "Why, what do you want to know?"

Ben swirled his beer in his glass. Damn, if he sounded like a sap, the guys wouldn't let him live it down—particularly Greg. "Uh... just wondering what humans usually do when they go out on the town." He took a nonchalant drink of his beer. When he glanced up, both Manuel and Greg were staring at him. Ah hell.

Manuel looked as if he were stifling a smile. "Catch a show on Broadway, maybe see a movie, take a stroll in Central Park..."

"In this weather, a movie sounds fun. Cheaper than a Broadway show. Just make sure to sit in the back so you can get handsy without people noticing," Greg suggested, bobbing his bushy brows.

Ben choked on his beer. "It's not a date!"

Greg sniffed at the air in front of Ben. "Oh, scratch that! You've already had that human's paws all over you. I can smell it. Looks like my boy doesn't need any love advice from me. The apprentice has become the master!" He threw back his head and howled. Manuel cackled, clapping his hands together.

Ben chucked his napkin at Greg, wanting to sink under the table as curious heads turned their way. "I hate you guys," he growled with as much venom as he could. His neck felt hot enough to catch fire.

"So, Ben, who's the lucky guy or girl?" Manuel asked, clinking his glass to Greg's while the historian struggled to catch his breath.

"There is no—Isaac and I are neighbors. We're friends."

"With benefits?" Greg asked.

"No!" Ben was sure he was as red as uncooked meat.

"Hey." Greg kicked Ben's foot under the table. "This Isaac guy, what's he smell like to you?"

"Nothing." Ben felt he'd already been softhearted enough for one day.

Greg scratched his chin. "Well, your favorite smell is after a rainstorm, right? Is that what he smells like?"

Ben knew Isaac's smell so intimately, just thinking about it awoke his senses and he smelled wet pavement and rain as vividly as if Isaac were there with him. "He does smell... different. Not like Heather. She smelled good but Isaac's scent is—" He quickly cut himself off.

Greg gasped, covering his mouth. "My boy's all grown up! You found your mate, didn't you?"

"He... he just smells good, okay?" Ben's face burned.

Manuel sighed dreamily. "The best scent in the world, isn't it? Anyone can smell good. But a mate, *your* mate, the one the goddess chose for you alone... they smell like every good memory, every happy thing that's ever happened to you."

Ben swallowed hard. He wanted to deny it. Isaac was human, after all. All he'd ever known about werewolf-human interaction had been painful. But after last night, the way he'd lost control, how happy his wolf had felt around Isaac... denying it was impossible. Shifting that night in front of Isaac had made him confront what he'd been ignoring since they met.

Isaac was his mate.

His mate was a human.

Fuck...

It explained everything. Why his wolf was so protective, so close to the surface and difficult to control. Why he wanted so badly to be there for him and protect him, even if he'd only known him a short while.

The She-Wolf, all-knowing and powerful, had touched another with a special scent only Ben knew and loved. He'd thought Heather had been the one, and it would have been so easy to love another shifter. Instead, they'd broken apart. For all Ben had known, he'd have to search the world over to find his missing half. Instead, his wolf had followed that scent to Isaac's door. A human, who knew nothing of the ways of wolves and their traditions, who would likely freak out and want nothing to do with Ben if he ever knew what Ben was.

The goddess must truly hate him. And Ben hated the She-Wolf right back.

Ben sighed, head in his hands. "Shit. What do I do?"

"Need some love advice?" Manuel guessed. He downed his shot and chased it with the last of his beer. "Humans really aren't that much different from us when it comes to love."

"Stop saying love," Ben grumbled.

Greg nudged Manuel. "Maybe you should, Manny. I know that face; when it turns that color, he's usually about to have an aneurysm."

Manuel rolled his eyes skyward. "Very well. When it comes to matters of the heart—is that better?—humans tend to move slower than shifters. They don't have the ability to sense a mating bond, so we shifters can sometimes come on too strong. We know who they are to us before they do."

"Right," Greg chimed in. "So you can't exactly walk up and say, hey, you smell frigging amazing! Wanna be my mate? Great! Let's fuck so I can bite you and claim you, baby."

"It's not like that for every werewolf couple," Ben mumbled. Shifters were perfectly capable of taking things slow. He sure as hell had no intention of talking to Isaac like that, as if he were nothing more than a piece of meat.

Manuel smiled. "Of course not, but the wolf knows what it wants. You should know relationships are fickle with a human. With shifters, we know right away this person is who we're meant to be with, and they feel the same. Most of the time, anyway. With humans, because they don't have that same sense, relationships fall apart more easily. It can be very hard to recover from that for us, when we believed so much that we were meant for each other."

Ben took a much-needed swallow of beer. Already, breakup scenarios were haunting him. "Humans know nothing about our ways. How can this work out?" He sighed, shoulders heavy with uncertainty.

Manuel offered a sympathetic smile. "Hey. These things do work out. Veronica and I had a bumpy start but we're both in this for the long haul. She's my mate; my wolf knows it, and so does she. Maybe we can't exchange mating bites or experience the magic that comes with that bond. It doesn't matter to either of us. We've both made sacrifices to make our relationship work and it was worth it. We love each other."

"You can't exchange bites?" Ben asked.

"Well, Veronica can't, obviously. I could, but she wasn't interested in walking around with a bite mark on her neck, for obvious reasons. So we agreed to be married instead of mating. It was important to Veronica and to be honest, I'd never understood the appeal of mating bites."

Ben frowned. Biting a chosen mate was important to him in the same way that wedding bands were important to some humans; it was the symbolic full circle of two souls handpicked by the goddess to become one, not just in body but in soul.

He hadn't thought about how important it was to him to be connected with his mate so intimately until he realized he might not get to have that connection.

Manuel clapped Ben's shoulder. "I'm not saying this to discourage you, Ben. But if your wolf has chosen a human as his mate, you will sacrifice more than you would if you'd chosen another wolf. There will be things you have to give up. That's why it's important to take your time with a human partner and figure out if the love you feel is worth sacrificing our long-honored customs and traditions."

Ben swallowed thickly. His friends had just given him way too much to think about.

Their food arrived, but Ben was no longer hungry.

"Gotta go." He lurched from his seat, desperate for some fresh air. He stumbled out into the cold and nearly slipped. The pavement was slippery with slush and ice, and clumps of snowflakes fell fast from the sky. The smell of the wet pavement reminded him of Isaac. He kicked a pile of slush into the street.

Isaac was his mate, huh? A human? Of all the people in the world, the goddess had picked a human for Ben. Was he really supposed to believe that? Well, he had his free will, independent of some deity's plans for him, and to this, he called BS. He flipped the moon the bird. "Fuck you too."

It couldn't be. Werewolves and humans barely got along; they couldn't be more different. There was no way he could make such a complicated relationship work. If the goddess really wanted to do him a favor, she'd have just left him the hell alone.

The door opened behind him. He smelled Manuel before he saw him. "Ben, I didn't mean to unsettle you. Trust your wolf's instincts."

Tangling his hand in his hair, Ben groaned. "For all I know, he hates werewolves!"

"If the goddess senses he's your mate, then it's because you two are meant for each other, despite all odds." Manuel looked down at his feet, running a hand through his hair. "Do you want things to work out between you two?"

"No! I don't even wanna look at him again! I—" Ben's protests died in his throat. His hands trembled and his throat thickened. When he'd held Isaac in his arms this afternoon, when Isaac had leaned in to kiss him and he'd realized Isaac wanted him as much as he wanted Isaac, it had been like a piece of himself, lost and alone, had finally come home.

And now he might lose that. He would lose Isaac. Just because Isaac smelled like rain and mate didn't mean Isaac felt the same way. He didn't belong to a wolf deity. He would never, could never, understand the ways of wolves.

"Ben, listen to me." Manuel grabbed his shoulder. "If you think there's even a chance he feels the same way, if he smells like everything that's good and right and pure—don't you let him go. No matter how hard things get. Trust the goddess. Trust that you're meant for him and him for you. Whether you're werewolf or human, it doesn't matter. We all love the same."

Ben swallowed hard around the lump in his throat. He couldn't seem to stop shaking. "I'll mess things up. I'll lose him. I'll—"

"Is that what you want? To let him go?"

He should. It would be easier on them both. The world was too complicated, and no one would understand. They would be judged by both humans and wolves. Isaac might suffer because of him if his peers found out he was with a shifter, and there were plenty of shifters who believed humans tainted the purity of a wolf's blood. And yet—and yet—the thought of losing Isaac was stronger than all his doubts.

"No. Damn it. I don't wanna let him go. I know I should, but—" Ben gritted his teeth. The fear was like quicksand, trapping him, but the thought of being with Isaac was enough to get him moving, one small, slow step at a time. "I'll talk to him. Let him decide how things will play out between us."

"Sounds good! When do you think you'll meet?"

Ben exhaled, feeling dizzy. "I'm meeting him tonight. Nothing crazy, just a date."

"I knew it!" Greg shouted from the doorway, making passersby jump and look at him as if he were nuts.

Ben rolled his eyes. "I'll tell him what I am and hope for the best." He patted Manuel's shoulder. "Now, let's go eat." He'd needed some guy time before the date. Now he could go in with some focus and fewer nerves. Or so he thought, but his nerves quickly returned when he got home and realized he couldn't remember the last time he'd been on a date.

He ran to the bathroom and checked his reflection. Should he trim his beard? And what should he do with his hair? He usually wore it long and loose. He tied it up into a bun and decided he didn't look awful. At least it would be out of his face.

In his closet, he searched through his best dress shirts and slacks and blazers. What if he was overdressed or worse, what if he was underdressed while Isaac looked sexy as sin? He whipped out his phone and sent a text Isaac's way.

Ben: Hey. I wanted to take you to a show. Do you like musicals?

He exhaled, hoping he'd struck a casual tone but didn't sound douchey.

Isaac: I haven't seen a play in a while! Sounds great.

Ben: As long as I don't have to sing.

He smiled, hoping Isaac got a kick out of that.

Isaac: LOL. I would pay to see that.

Ben: Tell me what show you want to see, and I'll take you.

Isaac: OMG no, let me pay for my ticket. Broadway is expensive!

But Ben insisted and Isaac caved and said he'd pick a show. There weren't any messages for a few minutes and Ben assembled what he hoped was appropriate theater attire: a black blazer, a button-up, and midnight blue slacks. His phone dinged.

Isaac: How does Phantom sound? Can you sing that?

Ben: A phantom?

Isaac: Man. I need to get you out more. I'll pick you up in five.

Ben bought the tickets online. It *was* expensive, especially for orchestra seats, but it was for his mate, so he knew it would be worth it. Five minutes later, the doorbell rang. Ben answered it so fast, Isaac jumped.

"Wow. Were you just standing by the door?"

"No." Ben had paced up and down, trying to figure out what he would say. Now Isaac stood before him in a fitted tee that hugged his muscular chest and dark jeans that teased the shape of his thighs. Ben swallowed. "You look... Oh no."

Isaac's eyes widened, and he ran a hand through his dark hair. "Uh." He laughed. "Is that a good 'oh, no'?"

Ben looked down at himself. "I'm way overdressed."

Throwing back his head, Isaac barked out a laugh. Ben's face warmed, and his eyes locked on the white column of Isaac's slender throat. He dug his hands in his pockets as his fingernails itched. He'd like nothing more than to nuzzle into Isaac's neck and scent him.

"Don't worry about it! Tons of people get dressed up when they go to the theater. You're making me look bad, if anything."

Ben snorted. As if Isaac could look bad. Ben had seen him puking behind a trash can after too many beers, and he'd still looked pretty damn good. "You look..."

Isaac grinned. "'Oh no' again?"

Ben laughed and stared at his shoes. "You look hot."

He was happy he'd found the guts to be so forward when a pleased smile tugged at Isaac's mouth. Storm cloud eyes raked up and down Ben's form appreciatively. "Yeah? So do you."

Heat simmered in the pit of Ben's stomach. He didn't know what to do with it, but he badly wanted to put his hands on Isaac and draw him close, hear him sigh as Ben claimed his lips.

"Why, Ben Stroud." Isaac tutted, and he had the gall to recline against the railing, body open and waiting. "Do you want to kiss me? Already? Before we've even gone on our date? What societal norms will you break next?"

Ben took one step, then another, until he'd cornered Isaac against the railing. Ben reached out and laid his hands flat on the railing on either side of Isaac's arms. Isaac exhaled, his breath warm against Ben's mouth. If Isaac knew what he was, would he feel frightened to have Ben so near? The uncertainty stole some of the fire Ben so desperately needed.

"Earth to Ben?" Isaac ran his hand over Ben's cheek. "You okay?"

Ben was great. Amazing, in fact. Isaac made Ben feel like a king instead of a confused wreck in a new city among so many new people.

"Yeah," Ben said, his voice oddly breathless as Isaac's nose brushed against his. He hesitated, afraid to take the plunge, worried even the brush of Isaac's mouth would wreak havoc on his control.

"Doesn't sound like you mean it." Isaac settled his hand on Ben's chest, the heat of his touch seeping into his clothes.

Ben's hands left the railing and he gripped Isaac's hips. "That's 'cause I'm better at showing it." He let his eyes fall closed as he met Isaac's mouth halfway. The sweetest serenity washed over Ben, and he didn't know what he'd been worried about or how he ever could have doubted they were meant to be when their bodies fit so perfectly together. A delighted shiver ran through him as Isaac ran his fingers through Ben's hair, his tongue dancing delicately over Ben's lips, tasting and exploring.

Ben opened up to him, unable to quiet a moan when Isaac pressed his tongue past Ben's lips. He tasted like peppermint yet also so faintly of ashy smoke, like he was burning up on the inside. Ben hated the smell of Isaac's cigarettes, but this taste... It was pure Isaac, and he wanted to burn it into his senses. Ben's arms went around Isaac's shoulders, needing him near as he tasted and teased Isaac's mouth to his heart's content.

Isaac pulled away, panting, and said, "We're gonna be late."

"Mm-hmm." Ben lunged forward, chasing Isaac's taste the way a man in the desert chased water. Their lips collided and Isaac stepped into Ben's body, leaving not an inch of space between them. Ben's breath quickened as Isaac ran his hands down Ben's back to squeeze his ass through his trousers, and the spicy scent of Isaac's arousal had Ben's cock stirring to life.

"We really are gonna be late, Ben." Isaac didn't sound like he cared, sighing as Ben nibbled his way down Isaac's neck, pausing at the juncture of his neck and shoulder to draw in a deep breath of his rainy scent.

"Then stop kissing me and we can go." Ben pinched Isaac's earlobe between his teeth. They should stop. He didn't want to get too worked up. Taking in a breath, Ben took a few steps back and immediately missed Isaac's warmth.

Isaac took both of Ben's hands in his. "Don't worry. We can make out during intermission."

Ben hoped he could wait that long.

They rode the train into Manhattan. Ben didn't like how noisy the trains were but Isaac's touch helped him stay grounded. The flashing lights of Times Square were downright blinding at night and Isaac held Ben's hand tight so Ben didn't get distracted by all the flashing advertisements and swallowed up in the crowd.

If anyone had told him he would be in Times Square on his way to a show, holding hands with a handsome New Yorker, he'd never have believed them, but here he was. They jogged to the theater and got to their seats just before the curtain went up, breathless and excited. Isaac didn't remove his hand from Ben's. It was perfect.

Ben would never forget tonight. The stunning costumes and set pieces, moments in the play that had him gasping and Isaac trying to stifle his laughter as Ben whispered, "Did you see that? How did they do that?" To which Isaac whispered, "Broadway magic," and kissed Ben sweetly.

They did wind up making out at intermission, and both jumped when the lights suddenly darkened and act two began. Ben still had the songs from act one stuck in his head and knew the music would stick with him for a long time when he found himself fighting back tears at the end of the show.

"You were crying." Isaac grinned, his hand in Ben's as they walked the streets of Brooklyn toward their apartment.

"So were you." Ben bumped his shoulder into Isaac's.

"Every time, man! I've seen that show twice, and the ending just gets to me." Isaac looked like he was choking up all over again. Ben put his arm around his shoulders.

"Sap."

Isaac tugged him into a kiss to shut him up, and Ben was never happier to stop talking. Their tongues tangled, and Ben thought he could kiss Isaac forever.

Somehow, they made it upstairs to Isaac's front door, a tangled mess of lips and roaming hands. "Wanna break another societal norm?" Isaac asked as he ran his hands down Ben's back to squeeze his ass. Ben thought he did, very much.

A sudden spur of doubt had him drawing back. He realized that if that was where their relationship was progressing, he had to be transparent about what he was. His wolf got riled up just smelling Isaac. If they went to bed, things would progress quickly. The last thing he wanted was for Isaac to freak out when he saw Ben's knot, or what if Ben flashed his eyes or his fangs?

"We don't have to." Isaac rubbed Ben's hand with his. "Tonight was great the way it was. Thanks."

Ben couldn't fight it. He leaned down for another kiss, one he couldn't bear to pull away from. Isaac's door creaked when he backed up into it. The little sighs and moans he made as their tongues tangled ignited Ben's blood. He was too nervous to talk now about what he was, but he wanted Isaac with a desperation he couldn't fight any longer. "Can I come in?" he asked against Isaac's lips. They didn't have to go all the way. Ben could find other ways to express his longing that didn't involve exposing himself.

"Don't even have to ask," Isaac said, fumbling with his keys.

Locked at the lips, they stumbled inside. It was dark, but Ben's eyes adjusted quickly. Isaac reached for the light switch, but Ben took his hand

and guided him to the couch. Having the lights off would help to conceal him. Isaac chuckled when he sprawled on the couch. "Like the dark?"

"Makes things exciting," Ben said, easing Isaac against the cushions. "Like this." He ran his hand down Isaac's stomach. His abs were taut beneath his shirt. "And this." He flicked open Isaac's jeans. Isaac was already hard, and Ben growled when he traced the bulge straining his underwear. "Love the way you feel."

"Fuck," Isaac whispered. He felt up Ben's arm and tangled his fingers in his hair.

Ben dipped his head, following the musky scent of Isaac to his inner thigh. He breathed in deep, his dick throbbing when the scent of Isaac's arousal hit his nose.

"I have condoms," Isaac said. "And it's been... I don't even remember the last time I was with anyone. I tested negative for everything recently."

"Recently?" Ben smiled. "Been wanting this to happen?"

Isaac chuckled. "Honestly? Since the moment I saw you. Wanted you on me, fucking me, any way I could have you."

Ben swallowed his delighted growl.

Ben squeezed his thighs. "I'm negative too. We can skip condoms. Wanna taste you when I suck your dick." Werewolves couldn't get STDs, so he felt comfortable going without the condom.

Isaac groaned. "God, Ben. Want your lips around me."

Ben mouthed his covered cock. He wanted to give Isaac everything he longed for. Wriggling down Isaac's underwear, Ben leaned in until Isaac gasped when his breath wafted over his cock. Isaac let out a hoarse cry when Ben lapped at the already leaking head.

Moaning, Isaac tugged gently on Ben's hair and pumped his hips in shallow thrusts. Ben bobbed his head, taking Isaac in deeper, then swirling his tongue around the tip. Kissing the head of his cock, Ben said, "Love your cock. Your taste. Want your load down my throat."

"Ben," Isaac gasped. "Oh God."

Ben swallowed him down and brought his fingers into play, fondling Isaac's heavy balls, rubbing his taint.

"Gonna c-come if you keep that up," Isaac panted, shuttling his cock in and out of Ben's mouth faster and faster.

Ben pulled off to nip his inner thigh. "Give it to me. All of it." He wrapped his lips around Isaac's cock, sucking from the base to the tip.

Isaac made a guttural growl a wolf would be proud of, spilling down Ben's throat. Ben swallowed every drop. He missed Isaac's taste when he popped his lips off his softening cock. Isaac was panting when Ben kissed up his jaw. Languid from his orgasm, Isaac tugged him into a kiss, and Ben's cock ached when Isaac thrust his tongue in Ben's mouth.

"Like the taste?" Ben asked, nipping Isaac's lower lip.

"Wanna taste you now," Isaac said.

Ben's heart stuttered. He was close after servicing Isaac, and he could feel his knot beginning to swell at the base of his cock.

"Can I?" Isaac asked, fingers poised at the clasp of Ben's jeans.

Ben cleared his throat. "Actually, I—"

He was about to say something about giving Isaac another turn when Ben's phone rang. He jumped out of his skin and snatched it up. It was Manuel. He never called this late, and he knew Ben was out on a date. Something must have happened. His stomach clenched. "Isaac, I'm sorry. I gotta take this."

Isaac kissed his cheek. "Yeah, of course."

Ben ducked into the bathroom and realized the phone had stopped ringing. Growling, he called Manuel back. "Manuel. Hey. Everything okay?"

"Listen, this is urgent, Ben. I forgot to tell you at dinner. There's supposed to be Moonborn cultists meeting tonight."

Ben was speechless, stunned by this turn of events.

"They're meeting in Inwood Park. It's a large forest where they'll be able to plot with ease. Supposedly, Jacob Morgan will be among them. We know there's ample support for the Moonborn in the city. The Council is flying in to shut down Stone's cult and I'll need your help. I don't know how many wolves to expect, so we'll need all hands on deck."

Ben bared his teeth. "Let's go crash a supremacist party."

He walked out into the living room. Isaac had turned on the lights.

"Isaac, I gotta run. My friend needs help."

Isaac's eyes widened. "Oh no. I hope it's nothing serious."

Ben tried to smile. "Probably not."

Isaac checked the time. "I actually have to head out in a bit too. Something at work came up."

Rubbing his shoulder, Ben said, "Thanks for tonight. It was great." Ben hoped Isaac knew just how much he meant it.

"Yeah. It was." Isaac's eyes were heavy-lidded, his lips damp and inviting. Ben kissed him one last time before he left, sighing at the sweet taste of him. Isaac moaned happily. "I'll see you soon, Ben. And hey, I'll make sure to return the favor." He squeezed Ben's ass for emphasis.

Ben licked the corner of his mouth. "Looking forward to it."

THE MAYOR HAD ISSUED a curfew for the neighborhood of Inwood. After nightfall, citizens were to remain inside while the Council prowled the streets, advancing on the shadowed trees of Inwood Park. Ben didn't see them, but he smelled them and often caught the movement of shadows in the corners of his eyes, only to turn and see nothing.

"They're here," Manuel whispered. Half-shifted, he walked on his toes, making each step soft and quiet. "The Council."

Ben held his breath and as the wind died and sudden silence fell over the streets, he heard the faintest click of toenails, the whisper of paws over snow. Then the wind picked up and obscured all sound. Clumps of snow hurtled into his eyes and the wind blew even colder.

"No police," Ben murmured.

"Good," Greg huffed. "They make so much noise, Stone's crazies would have heard them a mile away. Plus too many of 'em got that human stink. At least we all smell like wolves. Chances are, many of Stone's wolves won't be able to distinguish us from his pack."

Discarding his clothes, Manuel dropped to all fours, melting into his shift. The black wolf loped into the trees and Ben and Greg followed. Fabric tore and when he looked, a chubby wolf trotted past. Greg gave him a wolfy grin, wagged his tail, and bounded ahead. As he kicked off his shoes, Ben's body morphed into a half shift and he switched to walking on his toes, his eyes scanning the shadows as fur grew thick on his arms.

The snow was marred with paw prints but whether they were the Council's people or Stone's, Ben couldn't tell. There were many pairs of prints and Ben sorely hoped it was the Council, and that there really weren't this many fanatics within his own city. The thought turned his stomach sour.

Suddenly, the black wolf stopped, scenting the air. A growl curled Manuel's lips, his fur bristling. "What?" Ben murmured. Beside him, Greg growled, his pale blue eyes flashing.

"*Silver.*" Greg's wary voice filled Ben's mind.

Ben sniffed. The tang of silver was unmissable, scorching his nose.

"*Who the hell would bring silver into the woods? The Council?*"

"*No,*" Manuel answered along the bonds connecting them to one another. The black wolf sniffed the air and growled. "*Wait. Smell that? It smells like a wolf, but also like...*"

Ben closed his eyes and inhaled the smells of snow-drenched soil, frosty leaves, and wet fur, untangling the web of smells until he caught a foreign scent. He smelled wet fur but also leather, silver, and—"*Humans,*" Ben said.

"*Not just any humans!*" Greg flattened his ears. "*Hunters.*"

Ben's stomach turned over.

"*Shit!*" Manuel snarled, fangs bared. "*These assholes won't distinguish between the Moonborn and my pack! I've got to find Alpha Hanson and warn him! You two, keep your eyes peeled!*"

The black wolf tore ahead, weaving silently through the underbrush before vanishing from sight. Ben listened, his ears picking apart the silence to catch the occasional crunch of snow, the call of an owl.

He crouched and his clothes ripped and tore as he shifted. On his paws, he moved silently over the snow. In this form he heard every sound concealed from his human ears and he could pick out the heavy trod of boots over the uneven forest floor.

Ben sniffed, breathing in leather and fur and—

Something protruded above the bushes—two pointed ears, a long snout, and beady black eyes that gleamed dully. It was too tall to be a wolf and the profile was unmistakably human. Ben froze, crouching low. The scent of silver combated all other smells and won.

He lurched to the side as a bolt exploded into the tree beside him, showering him with snow and bark. Ben shifted to a man, hands raised. "She-Wolf's tits! Just let me explain. We don't need to fight!"

The hunter wore a wolf-skin cloak with the head still attached, concealing his face. "Ben?" There was fear and confusion in that voice, but it was familiar.

No...

Ben's heart shattered in his chest and he struggled to breathe as the wolf-skin hood fell down and revealed a familiar mop of curls tied back tight and the gleam of blue-gray storm cloud eyes.

The crossbow trembled in Isaac's hands and a shuddery gasp spilled from his lips. "Ben. You're... you're a wolf?"

The shock left Ben too numb to reply. He nodded, his lips settling into a tight line as he struggled to take the ache of hurt and betrayal and turn it into the anger he needed to survive. To kill if he must. His claws wouldn't come out; his fangs wouldn't sharpen. His wolf rebelled against the very thought of hurting a hair on his mate's head. "And you're a hunter."

Isaac's voice trembled. "You're one of Stone's fanatics? God. Ben, why?" The pain in Isaac's voice cleaved right through Ben.

"No." Ben raised both hands, his breath hitching when Isaac's crossbow came flying up and took aim at him. "Isaac. Listen to me. I'm not with Stone's pack. I'm here to stop his cultists. With my friends." By the goddess. Manuel and Greg, the Council... they would die tonight, torn apart by the Moonborn and the hunters. By Isaac. "Please, Isaac. Call off your people. Leave."

"I can't," Isaac said, voice tight with panic. "They're not mine to control."

Ben took one step, then another, hands still raised. "Then you're not leaving here."

"Ben, don't." Isaac's voice shook.

He gritted his teeth, fighting not to break under the pain in that voice. "I can't let you hurt my friends."

"And I can't let you hurt mine!"

Ben growled, "Those hunters are your friends, Isaac? They kill people!"

"We kill *monsters,*" Isaac hissed, his crossbow trained on him. "Feral wolves, or beasts who delight in taking lives like Stone and his fanatics. Are you a monster, Ben? How many innocent human lives have you taken?"

His words were like a dagger in Ben's heart. "*None.* I'd never take human life, not unless they threatened me and mine. I thought you knew that about me. I thought you trusted me!" Pain constricted Ben's throat. "Was it all a lie? Were you waiting for me to lower my guard so you could kill me, wear my skin like the thing on your back?"

Isaac shook his head. "It wasn't a lie, Ben. I do trust you—I did. But that was before I knew what you are. Ben, I don't want to hurt you." Isaac's voice broke.

Ben siphoned every ounce of fury he could and finally his fangs came out. "Why? What's so different about me, Isaac? How many people like me have you killed? I'm just a monster to you, aren't I? So pull the trigger and walk over my corpse. 'Cause I'm not letting you walk away." Ben opened his arms, exposing his racing heart. "Do it. I know you've done it before.

It'll be no different. I'm a monster. Aren't I?" The fury turned his voice to a roar. "So do it!"

The crossbow trembled, Isaac's finger poised upon the trigger. His eyes glistened with tears, every frantic breath misting in the air. The shift came over Ben and he turned and ran. He had no other choice; his wolf would rather die than keep baring his fangs at Isaac.

Something flew from the shadows, rattling as it hurled itself over his neck. With a tug, the chains tightened and burning pain sliced into his neck. He crashed into the snow, paws flailing, thrashing to try and escape as his skin burned white hot from the silver chains around his neck.

"No!" Isaac's voice was shrill with terror.

Ben lost the energy to maintain his shift. His paws turned to hands and he shuddered, naked on the icy ground.

"Damn, I got a big beast here!" a woman's brash voice jeered. Ben snarled, blinking away the pain blurring his eyes. A hunter leered at him, teeth bared in a cruel smile. "Isaac, what's the matter with you, eh? You almost let the bastard get away!"

"Let him go, Jocelyn!" Isaac demanded. His eyes met Ben's, wide and full of fear. Ben's heart soared with hope. Isaac still cared.

"Why should I?" The hunter yanked the chain around Ben's neck. His fingers clawed at the snow, and he gritted his teeth against a lash of pain.

"He's my prey." Isaac's eyes hardened, his face so cold and merciless Ben hardly recognized him. "I found him first, so I'm the one who gets to kill him. Got it?" Ben's hope dissolved. Isaac's boots crunched in the snow, his crossbow gleaming in the silver moonlight as he raised the bow to eye level and looked down the sight.

There was nothing in Isaac's eyes or stone-cold face to show he was still the man Ben knew. But Ben had never known him at all, not until tonight. His mate, who'd smiled as bright as the sun shone after a rainstorm—he'd been nothing but a mirage.

He was a hunter, and Ben was a wolf. Love that could have been had ended before it began. They'd been doomed from the start. Ben bowed his head as his heart shattered, and he closed his eyes tight. All he could do was wait for the bolt to pierce his skull, to die at the hands of the man he'd almost called his mate.

Ben heard the crossbow buck in Isaac's grip, the bolt whistling as it carved through the air—and exploded near his head, shattering the chains binding Ben to the hunter.

"Isaac, you idiot!" the hunter roared.

Ben came alive. Isaac hadn't missed; he'd just saved Ben's life. He threw off the chains and wrapped them around the hunter's neck. She sputtered and choked, thrashing like a fish until she croaked out a gasp and passed out, and Ben dropped her like a sack into the snow. Isaac slumped, hands on his knees. "Fuck... I thought I might hit you for a second..."

Ben rubbed his neck. The burns from the silver were healing fast. "Me too." He was honestly surprised Isaac hadn't. Isaac offered a small smile and Ben's heart lightened. "Isaac, I—"

Turning away, Isaac said, "Get your pack out of here, Ben. I can buy you time, but—"

A hoarse growl rumbled from above like thunder.

"Looks like I've hit the jackpot. A hunter *and* a traitor to our species." Ben recognized the naked man looking them over from the boulder at once. It was Jacob Morgan, murderer of humans and hybrids. "John Stone sends his regards!" He shifted to a huge white wolf and lunged, crashing down on Isaac.

The crossbow fell into the snow and Isaac seized a stick. The wolf's jaws crunched around the stick, shaking it in Isaac's grip. Ben's wolf came out in full force and he hurled himself upon Morgan, his jaws burrowing beneath dense white fur to the cultist's neck. He ripped Morgan from Isaac and hurled him across the forest floor, spraying snow.

Ben shifted to a man and positioned himself between Isaac, still lying prone, and Morgan's wolf. "Isaac, run. Now." He showed Morgan his fangs. "You touch him, and I'll rip your fangs out one by one and cram them down your throat."

Morgan snarled, charging them. Ben dropped to all fours and leaped as a wolf. Explosive pain knocked Ben out of the air. He yelped and cried, tugging at the bolt lodged in his leg. The pain was a constant ache deep in his bones, and the silver burned him to the marrow. Morgan thrashed on the ground nearby, smelling of blood and silver.

"Wait!" Isaac stepped in front of Ben, hands raised. The silhouettes of hunters loomed in the woods, their crossbows gleaming. "This is Jacob Morgan, Stone's wolf, and Ben Stroud of the Council. Don't kill them! They're more use to us alive!"

Ben panted as he shifted back to a man, squinting at Isaac. "The hell are you playing at?" he said, seething. Once the hunters learned he wasn't with the Council, they'd kill him anyway. "You're gonna get me—"

Isaac's boot flew into his face and Ben saw stars.

A hunter is my mate, huh, She-Wolf? Well, fuck you too...

CHAPTER 8

TRUST ME

Isaac couldn't stop shaking. He kept his face as, hopefully, blank as he could during the drive back to the cathedral. The cages rattled beneath the tarp as they drove. In one of those cages was the Moonborn cultist—and Ben was in the other one. Isaac's stomach gurgled sickeningly.

Outwardly, he held himself together but in his mind he was screaming, *Ben's a werewolf! My hot neighbor's a werewolf. I kissed a werewolf. I made out with a werewolf. I had sex with a werewolf. Ben's going to die unless I get him the hell out of here!*

When he thought about how easily Ben could have died tonight, his blood ran cold. But should he even care at all? Ben had kept who he was a secret the whole time they'd known each other. Then again, Isaac thought bitterly, so had he. He was hardly one to judge Ben for keeping secrets. They hadn't known one another at all, dancing a careful tango of secrecy and lies interwoven with friendship and mutual desire.

And yet Isaac still cared for him. The thought that he might be the one to drive a silver blade through Ben's heart made him sick with dread. Ben wasn't a monster. He was the opposite of everything Isaac had been told about werewolves: tender and gentle, grumpy but always soft-spoken and considerate. He'd been there for Isaac when no one else had, and regardless of his beast blood, Isaac couldn't look at Ben and see him in the same light as the monster who'd killed his son in cold blood.

Ben would never hurt him or anyone else. Werewolf or not, he was good. Isaac couldn't speak for the councilmembers in the woods tonight, but he trusted Ben and the company he kept. Ben wouldn't associate with killers and criminals like the Moonborn.

Isaac's thoughts warred with one another as the hunters stopped outside the cathedral. The streets were empty at this hour, so the hunters hoisted the cages and carried them into the refectory where Don lived. Isaac followed, each step slow as he trailed behind the other hunters. He would have to decide what to do. Soon. The hunters would realize Ben wasn't affiliated with the Council when they asked questions he couldn't answer. Then Ben's fate would be out of Isaac's hands. Fear formed a lump in his stomach.

Don awaited them within. He hadn't joined the hunt and Isaac thought that was insulting. He'd sent the hunters on their way, declaring God was on their side and would walk beside them in spirit. Don looked as if he'd sat around and watched television while they were gone, relaxed as could be with an ankle over his knee and his hands folded in his lap.

"My hunters!" Don rose, arms open to greet his flock of bedraggled hunters.

"Where the hell were you?" Gina snapped, throwing down her crossbow when she entered the refectory.

"Gina," Isaac began, but she ignored him.

"There's no need for such language, Sister," Don said, narrowing his eyes at her.

"Did you know there'd be Council wolves stalking around the woods?"

Don glanced in Isaac's direction, seeking support.

Isaac cleared his throat. "Gina, how would Don have known that?"

She glared at him. "Oh, shut up! We all know you're his favorite pet."

Isaac gritted his teeth. "What's that mean?"

Don countered, "I'm not all-knowing, Sister. That right belongs only to God."

"The Moonborn and Council wolves tore through our people! You should have been there! What were you doing while we were gone?"

"I am sorry to hear we suffered losses, but such is the way of this life. You all knew the risks. This is what you signed up for when you swore your life to become a holy warrior of God."

"Because I thought you cared about us!" Gina shouted, her voice echoing through the room.

Isaac said, "He does!"

"Then why wasn't he at the square? Why wasn't he there tonight in the woods?" Gina rounded on him.

Isaac opened his mouth. "Because..." He didn't know why. But he was sure Don had his reasons. "He... he trusts us to handle things on our own."

Don smiled warmly and appreciatively. "Precisely."

Gina shook her head. "You're brainwashed. All of you!" She kicked aside her crossbow and stormed out of the refectory.

Isaac's stomach churned.

"What if she doesn't come back?" Jocelyn asked Don.

Don curled his lip. "Then we will do what we must to keep our secrets. But it won't come to that. She'll return, mark my words. Now, what of the hunt?"

Isaac had trouble focusing. Don didn't mean to kill Gina if she left, did he? Surely he wouldn't go so far. The Cross was a family. He hoped Gina would return once she'd cooled her head.

"We caught the beast Jacob Morgan!" A hunter ripped away the tarp concealing Morgan's cage. The man lay beneath, pale and unconscious, his unkempt hair concealing his face. Don knelt wide-eyed before the cage. "And we caught a member of the Council."

Isaac's heart clenched at the sight of Ben lying still behind the bars. The light cast shadows over his rippling muscles. Brown hair hung wild about his face, some strands gleaming in shades of auburn and gold. He looked like a fallen warrior, deadly yet graceful.

"Incredible work, my friends," Don declared in hushed tones, his eyes roaming over the captive beasts with something akin to reverence. "This was a fruitful hunt, praise be to God." He crossed himself. "Go and get your rest. Isaac." He smiled warmly and Isaac tried to smile back. He hoped it looked more convincing than it felt. He couldn't understand why Don hadn't come tonight. "Thank you for having my back."

"Of course."

Don squeezed his shoulders and leaned in to touch their foreheads together. Isaac closed his eyes and tried to ignore the doubt gnawing at him. This was his mentor and closest friend. He'd pulled Isaac from his grief and despair, given him purpose.

"You alone understand me, Isaac. You have faith in me when no one else does. I hope you know how much I appreciate you, my son."

His words soothed the doubt in Isaac's soul. "I do, Father." Even if at times he doubted Don's leadership, he would never doubt his friendship.

Don patted his cheek with a warm, calloused hand. "You did well. You're every bit the hunter I knew you could be."

"Thanks, Don." Isaac glanced at Ben. "What will happen to them?"

"Nothing tonight. Once they're awake, they'll be questioned. We need to know where Stone's cultists are, and this councilman could provide us with inside information on the Council's movements. Once we've learned everything we can, Morgan will be handed in to the police and we'll all share in the bounty. The councilman... well, we'll have to see. But the Council can't know we're onto them. He'll have to die."

Isaac's stomach lurched. He had to get Ben out of here. Tonight, without alerting his huntsmen. He bowed. "Good night, Father."

"Yes, very. Well done, my son."

Isaac walked on legs like Jello out the door and into the frosty snow. He exhaled and couldn't get back enough air. Ben would die tomorrow unless he got him out tonight. The cold seeped through his boots as he waited, lurking in the shadows of the cathedral, the refectory always in his view.

The lights within eventually went out and Isaac's hands were freezing by then. Sitting in the shadows beneath his wolf cloak, he probably looked like a gargoyle. Snow gathered heavily on his shoulders and the wolf fur smelled like a wet dog. He stood, legs as stiff as if he'd almost frozen solid.

Don would have the keys to the cages somewhere within the refectory or in his bedroom above the refectory, likely on his person. The thought of retrieving them was as daunting as actually finding a way inside the refectory itself. The door was locked tight, the handle ice cold to the touch. It was an old building and currently undergoing some maintenance along the northern side. There was a small scaffolding that ascended to the roof. Isaac climbed it, wincing as the boards creaked under his feet.

He froze as he approached the windows on the second floor. Holding his breath, he leaned over to peer inside. It was as dark as the rest of the cathedral except for a few candles burning in small cones. In the dim light, he could just barely make out the shape of a bed and a lump beneath the blankets.

Isaac tried the window and nearly jumped out of his skin when it actually opened. Don had forgotten to lock it, much to his eventual chagrin and Isaac's luck. Was it really luck, he wondered, petrified to breach the threshold. If he were caught, there was nothing he could say or do to explain himself.

If he didn't try, then he would have Ben's blood on his hands. Isaac eased the window open inch by silent inch until he could just barely crawl over the frame. He landed lightly on his toes and held his breath as he sank soundlessly onto the floor. Knees bent, he didn't even breathe as he inched toward the bed. The closer he got to it, the darker it got, and he hoped he didn't walk into anything and make a racket.

Following the candlelight like a lighthouse beacon, his fingertips touched the bed. Don's back seemed to be turned toward him. Isaac clasped the candle by the holder and extended it over Don. He wouldn't sleep with the keys on him, surely. Isaac hoped not. But perhaps he kept them in the desk next to his bed?

Isaac eased a drawer open and tensed when it creaked. A glance at Don revealed he was still asleep. The drawer contained a Bible and nothing else. Isaac closed it as softly as he could. The next drawer was just as unremarkable. Isaac gritted his teeth against a surge of panic rising to his throat. Where the hell were the keys?

In his coat, Isaac thought. He looked around for a closet and spotted a wardrobe in the corner. Each step seemed to take a year and he cast frequent glances over his shoulder. He sure hoped Don was a heavy sleeper and that he'd pissed before he'd gone to bed.

The wardrobe groaned when he opened it. Isaac winced but Don slept on. He thought back, trying to remember what Don had worn when they'd returned from the hunt. Not his church attire, not a coat... A blue silk robe hung in the far back and looked familiar. Isaac reached into the pocket and stifled a gasp of delight as his fingers clasped cold keys. Yes!

Already dreading having to return them, Isaac made his painstaking way toward the bedroom door and eased himself into the hallway. It was so dark, he felt as if a cloth had been placed over his eyes. He almost missed the first step going downstairs and shuddered at the thought of all the noise he'd have made. Isaac felt to either side, touching the cool plaster of the walls.

From what he remembered of the layout, to the left of the stairs was the entranceway and kitchen and living room. To the right, the bathroom and the basement door where the wolves were kept. Isaac stumbled into the wall and clasped one of two doorknobs. He opened it and smelled air freshener. The bathroom, so the next door must be...

This time, Isaac really did trip. He flew down into total darkness, bouncing down the stairs on his ass before coming to a painful stop on his back. He groaned, his eyes watering from where he'd smacked his elbow on the bottom step.

"Isaac?" It was Ben's voice.

"Here." Blinded in the dark, Isaac eased himself to his feet. He felt around and his fingers fumbled over a switch. Blessed light flooded the basement. Unpleasantly, the first thing he saw was Morgan grinning wolfishly at him from where he lay in his cage. The huge white wolf watched him unblinkingly, and Isaac felt like a lamb beneath the wolf's blazing eyes.

Ben was in the cage below Morgan's. It was big enough for a wolf but hardly big enough for a grown man. He could only huddle into himself, his legs pulled up to his chest. Isaac threw himself to his knees and reached for the keys in his pocket. He froze, remembering all his questions. He met Ben's cool silver gaze. "You're a werewolf."

"And you're a hunter," Ben stated. "We done stating the obvious?" He squirmed uncomfortably in his cramped cage.

Isaac squeezed the keys tight but held them away from the lock. "Were you ever going to tell me?"

Ben's brow furrowed and his eyes hardened as he looked into Isaac's. "Think I should be the one asking the questions, considering *I* was never the one who had any intention of killing *you*."

His words cut deep, but Isaac didn't feel undeserving of his coldness. Despair gripped his heart. There was no way they could move past this, was there? "Do I look like I came here to kill you, Ben?"

"Suppose not. But that's the thing," Ben growled. "I don't really know who you are, Isaac, or what you want with me."

Isaac knew what Don would say, that Ben had to die. He was a werewolf, and sooner or later they would go feral and threaten innocent people. But Isaac couldn't see Ben that way. Isaac shoved the key in the lock and turned it. "I want to help you."

Ben eyed him with mistrust, then eased open the door. Isaac looked away for the sake of Ben's modesty as he crawled out on all fours and stretched gratefully. "We should get you some clothes," Isaac said, feeling his face warm as Ben stood.

It was hard to keep his eyes to himself. Ben had the body of a warrior—tall and muscular, with a broad, hairy chest. Isaac couldn't see his backside, but if Ben's front was anything to go by, he was likely chiseled there too. Isaac turned away fast. Now was not the time to start appreciating Ben's natural beauty. He was built like a predator because he *was* one.

"No need." Ben rolled his wide shoulders and they cracked. "The streets are quiet. I'll shift and make my way home. What do we do about him?" He curled his lip, eyeing Morgan with distaste. The wolf panted, his long tongue dangling and eyes narrowed.

Right on cue, the floorboards creaked upstairs.

"Shit," Isaac whispered, instinctively touching Ben's chest to urge him toward the door. "Don't worry about him. I'll be here. I'll make sure he's handed off to the cops." Isaac urged Ben up the stairs and turned off the light, leaving Morgan in the dark.

He held his breath as a door upstairs closed. The bathroom door. Knowing he had only seconds, he crept up the stairs and slipped into Don's room. He shoved the keys back into the robe and went out the window, closing it behind him.

He jogged to the road beyond the cathedral. A wolf stared at him from the shadows. Ben was here, and Isaac's car was not far away. He motioned for the wolf to follow. Isaac climbed into his car and shivered, turning on the heat. The wolf, Ben, jumped into the back seat. Isaac looked down, uneasy when those silver eyes blinked at him, and a rush of familiarity hit him. "Ben the Second, huh?" he murmured. "So it was you that night..."

Ben had been there for him the night he'd come back from the riot at Union Square. They'd shared steak and the wolf had consoled him. Ben had consoled him. Blinking hard, Isaac was both touched and embarrassed that Ben had seen him so vulnerable and yet still been so sweet the next morning. Did he remember? Don had told him wolves couldn't remember their shifts.

The sun was beginning to rise when they arrived back at the apartment. Isaac climbed the stairs, each step heavy. He didn't know what awaited them. There was no way Ben would still want to be his friend, let alone anything more.

When he looked up, his face warmed and he quickly looked away. Ben had shifted and stood buck naked, scowling at his door. "Damn. Left my keys in the car back in Inwood. Fuckin' hell." He rammed his shoulder into the door a few times and the door buckled and opened.

"Ben." Isaac's voice was a croak. "I want to explain."

Ben's eyes became pinched and he couldn't meet Isaac's gaze. He bowed his head and shouldered his way in, leaving the door open. Exhaling, Isaac followed him inside. He sat on the couch, squeezing his hands together in his lap while he waited for Ben to get dressed. The faucet dripped in the quiet and the radiator clicked.

"How many?" He jolted awake. Ben wore a robe tied tight, perfectly illustrating the shape of his waist. A sliver of chest hair showed through the V-shape in his robe's collar. Ben's eyes were hard. "I know you've killed my kind, Isaac. You smelled like a wolf that time you were hurt. Were you bitten in self-defense, or were you attacked?"

Isaac exhaled, his mouth unbearably dry. "I was at Union Square. During the riots."

Ben's jaw tightened. "Did you... kill anyone that day? There were casualties. Tell me you weren't responsible, Isaac."

Isaac winced at the desperation in Ben's voice. "Not that day, no, but I have killed, Ben." He forced himself to look Ben in the eyes. "No one who didn't deserve it."

"And you decide who deserves to live and die, do you?" Ben's voice was like ice.

He tried not to flinch. "I killed feral wolves who relished in bloodlust, who hunted humans for sport. Not people out doing their shopping, Ben!"

Ben folded his arms tight over his chest as if to protect himself from Isaac's words. "If you knew..." Ben hesitated, wetting his lips. "If you knew what I was, would you have—"

"No." Isaac spat the word out, hating the very thought. "No, Ben. You're not like them. You're good, you're—"

"Them? You mean, people like me?"

Isaac searched for words but they wouldn't come. "No. No, Ben. Not you, I meant…" What had he meant? "S-sorry. I shouldn't have—"

Ben straightened up from the wall, his feet pounding over the floorboards as he approached. "I'm a decent guy, Isaac, sure. But I'm still a werewolf. I'm not some gold standard for you to judge others."

Isaac looked him in the eye, wishing he could convey just how sorry he was. "I know. I'm saying that I trust you. You don't hurt people. You don't prey on others like the monsters—the wolves I've hunted."

"So, you trust me then?"

"Of course." Isaac looked at him head-on but his voice wavered.

A low growl rumbled in Ben's throat. Isaac's heart lurched. He'd heard growls like that so many times from shifters just before they pounced.

This is Ben. Ben! He wouldn't hurt me, Isaac told himself, balling his hands into tight fists.

Ben's nails sharpened; he bared his fangs, and fur grew thick on his arms. "I'm still me, Isaac." His voice was distorted, barely more than a growl. Isaac's mind screamed at him to run. He felt like prey under the glare of those animal eyes. "This is what I am. I'm the monster your hunters have told you all about." He seemed to grow taller, looming over Isaac. "Are you okay with this? Do you trust me now?" His voice thickened to a snarl, fangs gleaming with spit. A clawed hand came toward him, ready to strike.

"No!" Isaac lunged, striking Ben's enormous hand away with all the strength he had. He lurched toward the door, terrified he'd hear the floorboards creak under the slam of heavy paws, that he'd feel fangs crunch through his shoulder into his bone.

But none of that happened.

"Then you should go." Ben's voice broke.

Isaac's breath hitched. The pain in Ben's voice robbed him of his fear.

Why did I do that? He hadn't been able to control his reaction. It was Ben, but he'd treated him like a monster.

Ben exhaled shakily and bowed his head, but not before Isaac saw the glimmer of tears in his eyes. A trembling hand came up and covered them, and his massive shoulders heaved. "Go," Ben said, choking out the word.

A painful lump rose into Isaac's throat and he wished he could take it all back. Perhaps it was for the best things ended now, he told himself. Isaac threw open the door and stumbled out, closing it softly behind him. Then he stood in the hallway, struggling to move as everything inside him cried out to go back to Ben and tell him how sorry he was.

Ben deserved better than him. Gritting his teeth, Isaac let the door to his apartment slam behind him. He collapsed onto the sofa, the weight of the world pressing him down into the cushions. His throat ached from holding in his grief and remorse. Isaac dropped his arm over his eyes, and the pain and regret disappeared as he slipped into a thin, dreamless sleep where nothing could touch him.

CHAPTER 9

MISSING

The drive to the cathedral seemed to take forever. Isaac's phone was heavy in his pocket, a constant reminder that Ben was just a phone call away. All he had to do was call and tell him he'd choose Ben—and forsake his morals, forsake his duty to protect citizens from werewolves.

He squeezed the wheel tight. He couldn't do it. Ben would never love him, knowing the things he'd done to Ben's kind. Isaac could never leave the hunters; he owed Don too much to turn his back on him.

Isaac laughed softly so he didn't cry.

The car lurched to a stop outside the refectory and Isaac headed inside to wait with the other hunters, but instead he found the door wide open. Bloody paw prints in the snow led away toward the cathedral. "Shit!" Isaac whipped out his pistol and loaded silver bullets into the gun. Sirens howled not far away. Someone had called the police and as he neared the cathedral, stepping in more bloody snow on the way, he understood why.

Wails and screams came from beyond the doors, which were wide open, but there were no howls or snarls. Isaac peered within. Benches had been overturned, and the light from the rose windows reflected in pools of blood glistening on the marble. Men, women, and children lay face down in blood. Isaac ran, nearly slipping in it, and helped prop a woman up. It was Jocelyn. She had been bitten and clawed, her face bloodless as she shook and gasped for her daughter.

"What happened?" Isaac whispered, retrieving some bandages from his bag and wrapping them around the bite on her arm. But he knew before she even answered.

"A beast attacked the cathedral. A giant wolf."

Morgan had escaped. How?

Paramedics stormed in. Once Jocelyn was safely tended to, Isaac stood on trembling legs. Where was Don? He ran to the altar and found Don lying crumpled, his robes pooling around him. Isaac felt for a pulse. He found it beating steadily and helped Don sit up. "Are you hurt?"

"I'm afraid so," Don choked out, cradling his arm. He'd been bitten too, and the bite looked worse than Joce's. It was already turning so red around the edges as if infection were fast setting in. Isaac helped him stand. "The monster, he escaped his cage, attacked us during the service." Isaac helped him toward the paramedics. "No, no, my boy. Take me to the refectory. I can cleanse the wound myself."

The other hunters had arrived, but too late. They worried over Don but he assured them he was fine and Isaac helped him clean and bandage the wound. "This," Don declared, "was a grave and terrible attack on humans. The lives lost today will not be in vain. We will say the names of the dead in a rallying cry when we smite the devils responsible for this heinous attack on our race!" The hunters echoed him.

"Father, what about the councilman we caught?" a hunter asked.

Don said, "It and Morgan had been freed from their cages sometime during my sermon. Someone used my keys to open the cages. I suspect a traitor in our ranks. A werewolf sympathizer." Don's lips thinned in anger. "It could have only been Gina. She's betrayed us."

The other hunters gasped. One of them said, "It had to have been! You all heard the way she was ranting last night! She's betrayed us!"

"Gina wouldn't! She's our friend!"

"Don, how could you let this happen?"

The Father gnashed his teeth, his jaw going taut. "I will find whoever is responsible, and make this right! Have faith in me, my hunters!"

Isaac felt isolated from them all as doubts warred in his mind. How could someone have stolen Don's keys during his sermon? He knew Don always kept them on him. Something wasn't adding up—he just didn't know what.

"What do we do, Father?" a woman hunter asked.

Don wiped sweat from his clammy brow. "We must hunt her down. She needs to answer for her betrayal." Don swooned in his seat. "Please, my brothers and sisters, leave me." The crowd slowly dispersed and Don peered up at Isaac through weary eyes. "My son, you're the only one I trust to see this through. If I ask, will you help me find the traitor?"

Isaac couldn't find the words. He'd joined the Silver Cross to protect people from werewolves, not to kill one of his own. "Do we know for sure it was Gina? It doesn't feel right to accuse her when we don't have any proof."

Don grimaced as if Isaac's words had struck him. "I need you, Isaac. I need you to trust me as you always have."

"I do, Don. I just think we need more proof before we hunt down one of our own."

"It was her! You heard her! She's been doubting me, questioning me at every turn!" Don snapped. "And now, you do the same! How can you doubt me now, after everything I've done for you?"

Isaac flinched back from him. "You're right, you're right. I... I'm sorry, Don. I'll do my best to find her. But just promise me you'll hear her out first. It isn't like you to turn on one of our own so quickly."

Don slumped in his seat. "Yes, you're right. It is unchristian of me. Your words shame me, my son."

"Hey, it's all right. I get it. You're in pain, and we just lost a lot of innocent people."

Don nodded. "Still, I mustn't lose myself. I promise that if we find her, I will hear her side of the story before I judge her."

Isaac smiled and gripped Don's shoulder. "Thank you, Father."

IT WAS ONLY AFTERNOON and Isaac was aching for a drink, so he stopped at a bar near the cathedral after leaving Don.

"Sir, werewolves only."

Isaac shoved twenty dollars at the hulking bouncer. A bar was a bar, and this was the closest one to the cathedral. The bouncer shrugged. "Fine. Just don't cause trouble."

He collapsed into a seat at the bar, every aching bone going slack. The bartender's shakers rattled, a table of rowdy shifters howled, and the permeating aromas of different roasting meats made Isaac's stomach growl.

"Can I have an old-fashioned?" If he didn't numb himself, he didn't know how he'd get through the day. He could still smell the blood, hear the wails of the injured. And the worst part? He didn't know what the fuck to believe. Someone had let Morgan out of his cage, and it sure as hell hadn't been Isaac.

The question was, who? Don had been preaching when it had happened and had the bite mark to prove it. One of the other hunters, then? Could it really have been Gina? Isaac hadn't known her very well, but she seemed a levelheaded person.

The last of his old-fashioned burned its way down Isaac's throat and he ordered another. They had a spy in their midst. Someone within their ranks was working for Stone. The last thing he needed was to play detective. He wasn't very good at that.

"Oops!" Someone bumped into his back. Isaac lurched against the bar, spilling his drink all over the countertop. He turned and encountered the hairy face of a half-shifted wolf, fangs bared in an unsettling grin. "Sorry there, ham shank." Clawed hands grabbed Isaac's shoulders tight and squeezed, the nails piercing his skin.

"Get off!" But the shifter let go before Isaac could start with him, and he backed away, clawed hands raised.

"Temper, temper, beef jerky. You're a human in a wolf den. And you smell an awful lot like silver."

Isaac growled. He didn't appreciate threats, least of all after two drinks and from a werewolf. Unsettled, he paid for his drinks and left without finishing the third one. Thinking he'd sleep in his car until his shift at the bar tonight, Isaac went in search of his vehicle.

When he opened his eyes again, the streetlamps were on and the streets were empty. Yawning, he checked the time. His shift was in an hour, and he really had to take a leak.

Sighing, Isaac stepped out into the cold. Looking both ways and seeing no one, he unzipped his fly and got down to business between two parked cars. Not his finest moment, but it was better than pissing his jeans.

Snow crunched behind him. Isaac yanked his pants back up, ready to apologize to any poor soul who might have witnessed his crass behavior. Instead, a hand wrapped around his throat. Isaac was bent over the back of his car, at the mercy of the creature towering over him. It was the shifter from the bar, and he had a friend with him.

"Knew you smelled familiar, beef roast." The werewolf sniffed the air and growled low in its throat. "A hunter. You were there in the park. You're the reason they captured Morgan. Oh, I'm sure he'll love to say hello to you!"

Isaac tried to call for help, but the blow across his face made stars burst before his eyes. The wolves laughed as he crumpled to the ground. The pain didn't last long; he was unconscious in seconds.

BEN SPENT MOST OF the day with a hole inside him. He worked hard, overseeing business at the estate, doing everything he could to ensure his hands weren't idle. When he wasn't busy, the hole opened up and his wolf howled for Isaac, a song Isaac could never answer with his own verse because he was human, and a hunter.

He didn't want to leave the agency headquarters. He didn't want to go home and stop outside Isaac's door, knowing they couldn't see or talk to each other anymore. But if they could, Ben would apologize for scaring him the way he had. He'd talk to Isaac and try and understand why he felt the way he did about wolves. He'd ask Isaac about these so-called monsters he'd killed so he could get the full picture of Isaac's life as a hunter.

Now that he'd had time to cool off, he was coming to understand that, like Isaac, he'd made a snap judgment about Isaac's life as a hunter. For all he knew, Isaac really did target wolves who preyed on humans and left innocent wolves alone. He wanted so badly for that to be true. Ben, of all people, understood that in this world, sometimes it was for the best to take justice into your own hands. He couldn't fault Isaac for that, if that was what he did.

Isaac was a good person, Ben knew this, and it was obvious a lot of his fear of wolves came from common misconceptions. But was Isaac capable of change, or did he want to remain willfully ignorant? In his heart, Ben wanted to believe Isaac was open-minded, that there was still a chance for them. But if Isaac saw all wolves as irredeemable monsters, then Ben didn't see how they could be together. He wouldn't know, though, unless he found the courage to ask Isaac.

Just as he got off work, his phone rang and Ben's heart began playing the drums. He hated the disappointment he felt when he saw Greg's name. He heaved himself inside his pickup truck and got the engine running. Commuting was a lot easier and less expensive on a daily basis with his new truck. Flipping open his phone, he said, "Hmm?"

"Hi, Greg, nice to hear from ya, man! Is that really so hard, Ben?"

"Everything okay?" Ben asked.

"Just checking in, making sure you haven't been dognapped again. Man, that really freaked me out. Hey, tell me how your date went with your new guy. We never got to chat after the fight in the park."

Ben sighed and backed out of the driveway. "About that... really rather not talk about him right now."

"Come on, Ben, I know I tease you, but I'm happy for you. Heather was a nice chick but I've got a good feeling about Isaac."

"Doesn't matter. I think we're through." Ben slammed his foot down on the gas and sped past the gate.

"What? Why? You can't be through. He's your—"

"No, he's not, not if I got any say about it!" Ben spun the wheel and swerved onto the road from the estate. "Which I do. Fuck fate."

"Yikes." Greg sighed. "Okay. What happened? Wait, you're driving, right? I'll meet you at the apartment. Then you can fill me in on your teenaged angst."

"Fine. See you there."

True to his word, Greg knocked on the door a few hours after Ben had finally arrived home. "Follow me. I know this great pizza place nearby. It's real popular."

It was a short walk and Ben realized why. "Can we eat somewhere else?" It was the pizzeria and bar where Isaac worked.

Greg sniffed the air longingly. "But their pizza's so good. The line for a table isn't that long—" He smirked. "Oh, I get it. You and Isaac went on dates here?"

Ben groaned and turned away. He couldn't smell Isaac, though he did smell yeast and cheese, and his stomach rumbled longingly. He glanced in the windows. It wasn't Isaac behind the bar, but he vaguely recognized the bartender. Gerard, was it? The bar was full but he didn't see Isaac taking up a seat. He wasn't in tonight. "As long as we don't have to wait fifteen minutes."

They got in line to order slices. There were three people before them but the wait wasn't long. Ben stepped over the threshold and into the night he and Isaac first met. The crowds disappeared and Isaac sat at the bar, nursing a drink and a broken heart. Ben hadn't known then how badly he was hurting. How could he have guessed when Isaac had still managed to smile so radiantly?

But in quiet moments, he'd disappear into himself, and though physically he'd stood beside Ben, he'd felt a thousand miles away. Ben had never believed he could help Isaac, and that hadn't been his goal in befriending him.

It had just happened and before he knew it, he'd wanted to see more of the man behind his sad mask who laughed and smiled so easily, who helped strangers like Ben and went out of his way to make sure they felt like they belonged.

"This table good for you, Ben?" Greg asked.

Isaac vanished, the noise of the crowd rushing in. Ben blinked at the tiny two-top that seemed far away enough from the music. He sat without complaint and they ordered a pepperoni pie to share between them. "Heard their pies are huge. Think we can finish it?" Greg grabbed his utensils in preparation.

Once they had their drinks, Ben raised his beer in a toast. "I believe in us." No matter how many other men or women came and went from Ben's life, Greg was a constant. He hoped that never changed. They drank and Ben asked, "So, you never clarified how you escaped the hunters."

Ben swallowed hard. "Isaac helped."

Greg gawked at him, beer half-raised to his lips. "What? That boy of yours must be a good infiltrator to get inside a hunter lair without getting caught!"

The bubbles in Ben's beer frothed to the surface, the glass cold as he squeezed it tight. "He's one of them."

Greg sprayed beer across the table.

Ben managed a smile but it fell fast from his face. "Still think we're fated to be together?"

Greg rubbed the table with a fistful of napkins. "I didn't see that one coming."

"Neither did I."

Greg's cheeks lost their color. "Damn, Ben. I don't know what to say."

Ben took a gulp of beer, at a loss himself.

"But he saved you. Why do that if he didn't care?"

Ben slammed down his glass. "It's not about whether he cares or not. Of course he does and I—I did too."

"So, I guess it's over between you guys, huh?" Greg frowned sympathetically.

Ben sighed. "I don't know. I need to talk to him before I make a decision. But what if he doesn't want to be with me?" He winced, hating how pitiful he sounded.

Greg sighed. "Man. What a shitshow." He waved over more beers. "Are you... you know, safe? If you need a place to lay low for a while, my door's open."

The bartender, Gerard, caught Ben's eye and jogged out from behind the bar.

Ben didn't want to impose, especially knowing Greg's reputation as a ladies' man. "I can manage." Perhaps he was an idiot, but he did trust Isaac. Isaac wouldn't betray him to the hunters. Isaac might be a hunter, but he still saved Ben's life. That had to mean there was a chance for them, right?

"Hey, Ben! Nice to have you back!" Gerard shook his hand. Ben squeezed firmly, accustomed to human greetings and comfortable with them now. "You hear from Isaac today, by chance?"

Ben's ears pricked up at the mention of him. "No, sorry."

"Shit. I've been trying to reach him all day, but he won't answer his phone."

Ben's stomach lurched. "Really?"

Gerard put both hands on his hips, shaking his head. "For him to just not come in, no warning, no nothing? That's unusual. Shit. Hope he didn't go off the deep end." He walked over to the counter when one of the pizza chefs rang the bell.

Ben lurched from his seat and followed Gerard to the counter. "Isaac was supposed to work tonight?"

Gerard grabbed a tray of pizza. "Yup. Just decided not to come in, I guess."

Ben's stomach twisted itself into knots. "Why would he do that?"

"Who knows?" Gerard carried the pizza to a table and Ben followed him. "He lost his kid, he's divorced, he hasn't got any friends—except you, of course. Knowing you really perked him up. He talks about you all the time, gets this big grin on his face." Gerard walked back behind the bar. He poured someone a beer, then reached for a bottle of bourbon. "I worry about him, you know. Guy in his situation can go off the rails at any time, know what I mean?"

Chunks of ice fell into Ben's stomach. Now that he and Ben weren't speaking anymore, Isaac was truly alone. He'd been just as upset as Ben the last time they'd spoken. Ben was hurting, but he had people he could turn to when he needed to. Who did Isaac have? Ben's hands shook as he grabbed his phone. He ran outside where it was quiet and waited for Isaac to answer, but the call went to voicemail. "Come on, Isaac. Come on."

Images came at him with claws. Isaac having one too many drinks and going to sleep, never to wake up. Walking off the fire escape of his apartment. Pale and lifeless in the bathtub, blood staining the porcelain. No. No, he wouldn't have.

"Ben! Hey!" Greg called.

Ben's feet slapped the pavement as he ran from the bar and back to his apartment, each breath like a knife in his lungs.

Please. Please, don't do this, Isaac. Don't you fucking dare!

Ben collided with the front door, his hand shaking as he twisted the key in the lock until he thought the key would snap. He barreled inside and jumped up the stairs three at a time, breathless and shaking as he stopped outside Isaac's door.

"Ben, what the hell's going on?" Greg asked.

Ben slammed his fist against the door. "Isaac! Open up!"

"Hey, slow down, buddy!" Greg grabbed at his shirt. "He's probably fine, and he won't like it if you damage his front door!"

Ben pounded on the door. "Isaac! Answer me!"

Fuck this. Ben rammed his shoulder into the door but it wouldn't budge. A snarl tore from his throat, and fur grew thick on his arms. His wolf snapped and snarled, hurling itself against his chest, howling for *mate!* for *Isaac!* The knob crunched like a tin can between his fingers.

With a roar, Ben kicked the door and it crashed open and slammed into the wall. He could barely fit through the doorway, he vaguely realized, squeezing himself inside. The floorboards were cold under his feet and he realized his sneakers had ripped apart.

"Whoa, Ben, what the fuck?" He whirled toward his packmate with a snarl. Greg's face had gone white. "Ben, calm down. Okay? Something's wrong with you, man. You're freaking huge!"

He ripped the door to the bathroom open and the hinges screeched in protest. He sniffed the air, his claws scraping the tiled wall as he fumbled for the switch. The lights revealed an empty room.

Mate. Not here. Have to find mate. Protect him. Kill anyone who hurt him.

"B-Ben..." Packmate's voice was a squeak.

His claws punched through the bedroom door, sending an explosion of splinters into the room. Another sniff revealed the room was empty. A howl of despair pulled from his throat, and the rage boiled down to dismay. He closed his eyes tight.

Mate. Where is mate? Where is mine? Never should have left him. Have to find him, have to.

"Ben. Ben! Easy."

The room spun and Ben felt as if he were falling down a long, dark tunnel. He stumbled into something round and soft, and clammy hands gripped his shoulders. "Sit down, bud. Breathe."

Ben sucked in one shallow breath after another. "He's not here."

"Ben, what was that? You changed! You got bigger, you—"

Scrambling to his feet, Ben said, "The windows are all shut, so he couldn't have jumped! So he must just not be answering his phone!" He forced himself to breathe, trying to stay rational.

"Ben!" Greg gripped his shoulders. "Listen to me, I'm telling you something weird just happened to you!"

A lupine growl surged from Ben's throat. "You don't get it! Something's wrong. Something's happened to him! I can feel it!"

Greg recoiled from him. "Okay, okay. So we'll go back to the bar, talk to the bartender. He probably knows where Isaac might be. Just don't wolf out again on me."

"I didn't wolf out."

"You did! You don't remember?"

Ben squinted at him. Was Greg absolutely nuts? "Remember what?"

Greg flung open his arms and shrieked, "Look around you!"

Ben's mouth fell open. The front door hung off its hinges, there were claw marks on the floor, and the bedroom door had a hole blown right through it. No way. He couldn't have. How would he have had the strength to do any of that? Something tickled his knuckles. Tiny cuts on his fingers were healing, pushing out splinters from below his skin. The blood roared in Ben's ears and he collapsed onto the couch. "I don't remember how I got these."

Greg wiped sweaty hair from his forehead. "You're not kidding, are you? Ben, has anything like this happened before?"

"No!" Ben's voice was too small to be a shout. "I mean, I lost control of my wolf once. I smelled Isaac's blood, and the wolf came out. He was so strong, I couldn't control him even after I'd shifted. Not for a while."

Oh fuck. His grandfather had told stories about Ben's great-grandmother. How she'd lost herself to bestial rage and turned into a giant bipedal wolf-woman monstrosity. The stories of the damage she'd done in that form had given Ben nightmares when he was a kid. What was it called? A gene. Some kind of gene. His mother had complained when Ben was a teenager and he'd gotten rowdy as a wolf. His father had just laughed and said, "At least our boy ain't a berserker wacko like my grandmother."

Berserker.

Was that what he was becoming? Had his great-grandmother's gene passed on to him? Pieces fell into place. This explained why his wolf went absolutely nuts when he thought Isaac was in danger.

But that wasn't what mattered. "We gotta get back to that bar and find out where Isaac is."

Greg swallowed. "Ben, you sure you're good for this? Maybe you should call it a night and I'll find Isaac."

"No!" The roar exploded from Ben before he could stop it, in a voice he didn't recognize as his own. He sucked in a gulp of air and tried to find the words. "I will find him, Greg." His voice was hoarse and trembling. "I have to find him."

Greg exhaled, his shoulders drooping. "Fine, but I'm coming with you. And you're going to a freaking doctor after this is over."

"You can drive me," Ben agreed, breathless, and he ran from the apartment.

Chapter 10

BERSERKER BEAST

Isaac woke in suffocating darkness with only the rumbling of the car engine to convince him he hadn't been buried alive. His arms were bound tight behind his back with his own silver cuffs. His head ached, blood sticky and damp in his hair from where he'd been struck.

He didn't know how long he'd been out; it could be daylight beyond the trunk and he wouldn't know. He didn't know where they were going, but the road was straight and long, and he couldn't hear any traffic, making him think they were on a road beyond the city.

A wave of dizziness washed over him as he struggled to suck in enough oxygen to breathe in this tight, dark space. He vaguely remembered that he was being taken to Morgan and the Moonborn; his captor had mentioned as much before he'd conked him upside the head.

No one would find him. No one knew where he was or cared. Maybe Gerard and his coworkers might notice he was gone, but they wouldn't piece together that he was missing—not until he was dead in the ground with his throat ripped out.

Ben. Ben would notice, no doubt. They lived right across the hall from each other. He would realize something was wrong and—but why should Ben care what became of him? Isaac hunted people like him. Ben had zero reason to give a damn what happened to Isaac just because they'd shared a few tender moments together. Despair clamped like a cold fist around

Isaac's heart as he was bounced around in the trunk of the car that was speeding him to his demise.

No, he couldn't give up hope. He wouldn't surrender. All he had to do was keep his head on straight, bide his time, and find an opportunity to escape. He wouldn't die alone in the wilderness, not without a fight.

GERARD HAD TOLD THEM that Isaac frequented the Cathedral of Saint John the Divine. That was true—it was the hideout for the hunters. If he wasn't home, perhaps he was there. Perhaps he'd been called away on a hunt, and if he wasn't answering his phone, then that meant—

A snarl tore from his throat, his nails sharpening to claws.

"Whoa, Ben! Cool it, man. We're gonna find him." Greg raised his hands.

Ben closed his eyes tight, taking in deep, slow breaths to calm his frantic wolf. "We will."

And so Ben and Greg found themselves at the western façade of the cathedral facing Amsterdam Avenue. The rose window above the doorway revealed no light from within. Caution tape prevented them from climbing the steps into the cathedral. "Did something happen?" Ben wondered.

"Looks like the cathedral is closed," Greg said, not sounding too bummed out. "Oh well, he can't be here."

Ben tried not to be annoyed by Greg's relief. He understood why—the smell of silver hung like a thick mist in the air. Just the smell alone made him feel woozy. This was the hunters' stomping grounds, and he was about as eager to sniff around the cathedral as he was to stick his hand in a bear trap.

If Isaac wasn't here, Ben wasn't sure where else to look. Panic twisted up his insides. "Let's go." He spun around on his heel. "Can't smell anything through all this silver." To his relief, breathing was easier across the street.

Ben paced, trying to think. Isaac wasn't at home, and he couldn't be at the cathedral since the entire area was closed off.

Then he smelled it; beneath the tangled smells of silver, sour dog urine, and garbage, he caught the unmistakable scent of rain-washed pavement and wet leaves. His frayed nerves soothed at once as he breathed the refreshing scent into his lungs. Isaac had been here. The scent was stale but not by much.

"Found him!" Ben jogged up the street, following the trail. Howls and barks echoed from a shifter bar across the street called The Den. Isaac's scent drifted toward the door. "He stopped in a werewolf bar?" Ben didn't like the sound of a lone human in a bar full of wolves. It'd be like a lamb to the slaughter.

"Well, someone's bound to have seen him," Greg said, waving and flashing a grin at the bouncer. The guy grimaced, arms folded tight over his barrel chest. "Hey. We're looking for a human. We think he stopped in your fine establishment."

"A human. Tall, depressed-looking? Yeah. I warned him not to come in. Why, he in trouble?"

Ben said, "He's missing. Look, I would appreciate anything you can do to help."

"Shit…" The bouncer looked away with a click of his tongue. "Knew I didn't like the way Reggie followed him out."

Ben's heart sank. "Who followed him?"

"Reggie. He's one of our regulars, a real asshole. He pays well, otherwise my boss would have kicked his ass out ages ago."

"Why, what's he do?" Ben's fingers curled.

"He likes to mess with humans. Scare them, harass them."

A growl built in Ben's throat, rumbling louder than the revving of a furious engine. "And knowing that, you just let him follow my friend? The hell do you get paid for?"

"Ben." Greg gripped his arm. "Cool it. We need to find this Reggie guy. Know anything about him, where he lives?"

"I'll ask the bartender. He's sent Reggie home in a cab occasionally."

Ben paced until the bouncer returned. Once they had the address, Ben and Greg drove fast to their destination. Reggie lived on Grove Street. It was a quiet, narrow street with rows of small apartments built in the Greek Revival style. So quaint and cozy, in fact, that Ben hardly believed a human-hating asshole could live there. He stopped outside the building number the bartender had given them, his heart racing. "He lives here."

Greg looked up and down the two-story brick building. He swallowed with obvious apprehension. "If you say so."

The lights were on inside. Ben pounded on the door and waited. Every second that passed, the wolf growled louder, pacing up and down beneath his skin. Ben slammed his fist against the door. "Reggie, open up!" His voice echoed down the quiet street and a dog barked in response.

"Yeah?" came a rough voice from beyond the door. "Who the hell are you, asshole?"

Ben's heart leaped into his throat. This was it. His chance to find Isaac. "I think we have a mutual acquaintance."

A bark of laughter. "Go the fuck away, man."

Ben kicked the door in answer. "I'm looking for my friend. I know you've seen him! He's human. You met him at The Den."

A heavy silence answered him, and it was all the confirmation Ben needed. Fury brought his claws out and turned his breath to sharp pants. "So, you know him." It was hard to talk through his fangs. "My wolf's in a hell of a mood. I'm giving you a chance to tell me now 'cause I can't hold him back for long and once he comes out, I can't control what he does to you. Tell me where my friend is, right now."

"Y-you know your friend's a hunter, right? I did you a fucking favor!"

Ben's wolf hurled itself against his restraints and he doubled over with a hoarse snarl. "What did you do?" He slammed clawed hands against the door. It shook, rattling in its frame. He heard a yelp from the other side of the door.

"N-nothing, I swear! I just—"

The fury surged from Ben in a tidal wave, roaring to the surface. "I warned you!" he snarled, voice thick with a guttural growl. A single tug ripped the door wide open. The scrawny man screamed and hurled himself to the floor, huddling into a ball. Ben seized a handful of the werewolf's scruff and threw him up against a wall.

"Tell me where he is!" Hardly human, the roar tore at his throat. All the blood had drained from the werewolf's pockmarked face.

Ben grinned. "So, it's fun for you to pick on defenseless humans, huh? Telling you right now, bud, you messed with the wrong one. Talk now."

"H-he's at Norwood Asylum. Some ruins in Westchester County."

Fear festered in Ben's gut. He squeezed tight around Reggie's scrawny neck. "Why? What do you want with him?"

"Not me!" The shifter wheezed, eyes bulging in fear. "M-Morgan. Told him I ran into your friend, and he ordered me to capture him so he could 'get even.'"

Ben's blood froze in his veins. Greg whispered, "You sent him to Moonborn cultists? You work for that traitor?"

Reggie panted, spraying Ben with whiskey-sodden breath. "Stone and his Moonborn are going to cleanse this city. He's a fucking hero to all wolves. Humans, hunters, mongrels—this city doesn't belong to them, not anymore!"

With a roar, Ben slammed Reggie's head into the wall, and he crumpled in a heap with a groan. Ben's hands shook and he couldn't catch his breath. A pack of the most dangerous wolves in the country had Isaac. He stumbled, catching himself against the wall. By now, Isaac could already be dead. A strangled noise tore from his throat and his knees buckled. "I never—I never should have let him go."

"Ben, listen to me." Greg knelt, his hands heavy and firm on Ben's shoulders. "Hey!" He patted Ben's cheek hard and the ringing in Ben's ears died. He sucked in one gulp of air after another. "Isaac might still be alive. Think about it. He's got a lot to offer the cult, doesn't he? Info on the hunters' plans, their locations!"

It made sense. Isaac was a valuable source of information. "You think he's okay?"

Greg shrugged. "Well, not 'okay' but there's a chance he's still alive. And we know where the cult is! I say we call up Manuel and tell him to give us a ride upstate."

The shaking stopped, and through his despair, Ben found the strength to stand. He was glad Greg was here—without him he would be lost. He held on to Greg's shoulders and bumped their foreheads together. "Thank you." His voice was husky with relief and gratitude.

Greg grinned and clapped his shoulder. "Anytime. Now, let's go save your mate."

ISAAC'S HEART SANK AS the car rolled to a stop and the engine cut off. Beyond the trunk, all was silent, confirming his belief that they were in the countryside. The trunk opened and it was just as dark outside as it was inside. There were no streetlamps to illuminate the woods and the moon shone brightly in the sky.

"End of the line, hunter," his captor growled. He wasn't the jerk from the bar who'd knocked him out, but Isaac still wanted to put his fist through the fucker's mouth. Grabbing Isaac's jacket, his captor hurled him from the car. Isaac landed on his shoulder on the icy ground, gritting his jaw to keep from yelping. The werewolf yanked Isaac to his feet, and he choked on the cloth crammed in his mouth. His throat prickled and he thought he'd throw up if he didn't choke to death first.

His captor gripped Isaac's arm hard enough to cut off his circulation and shoved him forward. Isaac looked back. Was it possible someone would see his abandoned car and call for help? The deep darkness of the woods and the never-ending silence shattered Isaac's hopes. There wasn't a soul out here. He couldn't count on anyone to save him but himself.

Frost left the grass stiff and crunchy under Isaac's feet, every snap of a twig echoing for miles in the chasm of darkness around him. A dog barked, sounding several miles off, but it was impossible to tell from where. Isaac couldn't fathom where they were taking him, and his eyes strained to penetrate the darkness until his head hurt. Meanwhile, his captor navigated the dark with ease, laughing when Isaac almost walked into trees or stumbled.

If I escape, I'm killing you first, Isaac vowed, his head throbbing from where he'd struck it on a branch.

Howls echoed into the sky and Isaac shuddered. He'd never heard wolves howling in the night as a pack. It was terrifying and beautiful in equal measure. They sounded so close, and as eyes gleamed green in the darkness, he realized they were all around him and he hadn't heard their paws moving deftly over the frosted ground.

Their growls and curious sniffs raised the hair on his arms. His eyes had adjusted just enough that he could make out what looked like a building ahead, surrounded by a stone wall. Half of it had fallen away while the other half still stood. Based on the architecture, Isaac wanted to say it was an old asylum—the perfect place for a cult to hide.

The wolves surrounded him on all sides, fangs bared and glistening, eyes gleaming like demons in the dark. They charged past him, making him jump, and fangs snapped at the hem of his jeans but didn't break the skin. All the while, they howled and barked like the jeers of a blood-hungry crowd before a witch trial. They were mocking him. Isaac wasn't blind to the irony; he was prey now and the creatures he'd hunted were the hunters. Maybe it was no less than he deserved.

The wolves shepherded him into the ruins, and he stumbled his way through the curtain of darkness, tripping on the rickety stairs that groaned under his weight. The building stank of rotting wood, wet fur, and the sour, pungent odors of urine and shit. The bones of small animals snapped under his feet.

A door creaked, hanging on its last hinge. A sharp hand to his back sent him flying and he crashed headlong into the door and then onto the damp, chilly wood floor. His head ached and spots popped before his eyes.

A clawed hand fisted his hair and dragged his face up from the soggy wood. Morgan sat in a shredded armchair above Isaac, wearing a stained white shirt and baggy, torn pants. A matted beard twitched into a yellowed smile that was sharp and fanged. A chill of dread went down Isaac's spine. He'd never seen a man so animalistic—just his smile alone made Isaac's stomach shrivel. The eyes so closely resembled those of a wolf—no, a monster—that it was hard not to feel like helpless prey, ready to be devoured.

"Good hunter. I was so hoping to see you again." Creaky laughter wheezed from Morgan's chapped lips. They were unnaturally red, as if stained with blood, and his breath stank of carrion. Isaac's gag reflex, already irritated by the cloth, prickled relentlessly and his stomach threatened to heave as he doubled over. The cloth was ripped free from his mouth and he retched, sucking in gulps of stale air.

"Wh-what do you want from me?" Isaac croaked, fury numbing his panic. "You wanna get even, that it? Why don't you untie me, then? Unless you're scared."

The surrounding wolves snarled and barked, reminding Isaac to hold his tongue. He was surrounded and chained. He had to wait for an opportunity, play along with whatever the cult wanted. If Morgan had only wanted him dead, there was no reason to bring him this far.

Morgan wasn't fazed and only barked laughter. "I wanted the pleasure of your company, of course. There's so much I can learn from you, hunter of beasts." He paced, his arms behind his back. He was naked, his skin pale like a ghost's in the dark. "See, John Stone, my boss, has something of a hunter problem."

So it was information. Isaac swallowed hard, trying to ready himself.

"He has big plans for New York, for the world, actually. Imagine, a world where werewolves rule over the masses, where those who taint our pure blood are punished, and humans are no more."

"Sounds ambitious," Isaac said.

"So you understand why you and your hunters are a thorn in our side?" Morgan's lip curled in fury.

"I... I can see why. What do you want?"

Morgan knelt, his eyes burning into Isaac's. "I want names, hunter. I want locations. I want plans for your hunts. I want you and your people out of John Stone's city."

The sweat was cold on Isaac's brow.

"How about you answer a question for me?" Isaac growled. "Who let you out?"

The werewolf tsked, shaking his head. "Oh, hunter. That's not how this game works. Answer my questions, and I'll answer yours."

The minute he gave Morgan what he wanted, he would die. He had to hold out, wait for an opportunity.

"Don't want to talk?" Morgan's fingers tightened in Isaac's hair, ripping strands from his scalp. He clenched his jaw tight to keep quiet.

Morgan motioned a werewolf over. "Make him talk."

The werewolf grinned, showing his fangs.

Morgan smiled. "I suggest breaking his fingers first. He'll spill his guts before you've gotten to the middle finger, I guarantee."

Isaac shuddered, cold with dread as the werewolf picked up a brick, weighing it in his hand. Isaac imagined it smashing his fingers and the terror nearly made him throw up. He couldn't betray the Cross. Don was his friend, and he'd given Isaac purpose. "I'm tougher than that, Morgan. Think you'll be disappointed." Isaac's voice trembled but he'd made up his mind. He'd no sooner betray the Cross than he would betray Ben.

Ben. He wished he'd seen him one last time. He wished he'd never walked out of Ben's apartment. They'd deserved a second chance. Isaac gritted his teeth as the wolves circled, hoping they didn't see the tremors racking his body. He wouldn't talk. No matter how badly they hurt him, he wouldn't break. He closed his eyes tight and thought of Ben, his gentle touch and gruff voice, those silver eyes like pools of moonlight.

They were in his apartment and this time, Isaac didn't run. He took Ben in his arms, as frightening and monstrous as he looked, and accepted him in his entirety. Those big arms held him tight, bundling him in warmth and security. Ben took hold of Isaac's hand with surprising gentleness, holding it as if he were made of glass.

A clawed foot across his face bowled him over and he struck his head on the floor. He writhed, curling in on himself as kicks and hits rained down upon him. His ears rang and he wished he would pass out, anything to escape the pain.

Morgan towered over him, blurry and swaying. "Yes. I think you'll talk, all right."

WESTCHESTER COUNTY WASN'T A long drive from the city, but every minute that passed was another minute that Isaac was at the mercy of a cold-blooded werewolf with hatred in his heart for humans and hybrids. Meanwhile, all Ben could do was sit helpless in his seat, praying to the She-Wolf that they got there in time. He couldn't imagine what Isaac was going through.

"I know, Ben." Manuel's voice was tense. "We'll be there soon. Just three more miles to go. What are we looking for again?"

"An old asylum," Greg answered, his nose in his laptop screen. "Built in the eighteenth century. It's somewhere around Lake Kitchawan."

Ben sighed and squeezed his knees, wincing when his claws popped out and cut his skin. "We're not going there to fight. We're outnumbered. If you two will cause a distraction, I'll sneak inside, grab Isaac, and get out. I'll howl when I've got him, and we can find each other by scent. Don't take any unnecessary risks. I know you wanna get Morgan, Manuel, but the last thing I want is for you to die on me. Veronica will hunt me to the ends of the earth."

"I got this," Manuel answered easily, wearing a confident smile. "You just find your boy."

Manuel drove them down Knapp Road. They were entering the woods now. The streetlights disappeared behind them and soon the only light came from the waxing gibbous moon and their headlights. Beyond the headlights was a wall of darkness. Ben's heart threw itself against his chest. Isaac was somewhere in these woods, at the mercy of creatures who had no love for his kind, who were much stronger than he was.

Hold on, Isaac. You hear me? I'm close now.

The car rocked to a stop. They'd reached the end of the road. The woods opened up, revealing a vast lake beyond the leafy curtain. Moonlight glimmered on the lake, the water rippling calmly. The quiet was so deep, the slam of the car door echoed for miles, and every snap of the twigs beneath their feet was as loud as the snapping of small bones. Ben shivered, though not from the chill in the air or the frost that crunched underfoot.

Manuel sniffed the air. "Smell that? Wolves."

Ben took a whiff of numbingly cold air, and over the smell of frozen grass and cold soil, he caught the unmissable tang of wolf urine. They'd established territory within these woods, warning away any intruders. A chorus of howls echoed over the treetops and coaxed a growl to Ben's throat. The winds changed and he could smell their wet fur for miles.

"This way," he murmured and followed his nose. Greg and Manuel left their clothes in the car and soon two wolves prowled at Ben's side. His eyes quickly adjusted to the darkness and he could now see that paw prints marred the freshly fallen snow. There were too many to count, spread throughout the woods, but it was clear the cult had amassed a big pack. Ben hoped he hadn't dragged his friends to their deaths. He had to ensure Greg and Manuel escaped alive.

Through the trees, the ruins of an asylum materialized. Vines crawled over a tall stone wall and frost clung to an iron gate rocking on its last hinge. Ben's ears picked up the panting, snapping, and snarling of wolves beyond the wall. It was impossible to tell how many.

"Hey!"

Ben whirled toward the voice. A werewolf muscled his way toward them, naked from a recent shift. Fur covered his arms and his eyes glowed dangerously. Ben positioned himself in front of Manuel and Greg. He forced a grin on his face and waved. "Right back atcha. Good night for a shift, huh?" An idea jumped into Ben's mind. "Sorry for intruding. My friends and I smelled you guys all over the place. We were just wondering if this was Moonborn territory. We were hoping to join, kill some hybrids..."

The shifter bared his fangs. He'd killed something recently, and his teeth were stained with blood. Ben's stomach writhed with terror for Isaac. "That so? You'll have to speak to Morgan. He handles the mundane stuff Stone's too busy to deal with. Between you and me, you couldn't have picked a better night to join. We just bagged ourselves a hunter."

A growl rumbled in Ben's chest and he squeezed his hands into fists. "Sounds like you boys run a tight ship here. I want in. Where can I speak to Morgan?"

The shifter spat blood into the snow with a wet splat. A clawed hand pointed to the eastern side of the building. "Where do you think? Only part of this dump that's still standing. Can't wait till we're outta this place. We'll take over the city, that's what Stone says. He's got big plans for our race."

"That so?" Ben's voice tightened with controlled disgust.

The werewolf frowned. "Hey... you look familiar. Don't know you from somewhere, do I, bub?"

The winds changed. Ben sniffed at the frosty air and his breath caught when he detected Isaac's signature scent. It was all over this werewolf... and it was mixed up with the coppery tang of fresh blood. His fangs jabbed his lips as fear and fury warred with each other.

"You stink like a hunter," Ben growled. His shirt stretched tight across his chest, blood warming his fists as his nails punctured his palms.

The werewolf bared bloody fangs and grinned. "Morgan's let us take turns with him. I got him good across the face. For a hunter, he's real pretty." He chuckled. "Well, he was."

Ben's hands turned to claws as he snared the werewolf's throat, squeezing until the blood drained from his face. "You fucked up. Know why?" The blood roared in Ben's ears and in his fury, he felt ten feet tall, towering over the werewolf, who kicked and thrashed as Ben lifted him easily from the ground.

"You put your hands on my fucking *mate*." He wrapped his hairy, claw-tipped fingers completely around the werewolf's neck, squeezing it like a soda can until the bones crunched beneath his grip. He hurled the corpse into the stone wall. The coppery stink of blood made his mouth water, driving any thought from his mind until all that remained was the need to bite, rip, *tear*.

As fur exploded across his body, he threw back his head and let loose a song of war that shook the treetops. His packmates answered his song, their combined voices igniting the roaring blood in his veins. The ground shook under the slam of his paws as he charged.

The Moonborn wolves weren't ready, not for this. They tried to fight back, their fangs like the pricking of tiny needles against his thick hide. He seized a wolf by the head, squeezing until the skull ruptured between his claws, soaking him with blood. He hurled the corpse into a charging wolf and bowled him over.

Another wolf came flying at him and he swiped, his claws catching in the earth, raining dirt down. Penetrating the soft flesh of the underbelly, his fingers sank into hot entrails. The wolf died, impaled on his claws. With a swipe, the wolf flew limply from his hand. The rest of the wolves yelped and cried in terror as they fled, pursued by his packmates.

The smell of blood hung in the air like a mist but beneath it all there was still the aroma of *Isaac, mate, mine.* He leaped and landed through a hole in the side of the building. Bending his snout to the ground, he sniffed deeply. This whole floor smelled like Isaac, and the smell led him up a rickety flight of stairs that crumbled under his weight. Isaac's trail led to a door that was hanging off its hinges. Beyond the door, he smelled the tang of fear, of blood. Of Isaac.

With a roar, he charged.

ISAAC SPAT OUT BLOOD from where he'd bitten his cheek. The wolves who were in their human form took turns hitting him and kicking him while a few fully shifted wolves lifted their legs, pissed on him, and went on their way. Morgan had gotten bored and had shifted to a great white wolf and lay dozing in the corner, as undisturbed by Isaac's screams as if they were nothing more than a lullaby.

All he could do was wheeze and whimper, his eyes too blurry to see through. To his credit, he hadn't said a word, not that he could even if he tried. His cheek was swollen and he couldn't think past the pain fogging his mind.

He'd thought dying was the worst thing that could happen to him. Now, death would at least be a release from the humiliation and constant pain of his wounds. Still, a stubborn part of his mind rebelled. Someone would realize he was missing. Someone would find him and save him.

Who? Isaac wondered. *Who's going to notice I'm gone? Who will care?*

He'd had people who'd loved him once, but he'd burned every bridge. Beau had changed his meaningless life. Realizing he had someone so small and helpless depending on him had kick-started him into getting his act together. He'd quit college and worked hard at bartending, planning on making a career of it even if he'd only done it to put money in his pocket before. His son had needed him and knowing that had saved his life.

Then he'd lost Beau, and all he'd had was grief and a desire for vengeance that had kept him going. Until Ben had come along and reminded him how to laugh and smile. Just when he'd thought he would never feel anything but a numb hole in his heart, Ben had taught him that in the depths of all his grief and guilt, there was something beautiful on the other side, radiating with hope and promise.

Even now, through mind-numbing pain, Isaac could have smiled at the thought of him. Short-lived as it had been, their friendship had been everything he'd needed and so much more than he'd deserved. Ben had saved his life.

Thank you, Ben.

Tears prickled his eyes when he realized he'd never see him again.

I'm grateful for the time we had. I just wish we could have had more. Let's face it—that would have been more than I deserved.

He hoped Ben would be happy, that he'd find someone truly deserving of his love and his tender heart, who could give him everything Isaac had failed to. If Isaac had known there would be no second chances between them, he never would have run from Ben.

He closed his eyes tight and clung on to the memory of a big gentle wolf with eyes as silver as the moon.

A roar echoed throughout the forest, rattling the windows in their frames. Isaac's heart jumped. That didn't sound like a wolf or any other animal Isaac had ever heard. It sounded closer to a bear but there was something unnatural about it; not even bears could sound *that* pissed off.

The wolves yelped and howled below. Isaac peered through blurry eyes at Morgan as the wolf lurched to his paws and uttered a deep bark. His wolves took to their paws and paced, sniffing at the door and barking and growling.

Had someone come for him? Or were the wolves below just getting rowdy? Fogged as his mind was, Isaac was sure he hadn't imagined the sound and was even surer when the pained yelps and frantic barks from below grew louder. There was a fight happening and as soon as the sounds had started, they suddenly stopped and all was quiet. Isaac held his breath and jumped when the building suddenly shook. The wolves whined and growled, their tails drooping. Whatever it was, they were scared of it too.

The floor shook under the slam of heavy claws tearing at the wood. Isaac's gut lurched. Whatever it was, it was heading this way. Now was his chance—the wolves would be distracted in the fight and Isaac could escape out the window. The fall would hurt, but he could limp back to the car and get away. Gasping, he heaved himself onto his rear, cradling his arm to his chest. None of the wolves had noticed.

Then the door crashed open in a shower of dust. The door hurtled off its hinge and slammed to the floor. A beast loomed in the doorway, and all thought of escape fled Isaac's mind as primal fear froze him in place. The doorway creaked and strained as the creature squeezed its enormous bulk through the narrow entrance. It had to be at least ten feet tall, its pointed ears scraping the ceiling. It stood bent-kneed, standing on its toes with nails several inches long. It was built like a wrestler with dense silver fur wrapped around tightly coiled muscles. Enormous clawed hands dripped with blood that dotted the floor. Blood-soaked jaws parted as it took in a deep gulp of air as if it could literally taste the fear thick in the air like sour urine.

Its eyes glowed a pale silver as if the thing had pulled the moon out of the sky and stolen its light. Isaac swallowed the heart that was in his throat, his brain struggling to comprehend what he was seeing.

"Ben." There was no other explanation. The eyes were just too familiar, no matter how hideously frightening the face they belonged to was. God. What had happened to him? Isaac had never seen a werewolf assume such a monstrous shape, as if it commanded both man and wolf all at once. They could be one or the other, but never both. He'd just never heard of it.

The pointed ears flicked and the snarling face turned toward him. Claws opened, nails clicking together. He breathed in deep, as if scenting the blood, and snarled. Those eyes flickered from silver to a blazing yellow light that obscured his pupils. Isaac knew what those eyes meant.

Ben was lost to his wolf, and Isaac feared he'd never get him back. The beast dropped to all fours and let out a roar that shattered the windows and quaked the roof. Isaac's ears rang, the sound deafening in this small room. The wolves yelped and bowed their heads, cowering.

Morgan uttered a commanding snarl, even as his body shook, and his wolves charged Ben. But it was over in seconds. An enormous paw sent one of the wolves flying into the wall. Its body shattered on impact, its paws twitching in the throes of death. The other wolves charged to their immediate deaths; Ben seized a black wolf by the skull, ignoring the beasts snapping and clawing at his lower body as if they were fleas. The skull crunched between his clawed hands as if it were plastic, raining blood and bits of bone on the wolves below. He hurled the broken corpse to the floor.

A single swipe disemboweled a brown wolf, intestines spilling from its stomach like gray snakes. Another wolf jumped right into Ben's jaws, which crunched down on the wolf's ribs. As the creature yelped and howled, two huge clawed hands grasped the wolf by the front and back legs and tore the body clean in half, throwing both halves to the ground like an unappealing halved sandwich.

The ground shook as Ben advanced on Morgan, who was cowering with his tail between his legs. Morgan turned and tried to run but was seized by the scruff of his neck as if he were nothing but a puppy and hoisted from the ground. Morgan shifted to a man, writhing like a fish on a hook as Ben suspended him by the throat.

"Look at you, Stroud," Morgan choked out. "You've turned yourself into a monster for this human. How poetic." Thin pale fingers grasped Ben's thick, furred arm. Ben's huge jaws clicked hungrily, strings of blood and spit dangling past his chin. "You came all this way to save him, but do you think he'll still want you now that he's seen what you truly are? A monster just like the creatures he hunts!"

"Ben!" Isaac shouted. "Ben, don't listen to him!"

The growl vibrating from Ben's throat died to a low rumble. His eyes flickered, flashing from pupilless yellow eyes to silver, the pupils dilating. Something very human entered those blazing eyes: fear.

"This isn't over!" Morgan croaked. "I'll kill you and your precious hunter! I'll—"

Morgan's words died with a grunt as Ben snapped his neck and hurled his lifeless body out the window. Isaac distantly heard it crash into the snow below. As the beast that was Ben turned toward him, Isaac tried to speak but couldn't summon more than a croak. His hand shook, aching to reach out to him, but he couldn't move.

There was nothing recognizable about Ben but those wide, fearful eyes. The huge claws, blood-soaked and dripping, reached toward Isaac and he flinched away, unable to help himself. A growl erupted from the beast's vocal cords. It sounded like a word. "I... saac."

Ben was still in there.

How could that be? Isaac had always thought that once a wolf's eyes turned yellow, they were lost completely to their wolf. Somehow Ben had come back to him. He was in there somewhere, hiding within that monstrous form, and he was scared.

Isaac reached out, fingers shaking, and touched the warm, wet fur on Ben's hand. It was so big, Isaac's own seemed no bigger than a child's as he grasped a finger. The claw-tipped finger curled, wrapping around the width of Isaac's hand. His touch was so gentle, as if he hadn't just ripped apart a small pack of wolves.

"Ben," Isaac said shakily, at a loss for what else to say. But as he reached out, the beast jerked away from him with a hoarse snarl. Isaac stumbled as Ben pulled his claw away, holding his huge hand close to his body. The beast's hands trembled, his wide eyes flickering to silver and taking in his blood-soaked state with newfound awareness. Ben whirled around, panting harshly as he looked from body to body. A whine tore from his throat.

"Ben, no," Isaac said, understanding. "You did this to save me. You're not a monster. Don't listen to Morgan. Okay? Come here."

But Ben backed away with a snarl, his back leg slipping in blood. A powerful shudder racked the creature's body. "What have I done?" Ben panted, voice breaking with harsh snorts and snarls.

"Ben!" But Isaac didn't have time to say a word. The beast lurched toward him and Isaac was lifted like a child carried in enormous arms. The walls shredded around them as Ben charged, smashing through the wood and shielding Isaac with his body.

They landed, shaking the earth, and Ben gingerly lowered Isaac to the icy ground. Two wolves ran toward him. They shifted, both nude. One was a man with thick black hair and a neatly trimmed beard. The other man was chubby and radiated boyish charm.

"You must be Isaac!" said the dark-haired man. "I'm Manuel Reyes. This is Greg. We're here to rescue you!"

Isaac shuffled his feet, a bit uncomfortable with their nakedness. "Thanks. Ben—" But as he turned, the huge wolf suddenly took off into the woods, spraying snow. "Ben!"

Greg sighed. "Let him go, Isaac. He's freaked out. He can find his way back."

Manuel motioned for Isaac to follow, turning away and giving Isaac a front-row view of his bare ass. "Come on, let's get you back to the car and to a hospital. Ben would want you taken care of."

Greg and Manuel each took Isaac's arms, supporting him as he limped slowly toward the car.

Isaac couldn't catch a glimpse of Ben but as he turned away, a long and lonely howl echoed over the treetops and into the night sky.

CHAPTER 11

A HUNTER AND HIS WOLF

THERE WAS SO MUCH Isaac wanted to say to Ben Stroud. How grateful he was that Ben had come for him in his darkest hour of need, despite how divided they'd become. That he was sorry for running away when Ben had shown him what he truly was. That, despite everything, Isaac wanted them to be friends, if they could. Perhaps maybe even more.

But Isaac hadn't seen Ben all week, not since he'd run away into the wilderness after transforming into that beast. The closest Isaac had come to seeing him was when a handyman Ben had hired showed up at his door to do repairs on his apartment.

Life moved on. The Cross continued hunting for Gina. Don was relieved Isaac was all right and pleased to hear Stone's second-in-command was dead. Isaac felt as if he were frozen in time while the world moved on around him.

Every day, Isaac knocked on Ben's door to receive only silence in response. Ben's mail was piling up, so Isaac started taking packages and letters into his apartment for safekeeping. He was never at the bar. Ben had gone completely MIA and Isaac was left sleepless with worry.

He still shivered when he thought of that enormous creature, a terrifying conjoining of wolf and man with a hunger for blood that defied everything he knew about Ben's gentle and considerate personality.

"Ben awakened his berserker gene," Manuel explained one night. The pizzeria was packed as was typical on Saturdays. Isaac pushed Manuel's beer and shot of tequila across the bar to him. "It's a gene some wolves are born with that activates when a werewolf is feeling especially volatile."

"A... what? A berserker? Like those Viking warriors that went nuts on the battlefield and wore animal fur?" Isaac darted away to hand an impatient-looking customer their IPA before he scurried back to Manuel. "He really looked like a werewolf from one of those movies. I've never heard of a shifter being able to take on a form like that."

Manuel took a big gulp and explained. "It is very rare among werewolves."

Handing a patron their check, Isaac hurried back to Manuel again. "Did Ben know?" Was the berserker gene yet another secret unshared between them?

"Based on how Ben reacted, this was likely his first change." Manuel downed his tequila.

Isaac wet his lips, feeling guilty. "And Ben became one of those things for me?"

Manuel's mustache twitched when he smiled. "He was so worried about you. His determination to keep you safe brought out his wolf's most powerful instincts."

"More like I destroyed him." Isaac sighed, accepting the signed slip and flashing the patron a thankful smile and a wave. He crammed the receipt in his booklet.

Manuel's face wrinkled. "No, no, I wouldn't say that. Don't be so hard on yourself."

Isaac leaned on the bar, needing the support. "It sure looks that way to me. You saw him, didn't you?"

Manuel waved a hand. "Ben was in shock. How could he not be?"

Isaac's heart clenched when he remembered those petrified silver eyes, the only thing remotely human in that snarling, fearsome face. "He looked so devastated. Frightened. He couldn't even look at me. Like he thought I hated him." And Isaac realized he didn't blame Ben at all for feeling that way. Remorse threatened to drown him. He'd treated Ben like a monster when he'd shown his fangs and claws. How could he possibly expect Isaac to have accepted him in his most frightening form?

But I did, Isaac thought, wishing more than anything he could reassure Ben that he didn't think any less of him. *He saved my life. He touched me so gently, like he knew the damage he could do and was terrified he'd hurt me.* When he'd seen those silver eyes, had felt that gentle touch, he'd realized the Ben he knew and cared about was still there.

"Do you think he's all right out there?"

Manuel patted his shoulder. "If it were anyone else, I would worry about them, but Ben's got a good head on his shoulders. He'll be fine." A grin split his face and he waved toward the door. "Hey! Finally made it!"

Greg huffed exaggeratedly as he dropped into a newly vacated seat. "They really couldn't have chosen a location in the city for the new LPA headquarters? Fire Island's such a slog."

Isaac poured him his usual lager and Greg took a hearty swig. "What's the LPA?"

Greg looked at him warily, and Isaac realized it must have something to do with werewolves. "Greg, the Cross only hunts feral wolves and assholes like Stone's cult."

"The Lycanthrope Protection Agency," Greg explained. Isaac must have looked confused. "It's Ben's family's lifework. A place for abused shifters to have a home and a place to recover. So if you send your hunter buddies there, Ben will never forgive you."

Isaac blinked. "Huh? But Ben told me he worked for human resources."

Greg smiled sympathetically.

Isaac sighed. "Damn it." Yet another lie between them. He hated that Ben hadn't trusted him enough to be honest. Then again, Isaac hadn't trusted Ben either. He was so sick of the lies, all the tiptoeing around each other. He needed to find Ben and make things right between them.

When the bell dinged, Isaac jogged to the counter and brought the pie to Manuel and Greg. "So I guess you're running the agency while he's gone?"

Greg didn't answer immediately, stuffing his face with several huge bites of greasy pepperoni pizza. Licking the grease off his fingers, he smacked his lips. "No way. Like hell I'd let Ben tell me what to do. He invited me over today, wanted me to see all the work he was—" He froze. Isaac didn't know why, and then it hit him.

"You've seen Ben?" Isaac exclaimed.

Greg took a hasty gulp of beer. "No…"

Manuel shot him a look. "Greg, start talking."

Greg slumped. "Damn it! I wasn't supposed to say anything."

Hurt walloped Isaac in the chest. Ben had been in New York all this time? He'd simply chosen not to come home. Not to see Isaac. Hurt turned to anger and Isaac tossed some ice in the shaker and shook it hard, needing to vent somehow. He wrenched the shaker open and forced a grin as he poured the next customer their cocktail. They looked frightened.

"Isaac, it's not what you think," Greg began.

"He doesn't want to see me, right?"

Greg looked away, drawing a frowning face in the condensation on his beer glass.

"So, it's exactly what I think, then." Isaac gave the shaker a rinse and slammed it down. Some drunk bikers started singing "Don't Stop Believin'" by the karaoke machine. Isaac turned his back on the remorseful werewolves at the bar and handed out checks and grabbed signed receipts to add to his book.

"Get you guys anything else?" Isaac asked, glowering at Manuel and Greg. "Another round of disappointment and realizing I fucked up the one good thing to happen to me in the last year?"

Manuel elbowed Greg, and he mumbled, "He didn't think you wanted to see him."

Isaac scoffed. "So he makes up my mind for me? Well, tell him he's right; I don't want to see him." The insincerity of his words hit him hard. He wanted nothing more than to see Ben, but clearly Ben didn't feel the same. "You guys mind paying up early? I've gotta clock out."

Once they'd signed their slips, Isaac went downstairs to sort receipts. He slumped, a sigh escaping him. He couldn't believe Ben had really let Isaac worry about him all week long. For all he'd known, the stupid wolf had been running around the wilderness alone. But no, he'd been in the city the whole time. He just hadn't wanted Isaac to know.

Scowling, Isaac took his cut of the tips and climbed back up the stairs. His back ached and exhaustion tugged at his eyelids. He couldn't wait to get out of here and go home.

"Isaac." Greg was waiting for him outside, his hands shoved deep in his pockets. "Look, you got Ben all wrong. What you think really matters to him, and he's sure you hate him."

"Well, if he'd just let me see him, I could tell him he's wrong!" Running a hand through his wavy hair, Isaac got an idea. "Take me to him."

Greg seemed to shrink. "I don't know. He'll bite my head off for that. Besides, I just got back from Fire Island and—"

"Greg, come on. Please?"

"Fine. But you're lucky you're charming." With a sigh, Greg opened his car door. Isaac sat beside him and Greg started the engine.

"Thanks," Isaac told him.

"Hey, someone's gotta play cupid," Greg answered, and Isaac's face warmed. He hoped it was too dark to tell. Greg chuckled beside him. "Ben's a great guy but he's pretty clueless when it comes to this whole mating dance."

"Mating what?" Isaac almost choked on his spit.

Greg rolled his eyes. "Oh, come on. He hasn't told you?"

"Told me what?"

Greg made a zipping motion across his lips. "Nope. He's gotta tell you himself. I can't do it for him."

At a loss, Isaac slumped in his seat.

"You really need to talk to him, Isaac." Greg's voice was strangely subdued. "He hasn't been himself all week. He's really worried you won't ever wanna see him again. It's hurting him."

Isaac's heart thundered and he looked out the window. "Why does it matter what I think?"

Greg exhaled. "'Cause Ben seems to think you're his... well, you're special to him. And for werewolves, that's a big deal. There are people Ben likes a lot, and then there's you. He told me you have this amazing scent."

Isaac sniffed at his underarms. "I do? Doesn't garbage also smell great to a wolf's nose?"

"Of course, but—that's not what I'm saying!" Greg groaned. "Look, in the werewolf creation myth—"

"You guys have a creation myth?"

Greg looked like he'd kill Isaac if he interrupted him one more time. "Yes," he said, with far too much patience. "The story goes that once upon a time, the She-Wolf created a world for wolves—the Hunting Grounds. And for every wolf, she created one special person just for them. But she fell in love with a human, or so the more progressive tales go. Don't tell the Moonborn that. She believed werewolves and humans were meant to live together, not apart, and so after she'd encouraged the wolves to embark for Earth to start new packs, she imbued a chosen person with a unique scent, special to each wolf, so that they would always be able to find their mate, even in this big new world, no matter what species they are."

Isaac tried to swallow but his throat felt oddly thick. He wouldn't have expected such a beautiful story from werewolves. So much of what he'd thought he knew was turning out to be wrong.

"Or so the story goes. No one really knows why a werewolf's mate smells so unique. But supposedly, the goddess brings two people together who she knows will be the perfect match and a werewolf will know by the smell."

"What are you saying?" The fluttering in the pit of Isaac's stomach showed he knew exactly what Greg was trying to say.

"Ben can tell you."

Isaac wet his lips. "So, you're telling me that Ben and I are destined by some cosmic deity to be together? Is that it? But we're both guys, and I'm a human."

Greg waved a hand with a snort. "It doesn't matter. In the old days before werewolves assimilated with humans, any mate, regardless of gender, was considered a gift from the goddess. The two were meant to be, and no one questioned it. Obviously, humans didn't agree and same-sex relationships became more stigmatized among werewolves."

Struggling to process this new lesson on werewolf lore, Isaac stared blankly out the window. Honestly, of all the men in the world, he wouldn't mind being destined to end up with Ben. Except there was a problem, one of many. Finally, Isaac found his voice. "I'm not a werewolf, Greg. Whatever Ben feels for me, how can I even return it?"

"An astute question! I have to say, for a human, you've got so many layers. Well, according to the old beliefs, mates were destined to fall in love, despite all odds and obstacles. You two will come together, one way or the other, if tradition has a say in anything."

"It doesn't!" He laughed, unable to do anything else. "Our relationship couldn't be less traditional, or normal!" Isaac scoffed. "He's a werewolf and I'm a hunter! I think your magic moon goddess got something wrong. I'm not obligated to do whatever some wolf god wants me to do!"

"Of course not! But just try and trust that you're meant to be together, no matter what. The She-Wolf is never wrong about these things, Isaac. I promise you."

Head spinning, Isaac watched the scenery rush past. He couldn't ask Ben to be with him, not knowing the different directions their lives were running in. A sigh pulled from his throat. "If I can't sense our bond like a wolf can, then does that mean it is one-sided?" Hopelessness sank heavily into his chest.

"I think you do sense it. Why else would you be going against everything you've been taught to keep Ben safe?" Isaac was at a loss for words. Greg smiled. "Just talk to him, man. Humans and werewolves can be together.

It takes work, like any good relationship. Between you and me, though, I think you're sensing the bond just fine, in your own way."

"What's that mean?"

"Well, you haven't given up on him yet, have you? You've had plenty of opportunity to let him go, and you haven't. That's gotta count for something."

Isaac had never given fate much thought. He believed, in a world this big and wide, that there was someone out there for everyone, and he'd just been told that was especially true for werewolves.

Was there really a higher plan for one lost hunter and a gruff, gentle werewolf? It was all too much for him to wrap his head around, but one thing was for certain: he wasn't letting Ben go, not without a fight.

THE WAVES CRASHED AND the smell of sea salt was refreshing in the crisp night air. Greg parked them beyond the agency gates. Wolves howled and Isaac's body tensed involuntarily. He'd always associated the howling of wolves with an imminent attack, but these howls sounded ridiculous, each note off-key and rough on the eardrums.

Greg grinned. "Sounds like they're having fun." He motioned for Isaac to follow.

The agency headquarters was as vast as a whole city block. Isaac had to wonder how many miles of land the estate owned; the palm forests beyond the estate were vast and dark. A shiver ran down his spine when he realized how close the wolves were. Greg pointed behind the estate. "They just put in a pool in the backyard. A garden too. There's a whole beach on the other side of the forest."

Wolves tore across the courtyard, their fur sopping wet. Isaac tensed but the wolves were preoccupied with playing, pouncing on each other and tearing around the courtyard. They seemed friendly enough, so Isaac took in a breath and urged himself to relax. He followed Greg up the stairs to the front door and into a check-in room. Greg asked the woman at the desk about Ben while Isaac looked around. Through a door to the right was a huge dining room with a dinner buffet of options ranging from meat to veggie dishes. Isaac's mouth watered; he hadn't eaten anything since his lunch break at the bar.

Adjacent to the check-in room was a big sitting room with a huge television, a roaring fireplace, and many plush sofas to sit on. After a day on his feet, a sofa had never looked more tempting—until Isaac realized every head in the room was turned toward him. Some stares were curious, some downright suspicious. Isaac swallowed, aware he was likely the only human here, and the werewolves could smell it.

He went back to Greg's side and hung out by the door, watching as people passed in and out of the room. Some of the residents looked worse for wear, sporting bandaged injuries or downcast faces, but for the most part, the shifters here seemed happy.

"Maggie says Ben's probably upstairs in the kennel. Follow me." Greg motioned Isaac to the elevator by the stairs. A quick ride to the second floor later and Greg stopped Isaac outside a doorway. Beyond, the snapping and howling of wolves could be heard. By comparison, this howling was much less friendly, the kind that made Isaac's skin prickle uneasily. Greg hesitated. "Maybe you should wait here? I'll be back." He squeezed inside and closed the door quietly. A storm of furious barking at Greg's entrance made Isaac glad he'd waited outside.

A bay window with plush cushions compelled Isaac to sit and he sighed, relieved to take the weight off his feet. He closed his eyes tight and tried to figure out what he'd say to Ben. The drive over had helped cool him down, but it still irritated him that Ben hadn't wanted to see him. He wondered if Ben would be angry at him for turning up anyway.

Well, if you'd just come and seen me, I wouldn't have had to come to you. So there.

Someone yelled within the kennels. Isaac's heart lurched. "Greg?" Picturing any number of scenarios—an escaped feral running wild or Greg being devoured by angry wolves just to name a few—Isaac nudged open the door and peered inside. It was a long, narrow room with rows and rows of cages. Panting wolves, their pelts matted with blood, paced. One wolf hurled itself at the bars of its cage, frothing jaws snapping at Isaac as he passed. "Greg, you all right?"

He turned the corner and found Greg on his knees, rubbing his ankle. "Get back, Isaac! The door isn't locked!"

Something tugged hard at his pant leg. Isaac caught himself on his hands but struck his knee hard. His leg was ripped out from beneath him and he crashed onto his stomach. Realizing he was under attack, Isaac rolled over and struggled to free his pant leg from the teeth of a wolf. The door to the cage hadn't latched properly, allowing the wolf free rein.

Yellow eyes wide, the pupils narrowed to pinpricks, the wolf growled as it shook his pant leg. It was only a matter of time before its fangs found his leg. Isaac kicked it across the snout, and it yelped, but his attack only aggravated it more.

A scream pulled from his throat as its jaws locked around his ankle. Greg was yelling something, but Isaac couldn't hear over the pounding of his heart and his own frightened yells. He kicked but the wolf refused to let go, shaking his leg in its bone-crushing grasp. A roar echoed over Greg's and Isaac's combined screams and the wolf's snarling. The wolf retreated to the back of its cage, shaking wildly. Greg kicked the door shut and bolted it. Isaac gasped, cradling his leg to him, blood soaking his pant leg.

When he looked up, Ben was standing in the doorway. "Isaac?" Ben's voice was hushed, his silver eyes wide and his face bloodless. Kneeling at his side, Ben gingerly lifted the hem of Isaac's jeans. He couldn't muster a reply, shaking too badly to stand on his own as Ben helped him to his feet. "Why did you let him come, Greg? He shouldn't have been in here." Ben's voice was harsh.

"I told him to wait!"

Grumbling, Ben kicked open the door and helped Isaac limp through it. They entered a small exam room. Isaac sat on the bed and finally found his voice. "What're you doing keeping feral animals locked up for?" What if they got out, terrorized the estate?

Ben threw open drawers, grumbling. He didn't answer right away, making Isaac wonder if he'd heard him or not. Ben grabbed handfuls of bandages and disinfectant and slammed them down next to Isaac. He knelt, rolling up Isaac's pant leg, and Isaac winced; the bite was deep. A terrifying thought gripped him. "Am I gonna become a werewolf?"

Ben laughed softly. "No. There was no venom in her bite. I'd smell it." He splashed disinfectant on a cotton pad and said, "This'll sting." Isaac had thought he was ready but cursed as the wound blazed and stung. Gripping onto Ben's shoulder, Isaac dug in his nails. Ben's brow puckered but he didn't protest. "The hell were you doing in there, anyway? Trying to kill my wolves?"

Isaac bristled, though he understood Ben's mistrust. "No! I was looking for Greg. He yelled. I thought he was hurt."

"What's that matter? Greg can heal his wounds instantly. You could suffer through this bite for weeks."

Isaac growled. Way to make him feel like a stupid motherfucker. "Well, I wouldn't be here if you'd have just come to see me, right?" Ben stiffened. Isaac had intended to be more tactful, but he was beyond pissed. Lips thin, Ben blotted at his wound again. Isaac hissed and clamped down on Ben's shoulder. "But no. You had to wolf out on me and run away with your tail between your legs rather than have an adult conversation."

"This conversation isn't too adult."

Isaac threw up his arms. "Then contribute!"

"So you throw yourself into a wolf's den to get back at me?" Ben mumbled.

Isaac suddenly wanted to jump off the table and walk out. "Yeah, this big ol' bite? I got it just for you. Guess you shouldn't leave me to my own devices from now on. Who knows, I might just die without you. How stupid do you think I am?"

Decidedly quiet, Ben twined bandages around Isaac's ankle. He was so quiet that Isaac thought Ben was ignoring him. Then a smile turned up the corners of Ben's narrow mouth. "Considering you'd be dead without me, yeah, maybe you do need a sitter."

Isaac kicked his foot out of Ben's grasp, ignoring the growl he received. "Why didn't you tell me?"

"Tell you what?" Ben snapped.

Isaac gaped. "That you were fuckin' alive, for one thing! For all I knew, you were lost, or starving, or—"

"Wolves can always find their way back to their den, and I can hunt for myself," Ben retorted.

"Yeah. I know all about you wolves. You're a bunch of assholes." Isaac hadn't come to fight, but his body was ready and raring for it. Every stupid word out of Ben's mouth got his blood boiling. He'd wanted to believe that the Ben he knew and cared for wouldn't have intentionally hurt him. But he had. Ben didn't care at all that he'd left Isaac alone for a week, wondering and worrying about him. "Fuck it." He stood and nearly collapsed.

"Isaac, sit down!" Ben grabbed his shoulder.

Isaac ducked out of Ben's reach, gritting his teeth as he put weight on his wounded ankle. "Make me."

Ben stepped closer, his hands heavy on Isaac's shoulders. "You really hate me so much you'd rather bleed all over the halls than spend another second with me?"

"I don't hate you! I could never hate you." He trembled as all the anger and hurt erupted from him, leaving him feeling breathless and sick. "I should. The hunters taught me to fear werewolves. But then I met you, and... You're amazing, Ben. You're so much more than I deserve, and I'm sorry I fucked things up between us. I'm sorry I ever made you question how important you are to me." Blinking fast, he looked away, at the walls, the ceiling, anything other than Ben Stroud. How could one man have such a hold of his heart like this?

"If you…" He swallowed hard. "If you don't want to see me anymore, then I understand. I just needed you to know that I care about you, and that I'm sorry I was such a jerk. I'll… I'll go."

A sharp whine filled the room just as he turned to leave. Ben slumped into a chair, folding into himself with his face in his hands as if Isaac had reached into Ben's chest and ripped his heart from his body.

"I didn't know what to do," Ben said, voice thick with fury and pain. His eyes glistened, blazing with emotion. His face had gone completely red. "I thought you hated me. I showed you who I was and you—you pushed me away."

Isaac's leg ached, but not as badly as his heart. He'd done so much worse than just push Ben away, and he wanted to make up for it. He sat in the empty chair beside him. He could see it now, so clearly. They were frozen, both of them, unable to move forward from that moment in the apartment.

"And then you saw the absolute worst of me. The ugliest, most horrific side of me that I didn't even know existed until you came along and forced it out of me." Ben's fists trembled and his voice broke. "You should hate me. I became a monster, for you. To save you. You're crazy if you don't hate and fear me."

Isaac couldn't hate him. He couldn't be afraid of him. He tried to say as much but his voice was so small. Instead what came out was, "Do you hate me?" He couldn't look at Ben, and he wanted to run from the room. It was his fault Ben had become something he hated. He couldn't imagine how Ben wouldn't hate him for it.

Ben made a strange sound like a laugh, but it was watery. "No. Never." Isaac looked at him and exhaled when he found a tiny smile on Ben's face.

"You said I turned you into a monster. How could you not hate me?"

"I became that way because the thought of losing you terrified me." Ben grabbed his hand and held tight. He clutched it close to his chest, and the warmth of his body seeped into Isaac's palm. "I could never hate you." Ben looked down at his hands as if he could still see the blood dripping off them. He seemed to disappear into himself then, trapped in that moment when he'd confronted the worst of himself.

"Ben? What is it?"

BEN GAZED AT THEIR hands and it brought him back to that dark night in the cold. The call of the hunt had left him blind and deaf to anything else until he'd seen him. It had all been for him, for Isaac. His humanity had come rushing back and all that had mattered was getting him to safety.

Then he'd held Isaac's hand in his, so small and fragile that the slightest wrong move could crush the bones to splinters in his grasp. A rush of hatred had swept over him, and he couldn't stand just how big his claws were compared to Isaac's hand. And he'd understood in that moment why humans were so right to fear and hate monsters like him.

He'd become a monster.

"Ben?"

His hands slipped from Isaac's grasp and back into his lap. He'd thought to stay away from Isaac, but the separation had driven a nail right through his heart. This past week had been the longest of his life. His energy had waxed and waned, his mind fogged.

Isaac had seen him at his lowest. He'd wondered how Isaac could still want anything to do with him. He'd thought he had to be the strong one and reject the goddess's plans for them by shutting Isaac out of his life entirely. For his own good as well as Isaac's.

Now here Isaac was, sitting beside Ben. It felt like a strange but wonderful dream, the kind Ben might awake from at any moment, struggling to hold on to every detail and vivid, joyful feeling before it vanished forever. Somehow Isaac didn't hate him. Ben realized with a stab of dismay that he was the one in the wrong, the one who was jumping to conclusions and deciding Isaac's feelings for him. By all odds, Ben should have blown all his chances with Isaac to hell and back by now. Yet Isaac still wanted him and was willing to give him a second chance.

He was done fucking up.

"Ben?"

Ben looked into gray eyes flecked with blue, like patches of blue sky breaking through storm clouds. Isaac shouldn't have any reason to be here. Ben had been told humans would always fear and hate his kind and he'd given Isaac every reason to turn and run, yet he'd had the audacity to stay.

Laughing softly, Ben reached for Isaac's hand once more. Isaac met him halfway and their fingers twined together. Just to be sure it was real, he squeezed tight. Isaac's pulse raced between Ben's fingers, fluttering madly. Or was it Ben's? He didn't seem to be able to quit shaking. Swallowing hard, he met Isaac's gaze. "I've been a jerk."

Isaac bumped their shoulders together. "No, Ben. I was. I was cruel to you, and I'm sorry. You're not a monster. You're one of the best men I've ever known. Thank you for rescuing me. You didn't have to."

Ben's eyes stung and he looked away. "'Course I did. I couldn't let anything happen to you."

"I'd have deserved it." Isaac squeezed his hand. "Honestly, I don't get why you didn't let the cult eat me after I ran out on you."

"I thought about it."

Isaac laughed, his breath puffing warmly against Ben's mouth. "Ben," Isaac began, his voice slow and thoughtful. "You showed me the worst part of you. Well, I showed you mine a while ago, the night I first saw you as a wolf. I was so damn depressed I don't know if I'd have gotten through the night if you hadn't come scratching at my door." He squeezed Ben's hand again and met his eyes. "How about we call it even?"

Heart slamming against his ribs, Ben had to remind himself to breathe. "Yeah. Yeah, that... that sounds great." They were so close, their noses practically touching. All he had to do was lean over the arm of the chair, and—

Right on cue, Isaac's stomach growled and his face turned the color of a beet. Ben chuckled and helped him stand. "Come on, let's get you some food. The buffet here is pretty good." Isaac winced, his face scrunching up in pain. Ben had held his tongue so far, but now that they weren't spitting fire at one another, he said, "You know, werewolf blood heals injuries like that." He snapped his fingers for emphasis.

Isaac's throat bobbed, his face blanching. "No way."

Ben squinted at his bloody ankle. "You sure? 'Cause I have plans for a fun evening and that bum leg's gonna put a damper on things."

"I'm not pumping myself full of werewolf blood."

"You'd only need, like, this much." Ben held his thumb and pointer finger a few inches apart.

"I'm fine," Isaac insisted. He took a step and sucked in a breath, his face scrunching up again.

Ben heaved a long sigh. "Guess we won't have a romantic dinner and go for a walk on the beach. Don't wanna drag you around the estate looking like a sack of raw meat."

Isaac heaved an even longer sigh. "Fine."

Minutes later, Ben generously gave a donation of blood and Isaac was hooked up for a transfusion, cringing as the nurse poked him with a needle. "This is so romantic, Ben. Never been on a better date."

Ben gripped his knee and ran a thumb over the rough denim. "I know, right? We're getting to know each other on such an intimate level." Ben did feel a bit bad, seeing how wide-eyed he was. Isaac exhaled, looking anywhere other than the tube of blood draining into his arm.

"I ever mention I hate needles? Specifically, needles in my arm pumping me full of blood? Hate it even more when they're sucking blood outta me," Isaac said, rambling. Ben chuckled and squeezed his knee.

"Big baby."

"Talk to me," Isaac snapped.

"Sure. About what?"

"Anything? Uh... Here, is it true that the full moon makes werewolves transform against their will?"

Ben shook his head. "Only if they are newly turned. It does make us horny as hell. It's the only time we can exchange mating bites."

"Oh." Isaac's face reddened. Ben smiled. It was a cute sight.

"Probably something to do with fertility. It's an old belief that the full moon is tied to reproduction, menstrual cycles, that sorta thing. Between you and me, though, I'm ready and raring anytime. Full moon or not."

"Good to know." The little smile beneath Isaac's blush made Ben's breath hitch. He wondered at the other ways he might make him blush.

Isaac cleared his throat. "What about transformations? Do you lose control when you transform? Do you forget stuff afterward?"

Ben rolled his eyes skyward. "You've been watching too many shitty werewolf movies. Plenty of shifters can transform at will and stay in control during their shift, but it can be fun to free our minds and let the wolf take over. Honestly, shifting is hardest when you're a little kid. My transformations were all over the place. Some folks learn to control 'em when they're older."

"But you remember stuff after, right?"

"Yup. Careful, Isaac. Your hunter friends won't like you asking questions like that."

"I know. Father Don thinks all feral wolves are a danger to society. I did too for a while, after what happened to Beau," Isaac murmured, averting his eyes. "Then I met you. You're the opposite of everything I ever thought about werewolves."

Ben smiled. "And I was told humans all hate us and cause nothing but hurt."

"Is that why you were so awkward around me at first?" Isaac asked.

Ben's face burned up. Had he really been awkward? "I was not. I just didn't know how to be around humans. I'd seen with my own eyes the damage your kind are capable of doing to mine." But he'd also been forced to confront the extent of his own feral fury, a part of himself he'd never thought existed.

Isaac jumped as the needle came out. "Whoa." He lifted the hem of his jeans. The wound had faded to a scar. "That's amazing."

Ben held out a hand. "Come on. All this talk of blood has got me hungry."

Isaac took his hand and followed Ben from the exam room. He didn't let go, and Ben's heart was glad for it. Their hands fit together perfectly, like two halves of one whole. Sometimes their shoulders bumped together and sent Ben's heart into overtime. Isaac's scent was so potent, wrapping around him like a gentle, invigorating mist. It was all Ben could do not to lean over and nuzzle into his neck, breathing him in deep.

Holding his hand just wasn't enough. He wanted Isaac closer, the warmth and thereness of him right up against him. Isaac squeezed his hand tight and prickles of heat ran down Ben's spine. Eyes glinting, Isaac shot him a quick smile. It was nice to finally move past the initial awkwardness of their last encounter. Like they were finally getting somewhere.

"That smells great," Isaac said, and his hand left Ben's as he went to explore the dining room. Ben missed his warmth, his fingers tingling as if every pore were alive and dancing with sensation. Grabbing a container, Isaac loaded it up with a little bit of vegetables, meat, and mac and cheese. Ben served himself but when Isaac went looking for a table, Ben nudged him. "This way. Got somewhere nice and quiet we can eat."

They left the warmth of the estate and walked along a dirt path with palm trees swaying on either side. In the still of the night, every footstep echoed and the distant roar of the ocean instilled a feeling of calm in Ben. He carried the bag with their food at his own insistence and considered taking Isaac's hand with his free one. Only, the last time Isaac had initiated it and it had seemed more of a natural impulse. Now, Ben wasn't sure how to go about initiating more contact. Should he just reach out and grab his hand? Testing the waters, he stuck out his pinky and poked Isaac's hand.

Laughing softly, Isaac snatched up his hand and held tight. Heat bloomed in Ben's chest, little ripples of warmth spreading throughout his body. He looked at the ground so Isaac didn't see the stupid grin plastered on his face. When they'd first met, Ben had been terrified to touch Isaac thanks to Greg telling him how delicate humans were. But Isaac was pretty sturdy for a human.

He turned the key in the lock of his bungalow, a quaint cottage with two floors. Isaac looked around the living room with admiration. "It's cute." Ben hummed his agreement. He couldn't talk; his heart was jumping up into his throat. They hadn't been alone together since that day in the apartment, before Isaac had run out on him. Ben squeezed his fists tight. *Please don't run again.*

Construction had just finished, and he finally had a place where he could stay the night without having to commute back and forth to the city.

"I like your place, but I hope I'll still see you at the apartment," Isaac said.

"'Course." Ben set their containers on the table. "Make yourself comfortable. I'll find us some utensils."

Once they had knives and forks, they dug in. When they were done, Ben threw the empty containers into the trash in the kitchen. Ben asked, "Want to watch a movie, or—?"

When he turned, he almost walked right into Isaac. All the air left Ben's lungs and he became aware he was cornered against the counter by Isaac's hard body. In the sudden quiet, every breath seemed deafening. Ben hadn't realized how cold he was, not until Isaac's breath warmed his lips, the heat of his body seeping through Ben's clothes.

Isaac shuddered, his wide eyes blinking fast. "I... uh..." He hung his head. They stood so close, his face almost nestled into Ben's shoulder. "When they took me, I was sure I was gonna die. That no one would know or care where I was, or what happened to me. For a while, I was okay with the idea of dying." Isaac's gentle hands encircled Ben's face, his fingers running over Ben's jawline, his cheekbones, as if Isaac wanted to memorize every detail down to his very bones.

"Then I thought of you," Isaac continued, his low voice oddly scratchy. "And I realized how badly I wanted to live again. I promised myself the first thing I'd do when I saw you was kiss you 'till I was breathless."

Ben had forgotten how to breathe. He was suddenly more afraid than he'd been before, but it was a different kind of fear. He wasn't afraid of losing Isaac, not this time; he was afraid the slightest wrong move might shatter this moment.

Ben's hands trembled as they settled on Isaac's hips, urging him to close. His heart slammed against his rib cage and he was certain Isaac could feel it as their bodies came together. It wasn't enough, not nearly. Ben craved him in a way he'd craved nothing else. He wanted everything Isaac was willing to give, and even then he wasn't sure it would ever be enough. His arms encircled Isaac's back, his fingers curling in the soft hair at the nape of his neck. A little gasp spilled from Isaac's lips, and the way he arched his body into Ben's roused his cock.

"You're shaking." Isaac's lips just barely brushed his when he spoke, and it was all Ben could do not to devour his lips then and there.

"Just... wondering if it's too much to say I wanna do a hell of a lot more than just kiss you."

Isaac's lips burned against the crook of his neck, and Ben's cock strained at his jeans. He likely had no idea what a turn-on it was. He was kissing him right where werewolves claimed their mates, and it was making Ben's head spin. Though Isaac couldn't claim him, if he kept that up it wouldn't matter. Isaac's scent would be all over him, and everyone from Manhattan to Staten Island would know he belonged to Isaac. The musky aroma of Isaac's arousal scorched Ben's nose and he growled low, making Isaac shiver in his arms.

"Permission granted." Isaac leaned in, touching his lips to Ben's. Ben's breath caught in his throat, his arms frozen in place. He wasn't paralyzed for long, not when Isaac was nibbling and sucking on Ben's bottom lip. Carefully, he placed his hands on Isaac's back, waiting to be thrown off or worse, to grow claws. But peace settled over his inner beast and Ben allowed himself to trust in the serenity Isaac brought to his wolf.

Ben dropped his hands to Isaac's hips and turned them so Isaac's back was to the counter. Isaac moaned and the sound made Ben lightheaded, made him crowd close so that their chests and stomachs touched. Isaac's scent wrapped around him like a blanket and Ben breathed in a lungful of him, breaking their kiss and leaving Isaac panting. He kissed Isaac's neck, rubbing the bridge of his nose against his skin. Isaac sank his fingers into Ben's hair and tugged, pressing him close and panting when Ben licked and sucked at his neck.

A chorus of howls erupted outside the house. Isaac jumped, practically crawling up Ben's body. Ben growled as a memory broke through the storm of lust that clouded his mind. "Fuckin' hell. I forgot. I promised the pack I'd run with them." Isaac peered out the window where the glint of wolf eyes winked like fireflies in the dark.

Ben could sense the pack's anticipation, but he was reluctant to untangle himself from Isaac's arms. "I really don't want to, but I did give my word." Excitedly, he was about to ask Isaac if he'd like to join them, but Isaac was so jumpy around wolves.

"What?" Isaac smiled, curious.

"Wanna run with the wolves?"

Isaac laughed. "Seriously?"

"Hell yeah. Unless you're too slow to keep up." Ben grinned when Isaac slapped his ass in answer. Isaac's eyes twinkled, his teeth bared in a bold smile.

"Try me."

CHAPTER 12
RUNNING WITH WOLVES

Even knowing Ben's pack was nothing like the cult, it was still hard for Isaac not to feel like prey as eyes gleamed in the dark. Howls, snaps, and snarls raised the hair on Isaac's arms. Moonlight glimmered on dense pelts, fangs flashed white, and twigs snapped under large paws.

The wolves came from the woods, their tails swishing and noses extended as they scented Isaac. He froze at their approach, holding his breath as cold noses bumped against his arms. Heavy tails smacked his legs as the wolves circled him. They hadn't taken a chunk out of him yet, but Isaac didn't want to test his luck and kept perfectly still.

A rough chuckle rumbled behind him, rich and low. "Don't worry, I won't let 'em bite you." Ben peeled off his shirt, his skin pale in the moonlight. His nipples hardened in the cold and goose bumps rippled over the taut muscles of his arms.

He looked like a wild beast before he even shifted—heavy pecs covered in thick chocolate-brown fuzz and shoulder-length hair flowing in rich, dark waves to his broad shoulders. Eyes of molten silver stole Isaac's breath and he'd only just gotten it back when Ben kicked off his jeans and boxers.

Pacing himself, Isaac's eyes followed the trail of dark hair over his rippling abs to the dark patch at the base of his pelvis. A heavy cock swung between his full thighs, stiffening in the cold before Isaac's eyes.

Naked in the moonlight with a pack of wolves at his back, Ben Stroud cut a very daunting figure, as dangerous as he was gorgeous. A Viking berserker. Isaac wished they were alone; he'd kill to make Ben howl at the moon. Ben's mouth twitched beneath his full beard as if his mind and Isaac's were on the same wavelength.

"I don't have to get naked, do I?" Isaac asked, hoping that would distract Ben from the swelling problem between his thighs.

Ben laughed, his chest heaving. "You're welcome to," he declared, and Isaac shivered as those eyes swept up and down his form as if he weren't wearing anything at all. "But it's a bit cold tonight. I just didn't wanna ruin perfectly good clothes." Ben scratched idly at his chest, thick hair rasping between his fingers. Isaac almost swooned at the sound. He'd bet Ben's furry chest and big arms could keep him warm.

"Okay. Cool," Isaac said, wishing he'd worn a longer coat as his cock twitched maddeningly.

Ben tipped back his head, and moonlight glimmered in the hollow of his throat. He cupped his hands to his mouth and let out a guttural howl that tightened Isaac's balls and raised the hair all over his body. The wolves answered Ben's song, though their voices were rougher than Ben's, and the moment quickly dissolved into ecstatic yips and barks as the wolves went wild, bounding around like giant puppies. Isaac scoffed, finally managing to smile. To see such fearsome predators acting like little lapdogs was amusing.

When he looked back toward Ben, his breath caught. A familiar enormous silver wolf strode toward him, the frost crunching under his giant paws. The wolf's fur rippled like waves in the night wind, moonlight shining on a glossy pelt. Bright silver eyes winked at him, and his mouth parted in a wolfish grin as he loped faster, moving with more grace than such a large beast should possess. Isaac tried to brace himself but the wolf's paws caught him in the chest and knocked him flat.

"Ben, come on!" he sputtered, laughing as the wolf gave his face a very thorough tongue bath. Isaac chuckled as Ben licked his ears, the wolf's body vibrating with happy, playful growls. Grinning, Isaac dug his fingers into the wolf's dense ruff of fur and wrestled him to the ground. Ben jumped up on him, trying to pounce again, but Isaac ran. Yelping and howling, the wolves bounded into the woods. They were fast, their paws slamming the ground and moonlight rippling off their fur.

Determined not to let them outrun him, Isaac put on a burst of speed, a rush of exhilaration sweeping over him as he ran with the pack. What would it be like to shed his human skin and run on all fours? The thought startled him. These wolves were so gentle and kind, it was hard to imagine they could pose a threat to anyone. They made being a werewolf look... fun and freeing.

If Don could hear what Isaac was thinking now, how would he react?

Before Isaac could lose himself in that worry, Ben nipped at his heels, then wove from one wolf to the other, nipping ears or pulling on fur. As a chorus of howls echoed through the woods, Isaac tipped his head back and howled with them, not caring how bad it might sound. The wolves sang with him and whether he walked on two legs or four, Isaac realized he was one of the pack.

Isaac never would have imagined a day where he would have fun with creatures he'd come to fear, but he was quickly accepting that so much of what he'd thought he'd known about wolves was wrong. Ben was a good wolf, and his pack was fun and friendly. He wished more of the Cross's hunters could see this side of werewolves. The side that ran and played like puppies, that groomed and licked each other lovingly, that sang beautiful songs of love and friendship to the moon above.

The cold air numbed his throat and the wolves tired him out faster than he wanted to admit. Isaac howled once more, grinning when the pack raised their voices to echo his, and then he turned and headed back to the bungalow. Unable to believe he wasn't lost in an amazing dream, Isaac wandered in through the front door. Ben was waiting, kneeling by the blazing fire, clad in jeans and nothing else. The firelight turned his bare skin golden and shadows danced across his body. Drawn to him as much as to the heat of the fire, Isaac went and knelt beside him.

Ben's mouth quirked, slanting his eyes. "Think my pack liked you."

"Yeah, they're... they're a fun bunch." Isaac still felt breathless from running. "How many people can say they ran with wolves?"

Ben chuckled. "Not many. You're a remarkable man, Isaac."

A tingle of electricity swept down Isaac's spine as their eyes met. He couldn't tell which burned hotter, the fire or the warmth of Ben's body so close to his. Big, gentle fingertips rasped over Isaac's cheek. He breathed in the salty smell of the sea breeze that still clung to Ben's chilled skin, closing his eyes as Ben leaned in.

The scratch of Ben's short beard tickled Isaac's skin, his breath fanning warm against Isaac's mouth. Ben kissed him, one hand coming up to cup Isaac's cheek. It was brief, as fleeting as the gentle flutter of a butterfly's wings, sending little ripples of warmth throughout Isaac's body.

A smile tugged at Isaac's mouth and he rotated his body toward Ben, framing his bearded jaw with his fingers, opening his mouth to Ben's tongue. Big arms went around his shoulders and Ben gathered Isaac close. He wasn't numb to the world, not anymore; every kiss, every stroke of Ben's hands over his body brought him back to life.

The ripples of warmth inside Isaac turned to roaring flames of lust as his hands wandered warm, bare skin. His fingers rasped through the fur on Ben's chest. Ben's muscles tightened in approval, or perhaps just to show off. He stroked Ben's chest, unable to stifle a gasp as Ben mouthed at his neck. A growl vibrated deep in Ben's throat, making Isaac's skin tingle. Once such a sound might have had him reaching for his crossbow. Now it did things to him he was embarrassed to admit to.

Ben suddenly pulled away, one hand slapping over his mouth.

Isaac laughed. "It's fine. The growling's pretty sexy."

Ben's face colored but he scowled. "It's never been like this before. My wolf's never been this close to the surface, not around anyone."

"Is that a bad thing?"

"It might be..."

Isaac knelt back, confused. "Is it about your cosmic mate bond thingy?"

Ben grimaced. "It's weird when you put it like that."

"So explain it to me. Greg told me some stuff, but I'm guessing there's more I don't know?"

Ben shifted on his knees, his eyes fixed in his lap. If his ears got any redder, Isaac thought they'd turn into tomatoes. "My wolf's got it in his stubborn head that you're my mate. The one destined to be with me. A human, and a hunter to top it all off. And, call me crazy, but I'm starting to believe Greg's whole soulmate spiel." Worry darkened Ben's eyes. "Being with me will be a complication for you, Isaac. It's a risk I'm willing to take. But are you? I don't want you to get hurt because of me."

Isaac didn't like how worried Ben was. He took his large hand and squeezed it tight as Ben kept talking. "We'll have to keep it a secret. If your hunters found out..."

A shiver ran through Isaac. "It's scary to me too. Being together will be a big risk."

Ben gripped his hands tightly. "I know."

"Ben, I'm scared."

Sighing, Ben nodded grimly.

"If we're together, it's going to be dangerous. If the hunters find out—"

Ben squeezed his hands tighter. "I don't care. I'm not letting fear divide us."

Isaac tugged, trying to free himself. "Would you listen to me?" he said urgently. "If the hunters find out, I'll lose you, Ben!"

Ben worried his lower lip. "Can't you leave?"

Isaac looked at the scar on his palm from the night he'd sworn himself to the Cross. "I can't leave them. If I leave them, I have to leave you too because they'll hunt me for the rest of my life." He thought of Gina, of how determined Don was to find her and ensure she never spilled their secrets. Of what might become of her if the Cross found her. "How can this end happily between us?" Ben's hands were like steel, his eyes burning as he held Isaac's gaze. "Maybe it would be better if I just left you alone."

Ben's eyes flashed. "You are my mate, Isaac Bennet." His voice was a low growl, breath hot on Isaac's mouth as he leaned in. Their chests touched, and Ben's hands fell to Isaac's waist, urging him closer. "You're mine and I'll be damned before I let you go. No one's coming between us. The goddess brought us together for a reason, and I'm going to trust her judgment."

Isaac looked into Ben's eyes, rallying himself against the storm of fear. "When I married my wife, I thought it was forever. That's how it seemed at first. I thought I'd get to see my son grow up, graduate, fall in love… He's gone now, and Melissa and I broke up years ago. Ben, nothing's certain. I know things will be dangerous. But I'm not letting you go."

Ben's eyes widened, soft and full of vulnerability. "Yeah?"

Isaac nestled closer, enjoying the rasp of Ben's beard beneath his fingers. "Yeah. Sound good to you?"

Ben hummed quietly, angling his head so his lips could caress Isaac's hand, rubbing gently against his skin. The hot touch of his mouth spread heat from Isaac's hand, tingling all up his arm and down his spine to pool hot between his thighs.

"Sounds so good in fact…" Ben mouthed at the shell of Isaac's ear. "I'm thinking if I had my way, I'd claim you as mine, right here and now."

Joy surged through Isaac. He knew they'd only met a few short weeks ago, that they were as different as could be, but Isaac couldn't imagine a future without him.

The heat in Ben's eyes made Isaac's mouth run dry. "But I know that's not how you humans work. You want things nice and slow. We wolves figure out pretty fast who we want, but I'm fine taking things slow with you. Maybe I don't know what the future holds, but I know what I want here, tonight. What matters to me is what you want."

Isaac swallowed, feeling hot around the collar thanks in part to the roaring fire and in part to Ben's attentive looks and touches. He didn't know what the future held either. He knew how easy it was to take the future for granted, to assume tomorrow would be the same as today.

For the first time in so long, Isaac knew what he wanted, and it was like surfacing from a cold, dark sea and taking that first gulp of air. Ben was the air in his lungs, the life flowing through his veins, the port in his storm. Isaac touched his forehead to Ben's, and his heart fluttered when Ben sighed and nuzzled into his touch. "I don't want to take things slow. Not tonight. I want you. Tonight, tomorrow, for as long as you want me."

Arms went around his shoulders and Ben leaned his cheek against Isaac's hair. "I think that'll be a long, long time."

Isaac smiled. That was fine by him. Their noses touched, their lips just barely brushing with every slow, uneven breath. Ben's hands burned against his skin, the heat of his body like a furnace enveloping him with smoldering warmth. As he leaned in, Ben suddenly turned his head away. Isaac barely refrained from groaning his disappointment. "Before we... uh... There's something you should know. About werewolf reproduction and mating."

Intrigued, Isaac knelt back, grinning at the way Ben's cheeks reddened. "Educate me."

Ben scratched at the back of his neck, sweeping aside dense locks of long brown hair. "For one, we can't get STDs. Not unless we're half human. So condoms are optional. But there's something that happens when we... finish." If possible, Ben's face went even redder. It looked painful to even spit the words out.

"Ben, I understand what an orgasm is."

"It's different for werewolves." He hesitated, his lips tightly pressed together as if he'd chomped into a lemon. "Ever heard of knotting?"

"Like a rope?" Knotting. That sounded familiar. Wasn't that a canine thing? Isaac remembered when his mother had wanted her two shih tzu to have puppies. He'd walked in on the dogs in obvious distress, seemingly attached at the—

"No."

Ben nodded.

"No fucking way."

Ben looked like he wanted to sink into the floor.

Isaac was sure he was as red as Ben by now. "Werewolves can tie? In human form? Even if they're both guys?"

"Yup."

"You've got some magic werewolf dick? What's it look like?"

Ben practically flew to the other end of the room. "It looks normal!" he squawked, his hands folded over the crown jewels.

"Wait. Wait. I'm sure I read some weird kinky fanfics about this. Oh shit. You can't get dudes pregnant with that thing, can you?"

Ben doubled over with a snort of laughter. "The hell have you been reading? No! But... but we can tie with the person we're with. For some people, it's kinky. It's about control, even ownership. For others, for me, it's... it's about connecting afterward, in body, soul." Ben looked away, wetting his lips. "I haven't actually done it with anyone before. But having that connection with someone after, it's something I'd want to do. If you're comfortable with it. I'm not sure how a human would like it, which is why I wanted to warn you in advance."

Isaac couldn't even wrap his mind around the idea, and he appreciated that Ben had wanted to warn him.

Eyes widening, Ben said, "I can always pull out before if you don't want to."

"What would it feel like?" Isaac wanted to please Ben, but the biting, the knotting—this was all a bit much.

Looking like he was about to drop dead from embarrassment, Ben asked, "Ever used an inflatable dildo, or a plug? Kinda like that. And we'd be tied together afterward for a while." Exhaling shakily, Ben crossed the room and took Isaac's hands. They were cold compared to Ben's, and his heat warmed them immediately. "We don't have to."

"But you just said it's important to you." Isaac couldn't look him in the eye. He understood Ben's fears suddenly. There was so much about being a werewolf Isaac would never understand. "Ben, if we do get together, there's gonna be things you want that I can't give you. I'm never going to become a werewolf."

Ben's lips thinned and he nodded, his eyes intent on Isaac. "I'm not asking you to. You're perfect the way you are. I've thought about this." Ben held on tight but Isaac tugged his hands out of Ben's grasp.

"I don't think I did," Isaac admitted. Ben knew what he wanted. Isaac had thought he did, but he was terrified of hurting Ben or disappointing him when he realized Isaac couldn't give him what he expected from a mate.

"Isaac, it doesn't matter to me. My wolf chose you for a reason."

Isaac swallowed, struggling to breathe as doubts and fears submerged him. "Ben, I don't want to disappoint you."

In answer, Ben cupped Isaac's face in his hands and claimed his lips. His body leaned into Isaac's, and it was impossible to resist melting into the surety of his embrace. Isaac's breath hitched as warm lips parted against his neck, his blood burning hot as fangs pricked at his skin. Ben breathed in deep, rubbing his nose against Isaac's neck. His beard scratched Isaac's skin pleasantly.

"I know what I want, Isaac. Who I want. But if you really need convincing, we can take things as slow as you want. Whether I bite you or knot you—none of that stuff matters to me." Ben's gentle fingers curled in Isaac's hair. "Being with you, that's what's important to me."

He'd had enough reassurance, enough talking. "Kiss me right now, you big softy."

His legs went weak as Ben crushed his mouth to Isaac's, his fangs nipping at his lower lip, his hungry tongue licking into him, his big hands grasping at Isaac's waist to bring him close. Isaac hadn't realized he'd kissed him back until he broke away for air, one hand still clasped in Ben's hair, his lips throbbing and warm from Ben's fervent attention.

Still, for all his bravado, Ben's hands were shaky as they clasped Isaac's waist, his chest rising and falling fast against Isaac's. Warm hands glided up Isaac's front, palms splaying wide over his racing heart. Ben brushed his fingers over Isaac's jawline, framing his face in tender hands.

Isaac had never been touched so gently, and knowing Ben was as nervous and excited as he was only turned him on more. An inquisitive tongue rubbed his lower lip. Smiling at Ben's shyness, Isaac parted his lips for him in invitation. The tentative touch of Ben's tongue sent a shower of sparks down Isaac's spine. Ben nibbled at Isaac's lower lip as if Ben wanted to devour him.

The next thing Isaac knew, they were sprawled on the sofa, Ben's body comfortably warm above him. Isaac wasn't sure when either of them had gotten out of their clothes, his mind incapable of stringing together thought when Ben squeezed handfuls of his buttocks. The heat of Ben's body made his own hands seem cold by comparison, and Isaac sought the warmth between Ben's thighs.

Ben's body stiffened, a growl rumbling deep in his chest as Isaac grasped him. He was thick and hot as hell in Isaac's hand. He rolled their cocks together, making them both pant and gasp between heated kisses. A shiver ran through Ben as Isaac caressed the bulge at the base of his cock. He was grateful Ben had warned him in advance or else he might have suggested Ben see a doctor. Ben's breath, warm against the top of his head, shuddered. Glancing up, Isaac caught him looking away fast.

"It's probably weird to you, right?" Ben murmured, hiding his face in Isaac's neck. His lips mouthed at it, kissing and sucking.

Isaac's stomach clenched. He felt bad for freaking out earlier. Werewolf and human anatomical differences aside, Ben had a beautiful cock—thick and long, filling his hand just right. He didn't want Ben to feel insecure. What he needed was acceptance, reassurance.

Isaac squeezed, enjoying the way Ben rocked into his touch. "I love your cock." Gasping as Isaac squeezed his knot, Ben was rock solid in his fist but his knot was soft. A shudder ran through Ben's body, and his fangs nipped hard at Isaac's neck. "Want you inside me so badly, you got no idea. No condom, no nothing. Make me feel every perfect inch."

A low rumble filled Ben's chest. "Sure you can take it?" Isaac laughed at the smug grin on Ben's face. "My knot, I mean. I don't want you to be uncomfortable."

Isaac squeezed hard and Ben hastily bit down on his lower lip, pumping his hips into Isaac's hand. Isaac could bust from how hot he looked. He wet his lips, suddenly apprehensive. "I don't know. If I can't..." He didn't want to disappoint Ben. He wanted to give him everything he craved.

Ben's lips settled against his forehead. "It doesn't matter to me. Whatever you decide."

Isaac wanted to see just how big Ben could get before he decided. Stroking Ben's cock in tight pulls, he made sure to pay special attention to his knot. Ben's chest rose and fell fast as Isaac worked him up and down until Ben was panting harshly. A shiver ran down Isaac's spine when he glimpsed Ben's sharp fangs.

"Holy shit," Isaac said as Ben's knot grew harder, larger. A moan escaped him as he imagined taking it, how his hole would stretch to fit him. "Fuck, Ben."

"Getting close. Gonna come if you don't stop."

Isaac let him go and they both panted harshly. Before Isaac's eyes, Ben's knot got smaller until it was almost invisible.

"So? Think you can handle it?"

Isaac tugged Ben down into a kiss, reaching down to palm their cocks. "Yeah. Want that thing stretching me open. Sounds hot as hell."

Ben's mouth attacked his neck, biting and sucking hard enough to leave a bruise. "Fuck, Isaac. I wanna be inside you," Ben confessed, rolling his hips to Isaac's every stroke, grinding his thick cock against Isaac's. His fingers spread Isaac's cheeks, caressing the tight pucker of his hole. Isaac ached for him. Whether it was his fingers or his cock penetrating him, he'd lose his mind unless they were finally one. "I need you."

Isaac covered Ben's mouth with his, teeth scraping and noses bumping in their haste. He hadn't felt whole in so many months but he was so close now. There was no stopping this. He was tired of feeling half-alive. For so long he hadn't wanted anything, he hadn't felt anything, but tonight all he could feel was *want* and *need* and *Ben* and *now*.

"Do you have lube?" Isaac regretted asking as Ben attempted to untangle himself. Isaac grabbed his wrists and urged him to stay but Ben was insistent. He left Isaac's side briefly and Isaac kept himself occupied, one hand on his cock, his fingers straying to tease his hole until Ben returned. He cut a breathtaking figure, naked and bathed in orange firelight, his cock long and stiff. Isaac lay back against the cushions and motioned Ben close.

Ben knelt, leaning down for a kiss. Thick fingers slick with lube rubbed at his entrance. Isaac was unable to stifle a gasp as Ben's fingers stretched him so perfectly. When Ben added another finger, opening him up wider and leaving him slick and wet, Isaac broke their kiss with a moan. His back arched, his breath escaping him as he wiggled his hips to get more of that amazing sensation.

A hot, wet mouth encircled his nipples, sucking one and then the other, making them hard as pebbles. Ben's attentiveness was enough to melt him. It was so good but not nearly enough. A strangled sound escaped him, and his hips rose with every curl of Ben's finger. He wouldn't beg but he was damn near close.

"Now, Ben. Now."

Ben answered with a lupine growl, his hungry lips crashing against Isaac's. Isaac sucked and nibbled at Ben's lips, panting as their tongues tangled. His legs flew around Ben's waist, and he had to bite his lip to stifle his groan as Ben entered him, going in slow. It had been a long time since he'd been with a guy, and the burning discomfort made his breath hitch. Ben draped over him, warming him with his body, their sweaty foreheads touching.

A few shallow breaths passed between them, and Ben covered Isaac's mouth with his. The discomfort was there, but the ache in his balls spoke louder. Isaac raised his hips and moaned into Ben's mouth. "More," he panted. "I need you." Ben's claws left dimples in the back of Isaac's thighs when he hoisted his legs back toward his chest and thrust, deep and hard, making Isaac's eyes roll back.

As their bodies met, every thrust growing in urgency, hoarse pants spilled from Ben's lips, his breath puffing hot against Isaac's mouth. Isaac shivered under those predator's eyes, a glowing silver. Hair grew thick on Ben's body, and his powerful frame vibrated with loudening growls.

"Don't be afraid of me," Ben whispered, his fingers trembling as they wove through Isaac's hair. "I'm still here. I'm yours." His voice was low and rough, but the tenderness brimming over was too familiar to doubt.

Something tightened in Isaac's chest, as if his heart had just swelled to accommodate every precious feeling Ben Stroud stoked within him. He guided Ben's mouth to his, panting, "Give me all of you. I need it." His legs tightened around Ben's waist, urging him in deeper.

Ben's wild eyes found Isaac's as a snarl thundered through his chest. "Mine," Ben snarled. "All mine."

Isaac couldn't stifle his cry as Ben sheathed himself completely inside him, his pelvis ramming Isaac's buttocks. He cried out as Ben's knot swelled inside him, nailing his prostate with every mind-numbing pump of his hips. The delicious pressure pushed Isaac over the edge, and he came messily between them.

Raining kisses down Isaac's neck, Ben shuddered through his release while buried deep inside him. Unaware of anything outside of the two of them, they held each other tight and caught their breath. Isaac's heart raced, and everything below his waist tingled and throbbed blissfully. Ben's hips shifted and Isaac gasped at the tugging sensation. Ben hadn't been lying; they were well and truly stuck together.

"Okay?" Ben's voice was hoarse and quiet. His lips settled against Isaac's neck.

"Yeah." The slightest movement left him arching off the bed, everything still so perfectly sensitive.

"I didn't hurt you?"

Isaac chuckled, sweeping damp hair from Ben's forehead. "It's... definitely different. In a good way. I'm not sure I'll ever go back to human guys again."

"No, you won't." Ben practically snarled the words. He rocked his hips and Isaac clung to him, a gasp driven from his lips. "You're mine, Isaac Bennet. No one else can have you."

Isaac shivered, gripping Ben's arms tight. "Don't want anyone else. Just you."

A satisfied growl rumbled from Ben, and he nuzzled into Isaac's neck. "How long does this last?"

"Thirty minutes, sometimes less. Why? Going somewhere?"

Isaac squeezed Ben's shoulders, running his ankles over the mounds of Ben's buttocks and enjoying the rasp of hair against them. "Just means we've got plenty of time to lie here like this."

Ben's mouth parted against his collarbone, kissing at a bruise, Isaac was sure. "Wouldn't have it any other way."

Isaac had to agree. He couldn't remember the last person he'd slept with that he'd been genuinely interested in lying with afterwards. No matter the guy or girl, he hadn't felt comfortable staying. With Ben, Isaac thought he could lie in his arms until the world outside came crashing to an end.

"Is that okay with you?" Ben glanced at him, brow furrowed.

Isaac had been hoping not to say it. His face warmed, and rather than speaking aloud his cheesy thoughts, he nibbled Ben's lower lip, seeking his tongue. Ben moaned quietly and the sound went straight to Isaac's cock. Exhausted as he was, his body still ached for Ben and he couldn't remember ever feeling this way. Nothing he'd had with anyone else had ever been this intense, emotionally or physically. "It's perfect. You're perfect," he corrected, and it was worth being cheesy to see Ben turn red up to his ears.

Ben nestled his face in Isaac's neck and breathed deeply. "You smell even better." Ben's cock twitched inside Isaac. "Like sweat and sex." Isaac shivered at the undercurrent of a growl deep in Ben's throat. "Like mine."

"What do I smell like usually?" Isaac wondered, his teeth closing gently on Ben's earlobe. Ben squirmed with a sound that could have been a chuckle, and Isaac's heart went into overdrive.

"Like... wet pavement." Ben's voice rumbled against his skin as he rubbed his nose against Isaac's neck. "Like moisture in the air before it rains."

Isaac smiled. "Why?"

Ben shrugged, propping his chin on Isaac's chest. His fingers swirled through the hair there, brushing over a nipple that stiffened under his touch. "Some of my favorite moments happened in the rain. I had my first kiss during a rainstorm. I hate summer, can't stand the heat, but everything would get so nice and cool after the rain came. The best weather always seems to follow a rainstorm. That's why it's my favorite. I met you during a rainstorm. Remember?"

Isaac did, vaguely. He'd been so miserable that night, on the brink of going off the deep end. He hadn't believed he'd ever be happy again, and then Ben had walked through the doors.

"You always reminded me of a rainstorm," Ben mused, brushing aside a lock of Isaac's hair the way a painter might brush paint across a canvas. "Your eyes, the gray and the blue... You seemed so sad that night, and then you smiled and it was like the sun came out. I think you're in the middle of a storm, Isaac, but the best is yet to come. One day it'll pass and the sun will shine the brightest."

Isaac swallowed hard. While once he'd been drowning, lost in a storm like the one Ben was describing, he was finally beginning to see a sliver of sunlight. He wanted to be better, as much for himself as for Ben, in the hope that someday he could be the man Ben deserved, the man Ben saw within him.

There was no room for doubt in his mind; he would never feel so complete with anyone else. If Ben wanted to bite him, to claim him, Isaac would let him without question, but it wasn't necessary. They were one, in body and in soul, and for as long as he lived, Isaac would never find what they had with anyone else.

Chapter 13

HUMANITY

Isaac woke on the sofa to the smell of cinnamon, nutmeg, and melted butter. Ben, clad in a fluffy white robe, handed Isaac a plate loaded with French toast and berries. The sight brought a smile to Isaac's face, groggy and sore as he was.

"Stellar room service. Five stars if you lose the robe."

Grinning radiantly, Ben leaned down and covered Isaac's mouth with his. Ben dampened Isaac's lower lip with his tongue, and his big hand squeezed a handful of Isaac's ass. Isaac was still groggy but his dick was waking up. He broke the kiss, shivering when Ben tugged down the blankets and kissed his way down Isaac's belly.

Ben's beard prickled against his stiffening cock, and Isaac moaned when Ben nuzzled his inner thighs. The scratch of his surprisingly soft beard made Isaac's dick throb. When Ben parted his lips and swallowed Isaac to the back of his throat, all Isaac could do was grip onto his hair and enjoy the ride.

The wet, hot suction of Ben's mouth provided the perfect sheath for Isaac to buck into. Pleasure overtook him until Isaac was incapable of words, only moans and pants as he lost himself in the bliss Ben was giving him.

"C-close," Isaac said in warning. "God. Ben. So good. Please."

When Ben pulled off, Isaac quaked and gasped, desperate to come. Eyes dark and wild, Ben draped his big body over Isaac like a blanket. Gripping both their hard shafts in his hand, Ben thrust hard against Isaac.

"Fuck!" Isaac cried, rolling his hips into Ben's hand and against his cock. "Yes, Ben, yes!"

Ben captured his lips with a moan that drove Isaac wild. Their tongues tangled and their hips rolled together. Ben came first with a broken groan, kissing Isaac through it until they were both breathless. Isaac clung to Ben with a hoarse cry as he spilled between them, lost in the pleasure of his relief and the sanctuary of Ben's arms.

They panted together, covered in sweat and seed, but Isaac couldn't tear himself away to clean up. "Want to stay here with you all day, just like this," Isaac whispered, combing his fingers through Ben's long hair.

"Goddess. Me too," Ben said, kissing Isaac's neck. He got up and returned with a damp rag, and they cleaned one another, sharing kisses until Isaac's lips tingled.

"Hand me some food before I throw myself at you again," Isaac ordered, squeezing Ben's ass. He'd love to spend the rest of the day on his back with Ben buried deep inside him, but he didn't want the food to get cold.

Isaac accepted his plate of French toast. Ben had carefully sliced and layered strawberries in between the slices of brioche, which were crisp and browned on the outside and soft and fluffy on the inside. Ben passed Isaac his coffee and tucked in. They ate side by side on the sofa, and Isaac felt comfortably warm beneath the afghan, nestled up against Ben's body.

"Thanks for last night. It was fun running with your pack."

Ben smiled as he forked some French toast into Isaac's mouth. "Thought it was important for you to see werewolves as something other than the monsters your hunter friends have told you about. Not that some of us aren't. But the people here, they're good, Isaac."

"The one that bit me in the kennels didn't seem so good. What are you gonna do with her?"

"We'll restore her humanity."

Isaac gaped. "You can do that?"

Ben rolled his shoulders like it was nothing. "Sure. In New York State, it's legal to kill ferals if they pose a threat to others. Most people still don't understand that ferals can be saved. That's why my family founded the LPA. I guarantee in a few years, killing ferals will be illegal. They'll be turned over to the LPA for treatment and if they can't be helped, then we've got wolf conservation shelters opening up everywhere who will take in feral wolves who can't shift back. There are always more humane ways of doing things."

Isaac stayed silent, his stomach churning. He hadn't known any of this. Was it true? Had he been taking lives unnecessarily when all along there'd been a way to help? No, he argued, repulsed by the thought. The wolves he'd killed had reveled in the loss of their humanity. Some had even still clung to fragments of it, bloodthirsty and on the brink of insanity.

"Ben, that's wishful thinking and it's dangerous. Feral werewolves can't be trusted." Ben's nostrils flared. Isaac quickly looked away, realizing he might have upset him. "It just contradicts everything I've been told. Okay? If feral werewolves can be saved, then why do we need hunters?"

"Because we don't," Ben answered, his voice sharp. "Not for ferals, anyway. Wolves like Stone and his cult are the only wolves I could justify hunting. Isaac, you saw what happened with me the night I became a berserker, didn't you? I was lost at first. The wolf had taken over."

Isaac nodded, remembering those glowing yellow eyes with a shiver. "But you came back. Your eyes changed color, returned to their silver color."

Ben nodded. "It was because of you. I heard your voice. Smelled your scent. You and the bond we share brought me back from my feral state."

Isaac wet his lips, his mouth painfully dry. Had the wolf who'd killed Beau been in control? Could he have been saved? Isaac shook his head. "What about when... when ferals kill humans and other wolves?"

Ben sighed. "If a feral feels threatened, it will react the way any wild wolf would to defend itself. But I promise you, ferals don't seek out humans to hurt or kill. If a wolf is a danger to themselves and others and can't be treated, then sometimes we have to make the difficult decision to put them down."

Isaac swallowed the lump in his throat. "My son, he was... he was killed by a wolf."

Ben's breath hitched. "Isaac," he began, voice shaking.

Isaac shook his head. He blew out a breath through his tightening chest. "The way this thing acted... He was far too human. He stole Beau right from our backyard. Dragged him into the woods. Everything about his actions was deliberate."

Ben blinked fast. He took Isaac's hand and squeezed tight. "Then that wasn't a feral wolf, Isaac. I promise you that. He was a killer, the same way any human might have been. No feral wolf would have done that. If you want, I can show you how we help them."

Blinking away memories of that nightmarish night, Isaac could only nod.

"Come with me." Ben took both their plates to the sink and jogged upstairs to get clean clothes. Isaac dressed himself before Ben reappeared and motioned for Isaac to follow him. Intrigued, Isaac jumped up and accompanied him to the estate.

Once inside the estate, Ben led the way to an exam room where a huge wolf lay drugged on the table. Isaac hesitated by the door, recognizing her as the wolf who'd bitten him. She growled weakly but in her woozy state it was hardly threatening.

"This is Kayla." Ben flipped open a file on the counter nearby. "Morning, Kayla. Your family is coming by soon to visit you."

"Do you know why she went feral?" Isaac asked.

Ben shrugged. "Not sure. She had her purse on her at the time, which is how we identified her. She had medication for anxiety in her purse. Werewolves who suffer from anxiety tend to shift when they panic. Is that what happened to you, Kayla?"

The wolf only shivered.

If she was so traumatized she'd let go of her humanity to forget, then maybe she didn't want to come back. He said as much and Ben said, "Maybe. It's hard for any werewolf to have a good reason to come back from trauma. We need to give her a chance. If she's too far gone to her wolf, then that's the way it is. Hopefully once her family shows up, their presence will be enough to bring her back."

Isaac's chest tightened. He'd never seen a wolf look so broken before. All the wolves he'd killed had been drunk on blood and carnage, but he could see the hurt in her eyes and he found himself hoping that she could emerge from the despair she was drowning in.

Ben frowned. "The drugs are wearing off. She's not dangerous. That's a good thing. She could go to a wildlife center if she refuses to come back... Still, that'll be hard to tell her family." Ben hung his head with a sigh. This was eating away at him.

Isaac thought of her family going to visit Kayla, their relative who'd forgotten them and wandered as an animal behind a fence like a creature in a zoo. The idea broke his heart. He had to know if it was possible for a feral shifter to regain their humanity.

Someone knocked on the door. Ben opened it a crack and smiled. "Come on in." Kayla's parents walked in, each holding the hand of a little girl. Isaac's heart melted. That little girl couldn't have been older than Beau was when Isaac had lost him. She even had a gap between her teeth like Beau.

The wolf sat up on the table. Her eyes flashed from yellow to green and back again. A whine was pulled from her throat. Kayla gasped as she broke from her shift. Isaac stumbled back, astonished to see a feral wolf regain their humanity before his own eyes.

"B-baby," she croaked, tears spilling down her cheeks. "My baby!"

"Mommy!" The little girl let go of her grandparents' hands and ran into her mother's arms.

Ben reached for a blanket to cover them as Kayla shivered, sucking in one breath after another. Her parents knelt and hugged her tight.

"H-how did you find her?" she asked her parents, hugging the child to her.

"Your neighbor called us," her mother explained, stroking Kayla's hair. "She's the one who found Cammy."

"What happened? Can you tell me?" Ben asked.

Wiping her eyes, Kayla said, "My boyfriend and I were in the park with Cammy. My ex-boyfriend confronted us, tried to start a fight. When Cammy saw him, she got so scared she ran away. I c-couldn't find her. I thought..." She kissed her daughter's hair, a tear gliding down her cheek.

Understanding softened Ben's eyes. "So the stress of seeing your ex and the fear that Cammy had been lost was what caused you to lose yourself."

Isaac backed into the door. She'd lost herself to her inner wolf because she'd believed she had lost her child. Understanding tore a hole in Isaac's heart. Who wouldn't lose themselves in despair at the loss of their child? Hadn't he fallen into the deepest, darkest pit after Beau's death, with no way out?

Needing air, he stumbled into the hall and took a much-needed seat in a chair nearby. For so long, he'd believed that once a wolf went feral, there was no other choice but to put them down. He'd demonized feral wolves as dangerous monsters when the truth was that they were only hurt and scared. He felt sick for being so wrong. He closed his eyes tight, trying to reconcile this truth with everything Don had taught him.

"This building is full of people like Kayla." Ben's voice was a deep rumble as he leaned on the closed door to the exam room, his arms folded over his chest, his eyes full of tender empathy. "But they can be saved, Isaac."

Bile scorched his throat. "Ben, I... I didn't know." Isaac couldn't breathe. If Ben had gone feral, Isaac would have killed him without question. They never would have met. Isaac would have acted as judge, jury, and executioner for Ben based on a bad moment, and it would have been the worst mistake of his life.

Ben sat beside him, his arm going around Isaac's shoulders. "You watched a werewolf kill your son. If that was your first impression of us, I don't blame you. Some of us are monsters, Isaac. Some of us are a danger to society, like John Stone and his fanatics."

"But not you." Isaac took his hand and held tight, looking at Ben through eyes blurred with shame and guilt. "Not your agency wolves, or Manuel or Greg, or the people here. I know that now." He had to make this right. He didn't know how many shifters he'd killed who could have been saved. How many of them had truly been bloodthirsty monsters, and how many of them had had their minds broken by abuse and grief? He didn't know and the uncertainty pulled him into a riptide of emotion.

"I'll help you," Isaac whispered, his throat so thick he could hardly get the words out. "I don't want to hunt anymore, Ben." The admission sent a chill down his spine, but it was the truth.

Ben's chin came to rest on his shoulder. "Are you okay?" His thumb drifted over Isaac's cheek. "I didn't mean to upset you."

He didn't know how to answer, sitting motionless as Ben's arms went around him, guiding Isaac's cheek to his chest. A part of him wanted nothing more than to hold Ben tight. Another screamed at him to run from Ben's embrace before he rained ruin down on them both.

Don called a meeting out of the blue the next day, demanding the hunters come to the cathedral. Isaac had never been less enthusiastic to meet with Don. His stomach churned at the idea of hurting wolves like Kayla, like Ben, Manuel, and Greg.

Perhaps Don could be reasoned with. He was his friend, and Isaac wanted to give Don the benefit of the doubt. Like Isaac, there was a chance he didn't know most feral wolves could be saved and shouldn't be lumped in with monsters like Stone's cult. Isaac would tell him what he'd learned about ferals and hope that Don would keep an open mind.

But the moment Isaac laid eyes on Don, his hopes were dashed. In the refectory, Don paced up and down, dragging a hand through his disheveled hair. He was dressed for the hunt, wearing an overcoat to conceal the utility belt where he kept his vials of aconitum, powdered silver, and his holstered handgun. He mumbled to himself, gnashing his teeth, and then he paused, sniffing. He turned toward Isaac and some of the tension left his face. "Ah. There you are, my son. I'm surprised you came."

Isaac sat in a chair at the dining table. "Why's that?" He wrung his hands together and internally cursed his luck. Don was in a bad mood. How could he bring up feral wolves now?

"You've been absent from our hunts ever since your unfortunate abduction. I hope you haven't lost your nerve for the hunt."

Isaac swallowed with difficulty. "Don, there's..." Gathering his courage, he rose to his feet. "I want to talk to you about something."

Don shook his head, his shoes slapping over the floor as he paced. "Whatever it is, it will have to wait until after our mission is concluded."

"Don, if we're going hunting, then I really need to tell you now."

The father whirled toward him. "If it was so urgent, you could have told me when we met for hunts during the past week you've been absent!"

Isaac took a step back, surprised by Don's anger.

He sighed, seeming to shrink before Isaac's eyes. "You are my finest hunter, Isaac. Tell me I still have your trust and devotion, because I need it now."

Isaac opened his mouth but the words wouldn't come.

The door banged open against the wall and hunters shouldered their way in.

"My friends," Don said. "Have a seat."

Isaac sat, at a loss.

Don splayed his hands on the table and faced the hunters. "I have news of Gina, the traitor who freed the Moonborn cultist and turned her back on us."

Isaac's heart lurched. The hunters murmured in agitation.

Don smiled. There was a harshness to it, making his teeth look sharper, his eyes narrower. "I discovered her location. She's in hiding in Yonkers, and she isn't alone." He slammed a fist down on the table. "She's with a wolf, and what's more, she's let him turn her."

Cries of outrage and disgust echoed through the room. Isaac's heartbeat roared in his ears.

"She's turned her back on this family. Spat in the face of our loyalty!" Don paced, fury turning his face an ugly red. "She's let the enemy lure her into sin!"

Isaac had never seen Don so furious. Clearing his throat, Isaac asked, "Has she revealed our location? Our plans? If not, can't we just leave her alone?"

Don looked affronted. "If she hasn't, it's only a matter of time before she and her filthy pack descend on us. We will confront her today, and she will answer for her sins. The monsters will know God's wrath! Who is with me?"

The hunters in the room roared, but all Isaac felt was a rising tide of dread. Was this the fate that awaited him and Ben if anyone in the Cross found out about them? Or was Don's fury directed at Gina for turning her back on the Cross and letting Morgan go?

He had to warn Gina and her wolf.

Isaac did the only thing he could think of. The moment he was in his car, he called Ben and told him everything. "I know this is a huge risk to you and your pack, but she's in danger and so is the wolf she lives with. Is there anything you can do?"

"It's risky, yeah, but this is the work I signed up for." Ben's calm voice did wonders to soothe Isaac's racing heart. "Are either of them feral?"

"Not as far as I know of."

"Then the hunters can't touch them. The hunters operate under a gray area of the law. Killing ferals isn't illegal, not yet, but if they've got their wits about them and the Cross attacks them anyway, that's murder. As the agency's leader, I have the authority to take Gina and her mate under my protection, but I can't imagine the hunters will approve of that."

Isaac squeezed the wheel, as the tires roared over the road. "Then you can help them."

"Yes, but... Isaac, I want you to keep your head down. I don't want you to become a target for the Cross, so don't do anything rash unless you think you can get away with it."

Isaac pressed hard on the gas. It was a delicate situation. If Gina had been responsible for the cultist's escape, then she had the deaths of innocent people on her hands. He had to get to her first and figure out what really happened. If her only crime was loving a wolf and taking their bite, then Isaac couldn't let Don hurt her.

Isaac exhaled. "Okay. Ben... don't make me regret calling you. Be careful. I..." A lump rose in his throat. "I need you. Okay?"

Ben chuckled softly. "Guess I'm not allowed to get hurt, then."

"No. You're damn well not."

"Got it."

Isaac could practically see the smile on Ben's face. He hung up and prayed to a God he didn't believe in to keep Ben safe.

GINA AND HER WOLF lived on an isolated stretch of road far upstate, a backdrop of dark woods looming over their small, unassuming house. Isaac didn't see Don's car or Ben's truck. He'd beaten the others here but they couldn't be far behind. He had minutes to get Gina to understand her life was in danger before Don and the hunters showed up.

He wanted to wait for Ben. Gina would likely blow Isaac's head off before she trusted a word he said but if another wolf were there, she might be more receptive. But there wasn't time.

A growl rumbled from within the trees, loud in the quiet of the country. A wolf's eyes winked at him from the woods. The wolf charged him, paws spraying snow. Whether the shifter was Gina or her wolf, Isaac wasn't sure.

He tore up onto the porch and banged on the door. "Gina! Open up! It's Isaac. You're in danger!"

"Why the hell should I open my door to you? You're Don's pet!" Gina's familiar brash voice growled from behind the door. "Get out of here!"

The wolf's claws raked over the wooden porch. Isaac swallowed, his heart in his throat at the sight of all those fangs. "Gina, Don and the others are on their way. You need to leave before they get here! I can help you escape!"

The wolf's ears twitched. He spun toward the road where several cars came into view. Isaac's heart sank until he recognized Ben's familiar truck. The door slammed and Ben marched up the driveway. There were only three other SUVs in the road behind him.

The wolf shifted to a man, naked and muscular. "Ben Stroud? What are you doing here?"

Ben said, "No time to talk. My wolves and I are here to help you escape hunters. They're only a mile behind us. You've gotta get out of here now."

The door swung open. Gina stood on the other side, crossbow in hand. She eyed Isaac warily but stepped out onto the porch. "I'll pack our bags," the man said, heading inside.

Isaac gripped Ben's arm. "Is that all? Don will have dozens with him." Don could easily outnumber Ben and his pack, killing them all.

A sigh escaped Ben. "Unfortunately, yeah. The agency is still so new, and these wolves were all I could spare. Hopefully, we can negotiate."

Gina asked, "What's going on? Since when do you run around with wolves, Isaac?"

Isaac chuckled. "Could ask you the same thing."

She looked over her shoulder at the man running around the house. "That's Frank. My mate. He was feral when we first met. I was supposed to hunt him down but when he smelled me, he regained his humanity." She shook her head. "All these years, I thought ferals were beyond saving. I... seeing him come back to himself like that changed everything."

Isaac sighed around the ball of nerves in his stomach, watching as Ben and the other wolves kept a lookout for Don. "I know what you mean."

"Don lied to us," Gina spat.

Isaac winced. "Maybe he didn't know."

She scoffed. "He's got his hooks in you good, doesn't he?"

"He's my friend. He's just... He doesn't understand, but maybe we can reason with him." Isaac wrapped his arms around himself, his heart racing as he waited for the quiet to break, for Don and the others to arrive. "Gina, I need to know... Did you let Morgan out?"

She wrinkled her nose. "No. Why the hell would I have done that?"

"Then do you know who did?"

She shrugged. "No idea. I'd already left after we captured those wolves in Inwood Park."

Frank bounded from the house, dressed in jeans and nothing else, a couple of bags over his shoulder. Gina raced after him but Isaac remained where he was. If Gina hadn't released Morgan, then who had? Not that it mattered right now. They had to focus on getting Gina and her mate out of here.

Frank started the engine and Gina climbed in. Ben leaned in through the open window. "We'll help you cross the border out of New York. I have a friend in the Council who could talk to Alpha Hanson about helping you two relocate somewhere safe."

"Thank you, Stroud," Frank said.

Just then, a group of cars squealed onto the road. Ten whole SUVs, filled with bloodthirsty hunters. Ben's pack was more than outnumbered. They would be slaughtered. Isaac's heart dropped as he recognized Don's black Camaro. Don braked, the car lurching to a stop mere feet from Isaac.

Hunters stormed from their cars and in seconds, the pack was surrounded. Don slammed the door and marched toward Isaac, his jaw squared with a rage that Isaac had never seen before.

"What is the meaning of this?" Don roared, his face red as he faced Isaac down. "Why are you with them? Explain yourself!"

Isaac balled his hands into fists and refused to cave to the guilt Don's anger tried to drag out of him. "Don, Gina didn't let the cultist out. The massacre wasn't her fault."

"I don't care!" Don bellowed, spraying Isaac with spittle. "She turned her back on me! She swore a vow to me, and instead she betrayed me and sided with the enemy!"

"Hunters!" Ben's deep voice cut through all the noise. He shouldered past the agency wolves and made his way toward Don. Don tried to lunge past Isaac, but Isaac grabbed his arm, terrified of what he might do if he got close to Ben. "Gina and her mate are under the protection of the LPA. You won't touch them!"

The hate in Don's eyes when he caught sight of Gina made Isaac's heart sink. He'd never seen Don so livid, so unrecognizable in his anger. "Animals," he snarled. "You have no authority. That is my hunter, and she must answer for her crimes against me!"

"I fell in love!" Gina snapped, standing protectively in front of Frank, her crossbow raised. "I haven't done anything wrong! Leave us alone!"

"Don." Isaac tugged on his arm, forcing Don's attention back on him. "She hasn't spilled our secrets. She didn't let Morgan go. Just... Just leave her alone. Please."

Don ripped his arm out of Isaac's grasp. The betrayal in his eyes when he looked at Isaac threatened to crumble Isaac's resolve. Don shook his head. "What a disappointment you are, Isaac."

"Don, I... This isn't you. I know what she did hurts, but we hunt wolves who prey upon humans. Not one of our own."

Don's thin lips trembled in fury as he glared around Isaac at Gina. He looked among the wolves and Isaac could see him weighing the odds.

The agency wolves and the hunters were evenly matched. It would be a bloodbath on both sides if they clashed. But Don cared for his hunters. Didn't he? Surely he wouldn't throw all their lives away over one petty betrayal.

"Don. Just walk away. You... you lost Gina, okay, but you still have the rest of us."

Don eyed him warily. "And you, Isaac? Do I still have your loyalty? Your trust?"

And Isaac didn't know what to say. Once, he would have taken Don's hand and said yes without question. But this man before him, bristling with anger and rage, hungry for blood... this wasn't the man he'd pledged loyalty to. "Don, I... Lately, I've been—Things have changed, okay? You're my friend. My brother. But I... I can't let you kill her."

"Even if she's taken his bite?"

Isaac gritted his teeth. He nodded.

Don's jaw tightened, his eyes narrowing. He took a step back, like Isaac had shoved him, and Isaac knew he'd hurt him.

"Don, I—"

"Very well!" Don snapped, face red with fury and humiliation. "Take the traitor and her pet dog. But I want them out of New York State. And Stroud? Watch yourself. If you try and come for my people, I will bring God's wrath upon you!"

Ben growled low in his chest. "Just get out of here."

Gina looked wide-eyed from Ben to Don. "That's it? How can you let him walk away, Stroud?"

"We didn't come here to fight, Gina." Ben turned to her and gripped her shoulder. "My job is to get you and Frank to safety. Now, walk away."

But as Gina's eyes turned steely with anger, Isaac's heart sank. "He'll come for us. You don't know him like I do. He'll kill Frank!"

"Gina, don't—" Ben grunted as she shoved him out of her path.

Gina flung up her arm, the sleeve billowing back to reveal the miniature crossbow strapped to her wrist. A single bolt flew free, whistling past

Isaac's ear. Straight toward Don. The Father was older than Gina, but he was a hunter. Don spun out of the path of her bolt, pistol gleaming as he whipped it from the holster. The blast of gunfire split the air.

Gina grunted, doubling over and clutching her stomach. Frank screamed her name and caught her in his arms.

Don only smiled, and it was the coldest thing Isaac had ever seen.

The agency wolves roared their fury, and some started to shift. The hunters drew their weapons. Isaac's heart sank. Don looked to him, a challenge clear in his cold eyes. "Come here, my son. Stand with your hunters."

Isaac was frozen in place.

"Enough!" Ben roared. "Do not shift. Gina needs help, there can't be any delays. Hunters. Get the hell out of my sight. You got what you came for."

Sneering, Don holstered his gun. "I will see you at the cathedral, Isaac." He marched back to his car, and his hunters followed.

"Let them go!" Ben snarled, his voice guttural and deep as the wolves growled around them. "Gina needs immediate care. She's our priority, not them!"

"Gina!" Frank sobbed.

Isaac's heart sank. He and Ben ran to Gina and Frank. Gina gasped for breath, clutching the bullet hole in her stomach. Her veins ran black with Don's potent blend of poison. Ben dropped to his knees before her. "Someone get my bag! There's an antidote!"

Isaac shook his head. "Not for this kind of poison," he whispered to Ben. "Don makes it himself. She needs a hospital." There wasn't one for miles, but they had to try. Isaac had seen this poison kill wolves in minutes.

Frank hoisted her and carried her to Isaac's car. Starting the engine, Isaac drove them back toward the town he'd passed on his way over. The agency vehicles followed. Frank sat in the back with Gina, and Isaac watched in the rearview mirror as tears ran down Frank's face. "Gina. Please, baby," Frank gasped, cradling her pale face in his hand.

Isaac squeezed the wheel so hard, he thought it would crack.

Gina's gurgling breaths slowed and stopped. Isaac waited to hear her breathing but she didn't take another breath. Closing his eyes tight for a moment, Isaac willed her to keep breathing. The anguished sound that tore from Frank made Isaac's eyes sting and burn. Fury and pain had Isaac gnashing his teeth.

Looking into the back seat, he saw himself bent over Ben's body. He saw himself pleading for Ben to open his eyes, to stay with him. It was *his* heart breaking into pieces in his chest. His tears wet on Ben's cold, still face.

And Isaac knew in that moment that if he ever left the Cross, Ben could never follow him.

If he left the Cross, then Isaac would be saying goodbye to Ben. He would do it if he had to. He would do whatever it took to keep Ben safe, even if it meant letting him go forever.

CHAPTER 14

WHAT HAVE I DONE?

"I HATE LEAVING YOU alone." Ben sighed, his arms squeezing Isaac tight. The noise of the airport seemed to disappear when Ben brought Isaac's head to his chest, and Isaac's arms went around his waist. He would miss Ben too.

"It's for the best. Your parents would freak out if you walked through the door with a human. You said yourself no humans live among your pack, and I don't wanna make anyone uncomfortable."

A frown pulled at Ben's lips. "Isaac, if you want me to stay, I will. I know it's gonna be hard for you without Beau."

Isaac had been trying to put on a happy face, but as always Ben had seen right through him. It was still hard to believe Beau had been gone for two Thanksgivings now. This time of year never got easier. He pressed his mouth to Ben's, closing his eyes tight and savoring the woodsy scent of his beard oil. Isaac enjoyed the rasp of it on his face—and against his thighs. "Of course I want you to stay. But you should be with family."

"Remember, you can always call me or go to that meeting I told you about. There are plenty of folks this year missing family."

Isaac rebelled at the thought of spilling his guts to a group of strangers but for Ben's sake he said, "I'll be fine. Come on, do I have to drag you to the gate? I want you to be with your family. It's important. So go, have fun. It's only for a day."

It really looked like he'd have to urge Ben to go, so Isaac planted his hands in his chest and pushed against him. Ben took both his wrists and linked their fingers together, leaning down to claim his lips. "I'll call you when I get there."

Isaac was sure they looked like one of those mushy couples, acting like a day apart was a year, and he loved it. He closed his eyes and leaned their foreheads together, and suddenly it was so hard to let him go.

"Okay, and listen, you did the best you could to get justice for Gina."

Ben sighed heavily, expression crumpling. "Could have done more..."

Fighting between wolves and hunters was outside police jurisdiction, so Ben had gone to Manuel for help. As a shifter representative for New York, Manuel was trying to renew talks with the human governor of NYC to crack down on hunters, but it would be a slow process. Isaac knew the Cross helped fund politicians who were sympathetic to hunters, so he wasn't hopeful.

"You're trying. That's more than most people can say."

Ben kissed his neck, making Isaac chuckle. "You sure have a thing for my neck, don't you? Sure you aren't a vampire?" Kissing his neck, nuzzling his neck. He'd never asked why.

Ben's cheeks colored. "It's where werewolves claim their mates."

Isaac frowned. "Huh?"

Ben brushed his fingers over Isaac's skin. "When werewolves... consummate the relationship, we bite our mate, leave our mark on their skin."

Hadn't Don told him something similar? The day Isaac had joined the Cross, Don had said that his son had been violated, that a female wolf had forcibly claimed him by biting his neck and then she'd killed him.

Isaac shivered. "Oh. And you want to do that to me?"

Coughing, Ben averted his gaze. "Only if you want it. A wolf's bite has to be consensual, otherwise the mark will fade. The pair has to want it."

So how had Don's son been able to be marked if the bite had been forced upon him?

Ben cleared his throat. "But we don't have to talk about that stuff now. Just forget I said anything—"

Isaac laughed and kissed him. "Ben, it's okay." He would take Ben's bite without question. He'd love nothing more than to be Ben's. Isaac realized how close he was to telling him that he loved him and quickly changed course. "Have fun. I'll pick you up right after you land in the city, okay?"

Kissing Isaac's fingers, Ben relinquished his hand and slowly turned away before striding toward security. Isaac turned toward the car and hit himself. What was he thinking? He couldn't start spouting "I love yous" already. Was he crazy? Yes, one hundred percent. Was he madly, hopelessly in love with a grumpy werewolf with the heart of a marshmallow? Beyond a doubt.

Maybe he'd tell Ben when he got back. Or never, he thought as the idea made his stomach spin like a washing machine. Isaac drove back to the city, his windshield wipers batting away thick flurries of snowflakes.

Today... today was going to be a hard one.

He was sure by now the Thanksgiving Day parade was in full swing. Thanksgiving had never been his favorite holiday, especially since it usually meant driving to Melissa's family home with Beau for an awkward dinner with his ex. He'd never hosted, not after the one time he almost burned the kitchen down one year.

Additionally, he'd never liked the parade, and after he'd told Beau that Thanksgiving glossed over America's genocide of the indigenous population, Beau had decided he didn't like it either. Still, knowing there were families there right now with their kids left an ache in his heart. He'd sit through a painful dinner with Melissa's family if it meant Beau could be there with him.

Isaac battled with the memories as he clutched the wheel. This was what he'd promised himself he wouldn't do—reopen wounds that were still struggling to heal.

With a lump in his throat, Isaac bitterly accepted that he hadn't been truthful at all with Ben. Getting through today without his son was going to be much harder than he'd been willing to admit. Last year he'd gotten so drunk he couldn't remember but this year he'd vowed not to pick up a bottle. Ben was only a call away, but Isaac didn't want to be selfish. It was important to him that Ben be with his family, and he didn't want to ruin that.

He parked outside his apartment in Brooklyn and had the keys in the lock of the building's front door when someone honked their horn multiple times. He glared down the street, but then his heart lurched.

Don waved out of the window of his black Camaro.

Isaac sighed. Once, he would have been thrilled to see Don. But now that he was so conflicted, he didn't know what to feel anymore.

"What do you want?" he asked, marching toward Don's car.

Don stepped out of his car. He hung his head and stared at his feet. "I only wanted to wish you a pleasant holiday and to offer you some company. I know how hard today is for you."

A little piece of Isaac warmed at Don's words, but all he had to do was remember Gina's death a few days ago for his anger to rush back. "That's it. That's all? You... you killed one of our own."

"Isaac." Don reached for him. "She attacked me! She left me no other choice!"

"I know, and she shouldn't have. We'd resolved the situation so there was no need for her to attack you. But she didn't have to die, either, Don." Stepping away, Isaac said, "Do you even care about us? I thought we were a family."

Don seemed to shrink from Isaac's anger. "Of course I do."

Isaac's heart ached. "Why don't I believe you?"

A shuddery sigh escaped Don. Isaac's own sadness made his eyes sting, and Don hid his face in his hand. "I'm so sorry, my son." Don's voice shook. "You're right. I've let the hunt turn me into a monster." He turned away from Isaac and leaned on his car for support, his body shaking with grief and remorse. "I... cared for Gina, too. She was once a trusted friend. I d-didn't want things to end the way that they did."

It soothed Isaac a little to know Don regretted killing Gina. Maybe the kindly man he thought he'd known was still somewhere in there.

"I know I've got no right to ask for your forgiveness." Done sniffed. "But please, let me make this up to you. Let me show you I'm still the man you believed in."

Isaac wanted that. He wanted the warm, kind man he'd pledged his loyalty to back. "Don... I don't know if you can do that. I don't even recognize you anymore. And lately, I've been asking myself why I'm still hunting. What it's all for. I just don't know anymore."

Don drew in a breath and wiped his eyes. He turned toward Isaac, his face dry. "We can go for a drive. You can tell me. I'll listen to every word, Isaac, I promise. Just get in the car. Please."

Wasn't this what Isaac had wanted? A chance to try and get through to Don? Leaving the Cross meant leaving Ben. If there was a chance he could help Don change the Cross for the better, then he would take it. "Fine," he said, swallowing down his annoyance at caving so easily. "But I need you to hear me out."

Don smiled brightly. "I will, Isaac. I will. Thank you!" He bounded to his side of the car and they drove off. The drive took them out of the city and into the countryside. Don played some music to pass the time. Isaac wasn't sure where Don was taking him but during the drive he told Don about what he'd learned of feral wolves. He had to make some revisions to his story to leave out any mention of Ben and the agency, but he thought he still made a convincing argument against hunting ferals.

The father nodded along, his eyes growing wide as he digested Isaac's words. "You're telling me these feral wolves can be saved?"

"Yes!" Isaac said, relieved Don wasn't angry or doubtful. "All I'm saying is, maybe we take on a broader approach. Of course we can hunt down wolves like Stone, who prey on innocents. But we should rescue ferals and take them to the agency for treatment."

Don frowned. "I have to say, Isaac, this is very concerning to hear."

Isaac's heart sank. "Why?"

"You should be very careful who in the Cross you speak to about this progressive idea of yours."

Isaac wrung his hands together. "But you'll think it over, won't you?"

Don exhaled, hands squeezing the wheel. "Making such a change to our methods would not be a popular decision, Isaac. My hunters could begin to doubt the Cross's legitimacy."

"Maybe that's for the better," Isaac said, knowing he was stepping into dangerous territory. "Maybe hunters shouldn't exist."

Don whipped his head in Isaac's direction. "Who have you been talking to?" The sharpness of his voice made Isaac wince.

"No one. Just been thinking a lot, that's all."

Don breathed in deep, nostrils flaring. The gesture reminded Isaac so much of a wolf that he was momentarily paralyzed. Shaking his head, Don steered them right. "I must say, I'm disappointed in you, Isaac. But I will give this some thought."

"Thanks," Isaac said, though it lacked warmth. They sat in icy silence until, with a frustrated sigh, Don stopped the car and Isaac's heart skipped when he recognized where they were. They were at the church where Beau had been laid to rest.

"I knew you'd be missing him today, especially," Don said.

"Don," he began, not sure if he was ready to face his son's grave for the first time in so long.

Don held out his hand. "Come, my son. I'll be right there with you."

Blinking hard, Isaac took his hand and they walked together among the graves until they arrived at Beau's little headstone. Isaac's eyes stung at the sight of his grave. He touched the cold stone. "Hey, bud," he whispered.

Don handed him a small bouquet from his canvas bag. "For your son."

Isaac's throat tightened. "Thank you." He laid the flowers on Beau's grave. It looked less lonely now.

Don clasped his hands and said a silent prayer. When he looked up, he met Isaac's gaze and smiled, his eyes warm and kind. He looked so much like the man who'd rescued him from darkness. And yet, Isaac wasn't the same lost, broken man who'd turned to Don for comfort. "This was a nice gesture, but Don you know I'm not going to let this go, don't you? Killing feral wolves is murder."

The smile fell from Don's face, and Isaac saw through this seemingly kind gesture to what it really was. A ploy to win back Isaac's loyalty.

Don's eyes narrowed and when he spoke, his voice was hard and cold. "You are being tested, Isaac. These doubts are a sign that you have strayed from God's intended path for you, but it is not too late. Do not lose your way, my son." He squeezed Isaac's shoulder, digging his sharp nails into the fabric. "I would hate for us to become enemies." Then he turned and walked away, boots crunching in the snow.

Isaac watched him leave, feeling like something had shifted between them for good. If Don couldn't be convinced to spare innocent feral wolves, then Isaac couldn't see how he could remain friends with Don in good conscience.

Isaac remained by Beau's grave in silence. He'd never been one to talk to the dead, but he decided to make an exception. "I'm getting there, kiddo. I wasn't okay for a long time but lately things have changed. I've changed, I think. I'm going to do right by you. I'm going to be a man you can be proud of. I promise." Isaac kissed his fingertips and touched them to Beau's grave. "I love you. I just... I hope you know that."

Thumbing the wetness from his eyes, he turned away and walked right into a woman with blonde hair that was swept back into a ponytail. Her bright blue eyes sent a bolt of surprise down his spine.

"Mel?"

His ex-wife blinked away the grief shrouding her eyes. "Isaac. Oh my God." Her voice was... different, somehow. Lighter, more pleasant.

To Isaac's amazement, he smiled. "Hey."

She smiled back, and though it didn't quite touch her eyes, it was a valiant effort.

"Thank God." Mel sighed. "I didn't want to come here alone."

"Neither did I," Isaac admitted. He was surprisingly happy to see her. The last time he'd seen her, he'd held her in his arms, all their animosity forgotten as they'd knelt before their son's headstone. Remembering made his stomach churn.

"How—" Melissa began, but then she shook her head, biting her lip. "Sorry. I guess I shouldn't ask how you've been."

Shuffling his feet, Isaac searched for words. "It's been..." He didn't know what to say. "Hard" didn't cut it. He felt better than before but still unsteady. Ben had been such a blessing. Isaac wondered if she'd been going it alone with her grief.

They hadn't been kind to each other, not before the divorce, not after, but losing Beau had brought them closer together.

"Hey, screw this holiday. I've hated it ever since Beau died. How about we go somewhere? Anywhere. I really don't—I can't go to counseling. Not today." She sniffed and wiped her eyes on her glove.

Isaac exhaled, a knot of tension loosening in his chest. "Yeah. Okay. That sounds fine."

"Where do you want to go?"

He shrugged. "Don't really care. I can't even stand to be in the city, honestly." It held too many memories of past holidays with Beau.

Melissa smoothed back her hair, a tell Isaac recognized. She was working up the nerve to ask him something a bit out there. In some ways, she was still the mischievous teenage girl he'd crushed on so hard. "Hey, since we're both lonely, do you want to come over?" She flushed. "And not in *that* way. I'm with someone now."

Isaac laughed. "Me, too. Sounds like a good time. Thanks, Mel."

She laughed with him, then beckoned him forward, a charmingly mischievous smile on her face. "Follow me."

Isaac didn't recognize her. She was still mourning, but there was an air about her that hadn't been there before. She seemed lighter. Freer. More open.

It was a bizarre turn of events, but fuck it. Isaac needed bizarre right now. Anything was better than being lost in a haze of grief. They got into her car and drove east from the church's cemetery. They didn't talk much at first. Isaac's head was still reeling from the fact that he was in a car with his ex-wife.

Melissa drove confidently beside him, bringing a memory to the surface of Isaac's mind. He laughed and she arched a blonde brow. "What?"

"Nothing. Just remembering the night after a certain someone got her license."

She smiled, though her cheeks reddened. "Our first date."

Isaac looked out of the window to hide his grin. "You were so excited to drive us to the movie theater."

"I remember."

He chuckled. "You were so smooth, pulling up with the windows down."

"So smooth," she agreed.

"I thought you were so cool. I hadn't gotten my license yet and you beat me to it. I climbed in, you drove, and you played that song we really liked. What was it?"

"Oh, I don't remember! We sang our lungs out, though. People were staring. We were so ridiculous."

Isaac grinned, remembering his favorite part. "Drive was smooth. No problems. We pull up to the theater and..."

Melissa hissed.

"You jumped the curb and plowed straight into a fire hydrant."

Melissa groaned. "Oh God. Mom was so pissed."

"I thought we were gonna die!" Issac guffawed.

She shooed him off. "We were fine!"

"You kept screaming, 'Mom's gonna kill me. Mom's gonna kill me!'" Isaac cackled when she slapped his arm.

"Honestly, I'm amazed you agreed to a second date."

"That wasn't even a first date, woman!"

She laughed and Isaac joined her. It felt... God. It felt amazing to laugh and smile, even if it was with his ex-wife. Or maybe because it was his ex. He'd never imagined in his wildest dreams they'd be on a good footing again. Why couldn't it have been like this when Beau was still alive?

At the same time, he couldn't regret too much. He would always regret that he hadn't been able to give his son parents who had a loving relationship, but if he and Mel had stayed married, Isaac wouldn't have found love with Ben.

Love.

Isaac's stomach fluttered. Fuck. It was too soon to be thinking that way. He didn't need to slap a label on what they had. Labels were overrated.

But what else could he call this wonderful feeling he'd found with Ben? He felt so good when he was with him. He smiled and laughed effortlessly after believing he'd never feel happy or normal again. Before they'd met, Isaac had been drowning, and Ben had helped him reach the shore.

Some days, Isaac still felt like he was drowning, but Ben was always there with an arm around him, keeping him afloat. Making him see the sunshine again at the end of the stormy seas he'd been lost in.

And there was sunshine. Some days it was bright, and other days it was only the faintest of glimmers. But Ben gave him the strength to persevere, to trust that he'd see the sunlight again. Like... What had Ben said? The clouds opening after a rainstorm or something like that.

"Penny for your thoughts?" Melissa asked, a curious smile on her face. "You've got one heck of a goofy smile on your face."

Isaac's face warmed. Hell. He was actually blushing. Over a guy. The normalcy of it shook him to his core.

"Isaac, what's going on? You're blushing."

He looked out of the window fast.

Damn it. Maybe he really was head over heels for Ben after all.

MELISSA'S HOME WAS QUIET and secluded. She had a big backyard surrounded by woodland, and the woods were so serene that Isaac could hear the way the wind whistled between the tree trunks. She opened the door and let them in out of the cold, then cranked up the thermostat. "I'll get a fire going too."

Isaac sighed. "That sounds amazing."

She opened a package of quick-burning logs in the living room. Isaac hung up his coat on the hanger by the door as Melissa reappeared, shaking her long blonde hair free of her hat.

"Get you anything to drink? I have tea, ginger ale, beer…"

Tea for me. I'm not drinking anymore." He hadn't had a drink since after he'd learned Ben was a werewolf. He'd realized that if Ben hadn't been there to lie on him the night Isaac first saw him as a wolf, Isaac would have likely drunk himself to death. So, he'd decided to quit cold turkey and hadn't regretted it.

She got some water boiling. "That's good. You were always a bit of a lush."

"Beau's death really tipped me over the edge," Isaac admitted, emotion clogging his throat.

Melissa sighed shakily. "I know. Do you want honey?"

"Sure, yeah." Isaac swallowed hard and fought away his grief. He looked around the kitchen to distract himself. There was a framed photo of Melissa and a hunky guy on the counter. "He's a looker. Anyone special?"

She laughed, her cheeks reddening. "Dave. We started dating just before Beau died. He's been my rock."

Isaac's heart warmed. He was glad for her.

They took their tea to the table.

A wolf howled somewhere far away. Melissa jumped with a gasp. Not long ago Isaac would have paled at the sound, but he knew better now. "It sounds friendly," he reasoned.

Melissa exhaled shakily and wiped her eyes. "I used to like wolves. I thought they were different, but in the same way we all are. But after what happened to Beau, I hated them. All of them. It consumed me. I hated werewolves. I hated the government for trying to force us to live together. I wanted to buy a rifle and go into the woods. Hunt them all down."

"I know," Isaac said through a throat full of gravel. His stomach clenched. He'd seen the feral fury of a man lost to his wolf. He'd seen the rage of a berserker beast when those he loved were threatened. He'd seen so much, enough to know that werewolves truly could be dangerous. But so could humans. "But they aren't all like that, Mel."

"Don't," Mel snapped. Her eyes blazed. "Don't you defend them. Don't you dare. If it weren't for them, our son would still be here."

"Yes, he would," Isaac said quickly. He didn't want a fight. Maybe once, he might have. Just so they could feel something for each other, even if it was spiteful anger. Sometimes, the worst feeling of all was the void where love had once been. Anger could numb that void, chase away the empty throbbing hurt like a drug. But hatred and anger couldn't heal it. "But a human could have taken him from us just as easily, Mel."

She blinked fast, her eyes bright and wet, but she couldn't argue with that. Her face crumpled and turned red, and Isaac took her hands in his and held tight as she warred with her grief.

"It isn't fair," she said. "That a monster went on living and our son didn't. It's wrong. Beau was good. He deserved to live."

Isaac's throat ached. He held on to her hands tightly and tried to breathe around the lump in his throat. His face was wet and every breath was like a dagger in his lungs.

She was right. It wasn't fair. Not a fucking bit. It was messed up and wrong.

"That monster isn't living. Not anymore." Through his grief, he found his voice. He wanted her to know. Wanted to give her any semblance of peace he could. "The monster who killed our son is dead, Mel." He blinked away the tears blurring his vision and held her gaze, needing her to know. "Do you remember Father Don? He officiated at Beau's funeral."

Her brow puckered and she shook her head. "I was... I was a mess during the service, Isaac. I don't remember a thing. What about him? What does he have to do with Beau?"

He exhaled, running his thumb over the back of her knuckles like he used to do when they were married. "Turns out, preaching and sermons is a side job for him. His true calling is werewolf hunting."

She scoffed.

"I'm serious."

"No, I can see that." She sipped her tea. "You were a lot of things, Isaac Bennet, but you were always straight with me. Well, until the whole bi thing." Isaac snorted into his tea, and she laughed with him. "Still, a father who's a werewolf hunter? That's... odd."

"Don and I became friends. I told him what happened to Beau, and he said he could help me get vengeance for our son." Isaac shivered, remembering that night so vividly. The confusion, the excitement, the fear, and then... the release, knowing he'd avenged his son. Although the gratification had only been brief, he would always be thankful to Don, even if his faith in the man was shaken. "He brought the beast to me and gave me a dagger. I killed him, Mel. He's gone, and he can never hurt anyone again."

Mel's chest rose and fell fast. Her eyes were wide but unreadable. Did she hate him for keeping this secret from her?

"Killing him didn't erase my grief," Isaac admitted. "But knowing I prevented more suffering, that I can still help keep innocent people safe from feral—from murderers like him." No, not ferals. At least, not all of them. Ben had shown him that they could still be saved. "It gave me purpose, but I wouldn't say it helped me heal."

Melissa gazed at their hands intertwined on the table. Her fingers were cold and a crease appeared between her brows. She was thinking, churning over his story.

"Don't believe me?" he asked. He didn't blame her. It was still a story he sometimes struggled to admit had truly happened.

"No, I—I do," she admitted, meeting his gaze with honesty. "But..."

It was Isaac's turn to frown. "But what?"

"You killed the wolf the day of the funeral?"

"Yes."

She shook her head in bewilderment. "But that doesn't make sense, Isaac, because the killings didn't stop after you killed that wolf."

Isaac's stomach churned. "There's been more killings?"

She nodded. "Another poor family had their daughter stolen from their own backyard."

God. It was too similar. Was it possible there had been more than one killer?

"When did this happen?" Don had brought that wolf to him the very night of the funeral.

She bit her lip. "A few weeks ago, maybe."

Isaac's head was spinning. "You're sure?" he said, pressing her further, and he squeezed her hands tighter than he'd meant to.

"That's what I said!" She yanked her hands away.

Isaac slumped in his seat, reeling.

No. No, this didn't make sense. "Some wolf is still out there murdering kids?"

"No, thank God. There was a big story just a few days ago. Some hikers found a cave in the woods full of... bodies. Human remains. The police hunted the monster down and killed him."

Isaac pushed himself out of his seat and paced. Don and Melissa had the same story. A wolf in White Plains that targeted children. Don had brought the murderer before Isaac. Isaac had driven a dagger into the wolf's throat. He'd watched life leave the creature's eyes. The murderer had died by his hands. And yet, the killing spree had never stopped.

No. No, Don wouldn't have lied to him. He'd had nothing to gain from manipulating Isaac like that. Isaac knew Don. He was a good man. He cared about helping others and about protecting humans. Another realization crashed over him, submerging him in dread. If Don had lied to him, then who had he *really* brought before Isaac that night? Who was the wolf who had been lying chained to that altar?

Who had Isaac killed?

Oh God.

Isaac lurched toward the door. "Can you drive me to the train station?"

"Are you feeling okay?"

"Just drop me off in town. I can take a train back home. You don't need to stick around."

She looked unsettled but nodded. "Yeah, of course."

MEL DROVE HIM TO the nearest train station like she'd promised. "Call me when you get back into the city, okay?"

"I will."

She gripped his arm. "Do I need to be worried?"

He shooed her away. "No. Go home, Mel. I'll call you when I'm home."

She shot him a look.

"Okay. Sooner."

She started the engine.

Isaac said, "You know, maybe the reason we didn't work is because you are way too much like my mom."

She barked a laugh. "Fuck you."

Isaac leaned on the car before she could drive off. "Thanks, Mel. I really needed this today."

She smiled, her eyes soft. "This was different."

"It was." He'd never imagined they'd be on amicable terms, but here they were. "We should have been better, for him."

She blinked fast. "I know."

Throat tight, Isaac pushed off from her car and let her drive away. Her headlights chased away the darkness until she rounded the bend and disappeared. Isaac was left alone on the side of the road, the lights of the houses twinkling in the woods around him.

Isaac rode the train home, but he was miles away from his body. Through the haze in his mind, one thing was clear: Don had deceived him. He'd taken Isaac's grief and sharpened it into a weapon, and it hadn't mattered who that weapon had been aimed at so long as they were a werewolf. Isaac didn't know who he'd really killed on that altar. But Don did, and Isaac was going to find out. Now. Tonight.

Isaac's phone rang and he answered the call without looking. "Hey. I just finished dinner!" The smile in Ben's voice soothed Isaac's fury.

"How was your flight?" he asked, his mouth unnaturally dry.

"I slept a lot. Pretty uninteresting."

Isaac's thoughts kept whirling. Don had lied. All this time. What else had he lied about to get Isaac to do what he wanted?

"Tell me about your family," Isaac insisted, closing his eyes tight before he spiraled. "What do you guys usually do for Thanksgiving?"

"Oh, my mom makes the best turkey. It's never dry. My dad doesn't cook, Ma won't let him, but he buys a pie from our favorite bakery down the street from our house." Ben sighed. "I wish you could be here."

Would Ben still speak to him with such tender fondness if he knew the horrible things Isaac wanted to do to Don? The fury he was struggling to rein in that, if unleashed, would make him even more of a monster?

"Isaac? You okay?"

He blinked hard. "Yeah. Just miss you. A lot."

"You too. I'm gonna tell my parents about you."

Isaac scoffed. "Ben, don't. They'll have a fit."

"I don't care what anyone thinks. Isaac..." Ben stopped, laughing almost nervously.

"What?" A smile tugged at Isaac's mouth.

"Nothing. I don't wanna tell you over the phone. Just... just want you to know that what we've got, it's not a passing thing. Not for me. So, that's what I'm gonna tell them, and if they don't like it, I don't care. Your opinion's the only one that matters to me."

"Are you sure?" Blood stained his hands. The wolf's green eyes dulled. It... *He'd* looked so young. "Even knowing the things I've done?"

"What are you talking about?" Worry filled Ben's voice.

"I just don't think you understand the gravity of the things I've done. Or what I can do. You know, sometimes I scare myself, Ben. It's like Beau's death awoke this side of me, this dark thing. Or maybe I just used his death as an excuse to be the person I always was."

"Listen to me." Ben's voice was low and commanding, grounding. "You're having a rough day. Just go easy on yourself. You're not a bad person, Isaac. You're a good man who's been dealt a shitty hand."

"I need to go, Ben."

A low sigh escaped him. "Don't make me jump on the first plane home, Isaac Bennet. I'll see you tomorrow, okay?"

Isaac missed him. "I'll see you tomorrow."

Ben added, "I'll be back later than I thought. My flight got cancelled, so I had to schedule a much later flight."

"Oh. That's too bad."

"Sucks. But I'll see you soon."

"I can't wait." He almost said "I love you," but held back. He didn't want to say it over the phone. "Sweet dreams, babe."

"Oh, they'll be sweet indeed. Good night, Isaac."

He hung up, taking in a deep breath. Outside the windows, the Manhattan skyline glowed in the night. Soon. He would have answers soon.

Chapter 15

MONSTER

It was after midnight when the Amtrak train pulled into Grand Central.

Isaac didn't ride the subway home. No, he rode the subway straight to the Cathedral of Saint John the Divine. His stomach churned the whole ride, and he had to remind himself to take deep breaths so he didn't hyperventilate. His heart rate sped out of control and his hands shook.

He exhaled and sucked in another long breath. He needed to talk to Don. He needed to know for sure. Forcing himself to breathe, Isaac departed the train at the Central Park North stop and walked up 110th Street past the dark and empty Morningside Park. The cathedral loomed, its spires reaching into the night sky. The rose windows glowed with light even at this late hour.

He pulled out his phone and shot Don a text.

Isaac: I need to speak with you. Are you awake?

He didn't expect Don to be up at this hour, but even if the father was asleep, Isaac knew where he lived. He'd pound on Don's door until he answered. His phone buzzed.

Don: I'm inside the hideout praying. I'm always happy to speak to you, Isaac.

His chest tightened with dread. He would have answers within minutes, and whatever Don revealed to him would change everything about himself, about Don and the Cross.

The path around the back of the cathedral was dark and secluded. Isaac headed to the mausoleum of the old hunters, turned his key in the lock, and stepped into the darkness. It gave way to light below the crypt, with torches flickering on the stone walls. Father Don knelt before the altar, his head bowed in prayer. Above the altar, a statue of Christ observed Don dispassionately.

"What's brought you to me, Isaac?" Don stood from his praying position.

Isaac's mouth was bone dry. His tongue felt fat and heavy. The dread swirled and churned in his stomach and he didn't know where to begin.

"Speak, my son." Don smiled warmly. "You can tell me anything."

He balled his hands into fists. Anger cut through him when he realized a part of him still loved this man, still thought of him as the savior who'd pulled him from the darkness and given him the strength to go on living.

"Isaac?" Don's brow furrowed. "What's the matter? Is everything all right?"

"No," Isaac said through gritted teeth. "No, Don. I don't think so." He couldn't look away from the blood on the altar. How many innocent werewolves had been murdered by monsters like Don and the Cross? Monsters like Isaac.

Don's mouth creased in worry. "Come and sit. Talk to me." He reached for Isaac's shoulder.

Bucking his shoulder, Isaac dislodged Don's hand as if his touch had scalded him. "Don't."

Don's eyes widened, and then something changed in them. He nodded slowly, then followed Isaac's stare to the altar. "I see. Your conscience is heavy."

Isaac tightened his jaw and didn't speak.

You. It's because of you, he wanted to scream.

"You feel for the beasts we have killed." There wasn't contempt in Don's voice, only understanding. "It is only human to feel this way, Isaac. This is nothing to be ashamed of. A werewolf cannot feel guilt, nor remorse. It is a sign from God that we are still human."

Isaac swallowed the anger that was like bile in his throat. "What about you, Father? Do you feel remorse?"

Don blinked at him slowly, pondering the question. With a sigh, he took a seat in one of the pews. Isaac remained where he was, frozen. "Perhaps I did, once," Don admitted. He gazed at the altar, shrouded in the shadow of Christ. "Perhaps. But I cannot remember. When you've been hunting as long as I have, you learn to compartmentalize your own feelings to get the job done. I could not do Christ's holy work if my mind was clouded by guilt. Perhaps that makes me a monster."

Isaac nodded. His hands and feet felt numb. "It isn't true, Fa—" He bit his tongue. "It isn't true. What you said. Werewolves do feel. They feel as strongly as any of us and sometimes, they aren't the monsters we should be afraid of."

Don turned to face him. The torchlight cast shadows across his face, darkening his eyes and hollowing his cheekbones. "It's true. There are demons in all of us, Isaac. They are there to test our faith, to lead us astray from God's intended path. Sometimes they win." He curled his fingers over his wrist, touching something hidden beneath the sleeve of his robe.

Jaw tight, he stood, his shoes squeaking over the marble floor until he stood before Isaac. "But we can always fight them. We can always return to God's love. He will forgive us our sins when we cannot forgive ourselves." He reached out and grasped Isaac's shoulders. "These are demons of doubt, Isaac. They want to lead you astray. Do not let them. I am here, and I will help bring you back into God's light."

Isaac laughed and the sound echoed throughout the chamber. "The only one who led me astray was you, Don." He stepped out of his reach, unable to bear the touch of those big, warm hands that had once felt so comforting, had once been an anchor in the storm.

Something changed in Don's face. His warm smile turned hard, his lips thinning. "Isaac, you are not yourself."

Anger curled Isaac's fists. "I'm more myself than I've been since you groomed me."

"*Groomed* you?" Don recoiled from Isaac's accusation. "I gave you everything you needed to avenge the death of your son." Don wasn't angry. Instead he sounded like Isaac had cut into him. The guilt lashed Isaac and he had to look away from Don's wounded eyes.

"Isaac, look at me."

He closed his eyes tight.

"Look at me, my son."

Isaac did, and Don's wounded face stole the anger he desperately needed.

"This is not who you are. You are a righteous warrior of God. You are my brother. My friend. My son. I love you, Isaac, like the son I had and lost."

Isaac took in a breath. "The son you killed?"

The blood drained from Donovan Steele's face. His hands dropped to his sides and he took one step back.

Isaac's body trembled. He'd gotten him.

Don opened his mouth, then shut it, his jaw working as he struggled for words. "How could you have…"

"Because I know you, Don. I know for a fact you would have killed your son yourself before you let him choose a filthy werewolf for his mate."

Don had told him his life story long ago. According to him, a massacre had taken place in his home. His nineteen-year-old son, his wife—they'd been murdered by a werewolf pack. Don claimed he had come home from work and found them dead. The son had had a mating mark on his neck, had been "violated," Don had said. In retaliation, Don had hunted down the wolf pack and killed them.

Except Ben had told him mating marks had to be consensual or else they'd fade.

Isaac wanted to give Don the benefit of the doubt, but he couldn't. Only this morning he'd believed Don's crocodile tears and had tried to justify his bloodlust. He'd made excuse after excuse for him, and all Don had given him was lies. He was done defending this man, this monster.

"Your son took a werewolf's bite, didn't he?"

"It was forced upon him!"

"No, Don. He took that girl's bite willingly because he loved her and she loved him. Otherwise you wouldn't have seen the mark. You couldn't stand that he'd dirtied himself, defiled his body from God's intended image. Isn't that right?"

Don covered his mouth with a trembling hand, his fingernails digging into his skin. His eyes blazed.

"You hated the girl who turned your son, so you hunted her down like an animal."

Don's eyes widened, crazed with fury.

"But your wife? What did she do? Defend your son's choices like a good mother should? Or maybe she was an accident, Don, I'll give you that. You've got a hot temper. I've seen it. You got into a fight with your son when you found out he'd let some dirty wolf bite him." Isaac's voice grew louder as his fury reached the breaking point. "You lost control like the beasts you claim you hate so much. You lost your head and shot them down! Didn't you?"

Don lunged, fisting Isaac's shirt and yanking him in close. His teeth were bared and he panted, his body shaking with fury. "What would you have done? Huh? I raised my son in God's image. I loved him as God loved his own son! And he chose lust and sin. He chose the path of the Devil!"

After how callously he'd killed Gina, Isaac shouldn't have been stunned by Don's unapologetic admission of his own guilt, but he was. What had he ever seen in this man? Isaac shoved Don, but Don's grip on him was strong. Something was cutting into Isaac's chest. Don's nails were sharp. "You don't know the first thing about love!"

Don stumbled back, panting. His eyes were blazing so bright, they appeared to glow.

"You've hurt people, Don. Good people. Gina, she was good. Those ferals you've had us kill who you claimed couldn't be saved only needed help! How many innocent people have we murdered, all so you can play God?"

Don barked out a laugh, his teeth glistening. "Oh, the ferals. You and the ferals. I know they can be cured, Isaac. I'm not stupid. I simply don't give a damn."

So that whole conversation in the car had been an act, a ploy to try to earn back the good faith Don had lost. Isaac shouldn't have been surprised, yet there was bile in his throat.

"Feral or not, it doesn't matter. There are no good werewolves! Haven't you learned anything? It's a travesty, my son, to see how low you have fallen. You truly have lost your way."

"I want you to tell me who I really killed that night, Don. Because I know it wasn't the wolf who killed my son."

Don's eyes widened, and then a smile curled his lips. "Of course. I suppose I should have guessed. What's done in the dark is always brought into the light. How did you guess?"

Isaac had known Don had deceived him, but to hear Don acknowledge his deception without so much as a shred of guilt made his blood boil. "Because the real murderer was still killing people! All this time, he was still hunting children for sport. And you didn't even care, did you? Not so long as you got me to do what you wanted!"

Don chuckled. "Yet you're convinced they aren't all bad. Do you hear yourself? You've just admitted that werewolves kill for the pleasure of it."

"So do you, Don." Isaac approached, backing Don up against the altar. "Tell me the truth. Who did I kill that night?"

Don sneered. "What does it matter? Your conscience will never be clean. What's done is done."

Isaac lunged, slamming Don down onto the altar, his elbow digging into Don's throat. "Tell me!"

The father laughed. His laughter became a howl that filled every corner of the room. Isaac wanted to choke the life from him. Don grinned up at him and his canine teeth were sharp. Almost like a...

"A wolf," Isaac rasped. "You... When..." He thought he knew. Don must have been bitten during Morgan's rampage in the cathedral. Which meant Don had been the one to let him out. The son of a bitch. Don's eyes flashed and he touched the sleeve of his robe. Isaac yanked it down. A scarred bite mark marred his skin. "Did you let him bite you?"

"Sometimes we must make compromises. I was weak, tempted by his power. The wolf and his people have no love for humans, but they still kill sinners who crossbreed with wolves. The human deaths on the cult's conscience are a necessary price to pay for the eradication of wolves."

Isaac felt sick. "You have lost it, Don. God damn it, you've fucking lost it! Tell me who—"

"I don't know," Don said, and smiled as if all were right and well in the world. "Truly, Isaac. I do not know who that beast was that I brought before you."

Isaac's hands shook and he took a stumbling step back. Don pushed himself up and sat upon the blood-stained altar.

"He could have been anyone," Don admitted, shrugging his shoulders. "A murderer. A rapist. A nobody. Someone's cousin, or brother—a son."

Isaac collapsed into a pew. The world was spinning around him.

Don stood and paced, the candelabras on either side of the altar casting his shadow across the marble tile. "I gave you the tools you needed to avenge your son's murder. Your son wasn't killed by just one werewolf. Don't you see that? They are, all of them, responsible for your son's death. It isn't enough to kill one wolf. You must kill them all if we are to save our species."

"You..." Isaac struggled to find his voice. "You used me. You turned me into a monster."

Don looked at him, a sneer twisting his mouth. "I put a weapon in your hand and gave you a choice. You are an adult, Isaac, and no one can force you to do something you do not want to do."

"How many?" Isaac rasped. "How many of them were innocent? How many innocent people did I kill because I believed you, trusted you?" His face was wet. His whole body was shaking.

"You aren't listening!" Don roared, his voice echoing. "We'll never know, and it doesn't matter." Don opened his arms wide, laughter shaking him. "*It doesn't matter.* Don't you see? None of the beasts are ever innocent! From the moment they take the bite, or are born into this world, they cease to be one of us! But I... I will use this curse as my blessing. I shall become a beast to hunt the beasts. It is what God has intended!"

"You're fucking crazy," Isaac whispered. The kindly mask Don wore had fallen off and now Isaac could see that the man he'd thought had been his friend and father had never existed at all.

Don stood, dusting off his robes. "Who are you to judge me? I could smell that wolf Stroud all over you this morning!"

Isaac's breath hitched. "Don't you say his name."

Don's mouth curled into a grin. "It all makes sense now! Why you turned away from me. Why you sided with Gina and her dog. He got inside your head and turned you against me, filled your mind with sob stories about innocent wolves. What nonsense!"

"Shut up," Isaac growled.

"Maybe I'll pay your wolf a visit." Don licked his lips, his fangs sharp in his mouth. "The full moon is rising tonight. It will be my first transformation. I've been in talks with my hunters and many of them want the beast blood for themselves too. You would have been the first one I offered my bite to."

He shrugged. "Oh well. Tonight, we will ascend. We will be stronger. We will come for you and your wolf, Isaac. Unless, of course, you'd like to join us?" He grinned. "There's still a chance, Isaac. Meet us tonight. Accept the bite. Become the warrior God wants you to be. Or I will make you watch as your filthy pet dies by my hand."

Isaac hated this man. This monster. He hated Donovan Steele, but he hated himself more. He lurched to his feet and turned his back on Don.

"Isaac, my son, come here."

"No."

"Look at me."

"No!" His voice echoed through the chamber.

"This is not who you are. I know you. You have been led astray."

Isaac ripped the silver cross from his neck and hurled it at Don's feet.

The father's eyes narrowed. "Think very carefully, *boy*."

"I am," Isaac said, seething. "I'm thinking more clearly than I have since I joined your fucking cult."

"You do not want us as your enemies."

Oh, but Isaac did. But not yet. It wasn't enough to kill only Don. He took a step back toward the door. "You turned me into a weapon, Don. I sure as hell hope you're ready to deal with the consequences."

Then he turned and walked out.

ISAAC RETURNED TO HIS apartment and ran around like a madman, gathering what he needed. He ripped up the floorboard under his bed and filled enough empty grenade canisters with silver to put down a whole pack of werewolves. The shrapnel would shred them to pieces. He threw some bandages and first aid supplies in his duffel bag in case he somehow survived the encounter and needed healing. He loaded his gun with silver bullets and crammed it in there too.

Isaac spent the rest of the day in his apartment making preparations. In two hours, the moon would rise. The cathedral would close its doors to visitors. The Cross would gather and Don would turn them all into bloodthirsty mockeries of wolves. They would come for Isaac. They would target the agency wolves and Ben. They had outnumbered the agency before, and they could destroy Ben and his wolves easily. Ben's flight had been canceled, so he was still out of state, but he would return soon. Don would target Ben, would kill him, all because of Isaac.

Unless Isaac made himself the target of the pack's rage.

He ran through a mental checklist and thought he had everything he needed. Then he sat on his bed and closed his eyes tight. There was a high chance he wasn't going to walk out of the cathedral. He could be dead two hours from now. Not long ago, such a thought wouldn't have given him pause. After losing his son, Isaac had craved nothing more than to join him in death. Don and his hunters had given Isaac a purpose for a time. Hatred had kept him going.

But now he was hesitating. A part of him wanted to live, and it was because of Benjamin Stroud. He wanted a future with Ben, when once, he hadn't wanted anything at all. If he died tonight, he would be leaving Ben alone to mourn him. After everything Ben had done for him, didn't he deserve better than that? Isaac gritted his teeth, trying to find the resolve to leave his room and face the hunters. Isaac couldn't let Ben be hurt or worse. He owed it to Ben to stop the hunters from hurting the agency wolves and destroying his life's work.

But before he met his death, he had to speak to Ben. There was so much he had to tell him. He had to say goodbye. That was the least Isaac could give him. Ben deserved so much more, but Isaac could never look him in the eyes again without despising himself for what he'd done.

With trembling hands, he dialed Ben's number and waited.

"Isaac?" Ben's groggy voice made Isaac's heart flutter. "Hey. About to start boarding."

He wet his lips and tried to speak, but he couldn't find the words. "Ben. Hi."

"Guess what?" Ben's voice came alive with excitement. "I told my parents about you."

Isaac closed his eyes tight as they stung with tears. He hated that he was going to hurt Ben.

"They're thrilled! They can't wait to meet you. Isaac?"

He sucked in a breath and smiled. It was easy to smile, even in the depths of his pain and guilt. "That's great, babe."

"I know humans move slowly, so you don't have to meet them until you're ready, okay?"

Isaac wiped his eyes even though his heart was cracking in his chest. "No, I'd love to meet them."

"You sure? I didn't freak you out?"

Isaac chuckled. "Yeah, no, I'm fine. Everything's fine. More than fine. I've been feeling great since I met you."

"Me too." There was a smile in Ben's voice.

Isaac looked out the window where the moon was beginning to rise. Their time was almost up. "For a while, Ben, I was lost in the dark. But you brought me back. You made me want to live again. You got me dreaming of a future when I hadn't thought I had anything left to live for."

Ben was quiet, his breath soft on the other end of the line.

Isaac closed his eyes tight and pressed the phone close to his ear, wishing he'd been better for Ben, been the man he deserved.

"I love you, Ben."

Ben's breath hitched. It was such a devastating sound.

"I love you so much." This wasn't fair. It wasn't right. He should have told Ben in person.

"Isaac…" Ben's voice shook. He sounded moved. Overjoyed. Scared.

Isaac swallowed hard around the lump in his throat. He hoped he made it out of that cathedral alive so he could see Ben again, even if Isaac was no good for him. If he didn't, he prayed Ben would be able to move on and forget about him.

"Goodbye, Ben," Isaac said, his voice all but gone.

"Isaac," Ben said, and Isaac's heart seized. He'd never heard Ben plead before. "Isaac, don't hang up. Whatever's going on, we can work through it. I'll come home. I'll be there as soon as I can. We can talk about this, okay? Don't. Please, don't."

Isaac closed his eyes tight against the pain. "I'm sorry." With a touch, he ended the call and Ben's voice cut out. He squeezed the power button until the phone shut off, then slumped over and held his head in his hands. He didn't let himself break apart, didn't allow himself to wallow. He'd made this choice that hurt them both. Drying his eyes, he found his feet and left his apartment for what could be the last time.

Downstairs, he hurled his bag into the trunk, got into the car, and started the engine. With the moon climbing into the sky, Isaac drove for the Cathedral of Saint John the Divine.

Chapter 16

A Pheonix from the Ashes

Ben's plane touched down in New York City a few hours after midnight. Isaac wouldn't answer his phone, and the fear made Ben nauseous. He'd prayed the whole flight for the goddess to keep his mate safe, but he didn't know if she'd heard.

Ben lurched into a cab, ignoring the woman who squawked at him for stealing it from her. The ride seemed to take centuries. Ben had one hand on his phone most of the ride and in his haste, he almost forgot to grab his luggage when they stopped outside the apartment building. He ran up the stairs, panting as he stopped outside Isaac's door. He knocked and waited. "Isaac? It's Ben." No one answered.

Wrestling back the wolfish urge to claw at the door until it crashed open, Ben knocked again. When no one answered, his fear surged. Where was Isaac? What could have happened to him? Ben's phone battery was running low, so he reluctantly went into his own apartment. Once his phone was charging, he used his home phone to call the bar where Isaac worked just in case someone there could give him information.

No one picked up the phone at the bar either, but Ben knew they stayed open extremely late. Ready to throw his phone out of the window, Ben left his bags in the doorway and jogged to the bar. The bar was empty except for the staff preparing to close. Ben didn't recognize the bartender yawning behind the bar but asked anyway. "Is Isaac in?"

Polishing a glass, the bartender barely spared him a glance. "If he was, I sure as hell wouldn't be here."

Ben grasped the bar, his claws leaving indentations in the wood. "What's that mean? He never came in?"

"Nope. Why, he a friend of yours?"

Ben swallowed with difficulty. His knees felt weak, his stomach queasy.

"Shit, man." The bartender looked at the TV above the bar. "They still haven't put out those fires yet?"

On the screen above, a cathedral was on fire. Ben thought it was a movie for a moment. There were crowds of firefighters armed with hoses, and the street to the cathedral was barred. Before his eyes, a spire crumbled, crashing into a sea of dust and smoke and flames. It looked familiar, Ben realized with a sinking feeling in his gut. Because it was.

It was the Cathedral of Saint John the Divine.

The floor disappeared beneath his feet. Isaac must have been there when the fire started. He wasn't answering his phone because he must have been inside the cathedral when—

His stomach lurched, and Ben was almost sick in the middle of the bar.

No. Isaac wasn't dead. He couldn't be dead. Ben would drag him from the rubble himself, comb every inch of debris until he'd found his mate and brought him home safely. The door slammed behind him and Ben slipped on the slushy pavement as he ran for his truck.

His mind was in turmoil. Only a few hours ago, he'd been planning their future. He couldn't be without Isaac. He didn't want to be parted from him. He wanted to wake up to him, eat meals with him, see the world with him at his side—he wanted to spend the rest of his life with Isaac Bennet.

He slammed his foot down on the gas pedal and drove faster than he should.

Please. Don't take him from me. Don't you do it.

The cathedral was barricaded off, the streets choked with fire engines and police cars. The ash was so thick in the air it coated the back of his throat, and smoke stung his eyes. Sirens howled as an ambulance barreled into the street, and paramedics rushed past the barricades.

Ben followed them, clutching the barricade and struggling to see through the smoke. "Was anyone inside?" Ben asked a passing firefighter.

He shook his head. "We aren't sure yet. There's too much debris we need to clear."

Beyond the barricade, a lone figure stumbled through the rubble then stopped, covered in so much ash and soot he was unrecognizable. The figure turned toward him. His face was smudged with ash, but there was no mistaking those gray-blue eyes. Jumping the barricade, Ben ran. His arms flew around Isaac's shoulders and Ben crushed him to his chest. Isaac trembled in his arms, his shoulders heaving. Ben kissed his hair, tasting ash. He smelled like burnt metal and soot, but Ben breathed him in with every lungful.

"Ben... Oh my God. What are you doing here?" Isaac coughed into Ben's chest.

He cupped the back of Isaac's head, tangling his fingers in the soft hair. "Was gonna throw myself into the fire itself if it meant I could find you. If anything'd happened to you..." Unable to believe that he was here, alive in his arms, Ben took Isaac's face in his hands, wiping away ash. He gulped for air, unable to look away from his eyes.

"I love you, Isaac."

A breathtaking smile broke across Isaac's face.

Ben covered his mouth with his, then crumpled into his shoulder. "I love you so much."

Trembling lips claimed his, and they held each other tight.

Later they lay close beneath the sheets, Isaac's head nestled into the crook of Ben's neck and Ben's thigh draped over Isaac's leg.

"Can you tell me what happened?" Ben's lips brushed Isaac's forehead. "What started the fire? Were the hunters all killed?"

Isaac's face was totally blank except for his eyes. They were dark and hard with cold fury. He bunched into himself, breathing long and deep into Ben's shoulder. "I did."

At first Ben didn't understand. "You... you started that fire at the cathedral?"

Isaac exhaled shakily and nodded. "Silver grenades. It was the only way I could stop them for good."

Ben struggled for words, his hand moving up and down Isaac's back. He couldn't understand. "Why would you have charged in by yourself?" He pulled back to look Isaac in the eye. He lay so close his breath warmed Ben's lips, but he felt a thousand miles away, a stranger in Ben's arms. "Isaac." Ben gripped his arms and urged him to sit up. "You could have died today. Did you think about that?" Anger overcame his numb shock. "Huh? Did you think about what your death would have done to me?"

It was impossible to tell if his words had reached Isaac. He seemed utterly impassive.

"Answer me, Isaac! Why didn't you tell me what you were planning?" Isaac's selfish impulsiveness cut Ben deeply and left him shaking with fear and anger.

Isaac sighed, nodding to himself. He blinked, glimmers of regret breaking through the layer of ice in his eyes. "I had to act, Ben. The timing was too good. The cathedral would be closed. There'd be no innocent casualties."

"Why?" Ben gripped Isaac's hands. "What happened while I was gone?"

"I..." Isaac opened his mouth, but no words came out. It was like he shut down.

Ben kicked off the blankets and paced, his stomach churning. "Fucking hell..." He couldn't fathom what had happened in the short time he'd been away. Isaac had seemed fine. Depressed, but not suicidally insane! "Was it worth it, Isaac?"

Isaac's eyes glazed over and he bowed his head. "No, not quite. Don got away, and so did the bulk of his hunters." An actual emotion broke through the monotony of Isaac's voice. Fury. "If he figures out I'm alive, he'll come after me, Ben. He'll come after you. He's got nothing to lose now. Your agency won't stand a chance against his pack."

That was true, even if Ben hated to admit it. The Cross had hunters all over New York State, and the agency couldn't afford to go to war when they were still so new. He could always ask his parents to send wolves to New York, but could they afford to with humans lurking at the town's borders? "Well, maybe you should have thought about that before you blew up his base of operations!" Isaac wouldn't even tell him why he'd done such a thing. "Was it about Gina? Or did something else happen?"

Isaac still didn't speak.

Desperation possessed Ben. He threw himself on the bed and grabbed Isaac's shoulders. "Listen to me. You're free, don't you get it?" Ben cupped his mate's face, but it was hard as granite to the touch. "We can be together. We don't have to hide anymore. Understand me? And you... you will never do what you did today again."

"No more blowing up buildings?"

"No more. No more secrets, no more suicide missions. Just us."

Isaac's mouth trembled and he moved away from Ben's touch. "I don't know if I can be with you, Ben."

A block of ice sank into Ben's stomach. "What are you talking about? You just blew up a cathedral full of asshole hunters and I still love you. I don't know what you could do that's crazier than that." Ben's heart thundered. He didn't know what to say to make it better, to make Isaac understand how much he loved him. "Try me, Isaac." He clasped Isaac's cold hands together and squeezed tight, trying to rub some warmth into them. "Tell me. You were saying stuff like this on Thanksgiving. What's going on?"

Isaac shook his head, blinking stubbornly. "I'm sorry, Ben. I wish I'd been better for you. Deserving of you."

Ben's heart raced because it sounded like Isaac was saying goodbye. Shaking, Ben took Isaac's face in his hands again and looked him in the eye. "You listen to me, Isaac Bennet. You are the best thing to ever happen to me. I don't care if it's too soon. I know how I feel. I—"

Fumbling in his jeans, he retrieved the velvet box and opened it. Isaac's eyes went wide, and a quiet gasp spilled from his lips. "I want us to be together. As mates, as husbands, whatever you want. Mated couples aren't protected in the same way married ones are, but if we find an open-minded lawyer, they could draw up some documents for us."

Ben's stomach tied itself into knots as Isaac gazed at the rings with a growing smile on his face. Ben wet his lips, too nervous to shut up. "Until then, we can wear these rings. Everyone will know we're together but that's not what really matters to me. Just that you're mine, and I'm yours."

Isaac's smiling mouth covered his and his arms tightened around Ben's shoulders. "I love you. So much." But when he pulled away, there was a deep sadness in his eyes. "I want that, Ben. I want you." And yet, Ben sensed a "but" in there somewhere.

"So, what's wrong?"

"I can't think about a future right now. As long as Don is out there, I can't think about anything, not when he could show up and take it all away from us."

Ben felt like he'd been hit in the stomach. "Yeah, I... That makes sense, I guess." He could understand his uncertainty, but it hurt. "It's been a long day. You've been through a hell of a lot." He dropped the box onto the nightstand. "I didn't mean... you don't have to give me an answer. Maybe I shouldn't have... I just wanted you to know how I feel about you." He felt foolish. "Sorry, this was dumb of me. Let's just get some sleep."

Without waiting for a reply, Ben rolled onto his side away from Isaac. His chest ached. Isaac hadn't said no. He wanted the same things Ben did, but he had a lot on his mind. Ben regretted pushing thoughts of their future on him.

Strong arms went around him, and Isaac's warm body cuddled close to his back. "You're not stupid for dreaming of a future for us, Ben. I'm the one who can't give you everything you deserve."

Ben looked over his shoulder into remorseful eyes as gloomy as an overcast sky. "You are everything I need."

Isaac's lips touched the back of his neck and Ben rolled over to kiss him, long and slow.

"I'll wait for you," Ben said, one thumb running over Isaac's lower lip. "No matter how long it takes, I'll wait until you're ready."

Isaac's mouth trembled, and he put his arms around Ben and held him until they were both fast asleep.

ISAAC COUNTED THE MINUTES, aware of every fleeing second. Ben's chest rose and fell, his chin tucked gently on Isaac's head. The clock behind him ticked ever closer to dawn. He had to let go. The pain made him close his eyes tight.

God. He didn't want to do this. All he wanted was to stay in this room, locked in Ben's arms for the rest of his life. He wanted that future they'd talked about, a future where nothing and no one could come between them, full of happiness and love.

But he'd relinquished the right to happiness when he'd driven that silver dagger through a young wolf's throat, and killed dozens of ferals who'd deserved nothing but compassion. He'd let Don turn him into a monster, and Isaac had to make it right. As long as Don drew breath, he would never let Isaac go. He knew this because he'd seen the lengths Don had gone to when he'd been betrayed. He would target Isaac. He would target Ben.

He'd done what he had to do and made himself the target of Don and his pack. It was time to leave, to lure them as far away from New York City as possible.

Far away from Ben. He had to give Ben the chance to heal, move on, and find the happiness he deserved.

Even if it wasn't with him.

Throat tight, Isaac untangled himself from the warmth of Ben's arms. He threw some clothes into the duffel bag with his crossbow and silver bullets. Unable to leave without saying goodbye, he found some paper and a pen and sat down at the desk to write. By the time he finished, his tears had dampened the paper, and his hand wouldn't stop shaking.

Wiping his eyes, he folded the note with Ben's name on it and left it on the bedside table next to the rings. He stopped before he could walk away, unable to turn his back on Ben, asleep in bed. The floorboards squeaked as he knelt, his chin resting on the mattress. He knelt there and watched Ben sleep, unable to tear himself away. He blinked hard as his vision blurred, and he swallowed through a throat thick with grief.

"You saved my life, Ben Stroud." He slipped his fingers into Ben's and squeezed, then brought Ben's fingers to his lips and held them there. Their love had raised him like a phoenix from the ashes. "Thank you."

He slipped Ben's ring onto his finger and was gone.

CHAPTER 17

SHE WAS ENOUGH

"MER! LOOK! HE'S COMING back to us."

"Oh, Ben!"

Ben's eyes opened to the sterile walls of an exam room. The breath caught in his throat, and he surged upright. His parents were here. Wherever here was. It was familiar but fog shrouded Ben's mind.

"Where am I?" A wolf's growl made his voice rough. "What am I doing here?"

"Easy, hon." His mom draped a blanket over him as he shivered from the shock. Somehow he was naked, and fur was thick on his body. Had he shifted? Why couldn't he remember?

He grabbed a fold of skin on his arm and pinched, hard. This couldn't be a dream. In the haze of fear and confusion, a name surfaced in his memory. Isaac. *Isaac!* A stab of pain arched into his ribs and he doubled over as a sudden wave of anguish crashed over him. It all came flooding back to him.

"Ben? Hon, what's wrong?" His mom rubbed his shoulders, but all Ben could do was curl in on himself and whimper like a wounded animal.

"I'm sorry."

The note Isaac had left on their dresser came back to haunt him.

"I love you, Ben, but I can't stay here. Don and his hunters must be stopped. Please don't try and look for me. I've got to lead them away so they can't hurt you or any other wolf.

I need you to know that I'll love you for as long as there is air in my lungs and my heart still beats. One day, the hunters will be gone, and I will be free. I never believed in fate until I met you, but I believe in us. We're meant to be, and we will see each other again. Goodbye, Ben.

Isaac"

Isaac was gone.

Ben had waited and waited. Contacted the police and filed a missing persons report, reached out to the guys at the bar where Isaac worked. No one had seen him. No one could find him. The days had turned to weeks and Isaac wouldn't pick up his phone. He'd refused to get in touch with Ben.

Where had he gone? Was he even alive?

For a time, Ben had felt a flicker of their bond. Every day, Isaac had felt farther away. Then one day the bond had disappeared, and something inside Ben had broken.

"I went feral. Didn't I?" he whispered.

His father squeezed his shoulder. "Greg hadn't heard from you, so he checked in. Found you lying in your bedroom as a wolf. He... he said you were almost catatonic. Never seen you so sad. He called us right away and got you to the agency."

"What happened, Ben?" his mother asked, stroking his back.

He took a gulp of water from the bottle his father offered but his throat was still bone dry. "I can't remember."

His father nodded. "I understand that. It will fade. It's normal after you go feral to be a bit out of sorts."

His mom tried again. "What happened? Something drove you to lose your humanity. Can you tell us what it is? Were you hurt?"

Ben couldn't speak. He couldn't breathe through the swelling lump in his throat. Yes. Yes, goddess, he'd been hurt. So hurt. Closing his eyes tight, he struggled for control. He had to get out. "Can you... open a window? Can't breathe."

"Sure, hon." His mother threw open the window and the cold scent of rain filled the room.

A stab of pain went right into his heart. The scent reminded him of Isaac. Rain-washed pavement. Lips trembling, he stood and leaned on the windowsill. Rain spattered his arms and dampened his skin. His face was wet, but Ben couldn't tell if it was rain or if he was crying. He sure felt close.

Where did you go? Why would you leave me?

"Ben?" He couldn't look at his father. He'd never felt so bare, cut open for all the world to see.

"He left." His voice came out choked and weak. "Isaac. My mate. The one I told you about after Thanksgiving. He left me. That's why I…"

His father sighed. "Shit…"

Ben laughed, or he tried to. "Serves me right, doesn't it?"

"No."

He scrubbed a fist across his eyes. "I should have listened to you. You were right. All they do is hurt."

Big arms went around his shoulders and Ben stumbled into his father's embrace. "I'm sorry, kid."

He laid his head on his father's shoulder but he couldn't cry. He wanted to, but the tears wouldn't come. He was angry. Angry at himself for giving his heart to a human, angry at Isaac for leaving him alone to wait for him.

"I can't go back home," Ben confessed.

"No, you shouldn't have to," his mother said. "How about you come stay with me for a while, back with the pack?"

"No. The agency—"

"I will handle the agency here," his father said. "Go back home, Ben. It'll be good for you."

Ben wanted to get out of this city where everywhere he looked, he saw somewhere he and Isaac had visited: a restaurant they'd frequented and stuffed themselves full to bursting, a movie theater where they'd made out in the back row, the parks they'd walked through on cold winter days. This city was nothing but a cage full of memories, a constant reminder of what he'd had and lost.

So Ben spent the next week at the agency prepping his father to take over in his absence. He only left the estate grounds the day before his flight to pack. He sighed as he pulled up outside his apartment. Like ripping off a Band-Aid. In and out. He wouldn't look at anything, just throw his shit in a bag and haul ass.

Someone knocked on his car window. A tall bald man was waving at him. If not for the dimples in his smile and that freckle next to his mouth, Ben wouldn't have recognized him. "Greg!" He hadn't seen him in the weeks since Isaac had been gone. Leaping out of the car, Ben wrestled Greg into his arms. "Hope they donated all that nice hair to someone." He rubbed Greg's shiny, bare scalp. "What are you doing back in the city?"

Greg shrugged, offering a sympathetic smile. "Came back when I couldn't get a hold of you. I know, I know, I wasn't supposed to be using tech at the monastery but turns out I was right to check in. How are you feeling?"

Ben just shrugged. "I'm hanging in there."

Greg scuffed his boot on the ground. "Your father told me. About he-who-shall-not-be-named. I'm real sorry, Ben."

Ben looked away, unsure of what to say.

"I really did think you two were—well, screw him. Come on, I'll help you pack."

Ben hadn't been back at the apartment in a while. He'd clearly done damage as a wolf, scratching up the walls and clawing at the door. Humming, Greg went into the bedroom. A picture had fallen off a bookshelf in the living room. Ben picked it up, and his heart stopped.

The sight of Isaac's face sapped the air from his lungs. Gerard had taken the picture at the bar just a few days before Thanksgiving. Isaac was laughing at something, and Ben was smiling wide at whatever Isaac had said. He couldn't remember what they'd been talking about, what had made him laugh so hard in the photo.

Neither of them were looking at the camera head-on or were faking cheesy grins. It was a moment between them, captured forever in time. A moment when Ben had been happier than he'd ever been, happier than he'd ever be again. He removed the photo from the frame, folding it and tucking it into his pocket.

"Hey, Ben, where you keep your suitcases?"

He froze, reluctant to enter the bedroom. Squaring his shoulders, he marched inside, going straight to the closet. He didn't look at the nightstand where he knew his ring was. Just his. Isaac had taken his ring when he'd left.

Ben threw his clothes into the bag and Greg helped him carry the other bag downstairs. "I'll drive," Greg said.

Ben's feet wouldn't move. "Hang on." He returned upstairs and opened the little velvet box. He traced the cool gold band. Was Isaac wearing his right now wherever he was? The thought brought a lump to his throat, but it also gave him hope. Hope that someday, they might see each other again and fulfill their promises to one another. He slipped the ring on and left the apartment.

NOT MUCH HAD CHANGED during his time away. The little stretch of town was as unchanged as ever, alive with the distinct howling of wolves in the twilight. The town had been lit up for Christmas, which was only a week away, and there was a huge Christmas tree in the main square.

She was waiting for him on the porch like she used to. Heather. The sunset turned her blonde curls golden, and she smiled at the sight of him. "Hey, Ben. I missed you."

As Ben took her in his arms, he found he'd missed her too.

His mother had cooked them her signature BBQ ribs. Smacking her lips, Heather said, "Tell me all about New York."

Ben's chest tightened. So much of New York was wrapped up with Isaac. Trying to talk about New York without mentioning him was like trying to untangle threads of yarn. So, he didn't try. He told her about the bustling city streets, the flashing lights of Times Square, and told her about the lost hunter with rain clouds in his eyes who still held all of his heart.

He'd missed talking to her. It wasn't at all as awkward as he'd thought it might be, considering how they'd parted. Before he knew it, the New Year had arrived and they were as close as they'd been before he'd left.

"I want to move to New York."

Ben chuckled and forked some of the Moonbeam Diner's famous meat loaf into his mouth. How he'd missed this diner. "You wouldn't last a day."

"I would too! I want to get a real job, meet a guy, start a family... I want all of it. I don't want to spend my life cooped up in this town. I want adventure."

Ben admired her bravery. "Okay. What sorta work do you want? Law, social work? The agency is hiring."

She snagged a spoonful of his mashed potatoes. "I want to work in a big firm, represent shifter clients who need help."

Ben smiled. She reminded him of Manuel, he thought with an ache. He'd spoken to him on the phone recently. Gabe's team had won his school's soccer game and Manuel had texted Ben pictures of Izzie's adorable arts and crafts projects. Veronica wanted another baby but Manuel was insistent they stop at two kids. He missed seeing the Reyes pack in person.

"I've been submitting applications to firms all over New York City. I finally landed an interview this week. Want to come with me?"

The thought of returning to New York wasn't as daunting as before, but the thought of Isaac was like a shard of glass in his heart every time. He couldn't stay away forever; his father would want to return to Ohio. But when Ben got on the plane back to the city, he wasn't sure if he would be flying back to Ohio soon or not.

The sight of New York flooded him with a lot of different feelings. A part of him was glad to see the familiar skyscrapers and to walk along the bustling city streets. He found himself holding his breath in anticipation that any second he might round a corner and see Isaac.

"Earth to Ben? Isn't this your building?" Heather motioned at his building's front door.

Ben wondered if coming back had been a mistake.

They ordered pizza, though not from Isaac's bar. He couldn't even think about walking in there—except he had considered it, just to see if maybe Isaac had come back or if anyone had heard anything, seen him.

"You smoke?" Heather asked, her eyebrows arched. "Since when?"

Ben hesitated, the lighter in his hand, one finger poised to flick on the flame. He shrugged, unsure how to answer. "'Bout a week." He'd tried to hide his newly acquired bad habit. The flick of the lighter ignited his heart. The smoke burned his lungs. The smell of it made his heart squeeze in his chest. If he closed his eyes, Isaac could be standing next to him, smoke curling from his lips, shrouding him in a gray haze. Ben once had hated the smell. Now, he craved it.

"Is that his ring?" Heather was staring at him over her uneaten crust.

The gold ring around his finger felt tighter suddenly.

"Sorry." Heather tucked a curl behind her ear and looked away. "I shouldn't have asked."

"It's fine." Ben reminded himself to breathe and polished off the last of his pizza.

"Ben." Heather's voice was tentative, like the first step onto ice. "Have you heard from him?"

Ben shook his head.

"Is he coming back? Do you know? Did he say anything?"

Ben couldn't speak. He couldn't answer her questions when he didn't know, or even believe Isaac was coming back himself. "I don't know." He rotated the ring on his finger.

"What's he expecting? That you'll just put your life on hold? That you'll wait until he's ready to come back whenever he feels like it?" she scoffed.

Ben shouldn't have felt angry at her words. She had a point. Isaac wouldn't have wanted him to sit around waiting for him.

"It borders on plain manipulative."

"I will wait for him." He growled out the words before he could stop himself. "I don't care how long it takes."

She flinched and dropped her eyes to the table.

"He's my mate, Heather. We're meant to be together."

She stood without a word, tossing the paper plates in the trash. She stopped by the bedroom door. "He left you, Ben. He broke your heart. There are people here, Ben. People who won't leave. Who care. Just know that."

She left, and the wounds Ben had tried so hard to ignore all day re-opened.

They spoke about anything other than Isaac during her stay, and Ben enjoyed her company. After her interview, he escorted her to the airport and they parted ways amicably. Ben remained in New York. He'd been away too long, and he'd missed the city.

A week later, Heather emailed him. She'd gotten the job and would be in New York within a month. She needed someone to stay with, so Ben opened his door to her gladly. Coming home to her wasn't the same as coming home to Isaac, but he was grateful for her presence.

The months flew by. Ben buried himself in work and Heather settled in nicely. She dated a few guys; he caught glimpses of them sneaking out the next day. None stuck around for long. Knowing she had someone to sleep beside her made Ben ache inside. He missed having that connection to a person, the intimacy of knowing someone in body and soul, entrusting them with his heart and knowing they had done the same. But his bed stayed empty. He thought it always would.

It had been five months since Isaac left him. Ben looked at the picture of them in his wallet from time to time, and each time he recognized the happy man beside Isaac less and less. He didn't think he'd ever be that happy again with anyone, and it was a lonely feeling beyond description.

Isaac wasn't coming back. He knew this and yet he couldn't bring himself to remove the ring around his finger, to relinquish what they'd had. He would always be haunted when he stopped and wondered where Isaac was now—if he was even still alive— and he still couldn't accept that he might never know for sure. No matter how much these truths hurt, he would never regret loving Isaac.

Isaac would have wanted him to move on, but maybe, just maybe, Ben didn't want to say goodbye. He wasn't ready, and he wasn't sure he'd ever be.

Two years passed. Isaac never returned. The loneliness inside Ben threatened to eat him whole.

"Have you ever thought about having kids?" Heather asked one night.

They were watching reruns of *Friends*. Ben's mind was elsewhere as it always was these days. "Once. With Isaac."

Heather sighed softly. "I'm thirty, and I haven't found my mate yet. I probably never will and I don't want to wait around for him to show up. I want to have a family now while I still can. Isn't that what you want too?"

Ben's heart skipped a beat. Surely she wasn't implying what he thought she was. "Of course."

She took his hands suddenly. "Ben, look at me."

He did and saw only sincerity in her eyes. There was nothing romantic about her touch, no longing in her scent. She was offering for them to be a family, but as friends who'd grown up together and known each other longer than anyone else.

"Then you can have it. We can have that together. It won't be the same, but it can be ours."

Ben was breathless, astonished by her offer. He wanted a house full of love, wanted pups of his own to love and care for. He'd wanted that with Isaac, but Isaac was gone. Life was passing him by. She wasn't his first choice, but Heather wanted the same things he did. Someone to come home to. A family. She was offering him everything he wanted. She didn't smell like rain-washed pavement. She didn't make his wolf sing.

But she was enough.

They signed papers declaring them a mated couple. New laws had been passed granting mated pairs the same protections as married couples, and they'd wanted to make sure their family was protected. Though they celebrated their union with a mating ceremony, it was mostly to please Heather's family. They had made it clear to their in-laws that they were friends first, but Heather's parents still insisted on a big ceremony.

They bought a house outside the hustle and bustle of the city with a room big enough for a baby or two or three. Through IVF, they became pregnant, and it wasn't long before Ben found himself the lucky father of twin boys.

After a year of ups and downs, sleepless nights, and countless diapers, the twins celebrated their first birthday. Ben loved it. He threw himself into his role as a father and was rewarded with the unconditional love of his sons.

He and Heather made a good team. It was hard work, especially when the boys were fussing while their parents were trying to cut the cake for their guests.

Heather, her arms full of a cranky one-year-old, said, "Ben, can you grab the knife?"

Setting down his camera, Ben went to the kitchen and fumbled in the drawer. A phone buzzed on the counter. It was Heather's, and someone named Ian was calling her. He was her coworker. There was an unpleasant taste at the back of his throat. Ben didn't answer. He didn't ask Heather about it either.

Only a day later, Heather sat him down and took in a breath. Her heart was loud and fast, scent sour with apprehension. "Ben, I think I found him. My mate."

Ben opened his mouth, then shut it. He'd known this was a possibility. Their relationship had never been about love. Sure, they'd dressed it up like love and they cared for each other as dear friends but their romance had ended long ago. So why did his heart ache? "Really?"

"I'm positive." Heather wrung her fingers in her lap. "Ben, I can just ignore the bond. I can. It will hurt, but I want to put our family first." Pain made her voice shake. "I don't want to hurt you. It's not fair that I get to have love while you don't. Ben? Please, say something."

He couldn't speak, but he knew he didn't want her to sacrifice love for her family. Just because he was alone didn't mean she had to be.

While he gathered his thoughts, she put the kids in the car, ready to drive them to preschool. She came back in for the car keys and didn't look at him.

"Heather," he said, "if this guy is your mate, don't let him go."

Tears glistened in her eyes. "Ben, what will the kids think?"

Ben took her hands. "We can make this work. I love you, Heather, and I love our life together. But—" His throat tightened. His eyes stung.

"Ben..." She was close to crying.

He blinked away the burn. "You deserve someone who can love you in all the ways I can't. I wish I could love you. I wish I could be who you deserve—"

"No, Ben. Stop that. You've been an amazing father to the boys. You gave me everything I've ever wanted." Heather wiped her eyes.

He pulled her to him and held her tight. "So did you. And that doesn't have to change. We'll still be a part of their lives. We can make this work."

Things moved fast between Heather and her mate. Before long, it was hard for Heather to explain why she was living with a man who wasn't her mate, and as understanding as her mate was toward their situation, Ben knew how to read the room.

He moved out by the end of the month. He and Heather would have joint custody of the kids and agreed to spend equal time with them. Before Ben knew it, he was alone again in an apartment in Brooklyn. He missed his boys. That was the hardest part, not being able to see his kids whenever he wanted to. He and Heather did their best to listen to their kids; some days they preferred to stay with Heather while other days they wanted to see Ben, and they compromised to make their kids happy.

Sometimes, on days when he thought the loneliness would kill him, his boys brought a little light into his life. They'd fall asleep curled against his chest while they watched a movie, and Ben would close his eyes and bask in the bonds that glowed between them.

At the end of the day, for all he'd lost, he'd found a pack. A family.

And they were the reason he was still alive.

SIXTEEN YEARS LATER

CHAPTER 18

GHOST

A FEBRUARY SNOWSTORM RAGED. Ben whistled, watching big chunks of snow spatter the windows. His stomach growled, reminding him to take his lunch break. He cracked his back and shook out his shoulders, already sensing a headache from hours hunched over the computer screen ordering new equipment for the clinic.

A smile tugged at his lips as he descended the stairs and the rowdy voices of his pack echoed from the cafeteria. As always, the sight of them filled him with joy; Gabe, teasing his sister, Izzie, over her new boyfriend; Ryan spoon-feeding his new mate, Zach; Eddie with his nose in his phone and Vicenzo sitting as far away from everyone as possible; and Max, Gabe's mate, sitting between his and Gabe's adopted kids, Tommy and Luna.

Ben loaded up a plate of meat loaf and mashed potatoes and dropped into a seat. "Hey, people." Smiles and greetings were exchanged.

"Hey, Viejo." Gabe was glowering. "Look at this joker dating my sister!" He shoved Izzie's phone under Ben's nose. Ben didn't see anything wrong with the poor guy. "He can't even pull his pants up all the way!"

Izzie snatched her phone back. "Rafael is sexy and a gentleman, and *you* will never meet him!" She squealed over the picture and did a weird little thrash in her seat. "Can you believe it? He's taking me to see a concert at Lincoln Center for Valentine's Day!"

Max smiled. "Nice. Isn't it?" He elbowed Gabe.

Gabe frowned, pushing his mashed potatoes around his plate. "Well, at least it isn't a fast-food joint."

Ben, for one, was pleased for her. Izzie had dedicated herself to the agency for so long, using her brains and tech-savvy smarts to unite missing shifters with their families and introduce them to the agency's services. It was about time she found a guy who knew how to pamper her. "Sounds like a swell guy. I hope I get to meet him."

Zach's chair screeched. "Ry, I'm gonna grab another plate. You still hungry?"

"A side of the mac and cheese. Thanks!" Ryan kissed Zach's cheek as if they'd be parted for years before he headed to the buffet five feet away, Zach practically skipping. Gabe mimed vomiting and winced as Max kicked him under the table. Ben gagged, then laughed when Ryan shot him a glare.

"Laugh it up. Watch me be too happy to give a damn." Ryan slapped a big grin on his face and watched Zach from across the room.

"What are you doing for V-Day? Somethin' special? It's your first Valentine's Day as a mated pair," Gabe said, letting Luna steal some of his mashed potatoes with a dopey grin on his face.

Ryan whispered, "I booked us reservations at that super fancy restaurant at the Hudson Yards!"

"The one at the top of the observation deck?" Izzie gasped. "I've been wanting to go there forever!"

"They have awesome views. You can see the whole city! And after, he's taking me to a game at the stadium. Totally re-creating our first date," Ryan declared, practically swooning. "Ain't he just perfect?"

"Can't believe I've survived the past seven months of watching you canoodling all over the agency." Ben took a bite of meat loaf.

"Canoodling?" Ryan repeated in both disgust and awe. "Who even says that?"

"How about you kids?" Ben asked. "Anyone special at school?"

Tommy choked on his food. "N-no! No one."

Luna snorted. "He totally has a crush on this guy."

Gabe and Max gasped and Gabe sniffed. "My boy is growing up."

"Oh no!" Tommy groaned, hiding his face in his arms.

Ben pointed his fork at Gabe and Max. "What about you two?"

They exchanged happy glances and Max squeezed Gabe's hand. "A movie, dinner at our favorite restaurant, and then we'll walk through Central Park and find the spot where we first met."

"That's so sweet!" Izzie swooned.

"Hey, Ed," Gabe said, giving Eddie's foot a nudge. Eddie jumped and smiled, his cheeks going a little red the way they always did when anyone showed him any form of attention. "You got a special girl, or guy?"

Vicenzo took a sudden interest in the conversation, his brooding stare zeroing in on Eddie.

"No. I'll probably just read and tend Ryan's alchemy garden. He's trying out these new potions and just ordered a ton of new herbs to use in them that will need to be transplanted!" Eddie's enthusiasm for botany was... charming, Ben supposed, even if he didn't really get it.

"Vicenzo, what about—" But Gabe had barely asked before Vicenzo abruptly stood and walked away. "Guess not."

Ben checked the time. He had to get back to completing the rest of the equipment orders. "Nice chatting with you all, but business calls." He left his plate in the sink and headed for the stairs. By the time he'd reached his office, he realized Eddie had followed him.

"Ben, hold up a sec."

In his office, Ben turned his computer on as Eddie lingered in the doorway. "Can I talk to you? It's important."

Ben was surprised. Eddie was friendlier than Vicenzo, but the former hunter generally kept to himself in Ryan's greenhouse, tending to plants. "Sure thing. Hit me."

Eddie blew out a breath. "Okay..." The scent of his anxiety washed over Ben. "Ah hell. Maybe I'm just bein' paranoid..."

He leaned back in his chair. "Spill it, Ed. What's wrong?"

Eddie's scent filled with fear. "You know my uncle is the leader of The Beasts." He touched the silver chain around his neck. Eddie had never asked for help removing it, even though the silver suppressed his wolf.

"Yeah. Hard to forget."

Eddie had never gone into great detail about his past, but he'd shared enough for Ben to get the general idea. Eddie and Vicenzo had grown up in a town that had been wiped off the map by The Beasts. Eddie had been captured by his uncle and forced to hunt his own kind. Three years ago, Ben, Gabe, Vicenzo and Ryan had been captured by The Beasts but Eddie had found the courage to turn on his kidnappers to help them escape. Over the years Eddie had been with the agency, he'd given Ben as much information about The Beasts as he could. Ben knew that they operated wolf fighting rings using wolves they'd abducted and tortured to rack in blood money.

Ben had shared the information Eddie gave him with the Council, hoping they could finally shut The Beasts down for good, but so far without any luck. The bastards were too slippery. He hated to disappoint Eddie, who still carried guilt for being complicit in his uncle's activities, though Ben knew Eddie had done what he'd needed to do to survive.

"I haven't seen or heard from him since I joined the agency, but I've kept my eyes and ears open for any news. Huntin' ain't what it used to be. They operate covertly nowadays but yesterday I heard some news and... I think he's on the move again." Eddie's voice cracked, and the scent of fear was so pungent Ben could taste it.

He stood and crossed the room, and Eddie sucked in a gulp when Ben touched the back of his neck. "Hey. Take some breaths for me, Ed. You're safe."

Eddie's eyes were wet, and he closed them tightly. "I-I know, I just..."

"You're safe," Ben promised him. He wished he could feel Eddie's bond, but the silver muffled his thread. All he could do was reassure him with words and his touch. "You're mine, and I won't let him hurt you."

"I know," Eddie whispered.

"Can you tell me what you heard?"

Eddie swallowed, blinking fast. "So, you know how some wolves live among humans while others prefer to live out in the wilderness, right? No technology, nothing. They're as good as wild."

"Yeah," Ben said, sitting back in his desk chair. "The Council tracks and collars werewolves who live in the wild in order to protect them from hunters."

Eddie nodded, wetting his lips. "There was a story yesterday, made the news. A pack of twenty wolves in Denali turned up dead. Most of 'em."

Ben's lunch formed an uncomfortable ball in his stomach. "What do you mean, most of them?" The thought shriveled his insides. "Some of them survived?"

As his anxiety grew, Eddie's chest rose and fell faster. "It's complicated. I, uh, called Alpha Reyes, and he says t-that while the weaker, sicker wolves of the Chelatna Lake pack had been killed, he... uh, he thinks the stronger ones were taken away."

Ben laced his fingers together and squeezed. "Why?"

"That's the thing, Ben. My uncle would save the stronger wolves and use 'em for huntin', for fightin'. This is his doin'. It has to be." His voice got small and high-pitched, his eyes widening in his panic.

Ben hated to see him so frightened. "Say no more." He stood and gripped Eddie's shoulder. "We'll figure out what's going on with those wolves." He called a meeting in his office over the intercom. Within minutes, Gabe and Max, Izzie, and Ryan and Zach had arrived. "Some assholes targeted a whole pack of werewolves in Denali."

"I think it was my uncle," Eddie said.

Ben went on. "I need volunteers to find these hunters. Denali is vast and wild. I need a team I can trust, and you lot are the best I've got. I'm leaving today as soon as possible. Who's coming with me?"

Gabe and Max exchanged glances, probably speaking through their bond.

Max nodded at Gabe, then turned to Ben. "I'll go."

Ben noticed Gabe's worried frown. "You two gonna manage without each other?"

Gabe exhaled and set his jaw tight. "Yeah. I need to stay with the kids, and Max's lunar powers will be helpful. If I can't go, it would make me feel better if at least one of us went."

"Thanks, both of you." Ben knew how Gabe worried for his mate, capable as Maxwell Gallagher was. Max possessed powerful abilities when the moon was at its apex. Gabe pulled Max to the side, his arm around his shoulders.

"Zach, you know what I've gotta ask of you," Ben said.

"Right," Zach said, as serious as always. "I'll make sure the agency doesn't burn down while you're gone."

"Count me in!" Ryan was bristling with excitement. "I've never seen the packs in Alaska! Is it true some of them don't even take their human form?" Zach nudged him and Ryan reined in his excitement. "Besides, my magic will be potent as hell among all that natural scenery. Whatever messed with that pack, they'll sure as hell regret messing with us." Ryan had only inherited his family's druid magic from his grandmother last summer, but thanks to his mate bond with Zach, he had become a powerful spellcaster.

"I'll come too," Izzie said. Gabe's frown got impossibly wider. His mate and his sister were both going into certain danger without him. "Don't look at me like that, Gabriel! I'll look after Max, and he'll look after me. Count me in, Ben."

Ben's heart warmed at his pack's support, but there was a problem. "We need more. I'll ask Vicenzo if he wants to join us."

Ryan sighed. "Stuck in the wilderness with Vicenzo. I hope no one minds if I don't break my back jumping for joy."

Vicenzo had never been the most social of the pack, or the most positive, but he'd lived among a wild pack of wolves in Italy after his home was destroyed. Ben wanted his insights.

Vicenzo was working in the kitchen like he usually did when he was off guard duty, and he froze when Ben mentioned Eddie's uncle. "That son of a bitch," he whispered, voice a low growl. "Say no fucking more. I'm in." Fur thickened on Vicenzo's arms, and his fangs glistened.

Ben raised both hands. "Hold on. You can't wolf out on us while we're there. I need you to be levelheaded."

Exhaling, Vicenzo regained his human features. "Fine. But if this really is Eddie's shithead uncle, then I'm ripping him to pieces."

Hoping he wouldn't regret asking him, Ben turned away.

"Hey," Vicenzo growled.

Ben paused. "What is it?"

"How is Eddie? Is he..." Vicenzo looked away. "Never mind. Forget it."

Ben didn't push him, but he smelled the concern mixed with the anger in Vicenzo's scent. Honestly, Ed and Vico's relationship couldn't be more complicated.

Before sundown, the pack had purchased tickets for the last flight to Anchorage. Ben threw his bags into the trunk. He looked at his pack and found their uncertainty reflected back at him, their sadness present as Max hugged Luna, Tommy, and Gabe tight, and Zach and Ryan shared a farewell kiss. "I promise you, all of you—we'll see each other again."

They piled into their cars and drove from the agency to the airport.

Ben hoped and prayed he wasn't leading his loved ones to an icy grave.

If it had been cold in New York, it was freezing in Alaska. Ben had packed his warmest clothes in preparation for the trip and he hoped it would be enough as he set his sights on the snowcapped mountain ranges of Denali National Park. Ryan looked out at the mountains in wonder. "Hard to believe the packs actually survive up there. They must never take their human form, it would leave them vulnerable to hypothermia. I guess they stay shifted and rely on their pack bonds to keep from going feral."

"Some of them are feral," Vicenzo grumbled, shouldering his backpack. "You spend long enough as a wolf, you forget what being human is like."

"Sounds terrible," Max said.

Vicenzo shrugged. "It's not that bad. All the worries, all the pain, it goes away. All that matters is survival."

Ben guessed he was speaking from experience. "Don't shift too much, Vic. We'll be vulnerable in our wolf forms if there are hunters around."

"Whatever," Vicenzo said with a shrug, his face expressionless. "Just glad to be outta the city. It'll be good to breathe some mountain air."

Ben checked his phone's map. "Come on, we gotta buy some climbing equipment and tents."

Eddie yawned wide. "Then what?"

"We're catching a plane that'll carry us near Moose's Tooth. That's where we're meeting Manuel and Veronica's pack." Ben led the way. He was tired too, but they could sleep once they'd set up camp. Once they'd bought their tents and camping equipment, they took a plane over Anchorage and out into the tundra. The rivers they flew over were clogged with ice floes, and the patches of dense boreal forests were frozen over. The plane made a smooth landing on the edge of an alpine forest within the rugged hills that were surrounded by untamed mountains.

Ben found park rangers and wolf conservationists pitching tents and setting up small radio towers for reception. Vast, snowy wilderness spread out around Ben and the jagged teeth of the mountain ranges touched the skies.

While the pack set up their tents and equipment, Ben waded through the snow toward Alphas Manuel and Veronica Reyes. Manuel had earned the position of Alpha a few years back, and he'd chosen Veronica to lead beside him. Together, they'd made history, Manuel as the first hybrid Alpha, and Veronica as the first human to serve in the Council.

The Alphas of the Council were bent over a map where they'd marked out various pack territories. Ben smiled at the sight of them. If only Greg were here to see how far their friends had come, but he'd passed away a few months before Manuel and Veronica had become Alphas.

Veronica was bundled under so many layers that Ben wouldn't have recognized her if he weren't familiar with her. "The troopers weren't able to investigate the other packs due to the weather, but I want to check up on them to make sure whoever's targeting these wolves isn't going after them too. The closest pack to Chelatna Lake is in the forest near the Yentna River."

Manuel pointed at Ben. "You take the choppers in the morning and go check on the Yentna pack. I'll have my team check on other neighboring pack territories."

Ben blinked snow out of his eyes. "Got it. We'll leave at first light."

That night the wind howled, shaking his tent. Ben had never known wind could be so loud but in the quiet desolation of the wilderness, it was like one endless roar. In the moments when the wind did die, the silence was nearly unbearable in this place where only the strongest predators survived.

In the morning, the choppers carried them over miles of tundra. Despite the severity of the circumstances that had brought them to Alaska, it was hard not to be humbled by the mountain ranges towering over them on all sides, as treacherous and deadly as they were beautiful and intimidating. He just hoped wherever those surviving wolves had been taken, they were somewhere warm at least.

They touched ground. The frigid air carried the faint smell of wolves. A black wolf Ben recognized as Vicenzo brushed past him. Nose bent to the ground, Vicenzo sniffed at the permafrost. He was certainly warmer than all of them combined with his dense fur. Ben only hoped he didn't shift too often. Unlike the others, Vicenzo had never taken to their pack bonds, and Ben feared too much time in the wilds as a wolf might make him go feral. Shifting for him carried risks that didn't concern the rest of the pack, closely bonded as they were. Ben shouldered his bags and pressed on. He doubted Vicenzo would care for a lecture, so he supposed he should let it slide and not worry.

"Got a scent?" Ben asked.

Vicenzo growled and Ben couldn't guess what that meant. Even in wolf form, he'd never been able to hear Vicenzo's thoughts. He was completely walled off from the pack, always had been. At times, Ben had wondered if he even saw them as his pack. It didn't matter. Vicenzo was one of his, and Ben would protect him all the same.

He sighed. "I'm gonna take that as a yes," he said as the black wolf padded with ease over the uneven ground and dense snow.

"Feeling okay?" Ben asked Eddie.

The former hunter was quiet and gazed at the ground. "I haven't seen my uncle in years. Any day now, we could run into him." Anxiety soured Eddie's scent.

Max bumped his shoulder against Eddie's. "We won't let him hurt you."

Vicenzo suddenly stopped with a low growl. The black wolf was inspecting a spatter of blood, dried and brown.

Ben's heart sank. "Shit. We're too late!" He ran ahead into an area rife with the smell of urine, scat, and wolf fur. A coppery tang thickened the air. Ben's heart galloped with dread as the snow turned crimson the farther into the woods he ran.

Dead wolves lay butchered like cattle. They'd arrived too late. Ben slammed his fist into the icy bark of a tree, strangling a roar of fury. Whoever was doing this had shown no mercy to these wolves.

Eddie's face went pale and he leaned against a tree. "Goddess. It's him... It has to be."

Izzie pressed herself close to Eddie. "Ed, we will find them. The humans that did this will pay."

Eddie's eyes widened as he knelt beside the corpse of a wolf. "Hang on. Whoever did this wasn't human. Look." The throat had been punctured and the belly sliced open but not by any tools. By claws and fangs.

Ben growled. "They were killed by wolves. Didn't you say your uncle used wolves?"

Eddie shook his head. "There ain't any human prints in sight! Look around! My uncle always accompanied his wolves on hunts. No way he'd miss out on the thrill of the hunt. This... this wasn't him." Eddie ran his hand along the hard imprints of wolf tracks tattooing the ground. "Look! This one doesn't have a collar!" Eddie knelt beside a large wolf. The fur around its throat was matted with blood. It had bled to death.

Ben's head spun. This was one of the attackers, not a Yentna pack wolf.

"Guys!" Max pointed to Vicenzo. The black wolf was sniffing behind some bushes. Bloody paw prints led away from the scene of the massacre. "Someone survived."

Ben was doubtful. There was a lot of blood. "It's worth following the trail."

"Even if they are alive, they might not be able to speak to us," Ryan chimed in, settling into a swift pace at Ben's side. "These people are as wild as it gets. It's crazy." He sounded utterly fascinated. "I mean, we're talking generations of isolation! They might not even know anything about our technology or human society!"

"It does hold a certain appeal," Izzie said. "To completely embrace your wild roots like that and be one with nature... What a life."

"Cool, guys," Ben grumbled, not really caring.

"Guys, I think the wolf's chances of survival just dropped," Max said. He was looking at two sets of wolf prints trailing the wounded animal from the scene. "They were followed."

Whether by friend or foe remained to be seen. Vicenzo led the way, moving at a swifter pace than the rest of the pack. The trees cast lavender shadows on the snow, which was stained red by the setting sun. Ben had misgivings about going farther as the land grew colder and the shadows deepened. Vicenzo became hard to follow, his jet-black coat blending easily with the shadows.

"Whoa! Check it out!" Ryan's upturned face shimmered with blue and green light. A chorus of gasps erupted from the pack. The aurora borealis lit up the night sky, weaving like a banner of purples, greens, and blues against a backdrop of twinkling stars.

"Amazing," Ben said, wishing he could truly enjoy the spectacle.

"Man... I know we're here on a deadly mission, but this is a once in a lifetime sight," Ryan declared before moving on.

"It's too dark to keep moving," Ben said. The cold was starting to get to him. "We've gotta make camp."

Eddie called out, "Vico? We're makin' camp!"

The black wolf had disappeared. Scowling, Ben approached the trees at the edge of the forest. He couldn't see any movement within. Vicenzo wouldn't just walk off into the wilderness and be gone forever. Would he? Misgivings heavy on his shoulders, Ben turned on his flashlight and ventured into the woods. Normally he'd shift but he worried about being caught unawares by hunters.

"Stupid kid. Vicenzo, come back! We're stopping for the night!" When no bark answered him, Ben's worry only grew. "He's just sniffing a tree or something. Taking a shit." But the pressing urge to investigate wouldn't leave him alone. He followed Vico's scent deeper into the trees until the voices of the pack faded.

Twigs snapped behind him. His flashlight caught the brief glare of glowing green eyes and a wolfish face before the wolf darted into the shadows. Ben nearly dropped the light. That hadn't been Vicenzo. He wished he'd been able to tell if the wolf was collared or not.

"Hey, come out. Are you with the Yentna pack?" He realized talking might be futile. "Right. You don't even know English. Just wolf speak." He sighed, shining the light around the woods.

A throaty growl rumbled like thunder above him. Ben whirled and his light illuminated the wolf towering over him from on top of a couple of boulders. Lips pulled back to reveal razor fangs, its eyes wide and full of fury. It didn't have a collar on. Ben's claws came out and his fangs lengthened. "All right, asshole, here's how we play this. You shift back and tell me why you're out here killing wolves!"

The wolf flew at him in a blur of fur and gleaming fangs. Ben's claws dug beneath the coarse fur and pierced flesh, but the wolf knocked him flat on his back. Spittle rained down on him and teeth snapped, grazing the tip of his nose. There was a whooshing sound, and the wolf's body tumbled from Ben with a pained yelp. He blinked, his eyes adjusting to the dark. The wolf's paws twitched, its sides heaving. A silver bolt protruded from its shoulder and another was lodged in its skull.

Ben whirled around, claws raised, and found himself staring down a crossbow's sights.

"Wait." He raised both hands. "Just let me explain. We don't need to fight." Hadn't he uttered those exact words once while staring down the sights of a crossbow?

"Don't move," a gruff voice commanded. His face was cast into shadow, the crossbow steady in his hands. "I'll put a bolt through your eyes if I have to."

"Easy," Ben rasped, acutely aware of every beat of his heart when he realized the next beat might be his last. "I don't want trouble." How many more were there? Was his pack safe?

"Trouble? That's what you call slaughtering a bunch of innocent wolves?" The bolt was close enough now to jab Ben in the forehead. "I want you to tell me where your leader is."

Ben tried to pop his claws and fangs, but his body was frozen. His wolf didn't want to attack this hunter. Why? He couldn't even summon the urge to bite this guy. His wolf was ready to roll over and submit to him before he'd even shed a drop of blood. In his panic, Ben said, "I don't know! She-Wolf's tits, would you put the damn crossbow down so we can talk?"

The hunter sucked in a sharp gasp. "W-what did you say?"

"Put the crossbow down so we can talk."

The hunter shook his head. "Oh my God..." His voice trembled. The crossbow clattered into the snow. "Ben? Ben, it's me."

Ben didn't understand. He couldn't. Not until the winds changed and blew the hunter's scent toward him. This guy reeked of wolf blood. He stank of sweat and dirt and faintly of pinecones and pine sap. And underneath that...

Rain-washed pavement. Damp, refreshing air, charged and heavy with moisture just before a storm. Wet leaves and grass.

All the air left Ben's body. He took a step back. "No," he whispered, shaking his head.

The hunter lifted a trembling hand and pulled down his hood. The ghost staring back at him was pale as an Alaskan winter, lined across the forehead, his brows and bushy beard streaked with gray. Hard and edged with crow's feet as they were, Ben could never forget those eyes, gray flecked with blue. Like the sky just after a long storm when the clouds opened and the sun returned. They squinted at him.

"Isaac." Ben's voice shook, and deep within his chest, his wolf howled like it never had before. Howled for his mate.

Those eyes widened and shone with tears. "Ben! I knew it. I knew that was you! How—ugh!" Isaac stumbled forward, and his eyes rolled back. At first Ben thought he was fainting. If Isaac hadn't, Ben would have for sure. Ben caught him just before he toppled into the snow.

"Gotcha, bitch!" Ryan grinned triumphantly, brandishing the rock in his fist.

"Ryan!" he snapped.

Ryan's grin vanished and he dropped the rock. "You're welcome?"

CHAPTER 19

WASTED YEARS

"I'm sorry, Ben! How was I supposed to know this hunter guy was your friend? Which, by the way, what the hell, man?" Ryan panted as he and Ben lugged the very unconscious hunter into Ben's tent and dropped him in the space beside the sleeping bag.

"He's not my friend," Ben growled, unable to look away from the hunter. In the light, there was no mistaking it. The hunter was sure as hell Isaac. He'd never grown a beard quite this long while Ben had known him, but he knew those high cheekbones at a glance, the Cupid's bow in his lip, the handsome Roman nose. With the overgrown mane of hair and a bushy beard, along with the many scars that lined his face, he looked a total stranger while being so achingly familiar all at once.

It just made no sense and now that the initial shock had worn off, the anger was setting in. "Actually, you shoulda hit him harder."

Ryan's eyes went wide. "Okay... Not gonna ask what weird relationship you had with him."

Max's head popped up over Ryan's shoulder. "What'll we do with him?"

"Good ol' Isaac will stay with me till I can question him. After, I'll feed him to the polar bears."

Izzie popped up on Ryan's left, giving him the illusion of having two other mismatched heads. She gasped. "Ben! Is this that Isaac guy? Your long-lost mate?"

Ben glowered at her. How had she known that?

She covered her mouth. "Oops. Gabriel asked me not to tell you he told me."

Max squinted. "Wait, Ben's mate is a hunter?"

"Guys, what's goin' on?" Eddie's voice was muffled from beyond the tent. "Did you find Vicenzo, Ben?"

He scowled and massaged his aching temples. "Would everyone cool it? Isaac's not my anything!" Shit. He'd completely forgotten about Vico. Seeing Isaac again had tipped everything off its axis, and he was still struggling to find his feet. "I... uh..." Clasping his head, he looked from the unconscious hunter to the tent flap. He couldn't think right now.

"That's okay. Maybe he went huntin'." Eddie's footsteps crunched away.

"Ben, man... you okay?" Ryan asked, brows puckered in concern.

Beginning to feel cornered, Ben took in a shallow breath of what little oxygen the pack wasn't hogging in this small tent. "Isaac and I go way back. Back when I'd first founded the agency in New York. That good enough for you guys?"

Izzie frowned. "Gabe told me he was your—"

"Well, he isn't!" Ben snapped. He reined in his anger and sighed. "But he may know something about the dead wolves." Might even be the cause of it, Ben thought with a sick twisting in his gut. "All of you go to bed. I'll plan our next move, and Isaac here's gonna help me." He could tell they were still curious, but they went their separate ways to their tents.

Finally alone, Ben allowed himself to be consumed by the man sleeping at his feet. Ben couldn't take his eyes off him. Isaac was here. He was alive. To his dismay, tears stung his eyes.

His hand moved of its own accord, sweeping overgrown wavy bangs from Isaac's forehead. His breath caught in his throat, and a rush of exhilaration swept through his heart. Isaac's weathered face relaxed, his mouth twitching into something that might have been a smile. Ben's heart cleaved in two.

"Isaac," he whispered, voice rough with feeling. "Goddess, you have no idea how much I've missed you." Ben thumbed a scar that cut through his bushy beard and stopped short of his mouth. He hadn't had that scar before. It was new and Ben wondered what he'd been up to for the past two decades.

Isaac had been alive for all these years and yet he'd never once thought to seek Ben out. Never thought to come back for him. The realization was like a knife between his ribs. Anger buried his tender feelings.

Those storm cloud eyes fluttered open, stealing the breath from Ben's lungs. He angled his head, nuzzling into Ben's hand. "Am I dreaming?" His chapped lips caressed Ben's palm. "Got no idea how many times I dreamed of waking up to your face."

A shuddery exhale escaped Ben. "Not dreaming. I'm here. This is real."

Isaac blinked fast. His eyes were wet. "Ben…" A tear left a track down his cheek, disappearing into his bushy beard. "I don't get it. How are you here? Now? After all this time?"

Ben's chest shuddered and he gritted his teeth against an onslaught of emotion. "Must be fate."

Isaac pushed himself up and reached out, touching Ben's face. His eyes widened when his fingers rasped through Ben's beard as if he'd expected his hand to pass through Ben like a ghost. "Can't believe it. What are you… how…"

A bitter look twisted his lips, and the smell of his guilt and frustration crashed over Ben. "No. This… this isn't good. Fuck. This is the last thing I ever wanted." He yanked his hand away and drew his knees to his chest, closing himself off. His sudden distance was like a slap to the face.

"What are you saying?" Ben asked, hardening his voice to try and hide how much Isaac pulling away from him hurt.

"You should have stayed away. Why in the hell did you come after me?"

"I didn't!" Ben snapped, crossing his arms over his chest to shield his heart. "I had no damn clue you were out here. I'm looking for the missing wolves. All these years I've thought you were dead and gone."

Isaac flinched. "Ben…" He raked a hand over his face, growling lowly. "Fuck. I'm so—"

"Skip it. You think a half-assed apology is gonna make up for what you did? I woke up and you were *gone*." His voice cracked into pieces. "Oh, but at least you left a fucking note. How cute." Wounds from years ago ripped wide open, and he was drowning in the same hurt and hopelessness he'd felt when he'd realized Isaac was never coming home.

Pain twisted Isaac's face. "Ben, please. I—"

"Stop." Ben was all but begging him. He couldn't talk about this. Not now. "Just... just tell me what you're doing here."

Isaac tugged his hat from his head and squeezed it. His long hair tumbled to his shoulders. It didn't look like he'd washed it in a while or had a proper bath by the musky male odor of him, yet nothing could mask the scent of rain. "I'm investigating the wolf hunts, same as you. I arrived too late to the massacre at Chelatna Lake and I missed this attack too."

"What's with the interest?"

Isaac's brow furrowed low over his eyes. "Donovan survived the attack at the cathedral."

Ben blanked on the name. "Who?"

"The leader of the hunter clan I used to run with."

Ben remembered with a rush of anger. "He's why you left."

Isaac didn't deny it and nodded. "After our fight at the cathedral, they pursued me from New York. He's tracked me for years, and I ran from him all over the country. Don brought a bunch of his hunters with him to track me down, but over the years, they split up. I've spent the past two decades running from them. Now and again, they caught up with me, and I've managed to pick off most of them, but Don was always a step ahead. A time or two, I lost Don's trail. Just when I thought it was safe to come home to you, I heard about the killings in Alaska."

Ben shook his head. "All this to get back at you?"

Isaac sighed, closing his eyes. "He has nothing but revenge and anger to keep him going."

Ben pressed his lips tightly together, trying not to speak. "And in all those years, you never thought to come home?"

Isaac's face fell as if he'd sensed Ben's thoughts. "I wanted to. Ben, I dreamed of coming home to you."

"But you didn't." Hurt cracked through Ben's voice. "You let me go on thinking you were as good as dead."

"*Ben—*"

Desperately needing air, he swept open the tent door and walked out into the cold. The frigid air numbed his throat. Footsteps pursued him.

Hands shaking, Ben yanked a cigarette from his pack and lit up, taking a deep drag of ashy smoke. "I don't want to hear any excuses," Ben said to the stars. "I don't care where you've been, what you've done, why you couldn't shoot me one fucking *text* just telling me you were alive, to tell me not to wait for you, or worry, or—" His eyes burned as his fury turned to hurt.

"I'm so sorry, Ben." Isaac's voice was a shuddery whisper. "I left to keep you safe so you could have the life you deserved!"

"Don't tell me what I deserved!" Ben whirled around, clinging fast to his anger as the sight of Isaac's watery eyes threatened to break him. "And you know what, that's a fancy way of justifying how you chose revenge over us. Doesn't take a genius to figure it out." He turned, ready to storm off into the wilderness.

Ben stumbled as Isaac whipped him around, his eyes blazing. Their chests touched, and Isaac's breath warmed Ben's mouth as he squeezed a fistful of Ben's coat. "Don found out about us, Ben. He was going to kill you to get back at me. So I made myself a target. I needed him as far away from you as possible. If I'd just killed him that night, I would never have had to leave." Isaac's face twisted in frustration, the scent of his anguish making Ben's eyes sting. "Ben, after everything you'd done for me, I couldn't be the reason you died."

Ben's heart cracked in his chest. Wouldn't he have done the same to keep Isaac safe, no matter the cost? Once, he would have sacrificed everything for this man. His mate.

"I won't pretend this wasn't about vengeance, Ben. I thought Don was my friend, and he'd lied and manipulated me the entire time I knew him. He tricked me into—" Isaac cut himself off, blinking fast. "Leaving you was the hardest thing I ever had to do, and my heart and soul has paid the price for it every day we spent apart. And I don't care if you believe it. Look at me!" Isaac's eyes were wild and bright with emotion. "I've been living half-alive for twenty-one years."

Ben couldn't speak because he felt the exact same way about Isaac. No one else had ever filled the void in his soul.

A howl echoed over the treetops, and Eddie lurched from his tent. "It's Vicenzo!"

Ben felt pulled in two. His pack needed him, but Isaac was standing closer than he had in years.

"Go," Isaac said, stepping out of his reach.

Ben's wolf howled in fear and longing and his feet couldn't move. "You gonna be here when I get back?"

Isaac nodded, and his eyes radiated with his promise. "I'm seeing this through to the end."

"Forgive me for being skeptical. Just know that if you leave, I'm gonna hunt you down." He backed away from Isaac in long strides, unable to turn his back. Another howl danced with the aurora borealis above, and Ben turned and ran into the woods.

Running among the trees alone, his anger and hurt blew away into the wind behind him. Tears stung his eyes, and he smiled wider than he had in years.

He's alive, his wolf sang in his heart. *He's alive. He's back. Isaac's back!*

VICENZO WASN'T ALONE. LIMPING at the black wolf's side was a young female, her fur matted with blood. She collapsed just as Ben reached her. Lifting the wolf into his arms, he carried her toward his tent. "Get some first aid over here!" Max came running with a kit and he and Ben set to work, cleaning and bandaging what they could.

"She might need stitches. I don't understand why these aren't healing," Max murmured, eyeing a deep gash across her side.

Ben didn't have to wonder. "Smell that? Silver. They've been in wolf form for so long, the stuff doesn't force them to assume a human shape like it does to us, but it has weakened her."

Ryan knelt. "Here. This might help." He extended a vial beneath the wolf's nose. "Someone open her mouth." Izzie opened the wolf's jaws and Ryan splashed the liquid in. Before Ben's eyes, the flesh began to knit itself back together.

"Damn, Ry. Last time I talk shit about your foul-tasting potions again."

Ryan glowed with satisfaction. "She's collared, so she must be a survivor of the pack that was attacked." He touched the wolf's big paw where a gash was healing. He ran his finger across a strap on her paw. "Looks like she was tied down."

Max visibly shivered. Ben touched his shoulder, knowing this had probably brought back memories of when he'd been abducted by the Moonborn cult.

Ryan knelt and placed a hand on the wolf's head. "I'm gonna do a calming spell, see if I can convince her to let us in on her thoughts. Otherwise, we'll sit here guessing what happened to her all night."

A low growl was all the warning they got before the wolf suddenly sprang up, jaws snapping at Ryan. Ben seized the wolf around the middle as it flattened Ryan to the ground. He tugged, trying to urge the wolf off him. She suddenly yelped as tendrils of moonlight wrapped around her. Flying off Ryan, she landed gently in the snow. Max lowered his hand, his fingers glowing with moonlight.

The wolf tucked her tail and backed away, her lips pulled back from her fangs.

"Easy," Ben said but she just snapped her teeth, eyes wild with fear.

"We don't want to hurt you," Izzie said, approaching slowly with her hands raised. The wolf's growling intensified but Izzie knelt and extended a hand. The wolf looked warily at Ben and the others.

Ben understood. "She's scared of men. Whoever captured her must have been male. Guys, back off and let Izzie handle this."

Izzie scooted closer to the wolf and offered her some jerky. The wolf inched closer and snapped it out of Izzie's hands, growling protectively as she ate. Izzie offered her some more, talking gently, and the wolf accepted the meat. "Can you tell us what happened to you?" Izzie asked. The wolf growled and hung her head. "I'm so sorry about your pack, but we can help avenge them, maybe even rescue any survivors. You just need to tell us who did this to you."

The wolf whined and before their eyes, her body shuddered. The wolf doubled over with a yelp.

"She's trying to change," Ben said in realization. "It's gonna be too hard on her."

"Don't shift," Ryan said to the female wolf. "I can use my magic to create a temporary pack bond between Izzie and you, okay? It won't hurt, I promise."

Izzie raised a hand to stop the wolf. "It's okay, trust him. Hang on." She removed her layers while Ryan started chanting in Gaelic. Before their eyes, a golden thread materialized, stretching from Izzie's chest to the female wolf.

"Alrighty, pack bond is a-go! Izzie, do your thing."

"Right. Werewolves. Naked." Isaac quickly looked away as Izzie stripped and shifted to a black wolf like her brother's. She approached and bumped her head against the wolf's. Their tails wagged, and then they were both still.

Izzie's voice, warm as sunshine, filled Ben's and the pack's minds as she relayed whatever the other wolf was communicating to her.

They were ambushed by other wolves. The ones they didn't kill were taken to a... a structure of some kind, I think. Some place full of other werewolves in cages. There was a man. He called himself Father Don. He hurt her. He told her she was an abomination, that she had to be punished. She would suffer forever unless she joined his pack and helped kill her own kind. So she... told him about the wolves at Lake Minchumina."

The wolf bowed her head and Izzie nuzzled her. *"It wasn't your fault. I'm so sorry he hurt you."* Izzie's wolf whimpered from pain. *"We'll make this right. I promise."*

Ben's stomach churned. He opened his map and found the lake clear on the other side of the Denali mountain ranges. "Shit..."

"Am I missing something?" Isaac's voice shattered the quiet. "'Cause from where I'm standing, you guys are just standing there staring off all serious into space."

Ben briefed him on what Izzie had learned from the wolf.

Isaac whispered, "It's Don. This is all his doing. I'm so close to finding him..." He looked ready to sprint off into danger, and Ben's heart lurched with fear.

Ben asked, "Hang on, you're telling me this werewolf hunter became a werewolf himself?"

"It happens," Eddie remarked, one hand on his silver collar.

"I'll tell you the full story later," Isaac said. "We've gotta get to the lake. You guys have transport?"

"A chopper's coming to get us in the morning," Ben said.

"They could be dead by then!" Isaac paced.

"What do you want me to do, Isaac? Cross a whole mountain in the dark?" Ben was worried for the wolves too, but there was nothing he could do about it right now.

"I just wish we could do *something*. Anything but sit here knowing Don and his pets are heading straight for an unsuspecting pack."

"Max, can you do a portal?" Ben asked.

Max shook his head. "Sorry, Ben. I'd have to have a strong connection to the pack to teleport myself to them."

Ben sighed. It seemed they had no choice but to wait until morning. "Right, let's settle in. First light, we'll have the chopper carry us over the mountains and toward the lake. Get some rest. I think we all need it."

"What about her?" The black wolf that was Izzie cocked her head, panting at the new wolf. She slept with her head on her paws, whining occasionally.

Ben considered what to do with her. She was a lone wolf, so she wouldn't survive long. "I'll radio your parents. They should be able to place her within a conservation center."

Exhausted, he dragged himself back to his tent. His heart lurched at the sight of Isaac propped against the canvas, and it wouldn't settle. Every time he laid eyes on him, Ben expected him to vanish like a ghost. He couldn't believe he was really here after all these years. And yet, he couldn't rejoice, not when he remembered the hunger for the hunt that had blazed in Isaac's eyes.

"If Don runs, you'll follow him to the ends of the earth, won't you?"

Isaac flinched like Ben had hit him. "That won't happen."

He gnashed his teeth against the hurt and fear, then forced out a cold snort of laughter. "Forgive me for not believing you."

"If you'd asked me that question a few hours ago, I'd have said yes." Isaac swallowed, years of longing burning in his eyes. "But then I found you again."

Ben's fingers curled into fists. "And?"

"And I'm done, Ben. I'm done running. If I told you that if he escaped, I'd choose you, no matter how much it killed me to let him go, would you believe me?"

The breath shook in Ben's chest. "No."

Isaac dipped his head, closing his eyes tight. Then he opened them and set his sights on Ben. He smiled, and it was a cocky thing that set Ben's blood alight. "Then I'll do everything in my power to prove that I mean it."

Blinking fast, Ben looked away.

If Don did escape and Isaac pursued him, Ben's heart would break anew, and he didn't know how it could ever be whole again.

Chapter 20

THE PATH TO REDEMPTION

Barricaded beneath his sleeping bag, Isaac woke with the cold eastern sun. The walls of the tent glowed faintly with sunlight, and the wind howled as it swirled around the tent. He rolled over and Ben's sleeping face stared back at him. A rush of tenderness swept through Isaac and he wanted to pinch himself just to make sure he wasn't having some cruel, beautiful dream.

Ben was close enough to touch after so long. They were different people now and not just in terms of the direction of their lives. Isaac had hardly recognized Ben when he'd first laid eyes on him; he'd shaved his head and his hair had migrated to a bushy beard streaked with silver, like waves of starlight.

He'd started smoking. The asshole. All the times he'd pestered Isaac to quit, only for him to start up too. Isaac had quit years ago—couldn't have Don scenting him from miles away.

Ben's silver eyes were hard and cold, his mouth ever scowling. He'd always been a broody sort, but he'd only gotten grouchier as he'd aged.

And yet last night Ben's walls had come down and Isaac had seen the heart he guarded so closely. Ben still cared, still felt Isaac's loss as deeply as he must have years prior. The guilt could have eaten him alive and yet... that had made Isaac so happy. Because Ben still cared, Ben still ached for him like Isaac had ached for him all these years. Isaac would take his anger, his cold dismissal, all of it.

And he would find a way to prove that everything he'd sacrificed, all those years they'd missed out on, hadn't been because Isaac didn't love Ben. God, he did. Still, with everything he had. He had to find a way to prove that to Ben.

Only a few days ago, Isaac had believed he'd be alone the rest of his life, his only company the ghosts he hunted from his past. His secret heart that he'd locked away had ached for Ben, had dreamed of the life they might still have. And it wasn't a dream, not anymore. Ben was back. Fate had brought them back together after all these years, and Isaac wasn't letting this chance go.

He would earn Ben's forgiveness. They'd kill Don and the last of his hunters. Then Isaac would finally, finally, go home with his mate and it would be like all the years they'd lost had never come between them.

That was the plan, anyway.

First, he had a heartbroken mate to care for.

Needing to take a piss, Isaac crawled from the tent and out into the cold. He walked some ways into the woods and found a tree. The world was silent at this hour. The howling of the wind that made the branches of every tree shiver was near deafening and every little twig that snapped beneath his boots echoed. The Alaskan sunrise seemed brighter than usual, a little ray of hope in the darkness that had been his life for so long.

As soon as Ben was ready to hear him out, Isaac would tell him everything. He wasn't excited about reopening wounds that had never fully closed, but Ben deserved the truth. He'd always deserved far better than Isaac could give him.

What if he never forgives me?

Isaac banished the thought. He didn't deserve Ben's forgiveness, but he'd grovel on his hands and knees to fucking earn it. First, however, they needed to focus on finding Don and ending this decades-long hunt. And then... then, Isaac and Ben could pick up where they'd left off. He had to believe they could still have a second chance.

He went back and grabbed his crossbow and roamed the woods, brushing past snow-laden branches that powdered him with frost. About an hour later, he slung a large rabbit over his shoulder and carried it back to camp. Of course, the pack had gathered their own provisions prior to the trip, but Isaac wasn't deterred. Jerky and canned food couldn't compare to fresh prey, and it seemed the pack agreed. They introduced themselves one by one, but Isaac only had eyes for Ben.

"You caught a rabbit?" Max exclaimed.

"Ben," Ryan chimed in. "Remind me why we don't like him again?"

The man himself wrinkled his nose at Isaac.

"Morning, grumpy wolf." Isaac flashed him a smile.

"Hmm," was Ben's response, but Isaac didn't miss the way those glowering eyes snagged on the rabbit. "What do you know? Guess you're not useless."

"Hey, I may not be a natural hunter like you wolves, but I can still hold my own." Isaac held out the rabbit to him, wincing when its neck flopped limply. "This is for you. I'll go out and catch some more for everyone. You like your rabbit raw, right?"

Ben licked his lips but said, "Actually, I'm vegetarian now."

Isaac deflated so fast, he almost dropped the rabbit. "O-oh." Ben was a vegetarian? Since *when?* God, he'd changed so much. "Well... I've got some canned veggies in my pack if you like. I can cook them up and—"

Ben just glared at him and went back into his tent.

Isaac felt like the world's biggest idiot.

"Thanks so much, Isaac!" Izzie said, readying a small, round stove. "And don't let him fool you. Ben's favorite food is rabbit, not veggies."

"I know. That's why I..." At their curious stares, Isaac cleared his throat. "Though he doesn't seem too interested." Isaac speared the rabbit and laid it on the stove.

Izzie rolled her eyes. "He'll probably eat some when you aren't looking. Ah, this would make a great stew with the beans and the broth we bought. Did anyone bring any herbs or potatoes?"

"Yeah," Ryan said, "I got a whole grocery in my backpack!"

"That's why you're so slow, huh?" The shifter with the silver collar grinned when Ryan wrestled with him. The pack gathered around to add various ingredients to the stew, using whatever they had on hand. Isaac hoped the rabbit wouldn't be ruined, and he wrapped up a few seasoned pieces to give to Ben.

The collared shifter noticed Isaac's curious stare. "Eddie. Pleased to meet you."

"You too," Isaac stammered, a bit embarrassed. "I'm Isaac. Sorry, just wondering, can you shift with that collar?"

"Nope." Eddie gave the collar a tug. "It doesn't come off either. It needs a key, and my uncle's the one who's got it."

"You know, we could find a way to remove it without the key," Izzie said, holding her hands out over the crackling fire.

Eddie shook his head, unease plain on his face. "It's fine. It doesn't bother me."

"But don't you miss shifting?" Max asked.

"'Course I do. But I've had this collar on for years. I've lost my connection to my wolf. I can't even feel the bonds of the pack. I have no idea how my wolf will react once the collar is off."

Isaac thought he understood Eddie's reluctance. "You think you'll go feral?"

"I'd rather not find out." Eddie twisted his fingers together in his lap.

"Your uncle put a silver collar on you? Why?"

Eddie tossed a twig in the fire. "Ever heard of The Beasts?"

Isaac nodded. "Yeah. Wolf hunters. Real horrible people." Thinking back, hadn't someone hired him once to track The Beasts down? It was too long ago now.

Eddie shivered. "My uncle is the leader. He taught me to hunt my kind. Whole reason we came out here is because I thought he was responsible for the dead packs. But even despite my past, Ben and the LPA put a roof over my head and took me in. If he can see past the things I've done, I'm sure he can forgive you too."

Isaac appreciated the thought. "I don't deserve his forgiveness. I'll be happy if he even speaks to me."

Izzie and Max served everyone some stew. Isaac took a tentative sip and his eyes watered. "Whoa that is hot stuff."

Eddie licked his chops. "This is perfect! Reminds me of chili."

Max coughed and reached for his water bottle.

"Little babies." Izzie took a big spoonful.

Ryan shoveled half his bowl in his mouth and shot her a look, cheeks bulging.

"Is he eating?" Isaac asked. A black wolf prowled the camp. Isaac hadn't seen him in human form. Something about that combination of black fur and blue eyes was oddly familiar, but he couldn't put his finger on why. Was it possible they'd met before?

"Vico! Hungry?" Eddie called.

The black wolf gave him what Isaac could only describe as a glare, then trotted away.

"Guess not." Eddie sighed.

Isaac was old enough to be their dad, but he liked these packmates of Ben's. It felt good to be part of a wolf pack again, for however long it lasted.

"So, why did you leave Ben?" Izzie asked, spooning some stew into her mouth.

Isaac choked on his food. "Subtlety is not your biggest strength, is it?"

"Nope. You hurt our good friend, and I think we deserve to know why."

Trying to talk about it still left him feeling raw and exposed. "I did it to keep Ben safe." He regretted hurting Ben more than anything, but he'd had no choice. Don and the Cross would have killed Ben, and it would have been Isaac's fault. He'd had enough blood on his hands.

Izzie's brow furrowed. "Why?"

"Yeah." Ryan's eyes narrowed. "Why?"

Isaac squirmed. "I didn't have a choice. Trust me, I never would have left him if I did."

Izzie frowned at him. "You hurt him. You know that, right? And I don't like people who hurt my friends." Her fangs were sharp.

"I know. I'm sorry." Isaac raised a hand in supplication. "I'll do my best to make up for it by helping you save these wolf packs."

He thought about asking whether or not Ben had any family back home but chickened out. Surely Ben would have shut him down if he did have a family. Right?

The helicopters roared through the skies and descended just as they finished packing up camp. The wolf from the night before was gone, much to Izzie's disappointment. Isaac hoped she found herself a new pack.

The helicopters took off and they flew over the Denali mountain ranges, a desolate land of ice and snow. Isaac doubted any animals lived this far up the mountains. The helicopters carried them over the mountains and they landed as close to the lake as they could as a heavy snowstorm hit. They could reach the pack territory in the morning.

When the sun rose, the snow had stopped overnight and left several new inches. Once they'd eaten, the pack prepared for the trek over snowy hills and icy ground to the lake beyond the woods. It wasn't far but in knee-deep snow it felt longer. Isaac fell behind the pack, most of whom moved with ease through the snow as wolves. Max jumped on Ryan's back and tugged on his ears. Izzie chased Vicenzo and nipped at his heels. They were acting like big puppies.

"Fucking werewolves..." he muttered with fondness. He envied how swiftly they moved. They frolicked with each other, yipping and growling playfully as they nipped at heels and pounced on each other. He had to admit, Ben's crew made being a wolf look like a blast. They were all clearly close-knit in that way only wolves could be. Isaac had once despised the idea of being a werewolf, but Ben's pack was so warm and friendly that Isaac thought, if he had to be a wolf, he'd love to be part of their pack.

Vicenzo strode farther ahead than the others and made Eddie run to keep up with him. "Vico, wait!" Eddie shouted. "We need to stay together!" But the black wolf just forged ahead. The two disappeared over the hilltop.

Ben strode up beside Isaac, churning up snow as he marched. Isaac looked away, his heart hammering and not from exertion. In the past two days, Ben had barely spoken a word to him, and Isaac was itching to talk to him.

"Ben—"

Ben's nostrils flared and his eyes blazed, but there were splotches of color in his cheeks. It felt so good to be looked at with something other than indifference, and the rush went straight to Isaac's cock.

"Been thinking a lot the past couple days," Ben said, eyes fixed determinedly on the ground ahead. "I won't make you choose between me and revenge. If Don escapes and you wanna follow, go right ahead."

The cold dismissal in his voice made Isaac wince. "I've told you, I'm not leaving you again." Isaac took in a breath, feeling as if Ben's words had physically hit him. "I understand why you don't believe me. I understand if you... if you hate me." He pushed through the hurt, needing Ben to understand. "I get it, Ben. I hurt you, but I've been hurting too. Leaving you wasn't easy."

"Sure looked easy." Ben averted his gaze.

Isaac winced. "Okay. Guess I deserved that." He needed Ben to understand why he'd left. "Ben. Can we just talk? You can yell at me all you want, be as mad as you need to. But I need you to just hear me out. There's a lot you don't understand that factored into my decision."

Ben shut his eyes, his face twisting as if he were battling a war within himself.

"I know we've got a lot on our plate right now. So if we can't talk now, can we at least talk later?"

"No," Ben spit the word into the wind.

Isaac struggled to hold back a sigh. His man was so damned stubborn. "Why?"

"Because I'm not interested in hearing you justify why you left. Until you prove to me that you're staying for good—through actions, *not* empty promises—then I've got no reason to believe you," Ben snapped.

"Okay. That's more than fair. I'll prove to you that I'm not leaving you, Ben. Not again."

Ben answered with a *hmph*, and then he held Isaac's arm in a tight grip. Isaac lurched to a stop, glancing at the pack as they crested the hill. Ben spared them a watchful glance, and then the heat of his silver eyes was back on Isaac. Before he could stop himself, Isaac tugged on Ben's arm and brought the bigger man crashing toward him. At the last second, Isaac flipped them so Ben was against a tree and Isaac was flush against him.

Ben might be older, but his body was as powerful as ever, strong and bulky against Isaac. His chest rose and fell quickly, touching Isaac's with each breath. They were so close it was impossible to miss the quiver in Ben's lips. When he stopped scowling, they were as soft and inviting as they'd ever been.

"If Don escapes and you really want to go after him," Ben said, each word humming in the thin space between their lips, "then... then just go."

"I can't leave after I've only just found you. It would fucking kill me. Ben, I was wrong, and I'm so sorry. I never should have left, but..." Fuck, where did he even begin? "I did it for you."

Ben snarled, his eyes flaring. "Don't. Don't ever try and justify what you did by saying it was for me. Fuck you. You left for *you*. For revenge. For whatever fucked-up reason you had. Did you even—" He cut himself off with a strangled snarl. His breath was hot against Isaac's face, his eyes a wolfish yellow. The sight of Ben's wolf so close to the surface had Isaac's heart thudding, and not from fear. "Did you ever... care at all?"

Isaac's heart broke to pieces in his chest.

"You can't say that." Isaac's voice was labored as if he'd been running. So many emotions pounded through him. Fear. Anger. Lust. Such intense longing it made his knees weak. "Ben, I..." The lump in his throat ached so much he could barely speak. "I care about you. I never stopped, not for one day we were apart. You were my last thought at night and my first thought when I woke for twenty-one fucking years. Tell me, Ben. Tell me what I have to do to make this up to you, and I'll do it."

Ben's breath sawed out of him, his big chest rising and falling. "You can leave and never fucking come back."

But Isaac didn't buy that. Not for one second.

Gripping Ben's hands, he dropped to his knees in the snow and gazed up into his heartbroken face. "Is this what you want, Ben Stroud? Me on my knees for the rest of my life? Because I'll do that. I'll beg, I'll crawl. I'll fucking die for you if that's what it takes for you to understand that I never once stopped caring for you, loving you."

Ben yanked his hands free and turned away, his shoulders rising and falling quickly.

"Ben, I swear to you, if Don runs, I will let him go. I will hate it. It will kill me. We could... I don't know, work something out. He doesn't have the force he used to and your agency is bigger now, right? You could use your resources to track him, or... or something. I don't care."

Ben just shook his head. "I'm supposed to believe that?"

Damn his stubborn man. "I hate to let him go, but losing you again would kill me. Do you understand that? I haven't had a home since I left you and I just want to go home. Home is where you are, Ben Stroud. That hasn't changed. Not ever."

Ben turned toward him, and Isaac thought he'd finally done something right.

Oh God. Isaac still loved him. Still wanted him. Wanted to put his hands on him, feel the scratch of his beard as he leaned in for a kiss.

And Ben said, "I have a family."

The ground cracked under Isaac's feet. The breath was punched from his lungs. The cold seeping into his knees spread throughout his body until it reached his cracking heart.

Ben clenched his jaw, eyes hard and wet. "Whatever we had, it's over. I don't want a thing from you. I don't need you. Not anymore."

Isaac couldn't breathe.

Of course. It made sense. Why should Ben have paused his life all these years? Isaac was... happy for him. He opened his mouth to try and say so, but the words were stuck and all that came out was a tiny, broken noise. All these years, he'd ached, hoped, prayed to see the man he loved again against all odds. In his secret heart, he'd wanted Ben to wait for him, even if it was selfish and unfair and cruel. He'd been such an idiot.

Isaac and Ben could only ever end in ruin. It was a tale as old as time for a hunter and his wolf.

His eyes blurred, and Isaac looked down at the snow.

Somewhere through the haze of hurt, he registered Ben still standing there above him. Thought he heard the crunch of snow as Ben took a step toward him. "Isaac, I—"

Beyond the hills behind them, a whistle sounded.

A sigh escaped Ben. "That's Eddie's whistle. Something's happened."

Before Isaac could do anything, Ben was running off. Isaac slumped into the snow and squeezed his eyes shut.

Away from the pack, he let his tears fall into the snow.

FUCK.

Why had he said that?

Why had he used his sons like a shield to repel the man he loved? The man who'd gotten on his knees and begged, and said words Ben had only ever dreamed of hearing?

Goddess, Ben wanted to take it all back.

His wolf was furious, snarling and pacing.

Back. Go back! Comfort mate. Hold him. Love him. Now!

Ben ground his teeth and snarled, forcing himself to push forward when his instincts were screaming to turn back.

There was no point in taking anything back. Their lives were so different now. For all he knew, Isaac had never wanted a family again after losing his own child so tragically. They might not fit together like they used to, no matter how much his wolf snarled that they were meant to be, that he was being an asshole.

Fuck it. Fuck all of it. He couldn't be hurt by Isaac Bennet again. He'd done the right thing.

Hadn't he?

For reasons Ben couldn't fathom, Eddie had wandered away from the others. He urged the rest toward the lake and took a detour through the dense trees, scowling when snow cascaded down on him from the branches.

Panting, Ben stopped running when Eddie's familiar profile came into view. "Ed? What gives? Get back with the others!"

The platinum blond looked every which way as if he'd lost something.

"Lose something?" Ben asked.

"Vicenzo's gone!" Eddie never raised his voice, but he was panicked.

"Again?" Ben sighed. He jumped as Eddie abruptly kicked a tree, cursing when snow came crashing down on him. He did a little dance, smacking snow out of his coat. Ben tried not to laugh. "Cool it, Ed, no pun intended. When's the last time you saw him?"

Face flushed, Eddie paced. "I know he left the helicopter with us. He was walking behind us a few miles back. I looked back just a few minutes ago and he was gone. His tracks led into the trees but there's too much activity." Many wolf prints marred the snow, some fresh and others old.

Ben wasn't sure what to do. Vicenzo had clearly never taken to the pack the way Ben had hoped he would, but to just leave him to his own devices out in the cold didn't sit well with Ben. On the other hand, a pack of wolves was in danger. "Ed..."

"I'm not leaving him, Ben." Eddie's eyes blazed, and his hands balled into tight fists at his sides.

"I ain't asking you to," Ben said, raising both hands. "But we've got a lot more at stake right now. Vicenzo can find his way back to us."

Eddie hung his head and whispered something.

"Speak up."

"I don't think he's coming back."

Ben's heart sank.

"He told me last night." Guilt choked Eddie's voice. "He said we weren't his pack, and that he wanted to try livin' alone for a while. I should have said somethin'! I—" He paced out of Ben's reach. "He didn't even try to give this pack a chance. He shut everyone out! I tried to get him to open up. But he wouldn't listen."

With a groan, Eddie clamped his lips into a thin line and shook his head. Ben folded his arms, unsure if there was anything he could say that might offer him some peace. "I'm an idiot for thinkin' things could ever be the same between us. Like they used to be, when we were stupid kids."

Eddie turned his back on the snow-laden pines and walked past Ben. At a loss, Ben followed his packmate. His stomach clenched at the thought of Vicenzo out in the wilderness, but they were in a race against the clock. "Ed, maybe he'll find his way back to us, okay?" He couldn't look for Vicenzo and find those wolves. He had to choose.

"So we're givin' up on him?" Eddie's voice shook with emotion. "I can't do that. I already failed him once. I can't do it again."

Ben squeezed his shoulder. "I failed him too, Ed. I didn't work hard enough to make him feel like part of a pack."

Eddie shook his head. "He wouldn't let us. Wouldn't come to Pack Night, barely ever ate with us, hardly spoke a word to anyone." He was right, but the guilt was still heavy in Ben's heart.

"You two must have been close once for you to care this much," Ben said.

A small laugh full of wistful yearning escaped Eddie. "Yeah. We were. Friends since we were kids, then well into our teens."

That wasn't hard to imagine: grumpy, loner Vicenzo and soft-spoken, shy Eddie. What a pair they must have been once.

"Besides," Eddie added. "It's my fault he's like this. More wolf than man."

"That's a bit harsh, don't you think?" Ben didn't see Eddie the way he saw himself.

Eddie sighed and shook his head. "It's true. I hurt him. It's no wonder he couldn't wait to get away from me... But I don't know why he joined at all if he was just gonna wind up leavin'!"

Ben shrugged, thinking. "Maybe being part of a pack's what he thought he wanted?"

Eddie stayed quiet as they left the woodlands and followed the pack's tracks up toward the lake. The wind howled, and Ben's ears prickled. He breathed in deep and smelled wet fur and coppery blood—and he ran, spraying snow. "The pack's under attack!"

Eddie's crossbow was in his hands by the time they reached the top of the hill. Ben nearly tripped over the corpse of a collared wolf, its eyes glassy and unblinking. Max and Izzie faced off against two werewolves. Isaac took aim and a bolt soared past Ben's head and struck a werewolf between the eyes just before it could attack one of the collared wolves.

The ground trembled as Ryan's magic awoke the earth, and snow erupted as sprawling roots cracked through the ground, swinging like whips and striking any nearby foe. Ben's claws sharpened and he charged, slashing a wolf's snout and spattering the snow with crimson droplets.

Ben whirled around and encountered a wall of brambles shielding him as a wolf hurtled toward him and crashed into it, yelping as thorns pierced its hide. "Thanks, Ry!" Ben called, sidestepping the barrier and driving his claws into the wolf's throat.

Don's werewolves hadn't expected Ben's pack and took off yelping with their tails between their legs. The ones who didn't flee were either dead or shuddering as naked humans on the ground, clutching at the silver bolts lodged in their flesh. Ben thought it was time to have a chat with these assholes.

He slammed his boot down on a naked man's ribs. The man squawked, "Don't hurt me! Please!"

"Oh, I will," Ben said reassuringly. "But if you tell me what I wanna know, I won't hurt you too badly."

Grimacing, the shifter gasped and panted. "Fine. Just get that thing out of me!"

"This thing?" Ben kicked the bolt lodged in the shifter's buttock.

"Ow! Yes!"

"Who wants the honors?" Ben looked to his pack.

Isaac, jaw tight, marched to the shifter and yanked on the bolt. The scream echoed into the mountains. Kneeling, Isaac seized the shifter's jaw in an iron grip. "Where's Don?" Isaac asked in a voice like granite.

The shifter's eyes went wide. "I can't. The father helped me open my eyes to my wicked ways. He's going to help cleanse my curse."

Ben scoffed. "You serious? You actually think the good father knows how to cure lycanthropy?"

"He does!" the shifter spat with vehemence despite his injury. "It's a curse from God. If we cleanse the impure and wicked, we'll be rewarded."

Ryan whistled. "Okay, I think we just got on the train to Crazy Town. Man, I hate to break it to you, but there's no cure for lycanthropy. Except death, maybe."

"Yes!" the shifter exclaimed as if they'd finally reached some sort of weird understanding. "In death, God will cleanse us of our beasthood! The father has told us the only path to redemption lies in the blood of the wicked."

Isaac stepped on the man's wound, earning a pained squeal. "I don't give a damn about your unholy mission! Tell me where Don is!"

The shifter grinned, eyes fixated on the woods behind them. "He's here."

Howls echoed through the forest. Ben turned and his heart sank as wolves emerged from between the trees in uncountable numbers and as wild as a coming storm. They were a huge pack, snarling and snapping, and leading them was one of the more hideous beasts Ben had ever seen. The wolf had suffered severe burns to its face and shoulder, which had seared away the fur to the raw flesh beneath.

"Don," Isaac growled.

The burned wolf threw back his head and howled, and the pack charged, shaking the ground beneath their paws. The ground rumbled, and a tank rolled toward them from the trees, the side painted with a cross and bloody paw prints. A shell exploded from the tank and hurtled toward them.

Isaac launched himself at Ben, knocking him to the ground as the tank shell hurtled over their heads and exploded behind them, leaving a scarred crater in the earth. The tank rolled closer, the rotting carcass of a wolf nailed to the front of the tank like a gruesome car ornament.

"Run!" Ben roared.

The gun atop the tank rotated in the pack's direction and opened fire. With cries of alarm, the pack scattered, using the trees for cover. Ben wrenched Isaac behind a tree before he got his head shot off, and Max and Izzie had taken cover. Eddie loaded his pistol and leaned around another tree, shooting down a wolf that came charging toward them. Ryan curled his fingers, and roots ripped from the soil and tried to wrap around the tank's wheels but to no avail. They had no choice but to retreat.

"Retreat, spread out! Don't clump together and become a target for that tank!" Ben shouted. One by one, the pack dispersed into the trees. Ben closed his eyes tight, fury making him grind his teeth. They didn't have a plan. With all of them separated, no one knew where to regroup. They'd have to track each other by scent. Damn it. There was no time to do anything other than run.

"Isaac, we gotta retreat. Isaac?"

He was gone.

"Son of a..." Ben peered around the tree and jumped when the turret gun sprayed the trunk with bullets, none of which hit him. He was stuck here.

There was an explosion near the tank, and the turret ceased firing. Ben risked a look. The turret had been blown to pieces. Ahead, Isaac leaned out from behind a tree and chucked another grenade at the tank. With a *boom*, the tank fired a shell at him, and Isaac barely avoided being blown to pieces. Ben's heart damn near stopped beating.

"Isaac! Get back here!"

"This is my only chance to get to Don!" Isaac hollered back, charging behind a boulder for cover.

Ben ran out from cover just as the tank lobbed a shell at him. "You're gonna get yourself killed!" Ben roared, his ears ringing from the tank's gunfire.

"Get out of here, Ben!" Isaac chucked another grenade at the tank. Its wheel lurched into a small pothole the grenade had left behind but rolled out of it with ease.

No. Like hell Ben was letting Isaac die on him. He charged, weaving between the trees. A shell whistled past his head and made the ground shake behind him. He collided with Isaac and yanked him away from the boulder just as a shell smashed it to pieces. "You're not killing yourself on my watch!" Ben snarled, rolling them both behind a tree.

"Ben, just go!" Isaac struggled to escape Ben's grip on his arm. "Don's my problem!"

Ben yanked him close as a shell soared past their cover. "And you're mine, damn it!"

A deafening crack split the sky. The ground rumbled. From where they were, facing the mountains, Ben had a perfect view as an avalanche came crashing down from above.

"Oh fuck," Isaac whispered.

A howl of warning echoed over the treetops. It was Max, telling everyone to evacuate.

The tank ceased firing and began to drive in the opposite direction. The wolves retreated into the woods, their tails between their legs.

"They've got the right fucking idea. Move!" Ben shoved Isaac ahead of him and they ran in the opposite direction, away from Don and his pack. The ground shook, and trees snapped and cracked as the force of the avalanche ripped them from the earth. They couldn't run fast enough as the avalanche sped toward them. There was nowhere they could go.

"Ben!" Isaac seized his arm and hurled him to the left, toward an opening in the rock face. A cave. They'd just passed the threshold when a wave of snow crashed down behind them. Ben flew off his feet as snow spilled inside the entrance. Isaac tumbled to the ground, shouting in terror as snow submerged his legs. Scrambling to his feet, Ben grabbed Isaac's arms and pulled. Kicking and clawing his way to freedom, Isaac gasped as he collapsed beside Ben.

The snow that blocked their only way out muffled all other sounds except the drip, drip, drip of water from the icicles on the roof of the cave.

"Well, shit," Ben panted. "Can't go out that way." Wiping his brow, Ben blinked a few times until his eyes adjusted to the dark. "It looks like there's a path that way." Deeper into the dark unknown. "Looks like we're in for a nice stroll."

Isaac stood, dusting snow from his ski pants. "Come on. Let's go. I think I feel a draft. Maybe there's a way out."

Ben made himself stand, his legs aching from all the running.

Stumbling, Isaac cursed. "Shit. Can't see a damn thing."

"I'll lead." He brushed past Isaac, who tripped over something and cursed. Ben scowled, wondering if he ought to stick next to Isaac and lead him through the dark. The thought of being close to him made his stomach twist and his heart... do things.

"Ow, motherfucker!"

Growling, Ben reached behind him and seized Isaac's arm. "Just shut up and stay close to me."

Isaac stumbled into Ben's side. Ben reached down and grabbed Isaac's hand. Heat rushed to his face, and he was grateful for the dark. Isaac's fingers were stiff in Ben's grip. Either no one had held his hand in a while, or he was uncomfortable holding hands with Ben.

He expected Isaac to give him shit, but he was oddly quiet. What, no stupid comments or smug remarks about how Ben was still in love with him? Somehow, Ben liked the quiet even less. He could deal with Isaac's teasing but this sudden shyness? Ben wasn't sure what to do with that.

"Better now that you aren't stubbing your toesies on a rock?" Ben grumbled.

Isaac snorted. "My toesies are fine, thanks. How about yours?"

Ben kicked Isaac's foot in response. In retaliation, Isaac crushed Ben's fingers. It didn't hurt. Instead, Ben's stomach did somersaults. Goddess, how long had it been since anyone had held *his* hand? Not that it mattered. This wasn't romantic by any means. Especially not with Isaac.

His memories stirred—the last night they'd touched. They'd been lying in bed and Isaac had smelled like ash and smoke. Then he'd woken the next day to an empty bed, and he hadn't seen Isaac for decades. A spasm of pain went through Ben's chest. How long before Isaac disappeared this time?

"Ow."

Ben realized he was squeezing Isaac's hand. "Sorry."

"No. That's not it. My ankle's killing me."

Ben stopped, and Isaac leaned on the wall for support and raised his leg. "Think it got messed up while we were running, and I just didn't feel it."

"Can you walk?"

Isaac put weight on his leg and hissed. "Yeah. Just gonna be slow going."

Ben didn't have time for slow going. "Here." He went to Isaac's side and grabbed his arm, draping it over his shoulders. Isaac frowned and adjusted his weight to his uninjured leg. Then Ben took a step and, though they stumbled along at first, they fell into a slow pace through the darkness.

"Think there are any bears in here?" Isaac asked.

"No. I'd smell them," Ben said.

"Phew." Isaac was so close his breath tickled Ben's ear and Ben could smell his rainfall scent. It was all he could do not to close his eyes and breathe in deep. Their sides touched. Isaac's body was warm and strong, and his labored breath was close to Ben's ear. Closing his eyes, Ben tried to force away the memories of heated touches and breathless kisses they'd shared.

Something caught on Ben's foot and he lurched forward.

"Shit!" Isaac lunged to catch him, one arm flying across Ben's chest. Ben stumbled to the right and collided into Isaac, and a grunt escaped Isaac when he bumped into the wall. They froze, their bodies pressed close together.

"You okay?" Isaac's voice was low and raspy.

Ben nodded. His heart was pounding hard in his ears. "You?"

"Fine. Can't see a damn thing." Isaac's hands fumbled up Ben's body. His hand stopped over Ben's heart where it was slamming against his ribs. Frowning, Isaac looked left and right. Ben was right in front of him. Isaac couldn't see him, but Ben could see Isaac. Every little detail of his face.

At last, he allowed himself to look without fear of being caught. There were stress lines on his forehead and mouth, freckles from time under the sun. He had a small scar just above his lips. His lips, which were the same as Ben remembered, full and just as tempting.

This Isaac might be more rugged and scarred than the man Ben remembered, but he was still hot as hell. Ben gave a start, realizing he'd leaned closer so he could count the freckles on Isaac's cheeks. In the dark with nothing but the howling of the wind against the rocks, it was easy to feel like time had stopped just for them.

Isaac sighed, his eyelashes fluttering over heavy-lidded eyes. His scent had changed notes, becoming spicy and warm and—

Ah shit. Isaac could sense how close he was. Isaac wanted him. Here, now.

It would be so easy to lean down and finally taste his lips. Ben's eyes threatened to close as his resolve weakened by the second. Isaac curled a hand in Ben's coat, pulling him close. A little gasp escaped Isaac when Ben's breath wafted against his lips. "Ben..."

The sound of his name, moaned by Isaac's lips, had Ben growling and curling his hand in the hair at the nape of his neck. He wanted to be angry. He was still so angry. But he was tired, so tired of fighting his feelings. All his wolf wanted was to bury his face in Isaac's neck and breathe in his scent, blanket him with the warmth of his body and keep him safe.

But he didn't. Nothing had changed. If Don went running off, Isaac would follow, and Ben would have to pick up the shattered pieces of his heart again. Unless he left the life he knew behind and followed Isaac into the unknown.

Isaac sighed. "Light," he croaked. He pushed at Ben's chest. "There's light ahead. Don't you see it?"

Scowling, he yanked his gaze away from Isaac. In the darkness, shafts of light glimmered.

"That's the way out! Finally!" Isaac tried to move and winced. "Ow! Damn leg."

Ben tugged him close. "Easy. Can't go busting your leg up even worse and expecting me to carry you."

Isaac chuckled. "That doesn't sound so bad."

Ben rolled his eyes and led Isaac toward the light, which was growing brighter and brighter with each step.

They left the dark cave behind and stumbled out into a vast wilderness. Ben sniffed the air. "Excellent."

"What?" Isaac asked.

Ben smelled wolves. "By the stink of things, Don and his wolves passed through this area recently. We can follow the trail they left, and they'll lead us right to their hideout. If we move fast, I could get back home to Jack and Colin in no time."

Isaac cocked his head. "Who and who?"

Ben hesitated. He hadn't meant to mention them out loud. "My sons," he admitted.

Isaac was quiet. "Right. Yeah. Your kids..."

Looking away, Ben tried to ignore the damned guilty feeling suddenly gnawing at him. Like hell if *he* had anything to be guilty for.

"Uh. How old are they?"

"They're both in college. My ex Heather and I co-parent."

Isaac looked down quickly, wetting his lips. "Yeah, of course you do. I didn't expect you to put your life on hold all those years." But from the forced casual tone in his voice, Ben suspected Isaac meant something else entirely. He stopped walking, guilt twisting through his stomach.

Isaac sighed beside him. "Ben, I—"

"I waited," Ben said, pushing through the mire of pointless guilt. "I waited as long as I could for you. Till I thought the loneliness would damn near eat me alive. Heather offered me everything I was looking for." *Everything I'd wanted with* you, he wanted to say. "And I said yes. You're not going to saunter back into my life after two decades and fault me for moving on, you got it?"

Isaac blinked fast and nodded. "Yeah. No, Ben, I... I'm glad you found that. You deserve it. I just..." He sighed. "I wish I could have given you everything you deserved."

Ben gritted his teeth. Why did he feel guilty? He had no reason to feel guilty, not one bit, but he did, and he could kill Isaac for having the nerve to come back into his life and rip his heart from his chest, just when he'd finally convinced himself that he was *fine* being alone, that he had everything he needed. No, instead, Isaac had ripped open the wound he'd left all those years ago, and Ben was bleeding for him all over again.

"I wanted all of that with you." Admitting it out loud sent a throb of pain through his heart.

Isaac closed his eyes tight and looked away. He muttered something.

"What?" Ben asked, his voice hoarse.

"I said, 'It's snowing.'" Sniffling, Isaac looked up at the clouds.

Snowflakes started falling in fat clumps from the sky.

"I don't like the look of those clouds," Isaac remarked.

Ben hated to admit it, but Isaac was right. The clouds were dark and angry, blocking out the sunlight.

"Those are storm clouds," Isaac said, pushing off from the tree he'd been leaning on. He winced as he put pressure on his bad leg. "We need to find shelter. I sure hope that pack of yours will be okay."

Ben nodded. "They will be. If they shift and huddle close, the snow won't be able to penetrate their fur. You, though, you'll freeze in seconds."

"Thanks for the confidence. Really appreciate it."

Had Isaac always been this sarcastic? Maybe Ben just brought out the worst in him. He went on ahead, wading through the ankle-deep snow.

"I'm sure I'll be fine," Isaac called out. "I'll just be back here. Sauntering. Which I don't do, by the way."

"Yeah, you do, and it looks stupid."

Isaac laughed softly.

Ben snorted, glad Isaac couldn't see the genuine smile he'd just provoked. The fucker. Ben doubled back and grabbed his arm. "Come on. Keep up."

The wind howled and snow fell thick and fast around them.

Ben sure hoped they could find shelter soon.

CHAPTER 21

BLOOD AND ICE

HIS SONS.

Ben had children. Colin and Jackson.

The realization sat heavy in Isaac's stomach as they journeyed through the snow, following the tracks left by the wolves. *Of course he has sons,* Isaac reasoned, feeling stupid for being upset. *It's been years. He's had a life. What, was I thinking that he'd put his world on pause while I was gone?*

Ben had offered to give him everything once. He'd handed him a ring and told him they could be mates, maybe even husbands someday. They could have had a family.

No, it didn't bother him that Ben had a family. He'd moved on and was finally happy, and Isaac was glad for that. It was realizing Isaac wasn't a part of it that ached deep in his chest, that he could have had the world and he'd squandered it. Now, all he could do was mourn the loss of a life he'd never had.

"See that?" Isaac stopped, making Ben stumble. Through the trees, he thought he could see a cabin.

"A cabin in the middle of the woods?" Ben grumbled. "Sounds like horror movie material to me." He sniffed the air. "No scents lingering around. Maybe it's empty."

They made their way toward the cabin. The windows were dusty and covered in frost, making it impossible to see inside. Ben knocked on the door. "Hello? Anyone home?"

When no one answered, curiosity compelled Isaac to grab the knob and turn, and the door creaked open without issue. The cabin was dark inside and empty. It was a small space, with all the necessities contained in a single room. There was an empty hearth and a dining table and chairs. Isaac thought he'd seen an outhouse between the trees a little way to the left. And of course, there was only one bed. Isaac tried hard to keep his mind tame, but he wondered if two grown men could fit in it comfortably.

Recalling how Ben had almost kissed him back in the cave, Isaac had felt hopeful they were growing together and not apart. Ben was stubborn and hurt, but Isaac knew he hadn't imagined Ben's breath against his lips. He just had to keep proving he was serious about Ben, and melt the ice around his heart. Probably literally. A fire in the hearth would seriously do this cabin wonders.

Ben wrinkled his nose. "Nobody's lived here in a long time."

Isaac breathed in the stale air and kicked away an empty beer bottle that rolled along the floor. "Well, it's something. Do you feel okay waiting out the storm here? What about the pack?"

Ben didn't look happy about the idea, but he shrugged. "They'll be okay. We've handled worse than this, believe me. We'll catch up with them in the morning."

The wind slammed the door behind them and Isaac jumped out of his skin.

Ben chuckled. "Scared?"

Isaac shoved him and eased out of Ben's hold, wincing when he put pressure on his foot. The ache was getting worse. Needing to sit down, Isaac sat on the squeaky floorboards by the hearth. He tugged off his boots and socks. "Shit." A big nasty bruise was blooming in purples and greens over his ankle.

"Looks bad." Ben stood a few steps away, looking over Isaac's shoulder.

"Had worse," Isaac said. All this needed was some snow to ice the bruise, and it would heal fine. "Could have turned out a lot worse, all things considered."

Ben rumbled an agreement. "Where'd they get that tank from?"

"Hell if I know. There are all sorts of abandoned military bases around Alaska. Maybe they're holed up in one." Isaac touched the bruise and hissed. "Fuck me sideways."

"No, thank you."

Isaac snorted. It felt good to laugh in situations like this. He really needed to ice his leg, or he'd be useless in a fight. He tugged on his boot and laced it back up.

"Where are you sauntering off to?" Ben asked, voice ripe with suspicion.

"Gotta ice this thing." Isaac tried to stand.

Ben shoved him back down. "Stay. I need to nab us some lunch anyway."

"And here I was, thinking you didn't give a shit."

His sarcasm earned him a glower. "Stay put. I'll be back."

"I've got this, okay? I've been looking after myself for years. I can help myself, you know."

Ben marched to the door and glanced back at him. "You're not *you* anymore. For however long this lasts, you're part of a pack." Surprise bloomed in Isaac's chest. Ben looked away and rubbed the back of his neck, a tell Isaac remembered fondly.

"I got this," Ben said, finally finding the words. "Okay? So sit your ass down and I'll be back in a bit." Ben walked out the door and the wind kicked it shut behind him.

As much as he appreciated Ben's concern, he didn't want to be totally useless. The cabin was freezing cold. The least he could do was get a fire going. Anything was better than lying around brooding over Ben's sons and wondering who the other parent was. If he'd loved this "Heather" Ben had mentioned. Isaac hadn't known he was bisexual. He supposed they still had one thing in common, at least.

Grunting, Isaac limped around the cabin until he found a walking stick. Outside, he kicked snow around until he found big enough sticks to use for a fire.

Since Ben had called her his ex, he supposed their union hadn't worked out. He wondered why and felt bad for feeling a rush of relief. That meant there was still a chance, if only Don wasn't still in the damn picture.

With the firewood under one arm, Isaac limped back to the cabin on his cane and chucked it in the hearth. Using a lighter and some kindling in his bag, he got a fire going and huddled close. He'd grabbed a chunk of snow on his way in and pressed it to the bruise for as long as he could stand it. The aching pain became numb.

Eyes heavy, Isaac curled up on the cold floor by the hearth. Before he knew it, he'd given in to sleep.

When he woke, the sun was just beginning to dip beyond the mountains. Ben still wasn't back, and anxiety coiled in Isaac's stomach. Hunting took a while, but it had been at least two hours. The wild was howling around the sides of the house, rattling the windows. The fire had long since died in the hearth, and only embers and ash remained.

The wind rattled the windows and when he glanced back, the snow was hurtling down again. Shit. Ben was out in that storm. Was he okay? "He's a wolf," Isaac muttered, his voice loud in the suffocating silence. "He's in his element." The snow wouldn't be able to penetrate the thick layers of fur that kept a wolf warm. He would be fine. Wouldn't he?

"Damn wolf." Isaac couldn't sit still. He had to make sure Ben was okay. He stood with a grunt and grabbed his bag. His leg throbbed, but Isaac put his weight on the cane and stepped out into the cold. The snow was coming down hard, stinging Isaac's face. "Ben?" he called. He closed his eyes and tried to do that thing werewolves did where they communicated telepathically.

Ben? You hear me?

He had no idea if humans could communicate with wolves like that, but probably not. He didn't get a response.

The howl of the wind was his only answer. The snow must have just begun to fall because Ben's paw prints hadn't been covered. Just in case, he checked to make sure his pistol was loaded, which it was, and followed the tracks into the woods. The minutes passed and Isaac grew colder, his lips and face going numb. Snow crunched under his feet, and the wind screamed in his ears.

Something roared within the woods, and Isaac jumped but couldn't tell if it was the wind or not. What creature would be out in the woods during a storm like this? He shivered, thinking that was a question better left unanswered. Another set of tracks appeared. Hoof prints. Antler marks scoured the trees. A male elk, Isaac would know the hoof prints anywhere.

Bright red drops of blood stood out against the snow. Isaac's heart dropped into his stomach. He knelt to inspect the spatters of blood. It was impossible to tell whose blood it was. If it was Ben's and he'd been stabbed by the elk's antlers, he hadn't been hurt badly. However, the blood trail continued into the woods. Then Isaac realized it couldn't be Ben's blood—he would have healed quickly. Perhaps he'd gotten a bite in?

He followed the trail of blood and lurched to a stop when something lumbered through the trees ahead. It was big, whatever it was, dislodging snow from the trees as it walked.

"Ben?" he whispered. He couldn't tell if it was a wolf, but it sort of looked like—

Something grabbed his arm and pulled. Before Isaac could scream, a hand slapped over his mouth. His back slammed into the trunk of a tree and he found himself face-to-face with Ben, eyes wild, face covered in silver fur... and very, very naked.

Ben lowered his hand and Isaac snapped, "What the hell are you doing?"

Ben shot a worried glance at the trees. "Don't whisper. We need it to know we're here. It should be afraid of humans, so hopefully it will avoid us."

"Need what to hear us?" Isaac asked, voice louder than usual.

"Told you to stay put. I was hunting. Finally found us an elk. Got a good bite in, but then..."

A rumbling growl echoed through the woods. Something snorted and groaned.

Isaac's blood turned to ice. He knew that sound, and it only meant trouble. "A bear?"

Ben nodded.

"Is it alone? Are there cubs?"

Ben peered around the tree. "Not sure. It stole my kill and ran me off."

"It's going the other way. Come on, let's get out of here." Isaac grabbed Ben's hand and led him out from behind the tree. They headed toward the house, stealing glances over their shoulders. Isaac exhaled and spoke loudly, hoping his voice would encourage the bear to keep its distance. "Okay. Bears don't wanna fuck with humans. It should avoid us, especially since it has food."

Ben snorted. "Who're you trying to convince?"

"Shut up. Hear me, bear? Just eat your food and leave us alone!"

Ben's laugh died in his throat. He yanked on Isaac's hand, tugging him up against his hard, hairy chest.

The bear wasn't avoiding them at all. Instead, it stumbled through the trees and out into the path right in front of them. Snow turned its thick brown fur white. Its enormous snout was caked in blood that dribbled into the snow. It was moving erratically, its jaws snapping, its head bent up at an unnatural angle. It pawed at its face, its head jerking, and began walking backward. The thing moved like a demon possessed its body.

"Oh hell. It's rabid," Isaac whispered.

The bear swung its enormous head toward them and snarled. Huge clawed paws thundered on the ground, spraying snow as it charged. Ben shoved Isaac behind him. "Run! I'll hold it off. Go!" Before Isaac could stop him, Ben dropped to all fours as a wolf and ran at the bear.

With a snarl, Ben hurled himself upon it, driving his fangs deep into its fur. The bear bellowed and reared up on its back legs. Roaring, the bear sent Ben flying, tumbling over into the snow. The bear slammed a paw down on Ben, crushing him into the ground. Ben yelped and snarled, snapping wildly at the bear's face.

Isaac couldn't do it. He'd left Ben once, and he'd be a bear's dinner before he let it happen again. He'd told himself he would die for Ben. Well, now it was time to make good on his word. Isaac took aim with his pistol and fired. He'd intended to hit the head, but the bear was moving too much. He struck it in the shoulder and the bear roared in fury and pain.

"Hey, you big fucker! Over here!" Isaac shouted, taking aim again. The bear rounded on him with a deafening bellow and lumbered toward him. Isaac had no hope of outrunning it, not with his bad leg. He chucked his cane at the bear, making it snarl as the cane bounced off its head. Roaring, the bear thundered toward him, shaking the ground. The beast slammed into him like a freight train. The ground disappeared from under Isaac and he flew head over heels down a slope.

Snow sprayed into his face and the breath went out of him as he landed on his shoulder, struck his back and ribs, then crashed onto the ground and slid over a slick, hard surface. The world spun around him and he struggled to rise to his hands and knees, gasping for air and wiping snow out of his eyes.

The ground beneath him was cold, hard, and slippery. Isaac's heart stuttered. He'd landed on a frozen lake below the hillside. The ice hadn't broken and felt solid enough under him, but he was still paralyzed with fear.

"Okay... take it easy. Take it slow." With so much snow covering the ice, he had no idea how to tell if the ice was safe to walk on. He didn't have the courage to stand and so kept his weight evenly distributed on his hands and knees as inch by inch he crawled toward the path he'd cleaved through the snow when he'd tumbled down the hill.

The ice cracked. His hand plunged into frigid water and Isaac yelped as cold numbed his arm up to the shoulder. He stumbled back onto his ass, cradling his soaking arm to his chest. "Fuck, fuck, fuck!"

A roar drowned out his curses, and the bear came crashing down the hill toward him. Isaac looked down into the hole he'd punched in the ice. "Oh, hell no." The bear's huge paw slammed down on the surface of the ice, and a crack split the air. Cracks formed in the ice, spreading from the bear's paw toward Isaac, and the ice creaked under him.

With a snarl, the bear charged him, and with a deafening crack, the ice shattered beneath the creature's immense weight. The bear plunged beneath the surface of the lake. It surfaced, thrashing wildly, its claws breaking up chunks of ice. It tried to climb out of the water, but the ice wouldn't support its weight.

"Isaac?" Ben's voice echoed. He stumbled down the hill, eyes wide in horror as he surveyed Isaac and the broken ice.

"Stay there!" Isaac shouted. "Don't come out here, Ben! I mean it!"

Ben's chest rose and fell fast, panic clear in his face. "Just... take it slow, okay? Make your way over to me." Ben followed the line where the ice met the shore, trying to find a safe spot to reach Isaac.

Isaac didn't dare lift himself onto his hands and knees. He belly-dragged himself toward the shore, his heart stuck in his throat when the ice creaked beneath him. He crawled around the hole the bear's body had left in the ice, shivering when frigid water lapped at his stomach. Ben got down on his hands and knees and crawled through the snow toward him, but a crack split the ice between them.

Ben reached out his hand. "Come on, Isaac. I got you. I got you. Reach for me."

Trying not to panic, Isaac eased himself onto his hands and knees and reached for him.

The ice exploded around them. The bear broke the surface and heaved its wet body onto a firm patch of ice. With a snarl, it rounded on Ben, a huge claw raised to slice into him.

No. Isaac wouldn't let Ben be hurt, not even if it killed him. Isaac lunged, wrapping his arms around the bear's huge, soaking wet neck and throwing the beast off balance.

"Isaac!" Ben's roar became muffled as Isaac and the bear crashed beneath the frigid surface. The cold paralyzed him. His body seized, his limbs jerking. For a moment he couldn't move. Panic robbed him of his senses, and then instinct took over. *Get to shore. Get warm.*

He kicked and clawed his way to the surface, but the bear's huge paw slammed into his ribs. The bear wasn't fighting him; it was struggling madly to get to the surface and blind to anything else. The breath flew out of Isaac's lungs and water rushed in. The light of the moon got farther away. Cold... he was so cold. He couldn't move. He couldn't breathe.

At least Ben was alive. He was safe. That was all that mattered.

The bear heaved its huge body from the water. The moonlight rippled violently, then stilled. Isaac kicked feebly, but his whole body was numb. He reached for the light of the moon.

A shape crashed through the water, blocking out the moon's light. The wolf swam toward him, its jaws open wide and snapping around Isaac's shoulder. Ben... Ben had come for him. Saved his damn life.

The wolf dragged Isaac to the surface and he gulped in air but couldn't get enough, choking on the ice water in his lungs. Two strong hands grabbed him and hauled him from the lake and onto the ice. A hand struck his back once, twice, and Isaac retched a whole lake from his lungs. He lay paralyzed on the ice, capable only of shuddering, his limbs jerking and seizing.

"Isaac, I got you. I'm here." Ben was soaking wet and as naked as could be, but being a werewolf had its advantages. He was only shivering lightly when he hoisted Isaac onto his feet and helped him toward the shore. A roar followed them.

The beast, twitching and jerking, lurched toward them, its jaws snapping.

Isaac closed his eyes and waited for death.

CHAPTER 22

FORGIVENESS

As Isaac shuddered and shook in Ben's arms and the bear lumbered toward them, something awoke in Ben. His fangs sharpened and his claws elongated.

Don't. Touch.

A snarl pulled from his throat.

"B-Ben?" Isaac stammered. Ben whirled them toward the bear. Fur rippled over his body and he bared his teeth.

The bear roared, its head jerking back at an unnatural angle. It came toward them, claws slipping over the wet ice.

Don't. Touch.

Ben's vision narrowed only to the bear. His arms tightened around Isaac. The bear roared and charged, its jaws gaping and frothing.

Don't. Touch. Him.

A roar shook the forest, chasing birds from the trees. The sound erupted from Ben's chest, surging from somewhere deep within. Isaac jerked and shuddered in his arms, his eyes wide and mouth slack.

The bear took a few staggered steps back. It tossed its head, its jaws clicking. Then it turned and thundered away into the trees.

A sudden wave of exhaustion crashed over Ben. He felt much smaller all of a sudden, dazed and weak. His wolf hadn't felt so out of control before, ready to burst from his skin and defend his vulnerable mate shivering against his chest.

His... No. Isaac wasn't... He couldn't still be. Not after all this time. That bond between them had died. Hadn't it?

"B-Ben... That was c-cool and all, but I'm freezing to death here," Isaac stammered, hardly able to speak through his numb lips.

Ben hoisted Isaac over his shoulder, ignoring his yelp of surprise. "I got you. You fucking idiot. How could you do that?"

"Told you I'd die for you. I meant it," Isaac gasped through chattering teeth.

"You're not going to die!" Ben snarled. Softly, he said, "You can't. I can't lose you, not now."

He couldn't lose Isaac, not now that he knew how far he was willing to go for him. Isaac still cared for him, just like he'd said from the start. Ben wished he'd believed him.

He ran up the hill as fast as he could with a soaked grown man in his arms. The wind lashed at them and snow stung Ben's eyes. His body burned hot from his beast blood, but even he was starting to feel the bite of the Alaskan wind. He ran, his lungs burning and cold numbing his throat. He couldn't stop. He had to get Isaac inside, get him warm.

When the cabin came into view, Ben barreled inside and set Isaac on the floor. Isaac's lips were blue and so were the tips of his fingers. The sight cleaved Ben's heart. "Stay with me, Isaac. You don't get to fucking die on me, you hear?"

With shaking hands, Ben unfastened Isaac's belt and yanked his wet pants down, then got to work on his coat and sweaters. It was hard work. Isaac's clothes were heavy and waterlogged, and his limbs were stiff and trembling violently. Ben had worked up a sweat by the time Isaac was naked. Lifting Isaac, Ben laid him in the bed, grabbed a few blankets from his pack, and rushed back to his side.

Ben draped himself over Isaac and tugged the blankets over them, desperate to warm him. Isaac's body jerked underneath him and he made a sound that might have been relief as Ben's overheated body touched his frigid skin. Ben grabbed Isaac's hand and massaged his fingers, trying to ease warmth back into them. They were so blue. Fear clamped around his heart. "Move, Isaac. You got to move. Wiggle your toes. Do something, anything."

Isaac's teeth chattered. His lips were a dark, frightening shade of blue. Leaning down, Ben kissed them before he could stop himself, pressing his mouth hard against Isaac's. It was like kissing an ice cube but Ben did it again and again, fueled by desperation. "Come on, Isaac. Come on. Don't you give up." Ben wrapped himself around Isaac, rubbing the ice blocks that were his feet between his soles.

Raking his fingers through Isaac's cold, wet hair, Ben pressed Isaac's face into his neck and held him to his body. There wasn't an inch of space between them. Of all the ways he'd imagined lying naked with Isaac again, and there'd been quite a few times over the years those thoughts had crept up on him, this wasn't the way he'd wanted it to happen. But he'd take what he could get.

They lay there for what felt like years and eventually Isaac's violent tremors subsided into shivers. Ben pressed his mouth to the cold shell of Isaac's ear and let his breath warm Isaac's skin. If his own hair weren't still soaked, he'd shift and let his fur warm Isaac, but he thought a wet wolf would do more harm than good. Isaac huddled against him, vulnerable and needy in ways Ben hadn't thought him capable of being. It threatened to melt his heart.

When he opened his eyes, the cabin was dark. The wind howled, and snowflakes battered the windows. Isaac lay curled against his chest. His lips and fingers were a healthy pink again. Ben exhaled his relief. Isaac's body ran hot against him, but not feverishly, and he didn't smell sick. Ben brushed Isaac's long hair from his cheek, shaken by the immense relief he felt.

After so much time, he still cared for Isaac Bennet. When he'd watched Isaac plunge through the ice, he'd been breathless with fright. He held Isaac tighter and drew him close. Things weren't the same between them, but Ben didn't want to lose him.

Fucking hell. He was supposed to be pissed. Angry. Fighting this… thing that still burned between them. But he was so tired. Tired of being angry. Tired of denying himself what he wanted. *Who* he wanted. Isaac shivered against him, his stomach growling.

Ben felt the overwhelming need to provide. To hunt and give his mate—*Isaac, give Isaac*—whatever he needed.

He sighed. He couldn't buy his own bullshit anymore. Not after that kiss last night. She-Wolf's tits, what was he thinking? *You could warm a guy up without kissing him…* It hadn't occurred to him at the time. All he'd wanted was to comfort him in any way he could, and keep him safe and warm.

Since they'd been reunited, Isaac had tried to talk to him and tell the truth. In return, Ben had pushed him away. Guilt gnawed at him. Now that he was finally ready, would Isaac still open up to him and give them that second chance?

Once he was awake, they would finally talk and Ben would listen to every word.

But first, he had some hunting to do.

WHEN ISAAC OPENED HIS eyes, he was blissfully warm and wrapped up in blankets. It was dark out, and a storm raged outside. The only light came from a fire, roaring in the fireplace. He supposed they were stuck in the cabin a while longer. He smelled roasting meat, and his mouth watered. He sat up and found Ben kneeling before the fire. He was, sadly, fully clothed and rotating a spit with a plump rabbit searing on it.

"Roast bunny. My favorite midnight snack," Isaac announced, wrapping a blanket around himself and going to sit before the fire.

Ben glanced at him, then quickly away. Huh. Someone was shy today. "How do you feel?"

"Well, my dick didn't fall off, so pretty good."

Ben's mouth did a strange half smile and he turned the spit. Isaac didn't understand why Ben wasn't looking at him, why there even seemed to be a patch of pink in his cheeks. Except... he thought he remembered something. A warm body against his. Hot breath on his ear. Lips, hot and urgent against his mouth, and the scratch of a rough beard.

Ben had kissed him before Isaac had fallen asleep. He remembered that much. It hadn't exactly been romantic and the intention hadn't been sexual in nature, driven by desperation most likely. Isaac's heart fluttered regardless. Damn. His heart hadn't done that in a good long while.

Isaac set his hand on Ben's knee, which made him jump and clear his throat, his eyes intent upon the roasting rabbit. "You saved my neck out there," Isaac said. "Thank you."

Ben grunted, looking anywhere but at Isaac. "Don't mention it."

If his face got any redder, Isaac thought he could fry an egg on it. Isaac ran his hand up Ben's knee to squeeze his thigh. "I'll have to return the favor sometime."

"Kill that crazy priest pal of yours, and we'll be set." Ben looked out the window behind them at the raging storm. "Guess we'll be here a while longer."

Ben removed the rabbit from the spit and cut off pieces of it, dividing it equally between them. It was gamey and unseasoned. "Too bad we don't have Ryan's spices," Isaac said and regretted it when sadness furrowed Ben's brows. "We'll find your pack, Ben. I'll put a bullet or a bolt or both between Don's eyes. We'll both leave happy."

Ben grunted and attempted a smile but it fell from his face. "Isaac, we need to talk."

Isaac's heart leaped. Was Ben finally ready to listen to him? "Really?"

Ben turned to him, determination hardening his eyes. "Yeah. I'm... I'm sorry I gave you such a rough time. But I'm ready now if you want to talk about it."

Acid left a sour taste in Isaac's throat. The only thing that scared him more than losing Ben was Ben hating him for the rest of his life.

Gripping his shoulder, Ben said, "Tell me." The desperation made his voice shake.

Isaac swallowed and suddenly he couldn't find the words. He blinked hard as countless variations of guilt and shame surged to the surface like a rushing tide against a dam about to break. Shaking, he turned to Ben and forced himself to look into his eyes.

"You know I had a son. Beau. He's been gone so long, I can't imagine what he would look like. Who he would be." Throat aching, Isaac swallowed hard and pressed on. "A wolf killed him. When I met Don, he was like a father to me. He empathized with my grief. He brought me comfort. He told me there was a way to avenge Beau's death and… and he brought me who he told me had killed Beau."

Ben's face was unreadable as he sank back onto his haunches. His hand squeezed Isaac's shoulder, whether in anger or comfort, Isaac couldn't tell.

"Don told me the wolf was a murderer. That he'd killed countless children like Beau, and he would do it again. He gave me a dagger and told me to kill him." Isaac swallowed with difficulty. "So I did. I didn't ask questions. I didn't doubt anything he told me. I let Don turn me into a murderer."

His hands shook and they were suddenly hot and wet with blood, the tile cold beneath his knees as he watched the light fade from the wolf's eyes.

"Who did you really kill?" Ben asked, his expression as reserved as ever.

Isaac exhaled through a tight throat. "I didn't know for a long time. I did some digging, looked up all the kids who went missing in the upstate area. Found a missing person report that matched the Cross's methods to a family in White Plains. I visited that family. I told them everything I knew… what I'd done. The only reason they let me walk out alive was because they knew I'd carry that weight for the rest of my life. And they were right."

Isaac blinked hard, the guilt thick in his throat. "His name was Cooper Laurent. He was fifteen years old. He was running in the woods with his family when men wearing military gear and silver crosses dragged him from his own backyard. He was a good kid from an honest family. He never hurt anyone. He was just a boy, whose only crime was being born a wolf in a world where it isn't tolerated."

Ben's indifferent mask cracked; his brow furrowed, and his lips trembled. Isaac understood. That boy could have been any one of his friends, his sons, his pack. It was a fear he constantly lived with as a werewolf, that those he cared for might be taken from him by monsters with hatred in their hearts for anyone born different. Monsters like Don. Like Isaac.

He held Ben's cold hands and squeezed tight as they trembled. "That Thanksgiving when you were away, I found out the truth because the real murderer had only recently been caught. It destroyed me, Ben."

"And that's why you left?"

Isaac shook his head. "Not... not quite. A woman I knew from the Cross ran away to be with her lover. A werewolf. Don... he hunted them down. Killed the hunter right in front me."

Ben's eyes widened. "Shit. I remember that day. That was awful."

Isaac shivered. "Before all that, Don got bit by Morgan. He was turning into a werewolf. He smelled you on me. Told me he was going to kill you. I... Ben, I couldn't let that happen. The only way to keep you safe was if I made myself a target."

Ben exhaled shakily. "So you blew up the cathedral."

"Yeah. I did. I got their attention, and I ran. Ben, do you see? Do you understand? I didn't leave because I didn't care or love you more than fucking life itself." His heartache brought Isaac to the floor, prostrated before Ben. His forehead touched Ben's thigh, his tears dampening the denim of his jeans.

"I couldn't let them hurt you. Not after everything you'd done for me. Knowing you, loving you—you saved my life, Ben, and I had to do what I could to save yours." Isaac sucked in a breath through an aching throat, clutching onto Ben's hands as the wind howled around the cabin. "I understand if you... if you can't ever forgive me, Ben. I don't deserve it. I just want to tell you how sorry I am for hurting you, for not being the man you deserved. I'm so, so sorry, Ben."

Ben's hands squeezed tight, enough that it hurt. He clasped the back of Isaac's neck and gave his hair a gentle tug. Gasping for composure, Isaac looked into Ben's face and nearly broke apart. Ben's face was wet with tears, his powerful jaw trembling as he wrestled with his emotions. Ben opened his mouth but all that came out was a choked sound before he pulled Isaac into his arms and crushed him to his chest. Frozen in Ben's arms, Isaac couldn't move as Ben clasped the back of his neck, his shuddery breath hot and damp across Isaac's cheek.

"I'm still angry at you, Isaac Bennet. I hate that you left me, that we lost so much time. I'm a stubborn old ass and I'll probably be angry for the rest of my life but—" Ben pulled back, his gentle hands framing Isaac's face. Then he blinked hard and a tear left a shimmery track down his cheek before it disappeared into his beard. "I forgive you. And I hope someday you can forgive yourself too."

Isaac crumpled into him, overwhelmed by the capacity of Ben's heart to forgive him, and Ben held him tight. Ben's forgiveness wasn't what he'd expected. It wasn't what he deserved. Isaac closed his eyes and threw his arms around Ben, unable to let go. He wouldn't let go. Now that he'd earned Ben's forgiveness, he was going to spend the rest of his life making sure he never took it for granted. Ben would never have cause to regret him again.

For a time they were quiet. They reclined against a wall near the fire, Ben's back to the wood and Isaac sprawled between his thighs, his head resting upon Ben's sturdy chest. "You've got a good heart, Ben," Isaac said, his voice muffled against him. "But I haven't done anything to earn your forgiveness."

He felt Ben tilt his head in confusion.

As explanation, Isaac said, "I still have too much to make up for."

Ben sighed. "I forgive you. Isn't that what you wanted?"

"You forgave me for hurting you." Isaac met his silver gaze. "But I killed an innocent boy, and I killed feral wolves who could have received help. So many people are still dead because of me, so many families torn apart. Until Don and his hunters are dead, I'll never be at peace."

"Okay, I get it. Just don't be so hard on yourself that you can't recognize forgiveness when you finally find it." Ben stroked Isaac's hair. "All these years, I just wanted to know why you left. I understand why you did what you did. Even if it was moronic. You should have just talked to me... I could have... Well, I don't know how helpful I could have been. The agency was still new, and Don might have targeted our vulnerable clients." Ben was quiet a moment, moving his hand along Isaac's chest. "Do you really think killing Don will just... make all that guilt go away?"

Isaac didn't like that question, so he didn't answer it. He closed his eyes tight, struggling to swallow. "Don being dead is better than him being alive, no matter how I feel."

Ben said, "Isaac, we need to talk about what the plan is when this is over."

Isaac's stomach clenched. "Don't know." It was a lie. Truth was, he'd thought about it constantly. He'd thought that once Don was dead, he'd turn the weapon he'd used to kill Don on himself. Other times, he'd thought that once Don was gone, he would go home to Ben... if Ben still wanted him.

"Think about this, Isaac. Okay?" Ben touched Isaac's leg, his silver eyes intent upon him. "'Cause once Don is dead, you're gonna have to find another reason to go on. You're gonna have to find something other than hate and revenge to live for."

Isaac gritted his teeth. "Yeah? And what's that?"

"I don't know. You gotta figure it out. It sounds like revenge kept you going all these years. What's gonna keep you going after?"

Isaac forced himself to breathe. He wasn't ready to ask himself those questions yet, to find a reason to live other than revenge. He'd spent so long strangling the desperate urge to return to Ben. Could they have a future together, still? Did Isaac even have a right to ask that of Ben after all the hurt he'd caused him?

"Just... think about what you want, okay?"

Isaac laughed, the sound harsh in his throat. He sniffed and stared into the fire. "I haven't wanted anything. For a long, long time. I've spent the past two decades running and hunting. Driven by revenge and living in survival mode."

Ben sighed behind him, remorseful eyes gazing at him.

Isaac's mouth trembled, but he kept on going, unable to stop. "I wanted death. After I lost Beau. After I left you. I've been living just to die, keeping myself alive so I could find Don, kill him, then maybe myself."

"Isaac," Ben began, voice rough.

Isaac grabbed his hand, unable to look Ben in the eyes. He was shaking. He had no right to ask. Ben had given him his forgiveness. He couldn't ask for anything more. And yet...

"Then I found you again. After all this time. And I want things again, Ben. I want things I've got no right to ask for."

Ben squeezed his hand tight. "Ask me." His voice trembled and he cleared his throat.

When Isaac looked at him, Ben's eyes were shining, wide and intent upon Isaac, as if the universe hinged on his next words.

"I want you, Ben. If I can't have you, then nothing else matters. As a friend. As more. However you'll have me, I don't care. I'm so sick of being apart from you. Let me have you, Ben. Please."

He was ripped open, all his insides on the outside. His future hinged on the next word out of Ben's mouth. One word from him, and Isaac would never leave his side again, or he would go as far away as Ben wanted him to.

Big, warm hands framed his face. Ben's eyes were wet, his cheeks damp. He hauled Isaac in close and kissed him the way a drowning man needed air. Unrestrained. Wild. Desperate.

Ben was like a lifeline amidst a swirling sea, and Isaac grabbed on and held him for dear life. For the first time in so long, he wanted nothing more than to finally reach the shore.

THEY MADE IT TO the bed. Ben wasn't sure how, but next thing he knew, he was crashing down atop Isaac. Isaac was older than he'd been, but his body was hard and hot underneath him. Isaac's big, rough hands were all over him, yanking at his sweater, ripping open the buckle of his belt.

Ben was so hard he could barely think straight, and all they'd done was kiss, lips colliding, teeth scraping, noses bumping, and tongues stroking and tasting. The air was thick with the spicy scent of Isaac's arousal and the smell of the rain-washed asphalt.

Isaac yanked down Ben's zipper and Ben groaned, relieved when the pressure around his cock let up. He squirmed out of his sweater and his eyes damn near rolled back when Isaac's hot mouth attacked his chest, sucking on his clavicles, squeezing his pecs so hard it hurt, licking his nipples until they hardened.

Ben wrenched open the blanket Isaac had bundled himself in and groaned at the sight of all that bare, scarred skin covering his abs and chest. He put his hands on Isaac's body, hard with muscle and furry across his chest with a dark pelt worthy of a wolf. Isaac's cock was rock hard, and when Ben took him in his fist, he marveled at the hot, velvety texture.

Arching off the bed, Isaac bit his lip to stifle his moan. Ben pressed his nose into the crook of Isaac's neck and scented him in slow inhales. Isaac shivered beneath him. His wolf rumbled deep in his chest, his fangs sharp in his mouth.

Fuck, did Isaac smell good... Good enough that if tonight were a full moon, Ben would have claimed him here and now, fucked him and knotted him and tied their souls together so that they could never be parted again.

"Want you." The growl rumbled from Ben's chest.

"You too," Isaac said, his voice breathless and low. Isaac looked so good, naked and fired up beneath him. "Fuck, we... we don't have lube, do we?" Isaac panted.

Ben grimaced. "No, didn't exactly come out here expecting any action."

Isaac laughed. "What do you wanna do?" He ran a hand through the silver hair on Ben's chest.

They couldn't go all the way. But... "There are other ways I can get you nice and wet for me."

Dipping his head, Ben kissed a trail down Isaac's bare chest, pinching and tugging on his nipples. He buried his face in the crease between Isaac's thigh and groin and breathed in deep.

"Oh fuck..." Isaac whimpered. "Why is that so damn hot?"

Ben felt woozy from the smell of him—hot, spicy arousal and the earthy scent of his skin. His fangs lengthened. He wanted to bite Isaac. Taking in a breath, he urged his fangs away. Isaac writhed when Ben's breath wafted over his hard shaft. Ben parted his lips and, for the first time since they'd parted, took another man's cock into his mouth. Isaac's cock.

Nerves writhed through his stomach. After so many years apart, Ben wanted this to be good for Isaac, but he was rusty. The vulnerable, desperate sound Isaac made when Ben swallowed his cock probably shouldn't have tugged at his heart as much as it did, but damn it, he was melting under Isaac's touch when Isaac whispered his name and cradled Ben's head between his hands.

He couldn't get enough of the taste of him. He lapped at the head of Isaac's cock, tasting the liquid lust accumulating at the tip, and Isaac bucked beneath him, his fingers curling in the sheets. With every bob of Ben's head, Isaac's pants turned to moans and grunts that filled the cabin. Ben cupped a hand beneath Isaac's balls, rubbing and enjoying the weight of them.

"Fuck. Ben, keep that up and I'm gonna come."

Ben moaned around his cock, loving the idea. He wanted Isaac's load in his mouth, down his throat. Wanted Isaac to fuck his mouth until he was screaming Ben's name as he came. Ben doubled his efforts, stroking and squeezing the base of his shaft and kissing the swollen head of his cock. "Fuck my mouth. Go on. Take what you need, Isaac."

Isaac's eyes rolled back and he moaned. Ben wrapped his lips around him, making sure to give him space. Isaac flattened his feet against the mattress and thrust, filling Ben's mouth completely, then drew back and thrust again, faster and faster. The sounds he was making went straight to Ben's cock, and it dribbled precum over the sheets. He was so wired, he worried he'd come from Isaac's moans and desperate thrusts alone.

Gripping Isaac's hips, Ben held him in place and took him in deeper and faster.

"Wait. Ben, stop!" Isaac said, his voice choked and desperate.

Ben pulled off, slightly disappointed.

His face flushed pink, Isaac beckoned. "Come here."

Unable to hide his smile, Ben crawled over to kiss Isaac's panting lips.

Isaac reached between them and grasped both their cocks, moaning when his slick flesh glided against Ben's shaft. "Together. I wanna come with you."

Ben's heart fluttered. He rocked his hips, and his whole body shuddered as their cocks slid together. He was floating on air, blissed out with pleasure. In all the years they'd been apart, nobody else had shared Ben's bed with him. He'd forgotten how exhilarating it was, to share pleasure with another person. But knowing it was Isaac in his bed, someone he loved with his heart and soul, made him delirious with longing.

Licking his hand, Isaac worked it up and down Ben's shaft. They thrust together and their voices filled the cabin. Ben crushed his mouth to Isaac's, pushing his tongue past Isaac's lips, and they kissed until their lips were sore. Isaac finished first, crying out as he painted Ben's stomach.

Ben smeared his cock with Isaac's cum and stroked, his hand covering Isaac's. "Yeah. That's it. Come for me, Ben. Give it up for me," Isaac whispered, his hand flying up and down Ben's cock. That was all it took. Ben held him tight, crumpling into Isaac's neck. Years of unrequited longing surged from his body, and Isaac stroked him through it until Ben whimpered, his limbs going slack.

Isaac caught him when he fell, and they panted together, weak and elated.

"I forgot," Isaac panted, his chest rising and falling fast.

"Me too." Ben groaned, high on post-orgasmic bliss.

"The way you look when you're all worked up," Isaac said.

"Huh?"

"Your fangs and claws get all sharp. Your eyes glow. It's so sexy."

Ben snorted. "You're one strange man. Here I was, getting mushy over how great sex can be with someone special. And you're hung up on the claws? Fucking humans." He wound his arm around Isaac's shoulders and sighed contentedly when Isaac curled up against him. Isaac ran his hands through Ben's damp chest hair and played with his nipples, making Ben shiver and squirm. Everything was still so sensitive.

Ben fumbled in his bag lying on the floor next to the bed and found his pack of Marlboros and a lighter. A cig would really complete the moment. He held out the lighter and Isaac shook his head. Arching a brow, Ben said, "You quit?"

"Years ago," Isaac said. "Couldn't have Don smelling me from miles away."

Not wanting to tempt Isaac back to bad habits, Ben dropped the lighter and smokes back in his bag.

"Since when did you start smoking?" Isaac asked.

Ben couldn't remember exactly. "Long time ago." After Isaac left.

"Damn. My bad habits rub off on you?" Isaac captured Ben's earlobe between his teeth. Just having Isaac's mouth on him made Ben groan.

"It kept you close," Ben admitted, running his fingers over Isaac's rough beard. "Reminded me of you."

"Shit. Ben..." Isaac leaned in to kiss the corner of Ben's mouth. It wasn't enough, so Ben leaned over and claimed Isaac's lips, stroking his fingers through Isaac's soft, wavy hair.

"It's not going to be like that anymore." Isaac took Ben's hands and squeezed them tight, brushing his lips over the back of Ben's knuckles.

"After Don's gone, Ben, I swear, things are gonna be different. I'm tired of going it alone."

"Even if he runs?" Ben asked, hoping Isaac didn't notice the pitiful way his voice wavered.

Isaac met his gaze, then tipped his chin up and down. "Yes. I could never leave you again."

Ben's heart began to flutter, sweet relief surging through his veins. "I'd follow you, you know. If you really wanted to pursue him, I'd chase you down and I wouldn't leave your side until it was done."

Isaac swallowed with an audible click, his eyes glimmering. "I know. I'd never ask that of you."

"I can't be away from you." Ben gripped his hand, twining their fingers together. "Not again."

Isaac nuzzled their foreheads together. "You won't have to be. You, me... us... this is all I'm ever going to need."

His chest aching, Ben said, "So, if he escapes, I can have my friend on the Council help us out. Remember Manuel?"

A smile brightened Isaac's face. "Yeah."

"He and his wife are Alphas on the Council. I can call in a favor, and they'll help us find Don. You won't have to find him alone."

Ben ran his thumb over Isaac's cheekbone, then leaned in to kiss along his jaw. Isaac's beard scraped his skin and ignited his blood. A sigh fell from Isaac's mouth when Ben captured his lower lip between his teeth, and he swallowed Isaac's deep moan with his lips.

This felt like a dream from his fantasies. Here they lay, sweaty and warm, smelling like frantic, messy sex, their bodies heavy-limbed and content.

A smile curled Isaac's lips. "So, your sons. Tell me about them."

Ben smiled. "My pride and joy. They're twins, but they couldn't be more different. Jackson wants to join the Council and study solitary packs like the ones in Alaska. Colin was born with a camera in his hand, so he takes pictures for the articles Jackson writes for the school."

"They sound great, like they're gonna change the world."

Ben chuckled, full of pride. He nuzzled his cheek against Isaac's hair. "They will, definitely."

Isaac wet his lips. "And their mother?"

Ben scratched his head, worried Isaac might be upset that he'd started a family with someone other than his mate. "She's a good person. Loves them to death. We dated for a while before I moved to New York. After you left, we reconnected."

Isaac's fingers stroked over Ben's cheek. "I'm glad you moved on."

Ben sighed. "I didn't, not really. She and I were always friends more than we were romantic partners. I tried to live without you, Isaac." Ben ran his hand over Isaac's hip. "Best as I knew how. I focused on the agency, raising my boys, and looking out for my pack. But my life just wasn't the same without you. What about you?" Ben asked. "What kinda life did you make for yourself?"

Isaac scoffed. "It wasn't any kind of life. I never settled anywhere, Ben. I can't call all those years without you a life. I was a shell of who I used to be."

Ben squeezed him, nuzzling into the crook of Isaac's neck. "It's going to be different. We don't have to be alone anymore."

Isaac held him tight, his lips warm against Ben's shoulder. "No," he said, his voice light and content, and sighed. "No, we don't."

They were quiet for a moment. Ben closed his eyes, ready to sleep.

"Ben? I gotta know something."

Opening his eyes, he found Isaac staring intently at him, his eyes full of fear and fragile hope. "Do I still smell like rain-washed pavement? Am I still..." Isaac wet his lips.

"My mate?"

Isaac nodded, eyes wide and uncertain.

Ben leaned in and covered Isaac's mouth with his as he swept his fingers through Isaac's hair. "Yeah, Isaac. Of course you are."

A broken laugh escaped Isaac and his eyes shone bright with joyful tears. A smile bloomed across Isaac's face, erasing all the years of hardship.

"Good." He lunged in and kissed Ben again, and again, and again. Ben's lips tingled as they panted and gasped together, their hands relearning their way around each other's bodies, their lips sharing bruising kisses.

The wind howled but not even the slightest chill could touch them. For the first time in decades, Ben fell asleep, spent and content, in the arms of the man he loved.

IN THE MORNING, THE storm had passed and tranquil silence had fallen over the Alaskan wilderness beyond the cabin. From far away, a pack of wolves howled.

Ben woke up to Isaac's face on the pillow beside him and could do nothing but smile. He wanted nothing more than to stay in bed with him, but now that they weren't snowed in, the time had come for action. Leaning in, Ben woke Isaac up in the best way, with a kiss.

"Hmm..." Isaac moaned quietly, his mouth quirking into a smile. "Morning to you."

Ben let his lips linger on Isaac's for a few seconds longer, then swung his legs out of bed. "Come on. We've gotta move."

"Yeah, but where? Any trail those wolves left will be gone." Isaac sat up and stretched out his back.

"It's hard to hide a pack that size, and I heard a few of them howling when I woke up." Ben pulled on his underwear and snow pants, then looked around for his sweater. Isaac tossed it to him, a dopey smile on his face. Ben's face warmed and he caught it and pulled it on. Last night was still on his mind too. He wanted more, so much more, but they would have all the time in the world once Don and his pack had been dealt with.

When he looked around, Isaac was dressed and grabbing his bag. Before he could walk out the door, Ben grabbed his shoulder. "We'll talk more."

Isaac nodded. "Yeah, of course." He smiled. "I hope there will be a little more than talking, though."

It took all of Ben's restraint not to yank Isaac back and kiss him on the mouth. "There will be." He slapped Isaac's ass when he walked past, earning him a surprised holler.

The wind was bitter cold when they left the cabin, sending clouds of snow billowing from the snowbanks. At last, though, the sky was clear and bright blue.

"Now, to figure out where those howls were coming from..." Ben murmured.

Right on cue, wolves howled in the distance.

Isaac bristled. "Don."

But Ben's heart had stopped and restarted, stuttering wildly in his chest. "No. Those aren't his wolves." He waded ahead through the snow and began to run. "They're mine!"

Ben cupped his hands to his mouth and howled, joy surging through him when the familiar howls of the pack answered him. A rush of warmth tingled in his chest, and he felt them for the first time in days. Max, Ryan, Eddie, and Izzie. They'd found him and Isaac!

Ben caught his breath at the top of a hill, blinking against the bright rays of sun.

But his hope shattered in his chest. "No!" he snarled, lunging forward.

Isaac grabbed him around the waist. "Wait, Ben!"

Ben's heart sank as he watched Don and a pack of twenty wolves close in on Max, Izzie, Ryan, and Eddie. Blood matted Ryan's white fur and Max stood protectively over him as a wolf. Eddie put his hands over his head, cursing when a shifter in his human form forced him to his knees and cuffed him. Izzie snarled as one of the hunters threw a length of silver chain over her neck. Her snarls turned to agonized screams as she shifted to a woman, writhing in the snow as the silver burned her.

Isaac held Ben to him, his breath hot against Ben's ear when he said, "I know it's hard, Ben, but we need to let them go. We'll follow them to wherever they've been taking the wolves. We'll wait for our chance, and we will save them. All of them. But if we run in now, if we die here, then those wolves Don's captured will be beyond saving."

Ben blinked away the burn in his eyes. He knew Isaac was right, but his heart cleaved in two as he watched Don corral his friends away.

"I'll save you," he promised along the threads connecting them. *"Wait for me. I'm coming for all of you."*

Max looked back, hope flaring in his orange eyes.

Don would regret messing with his pack.

CHAPTER 23

REDEMPTION UNDER THE MOON

THROUGHOUT THE DAY, THE clouds darkened and snow fell. Isaac hoped it wouldn't storm again as they followed the wolf tracks through the snow. The tank's tracks weren't among the paw prints, so Isaac assumed it had been buried under the avalanche.

"Hold up." Isaac almost walked into Ben, who'd stopped, one hand raised. He squinted through the heavy snowfall. "You see that?"

It was Don's pack loping through the snow toward what appeared to be a fortress, its towering walls covered in snow and ice. The hunters waited until the agency wolves had passed through a hole in the wall and disappeared.

"Shit. That place is huge," Ben growled.

Ben and Isaac walked for a time as the ground sloped up to a cliffside where they had a view of the fortress below. It must have been here for a long time. Isaac had been in Alaska long enough to know there were dozens of abandoned forts scattered throughout the state, mostly going back to World War II. He supposed this must be one of them. It was the perfect place for a pack of werewolves to hole up in. The thought made his fists curl.

He was so close to killing Don tonight. Isaac wouldn't let him hurt wolves ever again.

Within the walls of the fort, Ben and Isaac prowled toward the ruins, Ben on four legs and Isaac on two. For such a big creature, Isaac was amazed at

Ben's ability to move so silently and he worried he'd make too much noise in contrast.

The ruins were much bigger than he'd assumed. There were dozens of old duplexes that must once have housed soldiers, and they passed snow-covered mounds that appeared to be bunkers. This was more than a military base—it had once been a town, Isaac realized as he passed a run-down police precinct and, chillingly, an empty playground.

"Not creepy at all," Isaac murmured, eyeing the silhouettes of playground equipment. He thought he could see the bell tower of a small church in the distance. Don likely spent most of his time there, no doubt.

Scenting the air, Ben changed course, loping toward a bunker. Isaac sighed, not looking forward to this. Ben sniffed at the bunker's gaping doorframe and growled.

"I can smell my pack! They're down here somewhere."

Isaac jumped as Ben's gruff voice echoed in his mind. "Whoa. What the hell?"

The silver wolf threw a look at him over his furry shoulder. *"I let you in on my pack bonds. This way I can stay in this form but we can still communicate."*

"Okay," Isaac said, then frowned and said in his mind, *"Got it."*

Readying his crossbow, Isaac stepped into the darkness. As his flashlight flickered and went out, he wished he had Ben's superior vision. He spread his arms, feeling for the cold stone walls and hoping he didn't miss a step.

Isaac was relieved when he got to the bottom of the stairs without falling on his ass. Scowling, he gave his flashlight a smack and sighed with relief when a cone of light illuminated the tunnel. There were rooms that connected to tiny sleeping quarters with old yellowed mattresses, rusted bunk beds, and storage trunks, and little else.

In the silence of the deep underground, Isaac thought he heard something. Barking. Ben's fur bristled and he took off at a swift pace. His huge paws slammed into a door, bowling it open to reveal an old mess hall full of tables and rusty chairs that no one had sat on in years.

The stink of rot and decay made Isaac's stomach lurch. There were two different hallways, and squinting at an old plaque, Isaac thought one hallway led to an infirmary. "Sounds like an ideal place to keep wolves, especially if they were hurt."

Ben trotted past in agreement, making for the infirmary. Something about abandoned hospital equipment ticked off unease in him, he realized, as his light wandered over rusty exam tables and racks of broken needles and abandoned tools that he hoped were just rusty and not crusted in old blood. The barking grew louder and louder as they neared the ward. Isaac readied his crossbow, realizing the wolves beyond this door could be either friend or foe. He kicked in the door and jumped in, crossbow raised in case Don's hunters prowled within the infirmary.

Wolves barked and howled, clawing to escape their cages. They went wild at the sight of Isaac and Ben, yelping loudly enough to draw the attention of wolves for miles. Isaac didn't have to be a wolf to know they were begging for help. Their living conditions were atrocious; the cages weren't big enough for the wolves to even turn around in, and they were forced to sleep in their own urine and fecal matter.

"Ben!" It was Eddie's voice. He'd been chained to a wall, his lip and nose bloodied.

"Ben, Isaac! Thank the goddess you're all right!" Izzie's black wolf pawed at the bars of her cage.

With a relieved whimper, Ben loped over to the cages and sniffed each of his packmates. *"Are you guys okay? Did they hurt you badly?"*

Max's red wolf reached his snout through the bars to lick Ben. *"We're okay, but we won't be. Not for long."*

Ryan whined and his ears flattened. *"Once they get back from their hunt, the hunters are going to torture the wolves in here until they go feral. Then they'll use them for hunting. It's going to be a damn bloodbath."*

Ben growled. *"That won't happen. I'll find the keys to these cages and free all of you."* He turned his shaggy head toward Isaac. *"Who has the keys? Do you know?"*

Isaac had a feeling he knew who. "The keys would be with Don." They just had to find him. He turned and made for the doorway, hungry to spill Don's blood.

Ben's fur bristled and his body vibrated with snarls. *"I'm gonna find him and strip the flesh from his bones."*

"Not if I beat you to it," Isaac growled. "And I think I know where he might be—in the church praying to God to save his ass from the fires of hell."

Isaac followed Ben back through the tunnels, racing toward the moonlight flooding in from above. The snow cut into Isaac's face like little daggers as they stumbled up to the exit. "Shit," he whispered, his heart sinking when the shapes of wolves emerged from the snow, flanking them on all sides. Ben grabbed Isaac's pant leg in his fangs and urged him to get down and out of sight. Was there any possibility they could make it out of this alive? If they met their deaths at the hands of this pack, who would rescue the wolves below?

"Isaac, I'll draw them away. You need to go for the keys."

Isaac's heart sank. "Ben, I can't leave you."

The wolf whined. *"You have to! If we both die, no one will rescue my pack and those wolves."*

"I know! You're right." Isaac sighed and he knelt, looking the wolf in his silver eyes. He took Ben's big, furry head between his hands and pressed their faces close. "I won't let you down, Ben. I need to do something good for once. Just like you do."

The wolf pushed closer, bumping his nose to Isaac's forehead. *"Be careful."*

His concern warmed Isaac's heart and brought a grin to his face. "Or what?"

"I'll bite you. Hard."

With a growl, Ben charged from the bunker and toward the wolves. Leaping through the air, he tackled one to the ground. Ben was on his paws again in seconds, and the wolves pursued him. Isaac waited until they'd disappeared into the storm, and then he forced himself to run, not allowing himself to look back. Ben would be all right. They would see each other again. He knew it.

The church towered over him, the rose window cracked and flooded with darkness. Isaac's hands shook as he seized his crossbow. Decades ago, he'd walked into a house of worship like this one, his heart full of grief and vengeance, and Don had taken his pain and turned him into a weapon, made him into a monster.

Tonight the monster would die when Don did, and Isaac would finally be free. In saving these wolves, he'd reclaim the humanity Don had stamped out of him. He eased open the door softly as he could and crept into darkness. To his surprise, candles were lit, glowing from candelabras along the aisle toward the altar. The wooden booths stank of rot, and icy water dripped from the ceiling onto moldering floorboards. Snow blew in through the cracked stained glass windows, piling on the floor and soaking into the wood.

A shape knelt before the altar, its robes flowing across the floor. What had once been a statue of Christ stood over Father Don, the face faded and unrecognizable. A crack echoed through the cathedral as Don flailed himself, the tails whipping across his back.

"Forgive me, Lord, for I have sinned." The voice had changed with age but a shiver still ran through Isaac. He'd once thought of that voice as so warm and kind, but now it ached with fear and sorrow. "I caved to temptation, and I have lost my way. Help me find my way back to you, Lord." A moment of silence followed. Isaac raised his crossbow. "You do hear my prayers, don't you, Lord?"

Bitterness seeped into Don's voice as he stared into the faceless statue of Christ. "I have served you well, and yet you've turned your back on me. I committed a grave sin, Father, but I am still your faithful servant! What more do I have to do to prove my devotion to you?" Anger made his voice tremble. Don took to his feet and roared, clutching his head in his hands. "I've flooded this land with the blood of the impure! I've brought servants of the Antichrist to their knees! Turn your face back to your loyal servant and cure me of this affliction!"

Don slashed out with his claws, and the statue of Christ flew from the altar and shattered on the floor. An inhuman roar tore from Don's throat and he brought the flail down on his back with a scream. "How much of my own blood must I shed before I am forgiven?" He lashed himself again and again until his own blood spotted the floor. Gasping, he dropped to his knees and threw aside the flail.

"If it's forgiveness you're after," Isaac growled, "it's far too late for that."

Don stiffened and turned toward him. He was half-shifted, and his eyes glowed. "Isaac Bennet." He bared his fangs in what was either a hideous smile or a snarl. "The betrayer who took everything from me. I gave you everything, and you turned your back on me and destroyed my hunters."

Rage tightened Isaac's throat and he aimed down the sights at Don. "How many families did you destroy just for being born different?"

A throaty cackle tore from the wolf's throat as Don turned toward him, bent-kneed as the shift slowly came over him. "And you really think killing me will erase your own guilt? God never forgets, Isaac. There will be blood on your hands for the rest of your days. The guilt will haunt you all your life."

Isaac swallowed with difficulty. "I know." The crossbow shook in his hands. "The regret and the guilt will always be with me. But you... you don't regret a thing, do you? Even after all this time, you still think you were in the right to kill innocent people. If there is a God, it's no wonder he can't forgive you, Don."

A snarl made Don hunch over. His fingers sprouted claws and his shoes ripped as his feet elongated. "He will forgive me in the end. Everything I have ever done, every corpse I've laid on his holy altar, has been for his good name. When I've cleansed the world of evil and I am ascended to his side, I will find peace. Your own guilt and self-loathing will haunt you until the day you die, Isaac Bennet. But I am merciful." A smile curled his lips, revealing his fangs. "I will end your misery, here and now."

"No," Isaac growled. "You're finished. I'll never let you hurt innocent wolves again. This ends here!"

Don dropped to all fours and pounced, ripping from his robes and leaping toward Isaac in a blur of dark fur. Isaac fired, but the silver bolt hurtled past Don. In the next moment, Don's fangs found his shoulder, biting down to the bone. Isaac crashed to the floor and a candelabra toppled over nearby. The spark from the candles fanned into a flame as the fire devoured the rotted wood like kindling.

Isaac smashed the crossbow into the wolf, bowling him off. Flames licked at his pant leg, and he ran for the stairs as a sea of fire consumed the first floor of the church. As he ran, he grabbed Don's fallen robes. The keys were heavy within, and he crammed them into his own pocket as he tore up the stairs.

The enormous wolf barreled after him, leaping up the stairs just before they crumbled beneath him. With the rose window at his back, Isaac took aim and fired. Don dodged the bolt and pounced with a furious snarl, sharp fangs bared and glistening.

As Don leaped at him, Isaac lunged for the blade in his belt. Don's weight crashed down atop him but Isaac plunged his dagger into the wolf's soft belly. Don howled in agony as Isaac hurled him off and found his feet. The silver in Don's stomach left him hunched over, blood pooling around his paws. Don shifted to something resembling a man, his claws ripping the blade free as he gasped and panted, clutching his stomach. The blood wouldn't stop flowing; he was too weak to heal.

With a roar, Don charged at him and Isaac tried to dodge but Don was too fast. His claws ripped across Isaac's thigh and warm blood soaked through his pants, but Isaac caught himself on his back leg and fired point-blank into Don's forehead. Don stumbled, and a river of blood poured between his eyes. With a roar, Isaac slammed his foot into Don's gut.

The rose window shattered, and glass rained down around Don as he fell. His body crashed into the snow and he stared toward the heavens unblinkingly as blood pooled around his head like a red halo.

Isaac's adrenaline faded, and he roared as much in pain as in liberation as the severity of his wounds brought him to his knees. He felt his fingers slipping in the blood soaking through his pants and didn't have to see the wound to know from the spurting of blood that it was fatal. He collapsed onto his back, suddenly chilled to his bones.

Hands shaking, he tore off a piece of his sleeve and bound it tight around the wound, trying to force the bleeding to stop. The blood kept flowing. Despair tightened his chest. He couldn't die. Not now. He couldn't leave Ben.

"Ben? He's gone. Don's dead."

He had to see him one last time. He had to tell him how much he—

A spasm of pain racked his body. His eyes closed as exhaustion overcame him.

"Ben. If you can hear me... I—"

"I LOVE YOU."

Warmth bloomed in Ben's chest, filling up the space Isaac's absence had left in his soul. The bond between them had risen like a phoenix. After all this time, their bond had been restored—and it was fraying, second by second.

Isaac's voice was so weak, it left Ben paralyzed with fear. Behind him, wolves howled as they gained on him.

"Isaac, don't do this."

He never should have let him go alone. This wasn't the way all those wasted years were meant to end between them. They were supposed to have a life together. He had to get to him, but the wolves just kept coming closer, their crosses glittering around their necks.

The wolves hurled themselves upon him. Ben toppled to the ground and the breath went out of him when a wolf's jaws locked around his neck. Another wolf grabbed his leg and pulled. Ben kicked and heard a wolf yelp when his claws struck their face, but the fight went out of Ben when claws raked into his belly.

The fear and fury left him shaking. He couldn't die here. He reached within himself, sought the golden thread that tied him to Isaac, and drew strength from it that he didn't know he'd had. Strength that for so long, he thought he'd lost.

Within him, there came a spark that ignited the blood in his veins, a berserker's rage awakening to protect what was his. It was stronger, so much stronger than when he'd faced the bear. His fury fed off the bond burning between him and Isaac and changed him. The wolves whimpered and backed away as he grew ten feet tall, dwarfing them. He rose on two legs fitted with hooks for claws, a roar building deep in his chest as primal fury surged within him.

A roar tore from his throat, cutting through the sky. The wolves buckled, pawing at their ears. Their eyes flashed to blank yellow hues. They were under his control. He could smell their blood, hear the pumping of their beating hearts. His mouth salivated, and his body burned for their blood.

How he longed to cut through every one of them, stain the snow with their blood, drive his snout into their organs and feast. The intensity of his fury threatened to drive him mad, but he latched onto the reins and held tight. These wolves were not hunters of their own choice. It was obvious in the scars of multiple lashings that cleaved through their fur. They were Don's pets.

"Go," he growled in a voice that rumbled down into the earth. "Return to your packs in the wild or make new ones. You are free." The yellow glow in their eyes faded as he relinquished control of their minds. One of the wolves whimpered and looked worriedly toward the hunter base. "The hunters are gone," Ben assured them. "They can't hurt you anymore. Go!" The wolves took off, howling their joy as they finally ran free.

Turning toward where Isaac's bond was pulling him, Ben ran, making the earth quiver with every slam of his paws. He easily outran the fleeing wolves back to the base, following the scent of rain-washed pavement until smoke hit the back of his throat. Terror drove a howl of dismay from him as the church burned. A body lay within a deep indentation in the snow. Father Don lay dead, snow and ashes slowly covering his corpse.

"Isaac? I'm here! Tell me where you are!" Ben roared, the wind whipping through his fur.

"Ben!" The voice was weak, nearly drowned out by the wind. A pale face loomed from the darkness of the shattered rose window and fire licked around the windowpane. Any second now, the building could come down and bury Isaac beneath it. "Don't come up here!" Isaac tossed something down. The keys sank into the snow at Ben's clawed feet.

Ben's heart raced as he clasped the cold keys in his huge fist. He wanted to jump to him but feared he'd bring the building down before he could reach him. He could die with Isaac if he tried, and no one would rescue his friends.

"Ben." Isaac's pleading voice called. "Don't leave them. They need you. Don't throw away your life for me."

Isaac was ready to die in that tower. Ben wouldn't allow it.

"This isn't the way we end, Isaac Bennet." Ben bunched his muscles and sprang. His claws found purchase in the walls and he climbed as the building creaked and groaned and planks of wood disappeared beneath his paws. He clasped the circular frame of the rose window and boosted himself inside, hurling himself away from the window as debris rained down from the ceiling.

Blood scorched his nose. Isaac was hurt, coughing and shivering on the floor as blood pooled beneath him.

"No!" Despair brought Ben to his knees as he fell out of his berserker form, gathering Isaac into his arms as gently as he could, careful not to hurt him. "Tell me," Ben rasped, feeling everywhere he could. "Tell me where it hurts. *Isaac!*" He patted Isaac's cheek, trying to make his eyes open.

They opened and then closed again, and Isaac pressed his face into Ben's chest. "Shouldn't have come."

"Shut up. You don't get to die on me, not like this!" There was still so much he had to tell him. Ben felt by Isaac's thigh, and his heart sank. It was soaked in blood. The femoral artery had been cut. Isaac had minutes at best. "No... No, no, no. Isaac, please..."

Isaac was so pale, his face covered in blood and ash. He gasped, coughing as he clutched onto Ben's shoulders. The blood leaving his body was slick between them. Ben's hands trembled as he grasped Isaac's face.

"I'm sorry, Ben," Isaac rasped, voice hoarse from the smoke. "We should have had more time. I shouldn't have left, I—"

But Ben leaned in and silenced him with a kiss, tasting the ash on his lips. "I love you too, Isaac."

A beautiful smile broke across Isaac's face, and tears gathered at the corners of his eyes. "Knew you couldn't hate me forever." A tear spilled down his cheek as his eyes closed. Ben crumpled into him, gasping as the air became too clotted with smoke to breathe.

The roof groaned above them, and debris rained down. Ben hoisted Isaac into his arms and leaped from the tower, landing on his feet in the snow. His knees gave out and he crumpled to the ground with Isaac. Behind them, the steeple tower came crashing in, and the church caved in on itself.

Shifting to his berserker form, Ben carried Isaac in one arm and gripped the keys in his fist. The ground shook as he ran, tearing toward the bunker. He needed to rescue his pack and get Isaac somewhere warm.

The wolves barked in their cages as Ben burst into the room.

"Holy—Ben? Is that you?" Max asked, eyes wide. *"You're a berserker!"*

"Is Isaac okay?" Izzie pawed frantically at the bars of the cage.

Shifting back to his normal form, Ben laid Isaac on an old yellowed mattress. He whimpered, closing his eyes tight. Ben uncuffed Eddie from the wall, and he collapsed onto the ground rubbing his wrists.

"Damn, feels good to be outta there!" Eddie groaned.

Ben ran around unlocking the cages. The wild wolves spilled from the bunker in a tide, eager to be back among the wilderness. Max crawled from his cage and shifted to a man, throwing his arms around Ben. "I knew you'd come for us!"

"Is everyone okay?" Ben asked.

Izzie grimaced and rubbed the burn on her neck. "We've had worse."

Ryan rolled out his shoulders. "What happened to Isaac?" He bounded to Isaac's side. "Whoa. Okay. That's a lot of blood."

"Can you heal him?" Ben asked.

Ryan's eyes widened. "Shit! Don's hunters shattered my potions when they captured us. I'm so sorry, Ben."

Ben sat on the yellowed mattress. "Isaac?" He took his mate's face between his hands. Isaac's eyes fluttered and his lips parted but no sound came out, only a bubble of blood. Denial turned to rage. The pulse beat feebly in Isaac's throat. "No. You don't get to leave me, Isaac Bennet."

"Ben..." Isaac's eyes opened, hazy with pain and impending death. His lips tried to form words, but he could only grunt in pain. Then he tried again. "W-want you to... turn me."

Ben's heart skipped. "Are you sure? Isaac, are you positive that's what you want?" He could still remember the hurt he'd felt when he'd asked once if Isaac wanted a wolf bite, only for Isaac to look disgusted at the very thought.

He dipped his head in a weak nod. "Yeah, Ben. I want that. I want a future with you and if I have to be a wolf, then so be it. I don't care." He tilted his neck, offering.

Ben covered Isaac's mouth with his. "Thank you..." Then his fangs came out. He could taste the venom on his tongue, willed forth by the drive to bite, to turn. "This'll hurt," he said to warn him, then brought his teeth toward Isaac's neck. He bit down, the skin broke, and Isaac's blood filled his mouth. Isaac writhed under him, a grunt escaping his lips, but he was too weak even to scream. The venom seeped from Ben's gums, dripping down his fangs into the open wound. He counted out ten seconds, then released Isaac's neck.

Ben kept his head close, listening to the feeble beat of his heart. Then Isaac's heartbeat sped up, pumping hard and fast in his throat. The bite mark Ben had inflicted mended itself before his eyes.

"He stopped bleeding," Max said. The blood spurting from Isaac's severed artery had ceased to flow.

Ben exhaled. By the next full moon, Isaac would be a werewolf. He only hoped Isaac wouldn't regret this choice.

CHAPTER 24

A SECOND CHANCE

WHEN ISAAC OPENED HIS eyes, the world around him was white. He supposed there was a heaven after all. Maybe he'd succeeded in finding redemption, and this was his reward? His body was heavy and comfortably warm. When he blinked, a bearded face loomed over him. Fingers rasped over his cheek. "God? Is that you?"

The bearded man smiled. "No, just Ben, but I'll take that as a compliment."

With another blink, the world came into focus. A wall of windows wrapped around them, framing a picturesque portrait of the snow-capped mountains that surrounded them. He lay in a luxurious king-sized bed with silk sheets and a heavy down comforter that kept out the cold. "Whoa. Where the hell are we?"

Ben surveyed the mountains beyond the windows with grim fascination. "A little resort at the base of the mountain ranges. I guess hikers and the like rest here before they hit the trails."

Isaac admired the view from his bed. "A nice enough place, as long as there ain't an avalanche."

Ben laughed and put a hand on Isaac's knee. "How are you feeling?"

"Okay, actually." Isaac peeled back the covers and checked where he'd been cut. There wasn't even a scar.

When he looked up, Ben wasn't meeting his gaze.

Isaac thought he knew why. Though so much was a haze after he'd killed Don, he remembered bits and pieces. He touched his neck where he'd felt the burning prick of fangs like hot daggers in his skin. "You had to turn me."

Ben flinched. "You gave me the okay to do so."

"I know. I remember that much..." For so long, he'd anticipated death, but when death had finally arrived, he'd realized he had a reason to keep on going. He hadn't wanted to leave Ben. He would have done anything to get another chance with him. So he'd made his choice. "When will it happen?"

"The full moon is tonight."

A rush of nerves swept through his stomach. "Will it hurt?"

Ben grunted, nodding his head.

"Shit. Will it be like in those old werewolf movies?"

Ben squeezed his shoulder. "Don't be a big baby. I'll be here. I'll help you through it."

Isaac wet his lips. "I know. But won't I lose my head? Werewolves need something to remind them they're human."

Ben pointed a thumb at himself. "That's why I'm going to be here. We have... something. You and me. It isn't as strong as it once was, but it's there. I can feel it. Once you're a wolf, you'll be able to feel it too. You'll use our connection to find your way back to your human form."

Isaac nodded, his heart racing. "Okay, think I get it." Another anxious thought poked him. "Will I survive the transformation?"

Ben's brow furrowed. "Born wolves shift with ease as early as a week old but they can struggle to control when they shift. For turned wolves, it's harder. Your body will go through changes in the span of a few minutes. Bones will reform."

Isaac grabbed his knee. "Will I survive?"

Ben's nostrils flared. "I wouldn't have bitten you if I thought there was a high chance you'd die. Wolves' and humans' bodies are different but similar in enough ways where it matters. You'll be fine. I promise."

Isaac was still nervous, but he trusted Ben.

Ben glowered down at his hands. "Are you angry at me?"

Isaac scooted closer to the edge of the bed. He lifted Ben's bearded chin and met his gaze. "I made my choice. All that matters is that we're here, Ben. You and me. So what if I'll be a little hairier than usual? I look forward to all the belly rubs and head scratches."

Ben laughed, his smile chasing away the broody aura. He grabbed Isaac's hand and tangled their fingers together, squeezing tight. "Why do I feel like I just made a big mistake?"

Isaac leaned over to kiss the tip of his nose. "Because you did. I'm gonna be the neediest werewolf ever."

Ben snorted when he laughed, which made Isaac laugh with him.

They shared a slow, lingering kiss that made Isaac's heart flutter, and then they lay down in bed together side by side.

"Wait, what about your friends? Tell me you found the keys. Tell me they made it out!"

Ben eased him down to the pillows. "Easy. They're all back in New York by now. I didn't wanna risk flying you across the country on the night of the full moon, so I stayed behind."

Isaac's mouth quirked. "You put me before your pack? I'm flattered." Ben's ears reddened and Isaac loved that he still had such a hold over him. "Actually, I remember a bit before the roof came in. You said something..."

Ben made a growling sound and Isaac grinned and scratched his chin. "I believe it was, 'I love you too,' and there was smooching involved." His memory could use a refresher. He scooted toward Ben and propped his chin on a broad shoulder.

Ben's whole body stiffened, his face practically radiating heat as he reddened further. In some ways he was still the shy, gentle man Isaac had loved.

Ben grunted. "There's a bathroom over there. Go take a bath, maybe have a shave. You really stink."

Isaac laughed into his shoulder. "I bet I do." He couldn't remember the last time he'd shaved. He stood and nearly fell over but Ben's big arms caught him round the middle. "Maybe you should join me? Make sure I don't fall over in the shower?"

Ben folded his arms over his chest. "Think you'll be fine."

Isaac took a long hot shower and shaved the animal off his face, leaving just a little scruff. He buzzed off some of his hair, leaving it shoulder length, and tied it into a bun. Ben was bald now, so it only made sense that Isaac should have enough hair for the both of them.

Ben sat at the table with a tray of dinner and a couple glasses of wine. Outside, the sun was setting, staining the snow orange and the shadows of the mountains a deep violet. When Ben looked his way, his silver eyes went wide, his breathing catching audibly.

"Doesn't look too great, does it?" Isaac rubbed the scruff on his face.

Ben's mustache twitched when he smiled. "It looks good. Just... You really haven't aged a day."

Isaac didn't feel that way at all. His face was lined around the mouth and forehead, his hair was more silver than he'd like it to be in places, and he had more scars than he could count. Hearing Ben's soft-spoken words made him feel more confident, though. He settled into the chair opposite him and they ate in comfortable silence.

Isaac cleared his plate and looked up in time to catch Ben staring down at the table where Isaac's hand lay, the golden ring glittering in the last of the sunlight. He didn't see Ben's ring, and he was afraid to ask. What did he say? How did they begin from where they'd left off so many years ago?

"You still have your ring." Ben's hand came to rest over Isaac's fingers. He traced the gold band, warm from Isaac's skin. "The day you left you'd taken it with you. I thought you were coming back. So I waited."

Isaac's heart ached for him and he squeezed Ben's hand tight. "I think," he murmured, finally finding his voice, "a part of me always wanted to come home to you. Held on to this subconscious hope that I'd see you again. That we could be like we used to." He laughed, realizing how wrong he'd been. "We're different people, Ben. You've made a life for yourself, helping others, and I've spent the last couple decades trying to make up for all the harm I've done."

"You did." Ben squeezed his hand tight and looked him in the eyes. "Don's gone, Isaac. You helped rescue innocent wolves, and you saved my pack. The Silver Cross will never harm anyone again. You made sure of that. You've done your part and then some."

Isaac pulled away before he could stop himself. Don's last words had been echoing in his mind, locked behind a door where all his other monsters dwelled. He was afraid if he opened that door, his demons would destroy him for good. "He's gone, but that doesn't erase the things I did, the lives I ruined doing his bidding. I don't know how many of the people I hunted were good people whose lives I cut short or if they really were monsters like Don claimed." Admitting it opened up a pit in his stomach. "I'll never know."

Don was right; he would be haunted for the rest of his life.

"I can't ask you to love me, Ben. I don't remember what it's like to wake up not hating who I am and what I've done."

Ben sighed quietly, blinking in silent contemplation. "First of all"—he reached across the table and clasped Isaac's hands tight—"you have my love. Whether you want it or not. You've never had to ask for it." He clasped the nape of Isaac's neck and drew him close. Isaac breathed him in, the woodsy scent of beard oil and freshly washed clothes. "It's easy to hate yourself. Forgiving yourself is a hell of a lot harder. Hating others is easier than helping, but helping people is healing."

Ben's eyes lit up and he urged Isaac to his feet, and Isaac couldn't help but smile. He hadn't seen Ben so excited before—he was practically on the balls of his toes. His smile took years off his face. "Come back to New York with me. I'll train you to work in the agency, teach you all about restoring a werewolf's humanity. Just like I said I would, remember?"

The hunters were gone and Don would never come for them. They could finally be together without anything between them—if that was what Ben actually meant. "It sounds great, Ben." His stomach churned. Did Ben mean what he desperately wanted him to mean? "But that would take a while. I'd need to find an apartment, and—"

Ben rolled his eyes skyward. He grabbed Isaac's shoulders and stared him down. "You're not the man I once knew, Isaac. You're different now, and so am I." Ben bumped his forehead to Isaac's. "But I loved you all those years ago, and I love you now. No matter how much time passed or who I was with, that never changed."

Ben pulled down the collar of his shirt and clasped a golden chain. He lifted a gold ring into the sunlight, one of two. "I never took mine off either," Ben said, and his voice trembled. He gathered Isaac close, his mouth touching his forehead. "I never forgot our promise, Isaac."

"Neither did I." Isaac stroked Ben's beard. "I'll do it. I'll come back to New York with you."

Ben grinned, and Isaac couldn't remember the last time he'd been so happy. He didn't know what he'd done to deserve a second chance with Ben Stroud, but he wouldn't squander it. He touched his mouth to Ben's and his lips softened at once at Isaac's touch. Ben's big hand, dry and warm, rasped over his cheek. The heat of Ben's body seeped through his clothes, and their chests touched with every breath.

Just kissing him wasn't enough. That little appetizer in the cabin had only given him a taste of Ben Stroud, and Isaac wanted the full-course meal. His lips tingled from Ben's kisses, and his stomach was fluttering from the sensation of Ben's hand on his waist.

Breathing shallowly, Isaac made his intentions clear, slipping an arm around Ben's waist to bring their hips together, and his cock stirred to life when Ben grunted his approval. Isaac rocked his hips, smiling when the hard swell of Ben's cock rubbed against his hip.

"Want to feel you." Ben's voice was rough, his fingers unsteady at the hem of Isaac's shirt. Isaac clasped his shirt and pulled it over his head. He didn't miss the widening of Ben's eyes, the little intake of breath. Isaac wasn't even naked yet but he felt as bare and vulnerable as if he'd been thrown naked into an open field.

This wasn't the same as those frantic kisses and touches they'd shared in that snowed-in cabin. This was different, monumental. There was no rushing things, not tonight. Tonight was the start of their forever together.

Isaac shivered under Ben's roaming eyes. His every scar was on display, reminders of every hunt from before he met Ben and long, long after. Reminders of the hunter he'd once been, and every scar had led to where he was now. To the man before him.

When he found the guts to check Ben's reaction, his heart raced when he saw that Ben was working away at the buttons to his flannel shirt, rolling his wide shoulders to push the fabric down past his elbows. The chestnut-brown fuzz on his chest had gone silver, making his skin appear to shimmer in the light. His body was hard around the chest and arms but softer in the middle than he'd once been. Time hadn't touched him; he was as beautiful inside and out as Isaac remembered.

Ben cleared his throat and Isaac realized he'd been staring. Fidgeting, Ben bunched his shirt into a ball. "Say something, would you?"

Isaac laughed, put on the spot. "You're still the sexiest man I've ever had in my bed."

Ben's mustache quirked when he smiled, his ears going modestly red. "And I'll be the last. Won't I?" He came close, his hands clasping Isaac's waist tight. His breath scorched Isaac's mouth, and Isaac could have drowned in the silver of his eyes. "The full moon will be out soon. Say the word, and I'm making you mine."

Isaac tugged Ben's mouth onto his, seeing stars as Ben rocked his powerful body against Isaac's. "I want you, Ben. As a mate, as my husband, or both, whatever we call it doesn't matter. Just as long as you're mine, and I'm yours."

A choked sigh spilled from Ben's lips, and then the sheets cushioned Isaac's fall and he pulled Ben to him—and his vision went white as Ben's forehead cracked against his nose. They both yelped.

"Shit! You okay?"

Isaac groaned, eyes watering in intense pain. "Is it broken?"

Ben tenderly raised Isaac's hands and checked. He smiled, red-faced. "You'll be fine. There won't even be a bruise once you shift." Ben kissed the bridge of his nose in apology. "Want some ice?"

Isaac did, but he didn't want Ben going anywhere. "I'll live." He tugged Ben's mouth against his, chasing the taste of wine on his tongue. Ben's fangs nipped at his lower lip, and his big hands squeezed Isaac's buttocks.

"Don't know how many times I dreamed of having you under me." Ben's voice was low and raspy as he kissed down Isaac's chest, sucking Isaac's nipples until they hardened to peaks under his mouth. Isaac struggled to catch his breath only to have it driven out of him as Ben squeezed his cock. He bucked into his touch, needing Ben's mouth on him, his fingers wrapped around him.

"I dreamed about you too," Isaac panted, raising his hips so Ben could tug down his jeans. "Woke up hard as a rock for years, wanting to touch you, feel you inside me." The dreams had tormented him, but as much as he'd ached for Ben's body when he woke, he'd wanted more than anything to feel him in his arms, to hear his voice. He'd resigned himself to the fact that Ben would be nothing more than a fantasy to him for the rest of his life.

The heat of Ben's mouth wrapped around his aching cock, his lips tightening as he sucked him down in one long stroke. Isaac bunched the sheets in his fists, unable to stifle a choked, desperate cry. Their eyes met, and Isaac couldn't look away, a shiver running through him. He couldn't get over it, this big sexy guy on his hands and knees, worshipping Isaac's cock and putting his pleasure first.

"Come here." He needed to touch Ben too.

Giving his cock one final lick, Ben draped himself over Isaac and their lips met. Isaac rolled them over and grinned at Ben's surprised gasp. Leaning over Ben, he took his time exploring and squeezing his heavy pecs, the muscles hard and yet perfectly padded and soft, and he splayed his fingers over the fuzz on Ben's stomach, his belly soft and warm.

Isaac tugged down his zipper. Ben's heavy cock strained his boxers, and Isaac rubbed the long length of him through the thin fabric. Ben's head rolled back, his lip between his teeth. "Fuck. Isaac, you're killing me."

Isaac grasped Ben's cock and let his fingers wander, rubbing the swell at the base of it. Ben groaned low in his chest and curled his fingers around Isaac's cock. Their lips met, parting around gasps and quiet curses as they stroked each other. Isaac caught his breath and looked into Ben's eyes, shivering to see his own aching desires reflected back in Ben's face.

Reaching over the side of the bed, Ben grabbed a bottle of lube from his suitcase. "Came prepared this time. Thank the goddess for vending machines," he said with a wink, then tore it open, drizzling some over his fingers. Once he'd pushed Isaac onto his back, Ben slipped his fingers between Isaac's cheeks. Isaac choked on a gasp, every nerve ending lighting up as Ben's thick fingers stretched him open.

Ben bit his lower lip, his eyes closing in bliss as if he were the one being fingered. "Fuck. I forgot how good it feels inside you." Ben pegged his prostate, and Isaac's eyes rolled back.

"Right there! Do that again." A shuddered gasp fell from his lips as Ben repeated the stimulation. Ben knew his body so well; it was as if they'd never parted.

Isaac rocked his hips and rode every curl of Ben's fingers, grinning at the curse he pulled from him. Ben's breath hit his mouth in short, quick puffs, silver eyes glowing like the moonlight.

A third finger filled him and stretched him open, the burn exquisite, the fullness inside him ramping his pleasure higher. Isaac pushed his hips back onto Ben's fingers, fucking himself in his desperation for more. "God, Ben. Give me more. I need you." He was ready for Ben, had been ready for years, waited and dreamed of the moment they could finally be one in body and soul again.

Isaac's knees were thrown across Ben's shoulders. Ben settled between Isaac's thighs and grasped himself, slicking himself with lube and getting into position. Isaac held his breath, unable to look away from Ben's heavy-lidded eyes. A groan tore from Ben's throat as he sheathed himself inside Isaac.

It burned at first, robbing Isaac of breath as Ben opened him up. A shudder ran through Ben's body, the desperation that gripped his face melting away to vulnerable bliss. Isaac raised his hips, urging him in deeper, and Ben thrust home. His pelvis struck Isaac's buttocks, and they came nose to nose. With their eyes locked and Ben's breath hot on Isaac's lips, they moaned and sighed.

"Fuck." Ben groaned. "Oh fuck, Isaac." He rolled his hips, drawing out nice and slow, then barreling back in. "So perfect."

Utterly incoherent, Isaac bucked his hips. They could be slow and tender later. Right now, he *needed*. Isaac arched up to meet Ben when he slammed back in, and he saw fucking *stars*. Whimpering, all Isaac could do was dig his nails into Ben's back and enjoy the ride.

Ben claimed Isaac's mouth, his teeth scraping, and Isaac didn't care that his fangs were sharp and painful. In fact, Isaac was surprised to realize his own teeth were sharp. He hadn't shifted yet, but his body still reacted to his mate.

Raising his hips to meet every thrust, Isaac felt like a god of sex when Ben cried out in euphoria. Isaac bucked mindlessly, chasing the sensation building deep in his balls. "Fuck, Ben. Not gonna last. That's so good. You're so fucking good."

A growl rumbled through Ben's body, vibrating deep in his chest. His lips pulled back, revealing the gleam of his fangs. A spasm of *want* left Isaac arching off the bed. "Need you to bite me, Ben." Isaac rolled his neck, exposing his throat. "Claim me. Do it. Please."

Fangs pierced the spot between his neck and shoulder, and Isaac screamed. The pain was white hot, and then warmth spread throughout his body. A wave of feeling enveloped him, filling him to the brim with countless precious emotions. Love, trust, and joyous relief so immense it brought tears to his eyes. He turned away, trying to hide it, but big gentle hands framed his face.

"I know," Ben whispered, wiping away Isaac's tears, and he was crying too. "I feel it too. You're mine, Isaac Bennet, and I'm yours." Ben grinned, sharp and white, and with such joyous relief it made Isaac's heart ache.

The love between them, warm and tangible, burned so bright Isaac would never doubt that he was loved again. Ben's knot filled him, pressing hard into his prostate, and Isaac's release broke upon him like a wave crashing to shore.

"Isaac!" Ben growled out his name, moving fast and hard and desperate inside Isaac, pulling away only to gasp when he came. Isaac's heart squeezed tight when he saw the glimmer of joyful tears in Ben's lashes. Ben went limp, sinking down onto Isaac's chest in a heap. His arms flew around Isaac, wrapping around his back to grab his shoulders. Holding Ben tight, Isaac swallowed the tidal wave of emotion that rushed into his throat. Ben's body shuddered and he rained kisses onto Isaac's neck.

Their lips met, tasting salty and coppery from Ben's fangs. When Isaac opened his eyes, Ben wore a smile that could have melted the snow from the mountain ranges around them. Eyes watery, he laughed in a way that made Isaac's heart clench, then buried his face in Isaac's shoulder, licking tenderly at the blood on his neck. It really was starting to hurt but they were tied together, unable to part, and Isaac wouldn't have it any other way.

"I want to marry you," Isaac whispered, watching as the northern lights danced across the crown of Ben's head and stained the surrounding sheets.

Ben's mouth curled in a grin. "Really?"

"Not gonna lie, marriage is important to me." He frowned. "Do werewolves get married?"

"Sure, some." Ben ran his fingers through the fuzz on Isaac's chest, tweaking his nipples. They were sore from Ben's attention and the sensation was wonderful. "Some werewolves would see marriage as an offense against the She-Wolf, but I ain't religious. And trust me, the goddess really isn't the type to care anyway."

Isaac bit his lip to stifle his grin. "So, that's a yes?"

Laughing, Ben pressed his mouth to Isaac's, their tongues stroking lazily. When they broke apart for air, Ben nuzzled their foreheads together. "I'll marry the hell outta you, Isaac Bennet. Just..." He frowned.

Isaac ran his hand over the smooth skin of Ben's scalp. "Hey. What is it?"

"Can you take my name? I don't know, Ben Bennet sounds stupid."

Isaac barked out a laugh and kissed his mate's smiling lips. "We can do whatever you want. What do I care? I'm the lucky bastard who gets to marry you."

Ben laughed low in his chest. "I'm luckier."

Happiness warmed Isaac to the bone as he held Ben close.

They were together, now and forever.

EPILOGUE

Isaac woke up and knew the change was coming.

The sheets were soaked with his sweat. His body burned feverishly and yet he shuddered from cold. His head ached. His bones throbbed, bringing back memories of growing pains from his teenaged years. His gums ached and he wanted to claw the skin from his body. Every pore itched.

"Ben..." His voice came out a growl.

Ben was awake in seconds beside him. The lamp flicked on. "I'm here." Ben loomed over him and Isaac's vision flashed. One second he saw colors, the next, only certain colors were visible to him, the rest gray. "Shit. Okay. Isaac? You're turning."

He groaned as cramps racked his legs. "Fuuuck... God. It hurts, Ben. It fucking hurts."

"I know."

Isaac's gums throbbed. He wanted to bite something.

"Come on. Let's get you outside." Ben hoisted Isaac to his feet and his head thumped against Ben's chest. He couldn't keep his eyes open. When he closed them, he felt like he was spiraling into a deep, dark pit. Ben carried him out onto the back porch. A blast of cold air made him shiver, freezing the sweat on his body, but he didn't feel as cold as he thought he should. His body was like a furnace.

Ben laid him in the snow, and the icy ground cooled Isaac down, if only a little.

The moon glowed full and fat. He could feel each ray of moonlight over his body. His skin itched as the hair on his arms grew thick and gray. The fur receded, leaving his arms bare, and then he groaned as the unbearable itching started again. He tore at the snow with dull nails that became pointed claws several inches long. He snarled up at the moon through a mouthful of fangs.

Everything was so loud. He could hear every snap of a twig in the woods. The crack of ice high up in the mountains. The hooting of owls. The scurrying of wood mice over dead leaves. The howling of a distant pack of wolves. God... their howling... A snarl ripped from his throat. They weren't his pack. They didn't belong here. They were a threat. An enemy, come to take away what was his.

So many smells accosted his nose. Wet leaves and dirt. The cold, crisp scent of snow that burned his nose. Sweat, his own pungent body odors. Something dead a few miles away—blood-matted hair, rotting entrails, and the musky odor of a male elk. His mouth flooded with saliva.

"Isaac."

That voice was familiar. A man knelt beside him naked, moonlight shimmering on his silver beard and chest hair.

"It's overwhelming, I know. You can smell things from miles away. Hear everything all at once. But find it. It's there, but it's buried underneath. It's golden and warm and to me, it smells like rain-washed pavement. But to you, it'll smell like something else. That's us, Isaac. That's our bond."

The man's hand closed around Isaac's claws and squeezed tight.

"Find it, Isaac. Find us. Our love will bring you home."

He didn't know why, but he wanted to listen to this man. Something was missing. There was a hole inside him. Something he needed. He needed it so badly.

But he couldn't think. There were so many smells. So many noises. And the moon... the moon was *burning* him, lighting him up from his very bones. Calling to him, singing to him the sweetest song he'd ever heard. His bones ached. He screamed, and his canines lengthened into fangs. His bones lengthened, and fur burst from his skin and darkened his arms and legs.

And then everything stopped. The pain, the discomfort. All he felt was the wind caressing his fur. The moon's soothing song filled his head with a light, fluttery feeling. He stumbled to his paws, tipped back his head, and sang to her.

Another voice joined his, and something burst to life inside him. The wolf turned and found another standing beside him, singing sweetly to the moon above. He was big and silver with moonlight shimmering through his fur. The silver wolf turned toward him and silver eyes pierced him.

The wolf whined. He pawed at his ears. Everything was so loud. The birds in the trees. The animals that stalked the woods. Even the insects writhing beneath the soil. He snarled at the rush of smells assaulting him. Dead things. Stinky living things.

And something else.

Something that smelled like a field of blooming flowers.

It was him. The silver wolf. He smelled like... like...

Death. Death had been nipping at his heels. For so long, he'd craved the release death offered. From pain. From guilt. From everything he'd done.

He whined. Memories tugged at him. A little boy lying dead in the woods. A headstone wet with rain. The taste of booze thick in his throat. Despair heavy in his chest. A wolf lying on the altar. Blood soaking his hands, the dagger cold in his grip. He'd hurt so many. He'd done horrible things. He didn't want to remember. He wanted to forget.

"Isaac."

A voice filled his mind. His chest flooded with warmth. The smell of blooming flowers, of *life,* overpowered everything else.

The silver wolf approached and pressed his nose to his forehead.

"Don't fight us. I know it hurts. I can feel it. All that guilt and pain that's been festering inside you is mine now too. We're one. It will always be there. It's a part of you. It's made you who you are. But it's a part of me too, and we're gonna carry it together, Isaac."

Life. There was *life*. In this sea of pain, hurt, despair, and self-loathing, there was life, and it smelled like blooming flowers and dewy summer grass.

And he wanted to reach out and take hold of it.

So he reached within himself, wading through the murky sea that dragged him down. Reaching, arms outstretched for the only light he could see. A thread, golden and bright, warm with the promise of life. He reached out and grasped it tight.

Isaac gasped like a drowning man breaking the surface of icy waters. He had hands again. His fur was gone. The smells were still potent but not overpowering. He covered his ears, wincing at the noises of the forest.

"I know. It's overwhelming." Big, strong arms enveloped him, and his head came to rest against a warm, solid, and bare chest. A heart beat soothingly in his ears.

"Ben..." Isaac whimpered, shaking and still struggling for air.

"I know. You did great, Isaac." Soft lips caressed his forehead.

"That was... I mean, that was... I could hear everything. Smell everything. I... Holy shit." He was a *werewolf*. "I'm... I'm like you now. Like your pack."

"Yeah, and you make one hell of a fine wolf." The pride in Ben's voice warmed Isaac to his core.

Isaac chuckled. "Tell me I at least look badass. I don't have a mangy tail or anything?"

"Nope. Your fur is a beautiful gray color."

Isaac raised a hand, looking for where his claws had been. "How can I do that thing you do? Where you make your claws come out?"

"That'll take practice and control. Otherwise, it'll probably happen when you—"

Isaac sneezed and yelped when his claws cut into his hands. "Motherfucker!" The wound healed quickly at least. "Okay, that's pretty fucking sick."

Ben rumbled out a laugh. "Let's get you inside."

He stumbled to his feet and leaned on Ben's shoulder as they left the porch and went back into the warmth of the cabin. Isaac collapsed into bed, and Ben curled up beside him. Isaac couldn't believe what had just happened. Rolling over, he inhaled into Ben's neck. A growl rumbled in his chest and Ben shivered.

"I smell any good?"

Isaac's fangs lengthened. "Fuck yeah."

"What do I smell like?"

Isaac pressed his lips to Ben's neck. "Like life."

"That's specific."

Isaac snorted. "It's hard to explain, okay? You smell like flowers. Like green growing things. You're the reason, Ben. You're why I'm gonna keep on going after all the shit I've been through. I want that future. With you. With your pack."

Ben wound his arms around Isaac and squeezed, bringing their bare bodies together. "I do too."

"You better. Or I'm gonna be real pissed if you turn me and drop me off at a shelter." Ben looked wounded. Isaac grinned and kissed his pouting lips. "You're stuck with me now. I can feel it. That bond you mentioned. It's warm and golden. It feels so right."

Ben hid his face in Isaac's neck. He sniffed and a powerful shudder ran through him.

"Hey. What's wrong?" Isaac framed Ben's face in his hands, surprised to see him blinking back tears.

Ben leaned in and kissed him. "Just... never thought I'd hear you acknowledging our bond. When you were human, you couldn't sense it. I knew how you felt for me, but... Shit. I'm so happy, sweetheart."

Fuck. Could Isaac be any more in love with him?

Isaac's fangs sharpened as he nuzzled into Ben's neck.

"Go on," Ben whispered, tilting his head.

His heart quickened. He wanted to ask, "Are you sure," but before he knew it, his fangs had elongated and his instincts had him surging forward until his teeth pierced Ben's neck. Ben squirmed beneath him, gripping Isaac's arm hard. The drive to claim that pounded through Isaac's blood subsided, and he licked the wound until the blood stopped flowing.

Ben caught his breath.

"Did I hurt you?" Isaac thought to ask.

Ben ran his hand through Isaac's hair. "When you bit me? Yeah, 'course. But then... I don't know. I felt this warmth. This relief... like that first gulp of air after holding your breath underwater for a while. It was..." Ben shivered beneath him and Isaac kissed the scarring bite on Ben's neck. "It was like I was breathing for the first time in a long time."

Isaac propped his chin on Ben's shoulder. "That's interesting. That's how I feel when I'm with you. Like I'm alive. Like I'm breaking the surface and taking a breath for the first time. You're my life ring, Ben. You're the air in my lungs."

"Life," Ben whispered, his voice thick. "It felt like life."

Isaac kissed the corner of his mouth and closed his eyes when Ben turned his head and leaned into the kiss. "You're my life, Ben Stroud."

Ben's trembling lips smiled. "And you're mine." He draped his thigh over Isaac's hip and leaned over to kiss him, and they held each other tight until Isaac's eyes grew heavy. Then he fell asleep in the arms of the man he loved.

BEN WOKE TO THE ringing of his phone in the dark. Reluctantly, he gently untangled himself from Isaac's arms, vowing to return at once. The northern lights had gone dark but a blanket of stars lit up the sky and the wind howled a soothing melody. He found his phone glowing faintly in his jeans. "Eddie? What's up?" He ducked into the bathroom so he didn't wake Isaac.

"I found him, Ben."

Ben yawned, his mind fogged. "Sorry, who?"

"Vicenzo."

He exhaled, relieved. He'd told the Council to search high and low for him. "Wait, you didn't leave with everyone else?"

"I stayed back and went looking. I found him."

"How is he?"

"He was nearly feral, Ben." Eddie's voice trembled. "He wasn't separated from us for long, but it did something to his mind."

Ben's stomach churned and he sighed. "That must mean…" Shit. "He's been on the verge of going feral for months now, Ed. He never took to us, and his humanity's paying the toll."

"I know." Eddie's voice was full of guilt. "He's agreed to come back with us, but he won't talk to me about how he's doing. I think he knows this was a close call, and he was scared, Ben."

He paced in the dark, then leaned against the wall. "He's gotta let us in. Something's stopping him. If he could just tell us what—"

"I know what." Eddie's voice was hard, but he wasn't angry at Ben. "He and I… we lost everything when our hometown burned. I've been trying so hard to have a fresh start, get to know the pack. But he can't move on."

Ben's jaw tightened. "We won't fail him again, Ed. Look, Isaac and I will be leaving in a few hours. Keep an eye on him till then. Be there for him."

"I've been trying, Ben, but it's hard when he won't let me." Eddie sighed heavily. "But you don't gotta tell me twice. Hey, how are you and Isaac? You guys on good footing again?"

Ben smiled, certain he looked like a happy fool. "Yeah. We're great, Ed. I'll see you soon."

"Talk to y'all later."

Isaac was awake when Ben returned. He opened his arms and Ben curled up against his chest and listened to the steady beat of his mate's heart.

"This is it." Isaac's voice was pleasantly low as he rested his cheek on Ben's head. "No more hunters, no more separation. I'm with you, Ben."

Ben squeezed him tight, his heart overflowing with a happiness he hadn't felt in years. He touched his mouth to the bite mark on Isaac's neck. His heart was finally complete. "I love you."

Isaac's eyes sparkled with joy and he squeezed Ben's hand. "You too."

In the dark, their lips met one more time before Ben pulled Isaac to his chest. Wrapped tight in each other's arms where not even the howling of the wind could touch them, Ben and Isaac fell asleep in the heart of the Denali mountains.

In the finale to The Lycanthrope Protection Agency series, will Eddie and Vico overcome childhood wounds and earn their Happy Ever After? Find out in...

Fire and Moonlight (The Lycanthrope Protection Agency Book 6)

THANK YOU!

Thank you for reading! If you enjoyed, please consider leaving a review on your preferred platform of choice. Indie authors like me depend on word of mouth reviews like yours. Additionally, please consider recommending this series if you enjoyed it! Thank you again!

Sign up to my newsletter to receive a free prequel to The Lycanthrope Protection Agency series, Before Moonrise. This novella features forbidden love, friends to lovers, possessive werewolves who adore their mates, and sexy times on a beach, in a barn, and a broom closet just to name a few locations. Additionally, you'll receive bonus content, cover reveals, and news about new releases. What are you waiting for?

Sign up now at www.CJRavenna.com

ABOUT CJ

CJ Ravenna loves to tell stories where the ordinary meets the extraordinary. Her books often feature an explosion or two, possessive and protective werewolves who adore their mates, steamy and swoony romance, and of course a happy ending. Connect with me on:

My website: cjravenna.com

My Facebook group: Ravenna's Ravens

Instagram: @cjravenna

TikTok: @cjravenna

Goodreads: goodreads.com/cjravenna

Bookbub: bookbub.com/authors/cj-ravenna

ALSO BY CJ RAVENNA

The Lycanthrope Protection Agency Series

Before Moonrise (Jin & Marcus. Newsletter exclusive)

To Hunt A Moonborn Beast (Gabe & Max)

Child Of The Moon (Gabe & Max)

The Moon Aways Rises (Gabe & Max)

The Moon Over The Oak (Zach & Ryan)

Redemption Under The Moon (Ben & Isaac)

Fire and Moonlight (Eddie & Vico)